MR CAMPION'S WAR

MR CAMPION'S WAR

Mike Ripley

This first world edition published 2018
in Great Britain and the USA by
SEVERN HOUSE PUBLISHERS LTD of
Eardley House, 4 Uxbridge Street, London W8 7SY.
Trade paperback edition first published
in Great Britain and the USA 2018 by
SEVERN HOUSE PUBLISHERS LTD.

British Library Cataloguing in Publication Data
A CIP catalogue record for this title is available from the British Library.

ISBN-13: 978-0-7278-8809-9 (cased)
ISBN-13: 978-1-84751-950-4 (trade paper)
ISBN-13: 978-1-4483-0161-4 (e-book)

All Severn House titles are printed on acid-free paper.

Severn House Publishers support the Forest Stewardship Council™ [FSC™],
the leading international forest certification organisation.
All our titles that are printed on FSC certified paper carry the FSC logo.

Typeset by Palimpsest Book Production Ltd.,
Falkirk, Stirlingshire, Scotland.
Printed and bound in Great Britain by
TJ International, Padstow, Cornwall.

For
Marcel Berlins – merci beaucoup

For three years he had been at large on two warring continents employed on a mission for the Government so secret that he had never found out quite what it was . . .

Coroner's Pidgin (1945) by Margery Allingham

'I did a lot of work before the war for a detective like – amateur mind, a gentleman – in fact I'd be doin' it now but that he took 'imself orf to the army and one of those 'ush-'ush jobs.'

Black Out (1995) by John Lawton

Author's Note

At the risk of irritating the population of France even further, I have used the pre-war spelling of *Mentone* (as did Margery Allingham) rather than the current *Menton*, and the curiously English spelling of *Marseilles* rather than *Marseille*.

Contents

Guests, distinguished and otherwise,
at The Dorchester Hotel,
Wednesday 20 May 1970, to celebrate the birthday of
Mr Albert Campion
7.30 for 8 p.m. *Black Tie*

Lady Amanda Campion

Mr and Mrs Rupert Campion

The Earl of Pontisbright — *accompanied by his daughter*

Mrs Sophia Longfox – *and her son Mr* *Edward Longfox*

Mr Christopher Campion – *nephew of Albert*

Johnny and Evie, Lord and Lady Carados

Guffy and Mary [née Fitton] Randall — *old friends and relations*

Jonathan Eager-Wright – *the mountaineer, now retired*

Robert Albrecht Freiherr von Ringer – *a German gentleman*

Dr Jolyon Livingstone – *Master, St Ignatius College, Cambridge*

Robert Oncer Smith – *an undergraduate*

Mme Corinne Thibus – *a French lady on a mission*

Mr L. C. Corkran – *a retired gentleman previously concerned with matters of security*

Miss Precious Aird – *an American*

Señora Astrid Vidal – *a couturier of growing reputation*

Señorita Prisca Vidal – *her daughter*

M. Joseph Fleurey – *of the Hotel de Paris, Nice*

Commander Charles Luke – *of the Metropolitan Police*

Mr Magersfontein Lugg – *a retainer*

And others, both uninvited and unexpected.

Prologue

Hôtel Beauregard, Mentone, Alpes-Maritime, Zone of Italian Occupation. February 1942

M. Étienne Fleurey had been a person of some importance in the self-contained world of the Hôtel Beauregard: the master of all he surveyed; an emperor who knew every bottle, knife, fork, towel, napkin, cocktail stick and fruit bowl in his empire and their exact strategic disposition at any given time. That, however, was before the war. Now he was little more than a flunky performing tasks which would have previously been delegated, with great and serious ceremony at a morning roll call, to a phalanx of smartly laundered busboys, housemaids, bellhops and waiters.

The defeat of France by the Germans in the north had given Signor Mussolini the chance to extend his greedy fingers in the south, to clutch at Savoy and Nice, and for a thankfully brief period in June 1940, Mentone had been in the front line of the fighting. The Beauregard had been fortunate. It had not suffered from the shells and mortar bombs which had destroyed the Hôtel Rives D'Azur and the nearby Majestic Bar; indeed, calamities such as those would, in peacetime, have been seen as good for business. But if the war had reduced the local competition, the price paid had been a concomitant reduction in both staffing levels and clientele.

Staff at the Beauregard, as with many hotels along the Riviera, had always been drawn from the bubbling cosmopolitan stew-pot of French, Italian and North African stock. The coming of war had seen the younger French employees, following patriotic impulses of one sort or another, decamp for 'Vichy' – the unoccupied southern half of France, which nodded allegiance to the German invaders but had, so far, avoided giving them house-room – whereas those of Italian stock had forsaken the Beauregard's kitchens and wine cellar to proudly serve Il Duce, and those of North African origin had scampered to Marseilles, seeking a passage to Algiers or Tunis in the mistaken belief that the war would not cross the Mediterranean.

The war had left M. Fleurey with few reliable staff, a host of additional tasks and duties to perform personally and, most depressing of all, a much-reduced clientele in terms of both quantity and quality. M. Fleurey longed passionately for the days when the hotel's lobby and cocktail bar bubbled with the refined chatter of young English voices, always polite if occasionally too loud, for the English had discovered Mentone and taken it and the Beauregard to their hearts. Up until that fateful late summer of 1939, the young English lords and ladies (as M. Fleurey referred to them with pre-revolutionary deference) had arrived in convoys of open-topped touring auto-mobiles, each with more equipment, it seemed, than the invading Italian Alpine Corps troops who replaced them the following season.

Now all M. Fleurey had to remind him of those golden days was a Lost Property cupboard stuffed with forgotten tennis racquets, discarded woollen swimwear, parasols, two bags of golf clubs, a picnic hamper, a wind-up gramophone and a dozen records, numerous garishly jacketed novels by an author called Francis Beeding (whose publisher insisted the reader would 'Sit up all night' with), two ukuleles with broken strings, a guitar with no strings at all, a trombone slide but no trombone, and at least five leather rugby balls – the latter being explained by the determination of visiting English males to play the game in the town where the Reverend William Webb Ellis was buried.

But that was not quite all, for M. Fleurey, a dedicated Anglophile, had also retained a series of photographs of his most distinguished English visitors – the ones who had always been polite, returned for several years running and whose accounts were always settled promptly, with generous gratuities. M. Fleurey had a gallery of such framed photographs hanging on the wall of the mahogany-lined sanctum which he called his office, the one place of peace and privacy he had managed to retain while the rest of the hotel was, in the main, given over to the Italian army and naval officers and their mistresses, many of whom, Fleurey was ashamed to admit, spoke in the Mentonasc dialect.

That night, however, he had three legitimate guests, which is to say paying customers who were not likely to require any of the more delicate, and unadvertised, services usually provided by the housekeeping staff in the dead of night.

They had arrived late in the evening, on the last train from Genoa, and had been urged towards the Beauregard by the Italian military policeman on duty at the station, who would no doubt be calling on Fleurey in the morning for his 'commission'. They were an unlikely trio, dressed in civilian clothes of good quality but in need of cleaning and pressing, and gave the impression that they had been reluctant travelling companions, for they regarded each other uneasily and seemed anything but relaxed in each other's company.

Their papers were spectacularly in order: two Frenchmen and one German, all with addresses in Marseilles. The younger of the Frenchmen – a tall, strongly built man of hard muscle and unblinking eyes, who spoke with a thick Corsican accent – demanded a double room with twin beds and specified that only one room key was required. His older companion, a smaller, balding man in his mid-forties, avoided eye contact with anything except his own dusty shoes and spoke not a word. He was, Fleurey guessed, an 'Israelite' – a French Jew – and oddly seemed warier of his Corsican companion than he was of the German, who spoke good French and courteously asked if the hotel kitchen could find them something to eat.

Fleurey himself prepared and served them a dinner of fish soup and what his English guests in happier days would have insisted on calling 'cold cuts' (Étienne was fond of most things *Anglais* but did draw the line at their culinary skills), and took some relief in the knowledge that, not being Italian, his guests would not complain about the quality of the wine he provided.

As they ate, Fleurey observed them through a peephole in his office; on his side a discreet sliding frame in the wood panelling, on the lounge side an unremarkable small round window high enough up the wall to be, it seemed, redundant.

The curious hotel manager, who was now also concierge, cook, waiter and sommelier, did not find his new vocation as a spy particularly rewarding, for he could see but not hear. Not that the three travellers seemed remotely interested in engaging in energetic debate or even polite conversation, although it did appear that the German, who had registered under the name Dr Haberland, was the only one making any attempt at conviviality.

Their sparse dinner devoured, the two Frenchmen, with the Corsican thug taking the lead, stood up abruptly and left the German at the table. M. Fleurey slid back the cover of his peephole and attended to his duties, collecting plates and glasses and apologizing to the remaining guest for not being able to offer coffee. The German, Dr Haberland, gave a suitably Gallic shrug of his broad shoulders, told Fleurey not to distress himself, and then concentrated on smoking a small, pungent black cheroot.

M. Fleurey paused on his way to the kitchen to make sure – for old habits die hard – that the two Frenchmen were climbing the stairs to their bedroom and requiring nothing further. The thought struck him that the young Corsican one was *escorting* rather than accompanying the older one up the stairs, but he put it out of his mind and made a perfunctory assault on the washing up.

If his German guest did not require his attention, then he too would retire for the night, but on his return to the lounge he found it empty and the door to his office ajar. Biting back his outrage at such an invasion of his sanctum, remembering of course that the Germans had recently proved themselves expert invaders, he approached his office door. His straining ears picked up a stream of guttural German and then the loud click of a telephone receiver being replaced.

'May I be of assistance, m'sieur?' he announced from the doorway.

The German turned to face him, blissfully unconcerned at being discovered.

'Forgive me, M'sieur Fleurey, for appropriating your telephone,' said Dr Haberland. 'I was making my transport arrangements for the morning. There will be a car coming at eight o'clock to take me to Marseilles.'

'Your journey has been . . . disrupted, I suspect,' said Fleurey, examining the face of the soft-spoken interloper in detail for the first time since his arrival.

'You could say that,' said the German with a resigned smile. 'Our ship was warned of the presence of enemy submarines and so we were diverted to Genoa under the protection of the gallant Italian air force. Consequently, we had to impose on your hospitality for a night.'

'It is no imposition, I assure you. It is a pleasure to have guests who are not in uniform.'

Instinctively the small Frenchman bit his tongue. These days one had to be careful what one said and to whom, but the word 'uniform' had escaped from his brain because the tall, athletic man before him would surely be as comfortable in a uniform as he was in his crumpled linen suit. With his clean facial features and his sharp blue eyes, he exuded the self-confidence often automatically thought of as arrogance among Germans. There was no doubt he would be considered a handsome man by the female of the species, and there was every indication that he was well aware of the fact. The only blemish that Fleurey could see – and he was a man who saw many every morning in the shaving mirror – was a livid purple scar some four centimetres long which snaked down the left side of his nose from the bridge almost to his upper lip.

'These must be difficult times for you, m'sieur,' said Dr Haberland, with a slight deferential nod, 'and not as life was before the uniforms came.'

The German pointed a finger along the line of framed photographs on the office wall, each one showing a group of happy faces smiling from bar, from beach, from harbour wall, outside St Michel Archange, inside the Jardin Serre de la Madone, or from around a well-stocked table into a camera.

'They were happy days,' Fleurey said wistfully.

'Your visitors were mostly English?' the German asked, but there was no threat in his question. Not yet, at least.

'Many of them, yes. It is fair to say we were popular with the young English. Some would come every year and we got to know them quite well.'

Dr Haberland's tracking finger paused, indicating one photograph in particular which showed four men in blazers, flannels and white, open-necked shirts, strolling on the beach, their arms looped over each other's shoulders, their legs outstretched as if in a chorus line. They were middle-aged men, not boys, but they all had youthful, almost innocently foolish expressions as they grinned – no, the word they had taught Fleurey was 'gurned', though he had no idea what it meant – into the lens.

'Were those four regular visitors?' asked the German conversationally.

'They had stayed here before,' said Fleurey, 'individually, that is, but I believe they were friends in England and perhaps two or three times they had holidays here together, or with their wives or girlfriends. They were all very pleasant gentlemen.'

'Have you thought that these pleasant gentlemen will all now be wearing uniforms?'

Fleurey shrugged his shoulders and opened the palms of his hands. 'I had not considered that, m'sieur. It is something I find difficult to comprehend.'

The German's finger closed in on the photograph like a slow-moving arrow, indicating one of the four happy faces shown, the tallest and thinnest of the group, with a shock of unkempt fair hair and large, round-framed spectacles.

'He for one' – said Dr Haberland with certainty – 'will certainly be serving his king and country in some capacity by now, take my word for it.'

Étienne Fleurey knew that for reasons he could not explain he should be worried and that mental alarm bells should be ringing, but instead he was consumed with curiosity.

'Do you, perhaps, know that gentleman?' he asked, determined to keep any trepidation out of his voice.

'Oh, yes,' said the German, and his hand moved, index finger still extended, until it was pointing at the scar wriggling down his face. 'He gave me this.'

ONE

Birthday Boy

The Dorchester Hotel, London. 20 May 1970

I t was said by almost all who knew him that the war had changed Mr Albert Campion.

It was as if the air of exuberant gayness he had worn in the 1930s, rather like a loud and vulgar waistcoat, had been exchanged, after 1945, for a more sober, sombre frame of mind, grey and austere enough to fit perfectly with the changing times. Mr Campion's supporters always maintained that this was the necessary psychological camouflage for a man who had made a career of not being noticed emerging into a new world.

Of the guests, mostly distinguished, who gathered at the Dorchester Hotel to celebrate his seventieth birthday, there were some who had seen the transformation at first hand, some who had suspected that a change in his character had taken place due to his embarking on both marriage and fatherhood in wartime, and there were those blissfully too young to have known Mr Campion before the war, or indeed the war itself.

Knowing that on such an august occasion his guests would demand a speech from him (much as an angry village mob made demands, though without the pitchforks and torches), Mr Campion had taken the precaution of making a few notes. Confident that at least some of his audience would appreciate his nod towards Horace's famous *Ab ovo usque ad mala* dictum, he intended that his personal life-menu from egg to apple would sweep gloriously from being a child of the Victorian era to a New Elizabethan pensioner. Along the way he would note numerous cultural and social milestones. The Wright brothers for one, or rather two, must certainly be mentioned, having started the craze of men flying which had culminated, last year, with man making a firm boot-print on the moon. The BBC, Campion was sure, was bound to be accepted sooner or later as a cultural institution, despite its diversification into television, a popular drug which really ought to be available only on prescription, and he really must make a point of thanking Al Jolson for inventing talking pictures, Mr Disney for the gift of Technicolor and the Duke of Ellington for providing the soundtrack.

'I don't think you are taking this seriously,' said Amanda.

'A leopard can't change his stripes,' rumbled Mr Lugg.

'Don't you encourage him! He really has to learn that music hall is dead and he doesn't have to play the fool. All the people at this party know what you're like and they've come because they love or respect you, not to suffer your end-of-the-pier act.'

Mr Campion smiled fondly at his wife.

'I notice you said love *or* respect, inferring that I am not entitled to both. So if I cannot persuade our guests to love me for my witty patter, do you think I can gain their respect by pointing out that I have, so far, lived under six monarchs and fifteen different prime ministers, perhaps sixteen if I can hang on until the election next month? Or are they just coming for the cake? There will be cake, won't there? I only agreed to have a birthday on condition there was cake.'

'Yes, there will be cake,' Lady Amanda relented and smiled, 'with thick white icing strong enough to stand on.'

'And marzipan, I 'ope. A proper birthday cake 'as a good half-inch underlay of marzipan.'

The Campions looked at the bald fat man, both of them thinking that the mere mention of cake, icing and marzipan should by rights have turned the straining buttons on Lugg's starched white shirt into death-dealing projectiles and his bow-tie into a garrotte.

'Haven't you got an elsewhere to be?' Mr Campion suggested airily as Lady Amanda tied his bow-tie for him, her delicate fingers manipulating the back silk as skilfully as a pair of spiders cooperating on the perfect web. 'Downstairs, in the party room perhaps? Surely there must be minions to intimidate, spoons to count, napkins to fold, guests to insult; things like that.'

Lugg's Easter Island statue of a head trembled in mock indignation, an expression the Campions were all too familiar with.

'I fort I was an 'onoured guest at this shindig, not being a flunky as per usual,' grumbled the fat man. 'But since you're taking your own sweet time getting dressed and having your hair done, I don't mind doing a bit of meeting-and-greeting downstairs while you keep the crowds waiting.'

'I won't be long,' said Campion, deliberately running the fingers of his right hand through his still luxuriant, if white, hair, 'but when you do have a good head of hair . . .'

'All right, don't rub it in,' grumbled Lugg, noticing in the mirror in front of which Campion was preening that the room's overhead lights were producing a reflective glow from his bald pate.

'You could go and say hello to the guests, I suppose, as long as you don't start frisking them or chucking bricks at any you don't like the look of.'

'We expecting the usual suspects, then?'

Mr Campion turned sideways on to the mirror, appreciating both the slim figure inside the sleek dinner suit and the slender arms of his wife around his shoulders.

'They're a motley crew but you'll know most of them, although there are one or two guests arriving from the Continent from whom I have successfully managed to conceal your existence for many years.'

'Foreigners, eh? I might have known,' muttered Lugg, making no attempt to hide his distaste; not at nationality but at being kept in ignorance.

'There will be an important French lady, a German gentleman and two ladies of Spain, so best behaviour, please.'

'And 'ow will I recognize 'em?'

'As they are neither family of mine nor friends of yours, they will be the ones standing politely to one side, behaving themselves, not shouting for a waitress and demanding more aperitifs and canapés.'

'Do you want me to converse with them, or do I just stand there like a wooden Indian?'

'Probably best if you say as little as possible. Get Rupert and Perdita to do the small talk. Oh, and you should know, the German gentleman is a Freiherr.'

'A friar? Wot, like a monk?'

'Freiherr; it's a title, somewhere between a knight and a baron, so show some respect.'

Lugg sighed dramatically and shifted his considerable bulk in the direction of the door of the suite. 'Another case of "up the workers", eh? Don't worry, I know my place.'

'I have never seen any evidence of that,' Amanda whispered in her husband's ear.

'And don't mention the last World Cup,' said Campion to Lugg's broad retreating back.

*   *   *

Two private function rooms had been booked for the party on the ground floor of The Dorchester, a dining room with a view out over Hyde Park and immediate but discreet access to the Grill kitchens, and an adjoining reception room which housed an exceptionally well-stocked bar and a small area of staging just big enough to allow a trio of jazz musicians to entertain without causing a riot.

It had fallen to Mr Campion's son Rupert and his wife Perdita to be in the front line of welcoming the guests. It was a duty they had volunteered for; or rather, Perdita had volunteered them in lieu of providing, in her opinion, a decent birthday present. As both were aspiring thespians, their thoughts on seventieth-birthday presents suitable for a man who lacked nothing and desired even less tended towards the theatrical, but when the best Rupert could come up with were tickets to the premiere at the Garrick of *Sing a Rude Song*, a show based on the life of Marie Lloyd which the pair had seen earlier in the year when it had been developed at the Greenwich Theatre, Perdita bridled that the gift seemed rather pusillanimous. Rupert's defensive pleading that the show did, after all, star Barbara Windsor cut no ice, and neither did Perdita's counter-suggestion of the new Beatles LP *Let It Be*. So they compromised by offering their services as unofficial maître d's for the event. They had even suggested that they could perform their roles in any character or period dress of the birthday boy's choosing, but Lady Amanda had rapidly and quite violently vetoed Mr Campion's immediate suggestions of 'Tarzan and Jane' and insisted on formal evening wear. Rupert had also been put firmly in his place by his mother when he had suggested, as he would be in a dinner jacket, that he might entertain arriving guests with a display of magic. 'Absolutely not!' Lady Amanda had thundered. 'If I won't permit your father to do his card tricks and his juggling act, I am certainly not allowing you.'

The younger Campions had therefore taken up their stations with solemn professionalism, making sure they were in position before Lugg could interpose his personality on the arrivals before they had taken off their coats.

'You really should have briefed me,' Perdita complained as the cars and taxis began to flock down Park Lane.

'About what, darling? It's a party, just enjoy yourself,' soothed her husband.

'About the guests, you twit. You've got to remember I won't know half of them.'

'And I won't know the other half,' said Rupert, 'so we'll cancel each other out, but we're not ushers at a wedding. We're supposed to get everyone to mingle, so let's introduce ourselves to everyone, whether they want to meet us or not. I'll try and whisper a few crib notes if any of the family black sheep show up.'

'Your family has black sheep?'

'A whole flock of them, so I'm told, and speak of the Devil, here's one now – well, not a black sheep so much as a grey one with black spots.'

Outside the hotel, a man was decanting himself in somewhat ungainly fashion from a black cab, the raincoat he carried folded over his arms seemingly acting like handcuffs as he hopped on one leg, freed a hand and began to search his pockets for the fare due.

'Is that a Campion?' Perdita asked as she frantically signalled for a waiter with a tray of drinks to come and stand by her side.

'Of a sort,' answered Rupert, 'it's a cousin of mine, Christopher, youngest son of Dad's younger brother.'

Perdita watched the man approach the hotel lobby. He tripped once, over a rebellious shoelace, and appeared sincerely relieved when a liveried doorman demonstrated how the glass doors opened to allow him entry. He had the Campion height but at least double the usual portion of Campion girth, and his decision to go hatless exposed a prematurely balding head and a half-hearted attempt at what Perdita understood to be called a 'comb-over'. As he came under the strident lighting of the hotel interior, she could see that his complexion was what – on a farmer in a Dorset field – would be called 'ruddy', but on a middle-aged man in a dinner jacket is usually classified as 'florid'. She also noticed that he had large, thick-fingered hands, which added to the initial agricultural impression.

The new arrival's rather horsey face lit up as he recognized Rupert across the lobby, but no sooner had he begun to stride purposely towards the younger Campions than he seemed startled by the fact that he was still carrying his raincoat, and he swivelled precariously on his heels through ninety degrees and set off with great purpose towards the cloakroom.

'Poor old Christopher,' said Rupert plaintively, 'he was always slightly odd. Lugg always put it down to the fact that his father had been "dropped on 'is 'ead" when he was at Eton, but I don't really believe any diagnosis which comes from the likes of Lugg. Still, some of the family had high hopes for Christopher at one time.'

'So what happened?'

'He went into public relations,' Rupert said smartly, then turned his attention to the main doors, beyond which several well-dressed guests were being decanted from a large and stately Bentley.

'The Earl of Pontisbright, unless I'm very much mistaken,' observed Perdita. 'We are duly honoured.'

'We are, actually. Hal is rarely in the country these days.'

'The woman is his daughter?'

'Yes, Sophia Longfox and the juvenile lead at her side is her son Edward; he'll be about seventeen now but he'll still probably get put on the kids' table with Cousin Christopher.'

'Christopher? But he's *ancient*! Well, you know what I mean; he's old if he's not quite ancient, like Lugg is ancient.'

'Christopher was thirty-four last birthday,' said Rupert grimly.

'Good grief! Public relations must be harder than they say. And who's that in the Rolls-Royce? I am *so* glad we left the Mini at home.'

'That, my dear, is a genuine war hero; if you believe his autobiography, that is. Lord – and Lady – Carados; Johnny was a Spitfire ace and Pa helped him out of a spot of bother at the end of the war.'

Perdita's eyebrows jumped to attention. 'I have come to know just what "a spot of bother" means in your family. I do hope the oldies are not just going to sit around talking about the war.'

Rupert sighed. 'I think that's inevitable, given the guest list I saw. I was warned there would be an important German gentleman coming and an equally important Frenchwoman, both people Pa knew in the war, though I'm not sure whether we're supposed to keep them well apart or not.'

'Well, should we need a peacekeeper or a bit of law and order, then here's the very man.'

Without having to check, Rupert knew to whom his wife referred and, sure enough, marching towards the hotel with the precision of a colour sergeant major showing a class of graduating officers how it should be done was the solid-oak figure of Commander Charles Luke of New Scotland Yard.

'I'm surprised they let you in here, you old recidivist.'

'Aw, come on, Charlie, draw it mild. You're supposed to be off-duty and having a good time at this 'ere party. In fact, I've been delegated to make sure you 'ave a good time whether you want one or not.'

The hapless waiter Lugg had summoned with an imperious flick of his neck, as though heading home the winning goal at Wembley, offered the pair a tray of champagne cocktails and surrendered two glasses as though paying a ransom.

'Well, I wouldn't want you to strain yourself, Mr Lugg, so I'll join in the fun and frivolities and start by wishing you the best of health.'

As the pair chinked glasses in a toast, Luke's eyes scanned the room.

'Checking for photographers?' Lugg asked with a sly grin. 'Wouldn't look good in the *News of the World* on Sunday, would it, the star copper of New Scotland Yard sipping champagne with the lower classes at a society birthday bash?'

Luke peered down from his considerable height at Lugg's already empty glass.

'I'd hardly call that sipping,' he said drily, 'but in fact I was looking for the birthday boy.'

''Im an' the boss lady is upstairs in the suite they've taken for the night. He's having his nails done and she's showing him how to tie his dicky bow so it doesn't look like a bat's flown into a mirror. He'll be down shortly to soak up the applause and adoration and take stock of all his presents. Speaking of which, what did you get 'is nibs?'

'What do you get the man who has everything?' Luke asked rhetorically. 'Especially when you know that if you asked him, he'd say that what he'd really like would be an electric train set or a Dan Dare annual, if they still do them. So we had a powwow down at the Yard, where there's plenty think very highly of him and even wanted to chip in.' Luke reached into the inside pocket of his dinner jacket and produced what appeared to be a fat sharkskin spectacles case. 'In the end we got him these as a bit of a joke, from All At The Yard, as it'll say on the card.'

Lugg took the case and opened it, then raised it closer to his bulging eyeballs. 'Strewth! Silver bracelets!'

Instinctively Lugg recoiled from being in close proximity to a set of handcuffs, even if they were clearly made for decorative rather than custodial purposes, nestling in a presentation case on a bed of red velvet. But curiosity conquered instinct, and he brought the open case up to his nose, peering intently at the shining object nestling within.

'I 'aven't got my jeweller's loupe with me, but that looks to me like the leopard's-head silver hallmark for London, and the date letter looks like a little aitch, which would make them . . .' his brow furrowed as he did some mental arithmetic, '. . . 1963, I reckon.'

'You haven't lost your touch,' said Luke, taking back the case and closing it carefully. 'They were commissioned in the Silver Vaults on Chancery Lane, but they were never collected. We had this theory that they were something to do with the Great Train Robbery, but when the silversmith's customer never came to collect them – and had left a false name and address anyway – they eventually came on the market. We thought Albert might appreciate them.'

'Oh, he will,' said Lugg, swivelling smartly on his heels to relieve a passing waiter of two more cocktails. 'They'll take pride of place in his own personal Black Museum, right alongside Jack the Ripper's second-best top hat and Rasputin's beard-trimmer. And them's two characters he personally brought to justice – if you believe the memoirs he's never written.'

'Now there's a thought,' said Luke, glancing casually – or as casually as a police detective ever could – around the room. 'Why hasn't Albert ever written his memoirs?'

'He's lazy,' Lugg confided, leaning in conspiratorially. 'Prefers to leave the hard graft to others; besides, you've heard some of the stories he tells. Who'd believe the half of it?'

'Well, there's plenty here tonight could tell a few tales about dear old Albert. There's one for a start: old L. C. Corkran, unless my eyes deceive me. He must be even older than you.'

'You be careful, Charlie Luke, or there'll be no cake for you,' growled Lugg, turning his head on its axis to follow Luke's gaze towards the stooped, elderly man who was testing the red lobby carpet with a heavy-calibre walking stick – as though detecting mines – as he slowly approached them. 'Mind you, Elsie is showing his age, right enough.'

All his friends, many of his acquaintances and the occasional past enemy, referred to Mr L. C. Corkran by the conflation of his initials into the deceptively twee nickname 'Elsie'. The soubriquet belied a long, dutiful military career, which remained deliberately inglorious as most of it had been conducted under the shroud of what was, perhaps too casually, referred to as 'Security'. After one working life quietly defending the nation's interests, Mr Corkran had, on reaching pensionable age, taken his retirement CBE and moved in to the private sector to protect and serve the international interests of Omega Oils. The work there had been equally discreet, and for

the most part kept well out of the public eye, or at least off the
financial pages of the press, and though it had not brought him any
further honours or recognition, the financial rewards had been spectacularly greater than those of a civil servant of equal experience.

'He's out of the oil business, I believe,' said Luke quietly.
'Maybe second-retirement doesn't agree with him. Some chaps
can go downhill pretty fast when they've not got an office to go
to every morning.'

''Specially if they're bachelors and haven't got a wife to find
them jobs to keep them out of mischief,' observed Lugg coldly.

The older man, still dapper, his white hair neatly trimmed to
conform to army regulations, limped towards them slowly and carefully, then leaned heavily on his walking stick.

'I thought I'd find you two here guarding the silverware,' he said
impassively, for it had always been difficult to discern whether Elsie
Corkran had ever possessed a sense of humour.

'Elsie,' said Luke and Lugg together, as if testing the hypothesis.

'Been in the wars, have we?' added Lugg, indicating the twisted
blackthorn walking stick, 'or is that for self-defence when the party
gets out of hand?'

Corkran glanced down at the stick as if it had appeared in his
hand by magic.

'Oh this? Spot of gout, that's all. One of the hazards of owning
a bit of property in the Douro region; still, it's provided me with the
perfect birthday present for Albert. I've sent him a case of the '55,
one of our vintage years. What did you get him?'

'A corkscrew,' said Lugg, keeping his face straight.

'Yes, Albert's not the easiest person to buy presents for,' Elsie
agreed, with an air of pedantic innocence. 'I thought of buying him
a book but . . .'

'He's already read one,' quipped Lugg, ignoring the impact of
Charlie Luke's elbow in his ribs.

'No, not to read, a book to *write* in. You know, one of those
leather-bound journals with blank pages, so he could jot down his
thoughts and memories. We used to call them commonplace books
at school, didn't we?'

'You might have; we didn't have them at my school,' said Lugg.

'Your school didn't have books of any sort,' snapped Luke, 'but
that's not a bad idea, Elsie. Funnily enough, we were just talking
about Albert's memoirs and what scandals they could reveal.'

Lugg leered in agreement. 'Nice juicy scandals, I 'ope.'

'And therein lies the problem, as I know to my cost. Albert and I both signed the Official Secrets Act thirty years ago and, as men of our word, that oath we swore, for it was a loyal oath to our generation, still stands. It's all very well to spread all those rather colourful stories about him helping the police out when they're baffled.' Elsie caught the warning lights flashing in Luke's eyes. 'I mean, in stories like that, the police are fair game, aren't they? But it's different when it comes to security matters, and especially Campion's war work. There are lots of stories there which will probably never get told, regardless of this Thirty-Year Rule business.'

'I 'appen to know that his nibs is rehearsing a speech about his distinguished career – that's his word, not mine, by the way – up in his room at this very moment,' said Lugg, 'but I don't know if he'll be mentioning the war as he's got this top-drawer German coming; a Freiherr, no less, which I'm told is a title and not an occupation.'

'Now that is interesting,' said Elsie. 'You wouldn't happen to know this German chappie's name?'

'As a matter of fact, I do, 'cos it's Ringer, which is Kraut for "wrestler" – a career I once considered pursuing when I was in my prime.'

Luke scowled at the fat man. 'To maintain diplomatic relations, can we refrain from calling people Krauts, Huns or Jerries for the rest of the evening? And when you were in your prime, I think you'll find they were called gladiators – and a centurion was a rank, not a tank.'

'Oh, hark at you, the laughing policeman.' Lugg recoiled in faux indignation. 'I know how to behave, thank you very much. Mr C. made it clear that this Ringer might be a German, but he's a gentleman and deserves to be treated as such. What's so special about him anyway?'

'Well, if memory serves,' said Elsie, whose expression confirmed that it did, 'that would be the same Robert von Ringer who, during the war, tried to kill Albert Campion. At least twice.'

TWO
Many Happy Reorientations

'Your French is better than mine,' said Perdita, arming herself with a second cocktail.

'I doubt that,' said Rupert, 'but I do speak almost fluent mountaineer, so you'll have to take the French lady. Don't worry; as long as you make the effort to speak French and not just shout at them in loud English, the Froggies don't mind how bad you are, they just appreciate the effort. Though you'd better not refer to them as Froggies.'

'You are wasted on the stage, darling, as the notices often say. You should have been in the Diplomatic Corps. Of course, I won't call her a Frog, but what has mountaineering got to do with anything?'

'There, behind the French lady coming out of the lift. The chap in tweeds hovering on one foot, giving a masterclass in looking uncomfortable in the presence of other human beings. Which, incidentally, he is; or so I have been forewarned. That's Jonathan Eager-Wright, the famous mountaineer. He's retired now, of course, but still prefers the company of a sheer rock wall or an ice shelf to anything resembling the warmth of human contact. He's a man who has contempt for society but also the manners not to display it in public.'

'You're quoting your father, aren't you?'

'They're old friends,' Rupert confessed. 'Had a few adventures together before the war. During the war as well, if the gossip is to be believed.'

'Gossip?' Perdita gasped in mock horror.

'Well, rumours, tittle-tattle and the odd unguarded word rather than gossip. Pop has never talked about what he did in the war, and of course I was nobbut a nipper, as they say in Rep, but I picked up a few clues along the way. Whatever he did it was pretty secret stuff.'

'You mean he was a spy?' Now Perdita's surprise was genuine.

'I wouldn't go that far,' said Rupert, 'more a sort of counter-spy, I think. He worked for L. C. Corkran, the old boy over there chatting to Luke and Lugg, who was something senior in what they call "Security".'

'He doesn't look anything like James Bond,' said Perdita with a small pout.

'The best spies never do, but forget about all that ancient history, we're supposed to be on duty. Come on, let's get this party started, or at least point people to the bar. I'll take the antisocial mountaineer and talk about crampons and pitons and other fascinating stuff; you take the nice French lady and discuss shoes or Paris fashions. I have to say she looks quite stylish.'

'All Frenchwomen do,' Perdita said in a low growl, 'and I'm sure we can find something slightly more intelligent to talk about. I think she looks about the right age to have been your father's lover. I think I'll start by asking if she was.'

'I say, steady on, Perdita!' Rupert gasped, but his wife was already striding purposefully across the lobby.

'*Madame Thibus? Bienvenue à Londres.*'

The older woman's reply was in English, and as elegant and silky as the evening dress which sheathed her figure.

'How charming to be welcomed personally, although I do not believe we have met, have we? Please forgive me if we have, but I could surely not have forgotten such a pretty face.'

Perdita nipped the end of her tongue between her teeth, an actor's trick to prevent blushing, she had been taught, although she suspected it was more an old wives' tale than an old thespian's.

'I am Perdita Campion,' she said, proffering a hand, which was taken graciously.

'You are the daughter of Albert?' She pronounced it *Alberr* and made it sound as sultry as only a Frenchwoman could. 'Then you should call me Corinne.'

'Daughter-in-law, actually; Rupert Campion is my husband. We have been recruited to greet the guests and keep them happy.'

'Is Albert not here?' The Frenchwoman raised her head and looked around.

'He and Lady Amanda are in their suite getting changed, so that he can make a dramatic entrance when everyone is assembled.'

Madame Thibus smiled briefly. 'Yes, that would be just like him, but it must be rather boring for you having to make conversation with all us old folk.'

'Madame is surely not including herself with the senior generation?'

'I have always lived and worked among older men,' Corinne Thibus said casually, 'so their company does not intimidate me, and I see few ladies of my age here.'

Perdita considered that the Frenchwoman had a point, and frantically tried to work out her age, angrily realizing that she was doing exactly what most of the males in the hotel had probably already done. Madame Thibus was certainly older than Perdita, though not as old as Lady Amanda, the distance between them being no more than fifteen years either way. This would put her in her very early forties, though with more flamboyant eye make-up, curls in her short blonde hair and some tie-dyed casual tops and a shorter skirt, she could probably pass for thirty. But then, Perdita reasoned, why should she have to? In her figure-hugging long yellow silk dress with its pattern of large red flowers – almost certainly by Givenchy – and bright red sling-back high heels, she looked supremely confident in herself. That was the trouble with Frenchwomen: they looked *chic* at any age. Her accessories gave no further clues, for she wore no jewellery apart from a small square Rolex watch on a thin white leather strap and carried a practical tapestry-weave handbag over her arm.

'The party arrangements are very informal,' said Perdita, 'so please stay close to me and my husband. Allow us to entertain you, rather than having to put up with some of the old buffers who will be here tonight who only want to talk about the war.'

She had spoken lightly and with a beaming innocence, but Madame Thibus responded in all seriousness.

'But my dear,' she said, patting the front panel of her handbag, 'that's exactly what I am here for.'

'I say, well done for capturing the Abominable Snowman, young Campion!'

Rupert had introduced himself to the solitary figure of Jonathan Eager-Wright – that noted misanthrope who was said to actively avoid contact with any human found below the snow line – and was attempting with some difficulty to make conversation. It was not that the short but muscular white-bearded man was unwilling to talk, it was that he was only willing to talk about a planned expedition (which he clearly expected Rupert to be conversant with) to climb something called the Great Trango Tower in a place called

Gilgit-Baltistan, and the devilish unfairness of the fact that he had been forbidden to participate in the 20,000-foot ascent on the grounds of his age! After five minutes of what was more a lecture than a conversation, during which time he had managed to narrow the geography down to northern Pakistan, Rupert was delighted to be interrupted by the deeply fruity tone of a jovial voice belonging to Mr Augustus Randall, land-owner, countryman and, for income tax purposes, farmer of Monewdon in the country of Suffolk.

'Evening, Guffy,' said Eager-Wright, frowning in annoyance at being cut off in mid-exposition of the geology of Kashmir, 'you're looking . . . ample. Mary, you're as delightful to look at as ever.'

Mary Randall, née Fitton, was now sixty, and although her hair had lost all the familiar family fire, she still exuded the natural Fitton grace.

'I couldn't agree with Mr Wright more, Aunt Mary,' said Rupert, leaning in to dutifully kiss the cheek being offered.

'Don't tell me you're taking lessons on how to charm women from old Eager-Beaver,' chortled Mr Randall, for whom the word 'ample' was a perfect description of how he filled his dinner suit. 'He gave up on women years ago when it became clear your mother had set her bonnet at Albert.'

'Don't be rude, or crude, Guffy,' scolded his wife. 'Delighted to see you Jonathan, you are looking extremely well. All that mountain air clearly agrees with you. And Rupert, you remain my favourite nephew, and one day I am sure we will be coming up to town to see you and the lovely Perdita gracing the West End stage. If, that is, I can ever tear Guffy away from his pigs or his pigeon shooting.'

One of the reasons Mr Augustus Randall had fallen head over heels in love with Miss Mary Fitton some thirty-seven years previously when he had first seen her in the village of Pontisbright, was that she had 'none of the modern nonsense about her' and shared Guffy's love of the countryside, estate management and long-haired dogs with uncontrollably friendly natures. They were living proof that a marriage could be made and sustained on fresh air, long walks in wellingtons across dew-soaked fields, ostentatious displays of support for the local church, harvest festivals and village fetes, making their own cider and, in Guffy's case, taking a slice of Suffolk ham, rather than bacon, with his eggs for breakfast every morning.

Rupert was fond of Guffy, and he could have nothing but affection for Mary, as she was a mirror image older version of his mother

Amanda, albeit a far more serious and unadventurous reflection. He knew the stories of how the Fitton sisters, and their younger brother Hal, had first met with Mr Campion and Mr Randall and indeed Mr Eager-Wright when in their younger, carefree – and in Guffy's case, less well-padded – days before the war. He knew that Guffy's slightly tart remark about Eager-Wright's relationships with women were very near the mark, as he had it on good authority (from Perdita, who had heard it from Amanda herself) that Eager-Wright had been initially quite smitten by the teenage Amanda, only slowly realizing that Amanda had set her sights, and fixed them, on Albert Campion.

'As soon as we get top-billing,' Rupert smiled at his aunt, 'then there will be front-row seats in your name, though Perdita's more likely to fly solo than I.'

'Long as it's not Shakespeare,' said Guffy. 'Never got on with the fella at school; too many strange words for my tin ear.'

'I've told you time and again, Guffy,' said his wife, 'just think of the dialogue being spoken in a Suffolk accent by a farmer staggering home from the pub, and it will all make perfect sense. And you, Rupert, don't you dare put yourself down, although I admit Perdita is very talented. Where is she, by the way?'

'She's over there,' said Guffy, rising unsteadily on tiptoes in order to look over Rupert's shoulder, 'talking to a very stylish piece of feminine pulchritude.'

'Oh Guffy, you sound just as ridiculous as you always did,' chided Eager-Wright although he, like the others, had sneaked a glance in Perdita's direction.

'He is ridiculous, Jonathan,' said Mary, 'but he's also right; she is very stylish and very attractive for her age. She's not English, is she?'

Rupert had long since ceased to be amazed at the instinctive radar embedded in the female mind.

'You're absolutely right, she's French,' he said, and Mary Randall nodded in confirmation. 'She's Madame Corinne Thibus and she was added to the guest list at the request of the French Embassy at the last minute.'

'Really? Do we know who she is?' Mary enquired, before turning on her husband. 'You can stop ogling now, Guffy: remember your blood pressure.'

'Sorry, old gal,' muttered Mr Randall, hiding his face in his champagne cocktail.

'I have no idea, Aunty, that's why I sent Perdita on ahead to scout the land. All I know is that Pop approved her inclusion on the list, saying it was a pleasant surprise as he hadn't seen her since the war.'

'Goodness, she must have been young,' Mary murmured to herself.

'Sure he didn't say *before* the war?' Guffy Randall grasped the shoulder of Mr Eager-Wright, who had shown no particular desire to bolt for the fire exit. 'I mean, we did do quite a few trips to France before the war, when we were all bachelors gay, of course. Down south mostly: Nice, Monte, Mentone. Good trips, although I seem to recall you always wanted us to head for the Alps or the Pyrenees so you had something to climb.'

Eager-Wright stared quizzically at Guffy as if wondering what point he was trying to make.

'Funnily enough,' said Rupert, 'there's another French person coming tonight, Monsieur Fleurey from Nice.'

Guffy's face lit up in the way it did, Mary was to say later, when one of his sows won a rosette at the Suffolk show.

'Fleurey did you say? Not old Étienne Fleurey of the Beauregard in Mentone? Goodness, we had some rum times there, I can tell you.'

'No, this is Joseph Fleurey, the son. He's in the same line of business but in Nice, and when Perdita and I stayed there he looked after us extremely well. He said something about repaying a debt of honour for something Pop had done at some time or other, but I didn't pay too much attention, I'm afraid. I was too busy keeping Perdita out of the casino.'

'Tricky things, casinos,' murmured Guffy. 'If I didn't know better, I'd suspect that they fixed the odds in favour of the house.'

'And I suspect they see punters like you coming a mile off,' observed Eager-Wright with thinly veiled sarcasm.

'Which is why Augustus is not allowed within *two* miles of one,' said Mary, 'and that includes the bingo stalls on Yarmouth pier.'

Mr Randall sighed wearily, as if this burden had been his birthright.

'That's Joseph Fleurey over there,' said Rupert, nodding in the direction of a tall, smartly dressed and really quite dashing young man talking enthusiastically with an even younger, equally attractive, fresh-faced blonde female wearing a chiffon 'little black party dress', with the emphasis on the 'little', in that it had a hemline so high there was nowhere else to go but down.

Rupert realized he had been looking at the couple – who seemed to have introduced themselves perfectly well without any external assistance, apart from that minidress – for perhaps longer than was diplomatic, considering Perdita was in the same room.

'He's chatting to Precious Aird. She's American, the daughter of a friend of Mother's and a bit of an archaeologist. We met her up in Sweethearting earlier in the year; she's quite something.'

'Young Monsieur Fleurey certainly seems to think so,' said Mary Randall. 'They seem to be hitting it off.'

'Precious seems to get on with everyone,' said Rupert.

'Just the sort of girl every birthday party needs.' Even as she spoke, Mary was aware that the three males in her audience were all looking at her quizzically. 'Because she's *young*. There are too many old fogeys here; we need the young ones to remind us this is a party. I rather hope she behaves disgracefully.'

'Rupert here used to be the life and soul of any party when he was in short trousers,' said Guffy, as if imparting confidential information. 'Whatever the occasion – birthdays, Christmas, even funerals – there was Rupert running around like a dervish shouting "Happy Reorientations", without fear or favour, to anyone who'd listen. Never had a clue what you were on about, but you did it with such charm and innocence that nobody clipped you round the ear, not even Lugg.'

'Perhaps somebody should have,' Rupert grinned. 'Perdita certainly would if I started doing it now, but we're both on best behaviour tonight.'

'Is Albert, though? He's usually got a party trick or two up his sleeve.'

'I suspect Amanda will have had a word,' said Mary casually.

'She certainly has,' Rupert confirmed. 'There will be no magicians, jugglers or surprise cabaret acts, just lots of good food, some fine wines, and that trio you can hear tinkling away in the background. They have strict instructions not to play "Happy Birthday" at any point in the proceedings, no matter how much Lugg attempts to bully or bribe them. There will, obviously, be a birthday cake.'

'And a few surprise guests,' Guffy observed. 'One or two faces I don't recognize, as well as that very chic Frenchwoman. I mean, who's that chap with a ramrod up his spine talking to Elsie Corkran?'

'Now he,' said Rupert in a conspiratorial whisper, 'is really interesting.'

*   *   *

Mr L. C. Corkran could not have agreed more.

'Freiherr von Ringer, it has been a long time.'

'Indeed, Mr Corkran. I do believe it to be ten years since we had cause to meet. It was Berlin, and we were observing some rather unenthusiastic bricklayers building a wall.'

The two men released their handshake.

'I have to admit I am surprised to see you here, Freiherr.'

'Robert, please. The title is rarely used these days.'

'But then you would have to call me "Elsie", as everyone around here seems to.'

'That is not seemly,' agreed the German. 'Not for two old warhorses of our age. I will call you "Brigadier" if I may, for that was the rank you retired with, was it not?'

'Technically, yes – and your sources are as good as they ever were. I take it we are *both* retired now, at least officially?'

'Happily so, for several years now. It will not be long before I am inviting Albert, and of course yourself, to my own seventieth birthday party in Germany. I have very pleasant house at Ludwigshafen on the Bodensee and you would be most welcome.'

'Ah, yes,' said Mr Corkran, remembering, 'you're a Schwabian, aren't you? I hear that Lake Constance can be very beautiful.'

'It is. You must visit, especially the island of Reichenau, which we call the isle of flowers, something which should appeal to you English gardeners. It is quite a short flight these days.'

'To Zurich with Swissair,' said Elsie thoughtfully. 'That would be the nearest airport, since they stopped landing Zeppelins at Friedrichshafen, wouldn't it?'

The German gentleman allowed himself a smile. 'Dare I suggest you have been doing some research, Brigadier?'

Mr Corkran dismissed the implication immediately. 'Checking up on you? Perish the thought! I'm out of all of that now; it is just that I am cursed with an excellent memory. Or perhaps I should say a selective memory. I can remember the war years, for example, and I can remember your fondness for quite disgustingly vile small cigars, but it took me over an hour to locate my damned cufflinks this evening.'

Freiherr von Ringer allowed his smile to broaden. 'On the way here I made a bet with myself, Brigadier, as to how soon the war would be mentioned and who would introduce the subject. That it would be mentioned was never in doubt, and now the cat is out of the bag, as it were, let me satisfy your curiosity without the pain of you having to ask embarrassingly oblique questions.'

'My dear chap, I have no wish to put you on the spot,' said Mr Corkran without much conviction.

'Let me assure you, you do not,' said Ringer, 'when I tell you that I am here because of what happened during the war. Mr Campion's war.'

'We have casinos in America too, but I guess they're not as swanky as yours.'

'Perhaps not,' Fleurey answered the delightful American girl diplomatically, without being too sure how 'swanky' might translate into French, 'but that is surely only because we have a longer tradition of them than you do in Las Vegas.'

Precious Aird cocked her head on one side. 'Are all you Europeans so goddamn polite?'

'Only if it impresses beautiful young ladies,' said Joseph with a delicate bow, 'but then I am French and it is expected of us, we being the most romantic people of Europe.'

'And the most modest,' said the girl, 'and that's something nobody's ever accused us Americans of. I guess the new world must look pretty brash to the old one.'

'I would say young and vibrant rather than brash, and the old always find the young more attractive.'

Precious bowed her head in deference to the compliment. 'You talk the smooth talk, as we would say, and you can probably do it in several languages.'

Monsieur Fleurey acknowledged this with an embarrassed grin, and sheepishly held up his right hand, displaying all five fingers.

'Wow! I can just about order a cheeseburger in kindergarten Spanish.'

'And there you have the advantage over me, for I have no idea what a cheeseburger is.'

'Long may it stay that way, though I don't think it will,' said Rupert, ushering a waiter with a tray of cocktails towards them. 'I see you have met our American friend, Joseph.'

Joseph shrugged his shoulders. 'As a Frenchman, I always make a point of finding the two most attractive women in any room, and your wife happens to be occupied.'

'Perdita is taking her duties as a hostess seriously and probably doing better than I am. She appears to have a full-time job on her hands keeping the old buffers away from Madame Thibus.'

Joseph nodded his head wisely. 'She is French, of course. Such style, so *chic*,' he murmured, then straightened suddenly as he caught Precious Aird's piercing glance of disapproval.

'Quite a cosmopolitan event,' she said to Rupert. 'I feel outnumbered, what with all you Brits, a German, the French contingent and those two Spanish ladies I met in the powder room.'

'Spanish?' said Rupert, reaching for the typed guest list he had stuffed into his jacket pocket as a secret crib-sheet. 'I don't think we're expecting any Spaniards here tonight.'

'Well, they said they'd flown in from Madrid, which is Spain, right? Nice woman, quite small, dark-skinned, black hair. Said her name was Señora Vidal. She has her daughter with her, a mousey little thing about your age called Priscilla – no, Prisca, that was it.'

Rupert gave a small snort of relief, folded the single sheet of paper and slipped it out of sight. 'Oh, the Vidals, mother and daughter. Of course they've been invited, but they're not Spanish. I think they're as French as Joseph here, it's just that they choose to live in Spain.'

Once again Joseph Fleurey shook his head, this time in mock bemusement.

'There is,' he sighed, 'as you English say, no accounting for taste.'

There was a movement in the air in the reception area. Conversations trailed off as if a volume control had been dialled down so that the sounds of ice tinkling in glasses and leather-soled shoes squeaking on the polished floor could be heard clearly. It was not a dramatic, ordered silence, more of a pregnant pause, as the waiters – scattered strategically through the throng of guests – automatically stood to attention. Upper bodies turned and heads strained in the direction of the staircase as a couple in evening dress descended with stately grace.

'Friends, Romans, countrymen . . .' Mr Campion began modestly.

THREE
The Unsurprising Surprise Party

'How wonderful it is to see you all here, to witness the empirical truth that you can't keep an old dog down however much you try, and especially not if there's a jolly party in the offing. I will now pass among you to say hello personally, while quietly accepting the lavish and far-too-generous, not to say extravagant, presents you will press upon me. And then the feasting can begin!'

There was a smattering of polite applause, naturally subdued by the fact that the majority of guests were holding a glass in at least one hand, but loud enough to drown out Lugg's half-hearted whine.

''Bout time, too. Me stomach's beginning to think me throat's been cut.'

Charles Luke, who had remained within earshot, gave him the 'policeman's eye', his gaze travelling downward from bald dome over the extensive midriff and ending at a pair of highly polished size twelves. Lugg was familiar with such unblinking scrutiny from officialdom and likened it to 'being measured for a coffin, but more in hope than expectation'.

'There are enough layers on you to see you through several winters,' observed the policeman, 'and you'd definitely be the hot favourite in a lifeboat if the subject of cannibalism ever came up. You could provide a few juicy cuts, I reckon, what with the muscles being so nicely relaxed due to lack of exercise.'

'Cheek!' grunted the fat man. 'I didn't come here to be insulted.'

'Where do you usually go?'

'Strewth, give it a rest, Charlie, or people will start thinking it wasn't so clever paying for our senior coppers to attend Clown School.'

'All right, then,' said Luke, drawing himself up to his full height, the better to survey the crowded room, 'let's get down to brass tacks. Who's the one we should be keeping an eye on?'

Lugg adopted his standard expression of shocked outrage. It was a familiar expression to those who knew him well, and one which Lady Amanda had once said reminded her of all three of *The Mikado*'s little maids from school having seen a mouse run across the footlights.

'I don't know what you mean, Charlie old cock. Must be an occupational 'azard, looking for ulterior motives all the time.'

'We're never off-duty when the likes of you are around.'

'Now that's harsh, Charlie, not to say mean.' The fat man reached out a paw to lessen the weight on a passing tray of drinks. 'Can I pass you another shampoo cocktail – oh, wait, I forgets, yer always on duty, ain't yer?'

The policeman planted his feet together and stretched his spine and neck, the better to allow him to scan the guests, or at least the tops of their heads, the most common hair-colouring being white, apart from the odd flash of red, ranging in shade from soft auburn to fiery copper, which betrayed a Fitton heritage.

Although Luke's eyes never stopped moving, his mouth and facial muscles offered few signs to the non-professional observer that he was still carrying on a conversation with the large bald man next to him. To the majority of the circulating guests sparing them a passing glance, they appeared as solid and as immobile as a pair of teak bookends.

'I'm curious, that's all,' said Luke *sotto voce*. 'Albert never made a big thing about his sixty-fifth, so why all the pomp and circumstance for his seventieth?'

'P'raps the old boy's feeling his age,' Lugg said blithely. 'The old threescore-and-ten finally hit home, simple as that.'

'Anyone who thinks that Albert Campion does anything simple is on a hiding to nothing; there are plenty of miscreants enjoying Her Majesty's hospitality to vouch for that. Now there's family and friends here aplenty, fair enough; but also a few surprises.'

'You mean the foreigners?'

'I've nothing against foreigners as such, and if a caravan of Bedouin camel-traders or the Mongolian state circus turned up to a Campion party, I wouldn't be at all surprised, but I get the feeling these ones are here for a reason. That German chap – officer class if ever I saw such – and that Frenchwoman Perdita's been assigned to, she's not here to make up the numbers. Then there's the other two women who are keeping themselves to themselves. Not sure what they are, but they're not British – they're still on their first drink and

they've not beaten a waiter to death to get at the canapés: both dead
giveaways.'

'You've not been sleeping on the job, 'ave you?' said Lugg with
reluctant admiration. 'Still, keeping yer eyes peeled is what bein'
a Peeler is all about, isn't it?'

'Very droll,' said Luke out of the corner of his mouth. 'How long
did it take you to think up that one? All I'm saying is that this party
is something a bit more than your average birthday bash, which
shouldn't be surprising knowing that Albert is centre stage.'

'Oh ye of little faith and giant enormous suspicious mind!' intoned
Lugg. 'What's wrong with the old boy havin' a few friends and relatives round to eat him out of house and home, blow out a few candles
and wish him more of the same? That's what relatives are for.'

'Friends and relatives is one thing, but there's some business
going on here; something official, maybe, I can sense it. I just can't
put my finger on what the connection is, but I'm sure there is one.'

'You've a suspicious mind, Charlie Luke, and it's probably stood
you in good stead in the past, but just switch it off for tonight and
enjoy yourself, will yer? It's a party wiv no surprises.'

'Now that makes me really suspicious,' said Luke. 'No surprises?
When Albert Campion's involved? That'd be a first.'

Lugg sniffed loudly, but whether it was in agreement or derision
was unclear. His attention had been drawn across the room to where
Mr Campion, with Amanda on his arm, was moving slowly towards
the dining room. Without pausing in his effusive meeting-and-
greeting of his guests, Campion caught the fat man's eye and bobbed
his head in his direction.

'*Allez-oop*,' said Lugg, 'that's my cue to bring order to the
proceedings.'

Charles Luke, guessing what was coming, took a pace backwards
and averted his ears as Lugg drew breath, inflating his chest until
the shirt buttons creaked in protest, opened his mouth and let forth
a majestic bellow.

'My Lords, Ladies, Gentlemen, and them that really should know
better! Dinner is served!'

There would be method in Campion's madness, thought Luke; there
always was with Campion. Not that madness was the right word,
eccentricity would be nearer the mark, but even that did not allow for
the careful thought Mr Campion put into most things – and then went

to extraordinary lengths to make it appear that nothing consequential ever crossed his mind. The seating plan for the dinner, Luke suspected, had been the subject of long and careful thought, despite the fact that Campion was faffing around like a drunken bridesmaid at a wedding trying to find his own place, even though it was obvious to all present that the centre seat on the top table was reserved for the birthday boy.

The dining tables had been laid out in the shape of an E, with the short centre wing missing; a pair of large printed charts displayed on easels in the doorway gave the key to the seating placements.

Somewhat to his surprise, Luke found himself allocated to the top table with the immediate Campion family and, it appeared, part of the contingent of guests Lugg had rather disparagingly dismissed as 'the foreigners'.

Luke was no stickler for the boy/girl/boy/girl seating arrangement at formal dinners; his experience of such events tended to be limited to police or civic functions, where the majority of the participants were male and females were in short supply. But he was slightly surprised that, given the number of couples present and even the availability of 'spare' women, the Campions had seemingly made no attempt to impose the formula.

Naturally, Amanda was on Mr Campion's immediate left, and next to her was seated the elegant Frenchwoman, then Rupert, Astrid Vidal and Hal Fitton. On Campion's right sat Perdita (could that be in some way a protective placement?) and next to her the distinguished, certainly aristocratic, German. Luke found that he himself came next and to his right, Guffy Randall. It was a curious order of battle – if, indeed, a battle was expected. At the far end of the two elongated wings of the truncated E-shaped table, in what were often referred to as the 'rear-gunner' positions, L. C. Corkran and Lugg sat in isolated but imperious splendour. Whether they were guarding against unwanted intruders or there to prevent deserters was not clear.

The thought flitted across Luke's mind that he had been placed next to the German as some sort of guard or watchdog, but he did not allow it to settle as, if the German had posed any sort of threat, Campion would never have seated Perdita next to him.

Mr Campion, as if he had been tracking that floating thought on his mental radar, leaned forward across Perdita to reassure his policeman friend.

'Excuse my rudeness, Perdita dear, but before we put our bibs on, I want to make sure that Charlie has been introduced to an old acquaintance of mine. Robert, this is Commander Charles Luke of New Scotland Yard. Charlie, please make yourself known, and by that I mean socially and not professionally, to Robert von Ringer of the BND, the West German . . .'

'*Formerly* of the BND, Albert,' said the German with a rueful smile, 'formerly. I am now retired to a life of growing roses and going fishing.'

'Sounds idyllic, Robert. Do forgive me.'

'The West German *what*?' asked Perdita innocently.

'Bundesnachrichtendienst, if I've pronounced that correctly,' Luke offered, 'is what BND stands for. Herr Ringer is an officer of the West German intelligence service.'

'Your pronunciation is perfect,' said Ringer, 'as is your deduction, apart from the word *retired*, which I must emphasize.'

He made that most awkward and un-English gesture of civility, the handshake from a seated position.

'And that is how you met Albert?' pressed Perdita. 'Working in this BND?'

'Oh no, I was in a completely different organization when I first met Albert.'

Luke felt the hairs on the back of his neck rise.

'Would that have been . . .?' he began carefully.

'Why, yes it would,' said Ringer smoothly. 'It was at Cambridge when we were students together at St Ignatius.'

Luke allowed himself a lengthy but discreet exhale.

'He almost killed me there,' Ringer continued cheerfully, 'so it was only fair that I tried to kill him when we met again during the war.' He turned to face Perdita and smiled. 'Of course, I wasn't trying very hard.'

Perdita, a 'useful and versatile actress with a future' (*Hampstead and Highgate Express*), assumed an air of polite curiosity, as if she were an honoured guest at a flower show trying to elicit the secret of forcing early rhubarb from a reluctant Yorkshire allotment holder.

'Are you teasing me, Herr Ringer, or Commander Luke, or both of us?'

'Don't you stand for any nonsense from Robert, Perdita,' said Mr Campion over his daughter-in-law's shoulder. 'He's dying to tell you how I gave him that scar.'

Now Perdita's staunch performance dissolved into an expression equidistant between shock and fascination, only a decent upbringing preventing her jaw from dropping open like a trapdoor. It was not so much what Campion had said in a stage whisper into her left ear, more the embarrassment of being caught out – as she was sure she had been – staring at the scar which wormed its way down the left side of the German's face.

'Oh, goodness, was I gawping?'

'I'm not sure what "gawping" means,' said Ringer politely with a toothy grin, 'but if you were doing it, it did not give offence. I am used to people noticing my little disfigurement. They see it and they hear my accent and immediately assume I am of the Prussian officer class and this must be a duelling scar. They are wrong on both counts.'

'Oh, come on, Robert,' said Mr Campion, wielding a butter knife in an ostentatious attack on a crusty *petit pain*, 'we were having a sort of a duel.'

Now Perdita's jaw did slacken, and her mouth formed a perfect, and perfectly pretty, 'O'. It prompted Ringer to reach out and gently pat the back of her hand.

'It was not a duel, it was a match – a fencing match – and we were using foils, not sabres. We were both trying out for the university fencing club, at Cambridge, when we were students there. Of course, Albert was older than I—'

'Thank you for that, Robert,' said Campion. 'I had quite forgotten how old I was. If only there was just one day in a year when one could be given a timely reminder . . . perhaps someone might send one a card or two . . .'

'Albert was quite good,' Ringer continued unabashed, 'and I thought he would go for his Blue, but after the accident he lost interest, I think. You see, he lunged, I parried, and the tip of his foil shot up under my guard helmet. It was a freak accident, and something I would think impossible to do intentionally. Fortunately for me, Albert was aiming for my nose and not my eye.'

'That sounds awfully violent,' said Perdita, who now found herself patting Ringer's hand in a reassuring manner.

'Nonsense,' said Campion, performing a swashbuckling parry-and-thrust with his butter knife. 'Real fencers – the ones you get at the Olympics – prefer the sabre or the épée; they dismiss a fight with foils as "aggressive knitting". It was a freak accident and I always blamed Robert for choosing a mask which didn't fit properly.'

'Don't be horrid! How did you ever forgive him, Herr Ringer? I'm assuming you have, of course.'

'But of course I have, my dear girl, and, to be fair, the fact that many of my countrymen *assumed* it was a Mensur scar probably helped my career in some small way.'

'What on earth is a Mensur scar, and how can it possibly improve your career prospects?' As she asked the question, Perdita felt Campion gently lean in to her shoulder, no doubt with ears pricked and a foolish grin on his face. Beyond Ringer, Charles Luke also leaned forward, making no secret of the fact that he was eavesdropping.

'The Mensur was a tradition in German universities, which taught students coolness and courage, although it often took more courage to avoid the tradition than to participate in it. Basically, two young men stand facing each other and hack away with large, very sharp swords, aiming for the left side of the opponent's head. Never the right side. That would be unsporting.'

'You call this a sport?' Perdita gasped.

'No. Fencing is a sport; the Mensur is a brutal ritual designed to satisfy a public opinion that was two hundred years behind the times, as a distinguished Englishman once said.'

'Jerome K. Jerome,' Mr Campion interjected, 'when he wrote about the Mensur in *Three Men on the Bummel*, and very scathing about it he was too.'

Perdita turned her head towards her father-in-law. 'The same chap who wrote *Three Men in a Boat*?'

'That's the feller. *Bummel* was the follow-up, though it is pretty much forgotten nowadays. Published in 1900, and I know that because an aunt with ridiculously high expectations and little experience of children bought me a copy for my first birthday. I seem to remember chewing on a corner at the time, but it was, I admit, some years before I got around to reading it.'

As was often the case, Perdita took a moment to decide if Mr Campion was being serious and, once satisfied, she asked: 'What's a "Bummel"?'

'I think it would translate as a slow journey or a wandering, or a stroll perhaps. Is that fair, Robert?'

Perdita swivelled back to Ringer, who was nodding in agreement. 'And what does "Mensur" mean?' she asked him.

'That I do not think can be translated. The Mensur is the event, the fight itself. Mensur comes from *mensura*, the Latin for measurement, referring to the distance the swordsmen had to stand apart during the ordeal.'

'Why didn't they run away? I would have.'

'So would I, but fortunately I managed to avoid the student fraternities which supported the Mensur. The scar Albert gave me – completely by accident – did however make people back home in Germany assume I had gone through with the idiotic ritual. Of course, the practice has been discouraged for many years now, but my mother told me that in her youth, young girls were very attracted to young men with Mensur scars.'

'Well, I think that's just awful,' Perdita said primly. 'It sounds the same principle as those awful tattoos which Hell's Angels have themselves covered with. I think they just make men ugly, though I know some girls . . . Oh, I'm so sorry, Herr Ringer, I didn't mean that you were ugly, I just meant that it was stupid when men try to make themselves look tough with tattoos. Charles, help me out here.'

Luke, who had been listening intently, but holding his peace until now, entered the fray.

'I've found it pays to keep an open mind on such things. I've arrested some giant bikers who have skulls and daggers – and worse – inked on their forearms and they've come along quietly, whereas one of the most evil, cold-blooded killers I ever met was no more than five foot four and weighed less than eight stone wringing wet. He had a single tattoo on his chest, a heart with an arrow through it and the words "I Love You Mother". You just can't tell.'

He locked eyes with Ringer, who showed no indication that he might flinch first.

'I'm guessing, Herr Ringer, that you have seen Albert since your days at Cambridge.'

The German smiled and took a moment to answer. 'Was that a question, Commander Luke, and if so, was it an official one?'

Luke returned the smile. Perdita, who was watching them closely, felt that some sort of bond had been formed; or, if not a bond, then at least territorial boundaries had been agreed, but the detail eluded her. She stole a glance at Mr Campion, who had turned to his wife and was, it seemed, giving her the recipe for the Consommé Mikado which would be their soup course.

'A policeman's curiosity, Herr Ringer; something I am sure you are familiar with as a policeman of sorts yourself.'

'A *retired* policeman, of – as you say – sorts, and I quite understand.

I know you are an old friend of Albert, and it must seem strange that a German you have never heard of suddenly appears out of Mr Campion's past. Your first thought will have been that it must be something to do with the war. Please, do not deny it out of politeness, for I am not offended. To answer your question, I did see Albert after Cambridge and, as you have probably guessed, it was during the war.'

'But you wouldn't have been on the same side,' interrupted Perdita, her hand flying to her mouth too late to stop the words escaping.

Ringer, still facing Luke, winked a mischievous eye. 'That was a problem,' said Ringer slowly, 'at least initially.'

'Are you going to tell us what Albert did in the war?' Perdita was almost breathless with excitement. 'He's never told us a single thing, has he, Charles?'

Luke attempted to strike an official pose. 'There may be very good reasons for that – reasons of state security, perhaps.'

'Tommy rot!' said Mr Campion, making Perdita jump in her seat as he re-entered the conversation. 'National security has nothing to do with it. I've kept Mum on the subject out of angelic modesty and monk-like humility, pure and simple. However, having reached a memorable age, I have decided to abandon modesty and spend my twilight years basking in your admiration. That is why I have seated you next to Robert, so he can tell you of my gallant wartime experiences in Vichy France, and I put Charlie there in the wings to satisfy his copper's curiosity, otherwise he wouldn't sleep at night. Ah, here comes the soup.'

Campion sat back in his chair and made a dance-of-the-seven-veils flapping show of tucking his napkin into his shirt front as a half-platoon of waitresses arrived bearing dishes as carefully as if they held nitroglycerine.

'Consommé Mikado was a long-time favourite on Atlantic liners going back yonks. Perhaps they even served it on the *Titanic*, though I'm not sure that's a recommendation, but I do know they've intro-duced it on to the menu of the *QE2*. There will be a rather fine manzanilla amontillada arriving momentarily to go with it.'

'Stop changing the subject!' complained Perdita.

'He's very good at that,' observed Luke drily.

'I want to hear about your wartime adventures in France,' said Perdita over a quivering lower lip.

Robert von Ringer took pity on her. 'Shall I be your biographer, Albert?'

'Good heavens, no,' said Mr Campion, 'if the story must be told, it must be an *auto*biography, because no one is more qualified to blow my own trumpet than I am. So, as we're sitting comfortably, I'll begin, and I'll start with Robert inviting me to the Riviera back in 1942 . . .'

'When the war was on,' Perdita said slowly.

'Oh, yes, bombs and bullets flying everywhere, it was quite a show; made all the newspapers.'

'And this gentleman here *invited* you to the south of France?'

'He most certainly did. It was a very clever invitation too. Well, it had to be; there was a war on, you know. Fortunately Robert was very clever, which is why he was such a good spy.'

'A spy? One of ours?'

'Certainly not. He was one of theirs.'

FOUR

The Man from the Minimax Fire Extinguisher Company

London. June 1942

They say things are classified 'Top Secret', not so much to protect the secret itself, but the source of the secret, and so it was not unexpected when my invitation to visit the Riviera came in such a convoluted way, although nothing very much could surprise us by that stage of the war.

We'd all seen it coming, of course – well, I had, ever since Neville Chamberlain had waved that ridiculous piece of paper at Heston airport in 1938, and now we were in the thick of it. The desert war was seesawing, as it always seemed to, Hitler was biting off more than he could chew in Russia, and dear old England was being invaded by Americans. At the start of '42 the US air force had seven men and no aeroplanes in England but, by Christmas, they'd turned East Anglia into an aircraft carrier flying the Stars and Stripes; we were very glad to see them, though.

In London, we'd taken an active dislike to good old Father Thames. Some even called the river London's very own fifth column, because all the Luftwaffe had to do on a starry night was follow its curves right into the heart of the city to find a target for their bombs. But London could – and did – take it, and American journalists were in raptures about the slogans on the sides of buildings which said 'Take Courage', not realizing that it was an advertising campaign for the Courage brewery in Southwark.

We were all frightfully tied up with our war work. In Amanda's case that was producing Rupert, whereas Lugg was doing his bit in the Heavy Rescue Squad, working with the ARP people and the fire brigade whenever there was a raid. It was rumoured that Lugg also had a nice sideline in rearing the odd porker or two to supplement the meat ration.

I myself, being naturally heroic, not to mention modest, had volunteered for frontline duty with the Light Brigade, even offering to supply my own horse, but for some reason no one took me seriously. They put a lot of obstacles in my way: I was too tall, I was too short, my eyesight wasn't good enough and, worst of all, I was too old. Oh, and there was something about the fact that we weren't doing cavalry charges any more. Anyway, the long and short of it was that the only enterprise willing to offer me gainful employment where I could do my bit was the Minimax Fire Extinguisher Company of St James's.

Now that may not sound terribly exciting, but the last thing we did was sell fire extinguishers – that was merely what the sign on the building, Number 54 Broadway said to fool the passers-by. We were in fact the offices of the very secret Secret Intelligence Services, although it wasn't *that* secret an address. Throughout the thirties, the Nazis had a man from their embassy posing as a blind matchseller on the pavement opposite the front door, monitoring the comings and goings. The regulars there actually missed him when he was rounded up once the war started.

Most of the building was kept busy supporting the forthcoming raid on Dieppe, which was supposed to be a dress rehearsal for the invasion of Europe, though it didn't turn out all that well. All the hard work was left to the professionals like L. C. Corkran and the secretarial staff, who really were brilliant. They were a fantastic bunch of young women, incredibly hard-working and very intelligent, most of them recruited from Oxford colleges. Oddly enough, the Service didn't seem too keen on recruiting from Cambridge. Can't think why.

So there I was, in a back office – only the top bods got offices with a view over St James's – with nothing very important on my plate, going through paperwork and stirring my tea to try and make the sugar go further, when a call came in from our colleagues in the SOE, the special operations people, over in Baker Street.

It was a major with rather a plummy voice, rather like a northern rep actor trying to do Shakespeare at short notice, which is a bit unfair as he became an actor after the war – quite a good one, as a matter of fact. I was quite surprised, not to say a little flattered, that he had requested to speak to me by name, but he just asked gruffly if there were 'any other Campions working at Broadway?' I had forgotten for a moment that there was little love lost between the competing secret services and let my guard down.

It turns out that this SOE chappie had heard that a Frenchman had just arrived in London and, while going through the usual vetting process, had insisted that the one man in England he was prepared to bare his soul to was little old me, much to the annoyance of our friends and allies the Free French, who tended to be rather protective in such matters.

Naturally, I was flattered to be in such demand, though not a little curious as to how my name came to be in the frame, so to speak. When I was told that the reticent Frenchman newly arrived in London was in fact Monsieur Étienne Fleurey, manager of the Beauregard in Mentone, I was at first delighted and then immediately in a state of panic, as my first thought was that he was after an unpaid hotel bill. But surely I would have remembered doing a moonlight flit on any bill big enough to risk chasing me across hostile territory to collect.

In those days, all refugees from France were dumped at Olympia so they could be sorted and vetted. We had to be careful in case the Germans tried to infiltrate their agents into the country posing as volunteers trying to join General de Gaulle, and anyone remotely suspicious was singled out pretty early on and interrogated by our chaps at the Royal Victoria Patriotic School, a Gothic pile down in Wandsworth, which was built as an asylum for young girls orphaned during the Crimean War. We called it, rather grandly, the London Reception Centre, and the hard-core interrogations were done by MI5's finest. Our customers, most of whom were genuine refugees, were detained nearby – the women in a school on Nightingale Lane and the men in various places on Trinity Road, which was very convenient because, if any of them turned out to be spies, they were marched over the road to Wandsworth Prison where they were hung.

I can't say I enjoyed visiting the Reception Centre, as it was a pretty depressing place, full, for the most part, of decent Frenchmen and women, who had gone through hell to get to England, only to find they were being quizzed and questioned by a Gestapo they thought they'd escaped from. But that was our job; we had to disbelieve everything we heard, question everything, trust nothing.

Étienne Fleurey had been held at London Reception for more than a week, bleating my name and pleading for an audience, before I got to hear about him. He'd already had a rough time of it, crossing from Vichy into the Occupied Zone and then making his way on forged papers to Brittany, where he made contact with the Resistance who'd smuggled him on to a fishing boat which was doing a moonlight run to Cornwall. An amazing number of little ships did that unofficially during the war, avoiding German patrols and minefields, and then our Coastal Command fly-boys and our submarines, but then the Bretons and the Cornish speak virtually the same language, and have never given a hoot about what Paris or London told them.

The old boy's face truly lit up when he saw my grinning mug. I think the Reception Centre interrogators had given him a bad time and, thinking about it, I could see why. I mean, Étienne wasn't exactly their usual sort of customer. He was too old for one thing, long past the age of the normal young bloods who wanted to join de Gaulle and fight the Boche, plus the fact that he'd come from the south of France, which hadn't been occupied by the Germans and was run from Vichy. Even if that was a puppet regime, standard wisdom was that life there wasn't as bad for the locals as it was in the OZ, as we called it – the occupied northern zone. And there was the fact that Étienne was a middle-aged hotelier and our war effort wasn't really desperate for his skills.

So, the question was: what had possessed that dear, harmless chap to make a very dangerous journey to Wandsworth, leaving behind the comforts of the Riviera? The only answer he could offer was that he carried an important message – a message just for me.

'My dear, dear friend,' he gushed when I found him, 'I was beginning to despair of ever seeing your kindly visage. It felt as though they were not comprehending me.'

Now, I don't want to give the impression that Étienne was some sort of end-of-the-pier caricature of a Frenchman. He spoke English well enough when he wasn't confused or under pressure, and to me he seemed to have all his marbles present and correct, even though he was in a windowless room being guarded by two of MI5's finest thugs. Certainly, he perked up no end when I told his watchdogs that I could not only identify him but vouch for him, though they didn't look too pleased when I suggested that old Fleurey be released into my custody. That had to be cleared and authorized in triplicate by their superiors, as they were naturally wary of an MI6 bod throwing his weight around on MI5 turf. There was little love lost between the two sections back then: the chaps in Five thought we in Six were prone to put on airs and generally act above ourselves, while we in Six regarded Five as a sort of jumped-up gendarmerie.

Still, they agreed to let me take Fleurey out for a walk on Wandsworth Common. It wasn't exactly the promenade along the front at Mentone, because quite a few bombs had been dropped there from a great height by the Luftwaffe aiming at Clapham Junction, but that had not put off the packs of roaring children playing on the swings that had somehow survived intact.

I had gone to Wandsworth well armed with some decent cigarettes and a hip flask of inferior brandy, and these seemed to put Fleurey at his ease, though he'd clearly been put through the mill by his MI5 inquisitors. We chatted about Mentone and the Beauregard Hotel in pre-war days and the larks we'd had there, and it took me ages to persuade him to stop addressing me as 'milord', but eventually he got down to business.

'I was told to speak only to you, M'sieur Campion, and to no one else,' he said after a healthy swig from my flask. 'I have a message.'

'That was brave of you, or very foolish, depending on what you have to say and who the message is from, old chum.'

He thought about that for a minute, or perhaps he was thinking about another belt of brandy, before he took a deep breath and answered.

'The message I bring you – the message I have carried in fear for my life – comes from an old friend of yours who is' – Fleurey lowered his voice and even glanced over his shoulder – 'a German.'

'I admit I have known Germans in the past,' I reassured him. 'Does this one have a name?'

'Dr Theodre Haberland,' said Étienne, with just a small touch of awe.

I knew in that instant that old Fleurey was being duped, and that what he was about to propose was almost certainly going to be a trap.

'There's no doubt that poor old Fleurey believes the yarn he was spun,' I said when I reported on our stroll on Wandsworth Common. 'It's the story behind the story that could be interesting.'

I was being debriefed – a word I had to learn to say without giggling – by my departmental head, Mr L. C. Corkran, whom we called 'Elsie', but only behind his back. He would sit behind a great oak battleship of a desk, trying to look like a headmaster disappointed in his pupils when we made our reports, but he didn't miss much.

'Do you trust this Frenchie?' he asked me in a voice which suggested that six-of-the-best would await me if I gave the wrong answer.

'As a diligent hotelier and a dedicated Anglophile, yes,' I said honestly, 'but that was before the war. Mentone was knocked about a bit during the Italian invasion in '40, and of course the Germans have trampled over the northern half of his country, neither of which does much for the hotel trade. I got the impression he didn't like having to suck up to the Italian occupation forces, as they are good at running up bills but not paying them, and he clearly doesn't have much time for the Vichy government and some of their paramilitary thugs, who seem particularly pusillanimous down in the Alpes-Maritime region. But I'd never have put him down as a Free Frencher or a Resistance man; he just doesn't seem the fighting type. Still, I knew him before the war and war changes people.'

'It does indeed,' said Mr Corkran wisely, 'and usually for the worse. What made him come over to England? It must have been risky for him, though he had the luck of the Devil getting through the Occupied Zone and over the Channel without being picked up.'

'I suspect he had help; in fact, I know he did. He told me as much.'

'From the chap who sent the message, I presume.'

'Indeed, and I think Monsieur Fleurey himself was part of the message. The sender was saying: look, this is an old friend whom you know and can trust. I am sending him to you safely as a sign of good faith.'

'The sender being this Dr Haberland?'

'That's not his name, at least not his real one.'

'But he has the power to get Fleurey out of Vichy France, across the Occupied Zone and even across the Channel, not to mention the skill to persuade him to make the journey in the first place. That's impressive.'

'I would expect nothing less,' I said, picking my moment carefully, 'from a Cambridge man of impeccable manners and high intellect, who is now a senior officer in the German military intelligence.'

If I had expected Mr Corkran to bite the stem off his pipe, or his head to simply explode, I was disappointed. He could be a very cool customer, our Mr Corkran; not an eyelid did he bat.

'This Haberland – he was a friend of yours at Cambridge? Why am I not surprised by that? You do know some rum coves, Albert.'

'I thought my rummier acquaintances – and I admit I have a bulging address book full of them – were the reason you recruited me, but I can't count the mysterious Dr Haberland among the rest of the riff-raff. True, he was a year below me at St Ignatius College, which in certain Cambridge circles makes us both riff-raff, but he was, possibly uniquely, both a gentleman and a scholar. His proper name is Robert Albrecht Freiherr von Ringer, but he rarely used the Freiherr title. The Germans went off the whole idea of aristocratic titles after the Armistice and, in these days of National Socialism, a title might be a hindrance rather than a help.'

'Well you'd know all about that sort of thing,' Corkran said, rather gruffly I thought. 'But you're sure that Haberland and Ringer are one and the same?'

'Absolutely. Étienne Fleurey confirmed it, though of course he only knows him as Haberland; but from the description of the scar on his face, and the story he told Fleurey of how he got it, then it's definitely Robert Ringer.'

'And just how did he get that scar?'

'Er . . . that would be my fault, I'm afraid. It was a complete accident during a bout of fencing. It was not, I repeat not, a duel.'

'So there are no lingering hard feelings there?'

'Certainly not on my part, and I seriously doubt if there are any on Ringer's. At the first sight of blood we stopped the fight, called it a draw and shook hands.'

'That the way you do things at Cambridge?'

'That's the way everybody does it on the fencing *piste*. It's required behaviour if it's not in the rules. After trying to stab or slash a chap in the name of sport, the least you can do is shake his hand.'

Mr Corkran did not seem convinced by this and murmured, 'Mmm . . .' in a sort of low kittenish growl before getting back to business.

'We have a file on Ringer, I presume?'

'A thin one,' I admitted. 'He's mid-ranking Abwehr, one of Admiral Canaris's blue-eyed boys, based in Marseilles. That ties in with what Fleurey told me; not that Étienne knows anything about German military intelligence, but he's not stupid. When the man he knows as Dr Haberland summoned him to Marseilles, provided him with the necessary permits and money to travel to the Occupied Zone and even pointed him towards Resistance cells in Brittany, it was fairly clear he was a man of influence if not power. I suspect Haberland had Fleurey's escape route carefully planned out, and was keeping a fatherly eye on the progress of his private messenger all down the line.'

'And Fleurey's motives for volunteering to be a messenger for German intelligence?'

'Threefold, I think. Étienne was always slightly deferential to, and very trusting of, anyone with good manners—'

'Clearly,' said old Corkran, but I ignored him and what I was sure was meant to be a slight.

'Sometimes too trusting, especially when it came to unpaid bar bills. Whatever else he may be, and I have not seen him for several years, Robert Ringer is a gentleman and impeccably polite. Fleurey would have trusted him, and certainly so once he'd declared that he was a former sparring partner of mine.

'Secondly, Fleurey is also an unapologetic Anglophile, not to mention a great rugby fan. They play rugby down in Mentone, you know, and his hotel was very popular with English tourists. He was clearly not happy living under Italian occupation, though I doubt he would be much happier living under the Vichy regime. The chance to get to England, albeit via a journey fraught with danger, would have been very tempting. The third factor which clinched it was that if he agreed to be Haberland's personal carrier pigeon, then Haberland would ensure that Étienne's wife and children were spirited away to Switzerland. That was an important consideration for the poor chap; you see, his wife's half-Jewish.'

'Yes, well that would be,' agreed Mr Corkran in his headmaster's voice. 'So that's the messenger sorted, what about the message?'

'Now that's what's interesting,' I gushed, perhaps playing the schoolboy trying to gain house points too much. 'Haberland told

Fleurey to speak to no one but me, which is why he clammed up when faced with his MI5 interrogators.'

'Those buggers from Five . . .' grumbled Mr C., as he often did.

'His reasoning was that anything Fleurey told them would get straight to de Gaulle and the Free French and they would almost certainly muck things up.'

'That's a bit harsh. We are fighting on the same side, after all.'

'True, but there are plenty in Vichy who trust the Germans more than the Gaullists, though I don't pretend to be an expert on French politics.'

'Winston calls them "caitiffs".'

'Who?'

'The Vichy leaders. I had to look it up.'

'It means contemptible cowards,' I said before I could stop myself.

'I knew you'd know. Now stop showing off and get on with your report.'

'Yes, sir. Fleurey went along with it and wouldn't say a word until he had the shell-like of yours truly at his beck and call. The message Haberland was sending was an offer of intelligence on some secret research being done on the Riviera, out of the French navy base in Toulon. A team of their naval officers under a Captain Jacques-Yves Cousteau are experimenting with a new compressed air aqualung, which would give their underwater divers a greater range and more flexibility than anything anyone's seen before. They are conducting tests in a cove near a place called Bandol, which is between Toulon and Marseilles, and Haberland seems to be offering me a ringside seat for the proceedings.'

'Why would he do that?'

'Because he knows I would appreciate a spot of spear-fishing or a paddle in the wine-dark sea – or is that the Aegean? No, perhaps not. I can tell from the look on your face you're not happy with that theory, but really, I think it's the most plausible.'

Mr Corkran aimed his frozen face at me in one of his famous 'looks', usually reserved for the receiving of bad news at inter-departmental meetings.

'Stop blathering, Albert. What's this Ringer feller up to?'

'He's inviting me to the south of France, but quite why I do not know. One thing's for sure, it's got nothing to do with the French navy's underwater experiments.'

'Why not? Sounds to me as if the chocolate sailors over in room thirty-nine at the Admiralty would choke on their pink gins over something like that.'

'Exactly, and Robert Ringer and his Abwehr colleagues would know that. They wouldn't try and give – or sell – me such a secret, they'd approach someone in naval intelligence. I'm sure they have channels for doing that.'

'Which begs the question of why the Abwehr is offering such intelligence to the enemy in the first place. Could this be an elaborate plot to get one over on the SD?'

Mr Corkran, as usual, had a point. It was common knowledge that there was no love lost between German military intelligence, the Abwehr, run by that cunning old fox Admiral Wilhelm Canaris, and SD or Sicherheitsdienst, the Security Service of Himmler's SS, run until recently by the late and unlamented Reinhard Heydrich. The two organizations were constantly jostling for power and doing each other down in a bloody rivalry which made the internecine sniping between MI5 and MI6 seem positively childish.

'At the end of the day, I suppose it could, though how getting little old me to go to Marseilles would score points for the Abwehr is a mystery.'

'The SD have a fondness for kidnapping the upper classes. They had a go for the Duke of Windsor not that long ago. That's why he was packed off to the Bahamas.'

'I hardly think I'd be a prize catch, and not worth more than half-a-crown in ransom money. No, given the trouble he's taken to send me the invitation, I think Robert Ringer wants to see me about something important. But I also think it has nothing to do with the aquatic adventures of the French navy.'

'Do you intend sharing your evidence for that theory?' asked Mr Corkran, as if awaiting a flimsy excuse for homework not handed in.

'Simply this. Robert is a clever chap; he was far brighter than I at Cambridge, though I admit that doesn't set the bar too high. Given the business he's in and the government he reports to, he has to be clever to survive. He has just taken a French citizen out of a zone of Italian occupation, sent him across Vichy France and then the Occupied Zone, and then helped him across the Channel into the arms of an enemy power, not to mention smuggling a wife with Jewish blood, as the Nazis would put it, and her children into neutral Switzerland.

'Now in doing all that, he was taking an enormous risk. The

Vichy police, the SD, the Gestapo or traitors within the local population could have wrecked his little scheme at any number of points;
even his own organization, as I'm pretty sure he's acting off his
own bat. Fleurey might even have given himself away. In which
case, Ringer would need a cover story, a story to cover himself
should Fleurey be picked up and asked some difficult questions.'

'In which case, Fleurey could only give the cover story because
he didn't know the real one.'

'Exactly, and Ringer would have prepared a position of deniability
or some plausible excuse for his actions, should anyone demand an
accounting.'

'So what's behind all this?'

'The whole point, I think, was to get Fleurey safely to England, where
he would demand to speak only to me and give me a message which
I would know could be trusted.'

'But you just said the message about these French deep-sea divers
was a red herring – if that's not one of your silly puns.'

'It was – it is, and I do rather like the idea of it being a herring
of any colour. The real message Fleurey carried was one that only
a few people in England – perhaps just me – would pick up on.'

'So there's a message within the message, eh? Well, don't keep
it to yourself.'

'It's not so much in the message as in the name of the sender,'
I said, perhaps a little too smugly. 'Ringer knew I would know who
sent the message because he'd told Fleurey about our little fencing
accident at Cambridge and to make sure he mentioned it. But he
never told Fleurey his real name, and Fleurey is convinced he's
called Theodre Haberland, which is the name of a character known
as 'the Professor' in the children's book *Emil and the Detectives*.
It's one of my favourite novels as it happens, and years ago Robert
sent me a German first edition, for which I never thanked him
properly now I think of it.'

'If that's a clue, what's it supposed to mean?' Mr Corkran bristled
to the extent that I feared for his blood pressure.

'It means that whatever Ringer's up to, it will be to our advantage
rather than Hitler's.'

'How do you work that out from a kids' book?'

'Because that particular book was one of Robert's favourites too,
and it was also one of the books that the Nazis made a point of
burning publicly.'

FIVE
Second Bureau

London. June – July 1942

Naturally I couldn't just throw my swimming togs and my bucket and spade into the back of the Lagonda and tootle down to the Riviera, even though Mr Corkran had approved the idea. There was a war on, after all, and that meant getting clearances and permissions in triplicate from all and sundry, but first I did the decent thing and took Étienne Fleurey up the West End for a slap-up meal.

It wasn't what any self-respecting Frenchman would have called a gastronomic experience, except perhaps ironically, but it was the best London had to offer at the time. Got the idea from a chap in naval intelligence who took two captured U-boat crew out on the razzle in an attempt to wheedle some secrets out of them as he got them squiffy. The wheeze didn't work, and at the end of the evening he ended up with two very drunk Nazis in the back of a taxi and no secret information. I think he got into a spot of bother with the Lords of the Admiralty over that.

I was not out to interrogate old Fleurey. I just wanted him to flesh out his story, pick his brains on a few details; anything which might help. Étienne was quite up for it and played along without making too many faces at the plates of stodge we were presented with, and made all the right noises about the bottle of claret I had scrounged up from somewhere.

It seemed that 'Theodre Haberland' had arrived unannounced at the Beauregard earlier in the year, in the company of two other chaps: a rough sort, possibly a Corsican, called Pirani and a middle-aged French Jew called Lunel. Being a good hotelier, Étienne had made sure they had registered legally, even though he had no idea if those were their real names. They had crossed from North Africa on a ship, bound for Marseilles but diverted to Genoa, but had not been travelling together. They were a curious trio. The young,

Corsican thug was clearly acting as a bodyguard, or perhaps just a guard, keeping a close eye on the Jew, who looked like some sort of businessman or lawyer. The polite German, called Haberland, was keeping an eye on both of them.

Fleurey had served his guests as well as he could under the circumstances and waved them goodbye the next morning, not expecting to see or hear of any of them again. When the telephone call came from a Marseilles wine importer that had never previously done business with the Beauregard, he was initially confused, and it took a while for the name Haberland to ring any bells. The offer of an expenses-paid trip to Marseilles, along with the required Letter of Transit, however, to discuss a recently arrived consignment of fine wines and sherries from Spain, of which the retail advantages were considerable, proved to be an offer he could not, in straitened times, refuse.

In Marseilles he met with the man he knew as Haberland in what appeared to be a genuine wine warehouse in the Old Port area, and they did indeed discuss, and sample, wine. But then Haberland had showed his hand and played two aces. The first ace was his connection to me, and he reminded Fleurey that I was the common bond between them. It seems the dear man has some holiday snaps of me and my chums pinned up on his office wall as if we were film stars. I had never thought of myself in competition with Betty Grable or Mae West before.

Haberland would have made it sound like the most natural thing in the world to choose Fleurey as his secret courier, and his second ace-in-the-hole was that while Étienne was off on his mission, his wife and children would be spirited away to Switzerland.

Now that really was the ace of trumps, because Haberland then tells Fleurey that the Vichy government, under pressure from their pugnacious Nazi neighbours, are planning a round-up of Jews in the southern zone – and we all know what that might mean. Poor Étienne has the devil's own choice to make: stick with his family and hope for the best, or trust Haberland and accept a temporary divorce, him sitting out the war in England and his wife and kids in Switzerland.

He chose a divorce which, hopefully, would be of short duration, and put his faith in two foreigners who had fought in a fencing match at Cambridge twenty years before. He was either very desperate or incredibly naïve: possibly both. He had also been incredibly lucky in his journey, and now I had to make some luck for mine.

My first port of call was to the Deuxième Bureau of the Free French Intelligence Service in their pokey little offices round on Duke Street, where I met with the incredibly charming and terribly bright Colonel André Dewavrin. He was known as 'Passy', because all their top agents had code names taken from station stops of the Paris Metro, such as Bobigny, Wagram, Tolbiac, and Étoile. I had once suggested that if I ever joined the Second Bureau they could call me whatever the French for 'Emergency Exit' was, but they hadn't seemed terribly impressed.

I had agreed with Mr Corkran that if I was going to pick the brains of the French, then a quid-pro-quo would be expected and, after checking with Room 39 at the Admiralty, I was to offer them the story Fleurey had brought with him about the French navy's research into aqualungs. I would not, of course, mention the source, and would keep Haberland/Ringer out of the picture.

There were some names I did want to float by Passy, though: Lunel and Pirani, the two guests at the Beauregard whom Robert Ringer had seemed so interested in.

Colonel Dewavrin could not have been more helpful, and even managed to rustle up a decent cup of coffee while one of his minions checked through their files. Monsieur Lunel, whoever he was, did not show up on the Bureau's radar, but there was a distinct *blip* when it came to Pirani, who had, for such a young man, a colourful and lengthy police record.

Paul Pirani, I was told, had wanted to be a gangster from the day he left school, and in a place like Marseilles that was a perfectly achievable career path if, that is, you had no moral scruples and a talent for fighting dirty with boot, fist and blade. He built himself a reputation as a hard man in the prostitution game, which had always been the core business of the city's criminal empires, but he had also shown considerable flair in the drug trade, importing opium from French Indo-China and in smuggling that most profitable of commodities, Parmigiano-Reggiano from Italy. I had no idea that a trade in illicit cheese could be so lucrative, but it seems it had been the foundation of several criminal fortunes.

The Bureau could not tell me anything of Pirani's current activities, although it was known he was an active, and probably enthusiastic, member of SOL – the Service d'Ordre Legionnaire. The SOL, which favoured collaboration with the Nazis, whose policies on race and Jews they particularly liked, was a pro-Vichy militia formed mainly of disillusioned army veterans, malcontents and criminals from the underworlds of Nice and Marseilles. On a scale of general nastiness, SOL was somewhere between Mosley's Blackshirts and the Gestapo, and was to be avoided if at all possible.

There was one name Passy would trust me with, and that was Olivier Courteaux, whom he described as the most important Resistance leader in Vichy France. Although Courteaux's base was in Toulouse in Gascony, he was sure to have trusted lieutenants on the Riviera.

Before we parted, the colonel gave me some wise advice: 'Be careful, M'sieur Campion, if you are planning to visit Vichy, which I think you are, though I will not ask your purpose. You must be aware that it is a strange place. Some call it the Free Zone, but it is not free. In 1940, France was beaten, and beaten well. Thousands of French soldiers were taken prisoner and remain hostages of the Germans. The Occupied Zone, which they control directly, contains seventy-five per cent of French industry, and in addition they demand occupation costs of twenty million Reichsmarks a day. Some say that the creation of the Vichy regime was defeatism, others that it was realism, if the alternative was for France to become another Poland. And now "Liberty, Fraternity, Equality" has been replaced by "Work, Family, Fatherland", which is much more pleasant to the Nazi ear, just as the laws Vichy have passed also appeal to the Nazis – they have banned women from wearing trousers, having jobs and holding bank accounts without the given permission of a husband or father, and encourage the denunciation of Jews. The Vichy police have a standing reward of one thousand francs for the denunciation of a Jew. Denouncing a communist or, worse, a Gaullist such as myself, earns a reward of *three* thousand francs.'

At this point, the colonel paused for a moment to brush, with great pride, a speck of imaginary Vichy dust from the collar of his uniform.

'You will find the Vichy regime cares little for the Allies; it hates General de Gaulle more than it hates Hitler, and there is no special love for the British. You will perhaps have heard the saying that "Britain will fight to the last Frenchman" and so, if you go there, be careful and do not be British. Canada still maintains diplomatic relations with Vichy and as your French is good enough and your accent bad enough, you could easily pass for a Canadian diplomat.'

* * *

I called in on the SOE chaps at 64 Baker Street (though they really should have renumbered it 221B in my opinion) to tell them that it was my intention to become a roving Canadian diplomat in order to grab a few weeks of holiday in the south of France. Two extremely young and fresh-faced captains agreed that it was an excellent plan, and quite frankly were astonished that anyone from MI6 had come up with it.

The SOE boys had never held us in high regard since the 'Great Pigeon Mission', and they clearly had no intention of letting us forget it. Somebody had had the wizard idea of parachuting crates of pigeons into northern France, not to the Resistance to carry secret messages, but just to the general population as a sort of mass observation study. Ordinary French citizens were asked to fill in a questionnaire about the hardships of life under the Germans and the pigeons would carry them back to the BBC in London where they would provide useful propaganda. The ordinary French citizenry made no effort to fill in the questionnaires and were very grateful for the pigeons, which I am sure they found delicious.

The two captains who had introduced themselves as Smith and Jones, which I thought slightly unimaginative given their Baker Street address (I had been hoping for a Holmes and a Watson at least), could not, of course, resist raising the subject. I would like to think I took their ribbing with good grace, smiling politely at their feeble witticisms about recipes for pigeon pie and trying not to wince when one of them used, for the hundredth time, the phrase 'coming home to roost'. Eventually, though, they came up with some valuable background information for me. I did not tell them the reason for my 'mission' into Vichy territory, and they knew better than to ask for details about what I would be doing there or how I would get there, but they were certainly the chaps to ask about getting out of France, hopefully in one piece.

I was sworn to several degrees of secrecy, each one accompanied by the fearsome threat that all SOE agents knew a dozen or more ways to kill a man with their bare hands; the fact that I assured them that I had at least two aunts who could boast the same skill did not cut any ice with Messrs Smith and Jones.

Clearly those SOE chaps thought I would need all the help I could get, and confided that should I find myself in trouble in Marseilles or its environs, then I should seek sanctuary in the

Protestant Seamen's Mission and Reading Room, run by a former
Royal Navy chaplain called Sandy Nevin.

Although British, or more accurately Scottish, Sandy Nevin had
found himself trapped, as many were, on the Riviera, when hostil-
ities had started in earnest. Technically retired from the navy, but
still wanting to do his bit for king and country, Chaplain Nevin took
over the running of the Mission, sometimes known as the English
Seamen's Hostel, to give comfort and shelter to lost, shipwrecked
or cast-adrift sailors. He had not been short of customers, among
whom he had numbered several successful authors of popular fiction
and numerous academic types, who had all failed to take the war
seriously, as well as a brace of Russian émigrés clutching Fabergé
eggs, and three Jewish families who had led a nomadic existence
floating across Europe for three years before washing up and into
Sandy Nevin's lifeboat.

For the Mission was certainly a lifeboat, which saved those lost
in deep and dangerous waters and ferried them to safety, or at least
sent them on their way. Sandy Nevin had an enviable record when
it came to smuggling people out of Vichy France and, for more than
a year, the Mission had acted as a staging post and safe house for
downed RAF aircrew who had been shepherded across France by
the Resistance.

At that point I was given a stern lecture by those bare-handed
killers from SOE, and I sat up straight and listened carefully. While
Sandy Nevin's no doubt brave and charitable activities were much
appreciated by the French Resistance and SOE, the chaplain was a
member of neither and kept a healthy distance from any of their
operations and operatives. It was safer that way. What he did not
know could not be tortured out of him in a Vichy prison cell.
Therefore, although he might just be the one person who could
facilitate an escape should I fall foul of spies, assassins, cut-throats,
or policemen – secret or otherwise – while in Marseilles, I was not
to approach him under any circumstances.

Thankfully, Captain Smith or perhaps it was Captain Jones – it
really was difficult to tell them apart – did not let me stew over this
conundrum for too long. Though I must not approach Chaplain
Nevin's Mission directly (not even, it seemed, in the guise of a
distressed Protestant seaman in need of reading materials), I could
make contact via an intermediary who, this being the world of SOE,
was naturally not to be trusted.

The fact that a former Royal Navy chaplain could be openly running a safe house and an escape line in the middle of Marseilles, right under the noses of the Vichy (and other) security services, was extraordinary enough. To be told that Chaplain Nevin's diary secretary was a leading light in the Marseilles black market and a British army sergeant to boot, was positively flabbergasting.

Needless to say, I was intrigued as to how two members of His Majesty's armed forces could survive and openly prosper in enemy, or at least unfriendly, territory two years after the fall of France.

To Sandy Nevin, as an ardent Francophile, as well as a man who believed in the power of charity and selfless good works, it had been only natural that he would stay where he thought he could do most good. When on shore leave from postings with the Mediterranean fleet, he had volunteered many times to help in the numerous Seamen's Missions in various ports, including Marseilles.

Nevin was a popular and trusted figure in the dingy back streets and pungent alleys around the Old Port area and the Bassin de la Joliette, and his dog collar seemed to protect him even in the dangerous Panier district, which was ruled by the Marseilles underworld. Because he made no attempt to preach or proselytize, Nevin was looked on kindly by the Catholic priests of the city, and he performed a useful service in return, as any lost and wandering soul, unable to speak adequate French and seeking sanctuary in an English accent, was quietly directed to the Chaplain's Mission.

If Sandy Nevin survived by keeping his head down and doing good works, the man who would supply me with an introduction should I need it seemed to specialize in exactly the opposite.

The one definite thing known about Magnus Asher was that, as a sergeant of a despatch-rider unit in a county infantry regiment, he had been part of the British Expeditionary Force, which saw action on the Belgian/French border in 1940. In the retreat to Dunkirk, Asher had either become separated from his unit or deserted; the jury was still out on that one. He had been listed as Missing in Action but then, according to a report from the Resistance there, had turned up in Lyons in early 1941, wearing an expensive suit and driving a hardly inconspicuous Bugatti roadster. His luggage included one leather suitcase bulging with paper money in at least four different currencies.

The expected scenario was that any British soldier (or deserter) trying to evade capture by the enemy and make his way home, would seek out the local Resistance and plead for assistance. In Lyons, Magnus Asher sought out the Resistance, seemingly unconcerned as to whether they were communist or not, and offered to help *them*. Sergeant Asher may have been missing in action for eight months, but he had certainly not been inactive. Somehow, in those eight months, he had abandoned his identity as a British army sergeant and reinvented himself as a successful black marketeer, apparently able to operate with impunity in both the Occupied Zone and Vichy. One SOE report contained the phrase that he had arrived in Lyons wearing 'the last good suit made in Paris'.

The Lyons Resistance members that Asher contacted at first treated him with the utmost suspicion and were determined to keep him on the circumference of their circle, but gradually began to do business with the shady Englishman. If they required supplies – batteries, torches, tools, boots, blankets, petrol, even occasionally weapons – Asher could supply them, if payment could be made in cash and delivery taken under cover of darkness.

With an extensive supply of official documents offering him the security of several identities, plus an inexhaustible supply of cash and tradable goods, he lived in numerous mid-range hotels in Lyons for six months, being arrested and released without charge at least twice. He then disappeared, and it was assumed he had sought refuge with his ill-gotten profits in Switzerland, only for him to reappear, with a spring in his step, in Marseilles towards the end of the year.

No one knew how he did it, certainly not my new young friends at SOE, nor any of their chaps on the ground in France. They had not, of course, asked our allies in the Free French's Second Bureau, as it would be terribly embarrassing to admit that we had lost track of one of our non-commissioned officers, who now appeared to be a leading light in the black market.

Army records had been checked and provided a few indications, though no definite clues. Magnus Asher had joined the Territorials at the age of twenty-two in 1936, while working as a clerk in the accounts office of a light engineering firm in Sheffield. An unblemished if undramatic military career had led to one stripe and then two, and the outbreak of war accelerated the award of a third on his unit's incorporation into the regular army. The only distinguishing feature on Asher's curriculum vitae up to Dunkirk was that, from a working-class background (his father was a foundry-man, his mother sewed cricket gloves on a piece-work basis), he had won a place at a respectable grammar school where he had excelled in French and German.

Such an aptitude, I felt, must have put him in line for a position in intelligence or field security once the army crossed the Channel on a war footing, perhaps even a field commission, but Asher remained an infantry sergeant. Statements taken from members of his platoon who had been rescued from the beaches of Dunkirk indicated that Asher had performed well enough under fire, but on the confused and chaotic retreat towards the Channel ports, the platoon's unity had been shattered during a sustained Stuka attack. When their sirens had stopped their screaming and the smoke had cleared, Asher had disappeared. Without their NCO – their officer had been killed, foolishly attempting to disable a Mark IV Panzer with a Webley revolver – the leaderless platoon wearily followed their noses towards the sea, few of them caring what had happened to their sergeant and none of them having the energy or inclination to search for him or his body.

But now, two years on, Magnus Asher – for SOE were convinced it was he – was alive, well, and prospering in a business no doubt shady in Marseilles, living openly and, by all accounts, in some style. And however dubious his business dealings, he maintained close links with Sandy Nevin's Mission and had, according to several escaping airmen who had sheltered there, provided the chaplain with clothing, food and excellent quality forged documents, though presumably at a price.

I asked if Asher had any sort of police record and was told that SOE had not found one, although the expressions on my two young captains' faces betrayed the fact that they had not looked very hard. To be honest, two years of air raids had destroyed many official buildings and documents, so it was feasible that Asher had got away with murder and no one was any the wiser. If SOE were not interested in him, he was beginning to sound like just the sort of chap my lot could find a billet for.

Should I need to get out of Marseilles quickly, I would have to find and approach Magnus Asher, though I would need to be armed with a suitably large amount of funds. To approach Sandy Nevin and his Mission directly could risk compromising his operation, and my SOE advisors felt it would be better 'for all concerned' if I put my trust, not to mention my life, in a deserter-turned-spiv. I told them that I quite understood.

They had some other useful advice on what I might expect in Vichy, which boiled down to the fact that while Vichy was technically not at war with Britain but in a state of armed neutrality, I could expect to be treated as an enemy should my thin disguise as a Canadian diplomat be stripped away to reveal a hated Englishman. Many in Vichy were bitter about how French ships in British harbours had been seized and then the French fleet attacked by the Royal Navy at Mers-el-Kébir, with 1,200 French sailors killed, and furious that Britain now offered a base to General de Gaulle, whom they regarded as a renegade and traitor.

It was nothing I did not know already, but out of politeness remained attentive and grateful for the information. I was genuinely grateful for the forged Vichy ration coupons they offered me, and tried to lighten the mood by observing that it was odd that the French actually called them 'tickets', which was an English word, while we called them coupons, which was a French word.

Captains Smith and Jones were not amused, but then neither was I when they presented me with a final gift – a handy, tooth-sized cyanide capsule.

'Just in case, old boy,' said Jones, or perhaps Smith.

That evening, during a walk along the Victoria Embankment, I threw it into the Thames.

SIX

Table Talk

The Dorchester Hotel, London. 20 May 1970

'Is my husband boring you, Herr Ringer?' asked Amanda, pressing a hand lightly but with firm intent on Mr Campion's shoulder. 'He is rather good at that, especially when he has a captive audience. They say he could bore for England.'

'Please do not be concerned, Lady Amanda. Albert is being most entertaining, as he always is, though I fear the younger ones . . .'

'Oh, don't worry about me,' Perdita gushed enthusiastically. 'I'm finding this fascinating.'

'Charles,' Amanda fixed Luke with her no-nonsense-to-be-tolerated face, 'as you have undoubtedly heard all Albert's stories before, I'm putting you in charge of telling him when to shut up.'

'I'm afraid I'm with Perdita on this one,' Luke said. 'I've never heard Albert talk about his time in . . .' then he caught the amused twinkle in the eyes of the German sitting next to him and finished limply, '. . . the services.'

Ringer smiled. 'Do not try to be diplomatic, Commander. It is perfectly acceptable for you to mention the war.'

'But should Albert be doing so?' asked Amanda. 'Seriously, darling, aren't you in danger of betraying state secrets or something? You've always said your war work was so secret that you never found out what you were doing most of the time, and surely you must have signed the Official Secrets Act.'

'I'm almost certain I did,' said Mr Campion vaguely, 'but in those days one had to sign chits for everything from paper clips and pencils to a Lancaster bomber, should you require one. In any case, I'm not giving away state secrets, merely catching up with old friends and reminiscing about events more than twenty-five years ago. There can be little harm in that. Should I overstep the mark, then Charles here is on hand to arrest me but, until he does, it is my birthday, my party and I'll gossip if I want to!'

'Well, I only hope you know what you are doing,' Amanda scolded him mildly, 'and don't stop your guests from enjoying this delicious meal.'

Mr Campion pretended to look shocked at the implied accusation.

'Heaven forfend! I will hold my peace until the main course is served, for it should be quite spectacular – and here it comes.'

At the far end of the room the doors opened, and in rumbled a pair of silver-plate domed carving trolleys propelled and flanked by half a platoon of starched and shining waiters. The trolleys advanced in parallel towards the top table, like the slow-moving tanks of the Great War growling towards an enemy salient with infantry support. They came to a halt in perfect unison and the commanding waiters of each vehicle stepped forward to present a long-blade carving knife and fork, as if presenting arms.

'To what are we being treated, Albert?' asked Robert von Ringer politely.

'Barons of lamb,' Mr Campion said, tucking his napkin into his

shirt collar, only to have it gently removed and placed in his lap by
Amanda. 'I thought two should be enough to feed this lot, if not
the five thousand, and I got special permission to bring in two
carvers from The Savoy: they are the experts when it comes to
dicing and slicing this particular cut.'

'They look like whole sheep,' squealed Perdita.

'Actually, the back half of two sheep,' said Mr Campion. 'We had
to borrow the trolleys from the French Embassy. They were made
by Christofle of Paris and I'm told they are quite expensive, so I
would appreciate it, Charlie, if you'd keep an eye open in case one
of the guests try to sneak one out under their coat.'

'You mean you don't trust your guests to behave themselves
impeccably?' said Luke with a broad grin.

'Of course not!' blustered Campion. 'That's why I invited them!
But please don't regard yourself as on duty, at least not where drinking
is concerned. I've chosen a fantastic Château La Fleur-Pétrus Pomerol
to go with the lamb.'

'You know I'd be quite happy with a bottle of Spanish Burgundy
for fourteen-and-nine down the local Berni Inn.'

'Oh, come off it, Charlie, don't play the Philistine. You'll enjoy
the wine – I insist you will. It's a 1961, which I am sure will be a
vintage that will outlive us all, even if the paltry supply I've laid
in probably won't see dawn tomorrow.'

Mr Campion turned to his German guest, indicating the two
waiters looming over their trolleys, silvery domes opened to reveal
roasted and glistening haunches of meat. The waiters dramatically
clashed their carving knives against their long-handled, two-pronged
forks and set about their business.

'Now watch these chaps in action, Robert,' said Campion. 'I
reckon they'd make excellent *sabreurs*.'

'I think Campion is reliving the war,' said Dr Jolyon Livingstone to
his fellow diner far down the stem of one of the table extensions.

His companion, Mr L. C. Corkran, allowed himself to be distracted
from his enjoyment of some of Bordeaux's finest produce.

'What d'you mean, Joly? I admit that all these chaps waving
long knives and pushing carvers as big as Bren-gun carriers looks
a bit like Trooping the Colour in mufti, but you need a squad of well-
drilled men who know what they're doing to serve baron of lamb to
this amount of people. Lord knows I've sat through enough official

dinners where the gravy's congealed into wallpaper paste before the potatoes have come over the horizon.'

'No, no, I wasn't referring to the menu, I was thinking about the guest list and especially the selection for the top table.'

'I suppose you think the master of a Cambridge college should automatically be placed on high,' said Mr Corkran, determined to concentrate on the rapidly disappearing contents of his glass. 'Must be strange for you to be placed below the salt for once.'

'Actually, it happens quite a lot these days,' sighed Dr Livingstone quietly, 'though any further below the salt and we'd be the other side of Park Lane. But I was thinking of the guest of honour up there shooting the breeze with old Rudolph . . . oops! I forgot. We must call him Albert, mustn't we?'

Mr Corkran, who did not believe for one second that Dr Livingstone's memory had failed, chose to ignore the deliberate slip.

'Are you referring to Freiherr von Ringer?' Mr Corkran dragged his adoring gaze from his wine glass and fixed the academic with the blank stare he had honed to perfection for use in interviews and interrogations over several decades. 'He is a German gentleman who is an acquaintance of mine and an old friend of Albert's.'

'I know very well who he is and what he did during the war.'

'You do? That's interesting. May I ask how?'

'You know very well, L. C.,' said Livingstone, keeping his voice low. 'I may not have been in one of your Boy Scout outfits, but I was in intelligence in the last few years of the war. Quiet code-breaking was our thing, not your shooty-bang games, but I did get the chance to meet a real live German spy in late 1944 when he came over to our side. Guess who.'

'Ringer.'

'Exactly. MI5 called me in to help with his clearance procedure as I had worked on the latest Abwehr codes, and they thought the St Ignatius connection would establish a certain level of rapport if not trust.'

Mr Corkran went into ruminative mood. 'Yes, the Cambridge chaps in Five always believed in the old school tie, or should that be cap and gown?'

'I know what you're implying, L. C., and I utterly refute it. There has never been any question of the loyalty of the alumni of St Ignatius, unlike some other colleges I could mention. Robert Ringer was an alumnus, as was I, though of a younger generation. It was logical that I should be involved in his debriefing. That fencing scar he got from Campion was an obvious point of mutual interest.'

'So you knew the story?'

'Of course, it was part of the folklore of St Ignatius. It happened ten years before I went up, but everyone knew of legends surrounding Rud . . . That Albert Campion, the chap who, to look at him, wouldn't say boo to a goose, had beaten a Prussian sabre champion in a duel over some outrageous slur on his honour.'

'It's a good story, if you know Albert,' Mr Corkran said thoughtfully. 'Except that it wasn't a duel, they weren't using sabres and Ringer is no Prussian.'

'You must allow us some small flight of fancy. Dinners at high table can be awfully boring in the long winter nights.'

'I've heard it said,' observed Corkran, 'but I think all we have here is some old friends celebrating a birthday. I wouldn't read too much into the table plan.'

'But as the master of a Cambridge college, I am trained to do exactly that. Ringer's not on the top table by accident; that's not Albert's style at all. And what about that very attractive Frenchwoman bending Lady Amanda's delicate ear? Who's she and what's she up to?'

'You worry too much, Jolyon. Now drink this excellent wine and pass the mint sauce.'

'I think this end of the table should devote itself to talking loudly about hemlines, shoes and handbags,' said Lady Amanda. 'We don't have to do it for long, but if we're loud enough, then the men will soon lose interest and stop listening in, so then we can talk about them.'

'You are assuming, Lady Amanda, that we might have something interesting to say about them,' said the elegant Frenchwoman. 'In either case, would we not be descending into cliché?'

'You are absolutely correct, Madame Thibus, so we will therefore discuss important matters of foreign policy, economics and religious philosophy. That will put the men off just as much, but not until you have admitted to me that your dress is Givenchy and that beautiful tapestry bag down by the side of your chair is a Walborg.'

'I admit to both offences, if there are offences,' laughed Corinne Thibus, adding, 'that bag may come from an America company but, like the dress, it was made in France. Does that suffice for the topic of foreign policy?'

'I am sure it ticks all the diplomatic boxes, but I will not be diplomatic and admit openly that I am jealous of both. Your bag, in particular. I have not seen that particular design before. Is it an heirloom?'

'No, but it is old enough to be one. I bought it in Paris almost twenty years ago from – how do you say it? – my first pay cheque. I was desperately in need of new shoes, but then I saw the bag I needed even more.'

'It is a good size,' said Amanda, nodding in agreement. 'Capacious, you might say. Looks as if it could contain everything a girl might need.'

'And more besides,' the Frenchwoman smiled thinly. 'Have we now exhausted the subject of fashion, or was it foreign affairs?'

'That rather depends on how you come to be here tonight.'

'Do I detect that the Lady Amanda is suspicious about something?'

'Not at all suspicious, but very curious as to how you know my husband as, I am afraid, he has failed to mention your existence before now; and although he can be notoriously absent-minded when it comes to the minor things in life, I would hardly put you in that category.'

Madame Thibus adjusted her smile in that knowing telegraphy which passes between women who instinctively know they are far too intelligent to be fooled by the playing of the coquette expression card, invariably accompanied by the fluttering of eyelashes as subtle, and as quiet, as wood pigeons mating in a tree in full foliage.

'Should I be flattered by that, Lady Amanda? Or perhaps a little worried?'

Amanda picked up her wine glass and drank slowly, observing the Frenchwoman over the crystal rim. She was not a threat, nor even an opponent, but she was an uncertainty and she had appeared suddenly, an immaculately dressed and supremely confident ghost from her husband's past.

'I was merely curious as to when you and my husband met,' said Amanda, pointedly emphasizing the *when* and leaving the *and how* merely implied.

'It was during the war,' said Corinne Thibus without hesitation, meeting Amanda's eyes.

'You must have been very young.'

'I was old enough. I had to be.'

*   *   *

On the other 'wing' of the table, Guffy Randall was beginning to admit what his wife had long suspected, that he was going deaf on his left side. No matter how discreetly he had cupped a hand around his ear, he had been unable to follow much of Campion's monologue, even though it seemed to have held Luke, Perdita and that starchy German fellow quite entranced.

It did not help that Campion was naturally quietly spoken, nor that he resorted to initials – half of which went over Guffy's head – and odd inserts of foreign lingo. From the little Guffy had managed to glean, Campion seemed to be talking about war, which was rather rum in his opinion as he regarded it bad form to mention the war in front of Germans.

Sensibly, Mr Augustus Randall turned his attention to the excellent roast lamb in front of him and to the diners on his immediate right: the young French chappie, Fleurey, and his wife, Mary, who seemed to be getting on *comme une maison en flammes*. Happily, they were conversing in English, as that very thought had exhausted Guffy's reservoir of half-remembered schoolboy French.

Mary Randall took pity on her husband and brought him into the conversation by speaking across Joseph Fleurey, aiming for Guffy's right ear.

'Darling, we simply must go down to the Riviera this summer. Joseph here has a casino in Nice.'

'I merely work in a casino, Mrs Randall. Sadly, I do not own it,' protested M. Fleurey.

'I don't know about casinos; not much fun to be had there with the fifty-pound travel-allowance rules,' Guffy grumbled amiably. 'But I've always had a soft spot for that bit of coast. Plenty of happy memories of Mentone, just around the corner from Nice towards Italy . . .' Joseph Fleurey nodded politely, indicating that he too was familiar with the geography of the area. 'Stayed at the Hôtel Beauregard there. The manager was a charming fellow called Étienne Fleur— But, of course, you must be the son.'

'I am indeed, and proud to represent my father here tonight. Sadly, he is too old and infirm to travel these days, so his invitation passed to me.'

'I hear you were very hospitable to my nephew Rupert and his wife when they visited Nice a year or so ago,' said Mary.

'They were delightful company, but terrible gamblers. I made sure they did not lose too much.'

Mary Randall placed a hand gently on Joseph's wrist. 'Should we visit your establishment, I would appreciate a similar watchful eye being kept on my husband.'

A wine waiter hovered in front of them, having judged psychically, as the best sommeliers always do, the exact moment that Mr Randall's empty glass was returned firmly to the table. The drinker paused for the required moment of considered thought that is expected rather than required, gave a nod of acceptance, and the glass was smoothly replenished.

'Got to admit that Albert knows his wine,' said Guffy. 'Must make a note of this – see if Lay and Wheeler can get us a supply. Got to hand it to you French, when it comes to wine.'

'I thank you on behalf of a grateful nation.'

'Grateful? That's a matter of opinion.'

'Guffy, really!' Mary Randall laughed lightly, but the tone was anything but light. It was a warning, and pure Fitton.

'Are we not, as a nation, grateful?' asked Joseph, keeping his voice as falsely light as Mary's laugh. 'I am certainly grateful to England for keeping my father safe during the war and for helping to liberate my country.'

'Wasn't actually thinking about the war as such,' said Guffy, his complexion reddening somewhat, 'more about that fella de Gaulle. We gave him shelter and succour during the war and then the blighter vetoed us joining the Common Market, not once but twice.'

'General de Gaulle is no longer in power,' Joseph pointed out, 'and I am sure it will not be long before Britain joins Europe.'

'Might as well, after all the currency's going foreign next year.'

'My husband has a bee in his bonnet about the change to decimal currency,' Mary Randall explained. 'He's dreading D-Day next February; regularly says a prayer for the soul of the half-crown and sheds a tear whenever he finds a crumpled ten-shilling note in a jacket pocket.'

'Steady on, old girl, you're making me sound like an old buffer.'

'But you're my old buffer, dear,' Mary said sweetly.

'And don't worry, I'll watch what I say about the French from now on.' Guffy looked around the room. 'After all, they seem well represented at this do. Who's that very smart one over there, nattering to your sister?'

'Guffy! It's the same woman who had your eyes out on stalks during the pre-dinner drinks.'

'Yes, yes, I know, dear, but *who* is she?'

'That is Corinne Thibus,' said Joseph Fleurey, interposing himself in the hope of defusing a family row. 'She is a prominent lawyer in France with – how would you say it? – a high profile. She appears on television and writes for the national newspapers. She is known as *l'avocat de guerre* – the lawyer of war.'

'What the devil does that mean?' asked a genuinely confused Guffy.

'It means she prosecutes war criminals, whatever the war, whenever the crime. More than that, she does not just prosecute them in court, she hunts them down.'

For a full minute, Mr Augustus Randall's brain digested this information before he reached for his glass, took a long draught and said: 'Be a rum do if she was here tonight on business.'

Rupert Campion, sitting at the corner of the top table, could not help but be aware that his mother and Madame Thibus were, if not locking horns, then at least flexing their feminine muscles and, showing a maturity beyond his years, decided to keep well clear of any potential storm front. Instead, he turned to concentrate on the woman on his left, wondering what he had done to deserve being placed between two formidable Frenchwomen; for, in his limited experience, all Frenchwomen were formidable, especially when they are mistaken for being Spanish.

'My second husband was Spanish,' Señora Vidal informed him in faltering English. 'My first was French and I was born French. Husband Number One was killed in the war but soon after I met Husband Number Two. Now he is also dead, but from the cancer of the lungs, not war.'

'I am sorry to hear that,' Rupert sympathized.

'Do not be; it was his choice to smoke the cigarettes so much. That is the trouble with Spaniards: they smoke too much – even more than the French.'

'But you live in Spain?'

'Yes, I have a small business as a *couturière* in a little town near Pamplona. The ladies of Spain seem to think they are better dressed if dressed by a Frenchwoman, even a Jewish one.'

Sensing he was being offered a nerve to prod, Rupert wisely changed the subject.

'And is this your first visit to London?'

'It is, and it may be my last, as your weather does not suit my blood. I cannot stand to be cold.'

Rupert drew on his admittedly limited thespian talents and mugged an expression of shocked surprise. 'But we have been counting ourselves lucky as the Met Office thinks this could be the warmest May since 1940.'

Señora Vidal was unimpressed by both his acting and his statistics.

'In 1940,' she said solemnly, 'the weather was the least of my concerns.'

Rupert straightened his face. 'You must mean the war.'

'Yes, I do.'

'Is that how you know my father?'

'It is, and it is why I have come here tonight.'

The woman leaned back in her seat to allow a waiter to remove her plate. It was as if, Rupert thought, the interruption had disconnected their conversation; as if she had chosen to hang up on a frustrating phone call. If only to avoid the embarrassed silence which often envelops strangers who find themselves adjacent diners, Rupert persisted.

'Have you been friends since then?'

'Oh no,' she said casually, dabbing her lips with her napkin, 'we were never friends. I came here out of a sense of . . . is the word "obligation"?'

'Well, it is certainly *a* word, but why should you feel obligated to my father?'

The woman turned her eyes – wide, brown and deeply soulful – on the younger man.

'Because he saved our lives.'

Several yards as the cruet flew down the table, Precious Aird was finding the younger Vidal female as unforthcoming as Rupert was finding the senior one. In her attempts to be sociable and to strike up a rapport with someone who was not only of the same sex, but roughly the same age group, give or take six or eight years, she thought, Precious was not helped by the overwhelming presence of Mr Magersfontein Lugg, seated solidly at the end of the table, as if he had been left by Horatius to guard the bridge across the Tiber on his own. He appeared impermeable and immovable but not necessarily displeased with his lot.

Mr Lugg had, over many years, become accustomed to being assigned by Mr Campion to 'the children's table' whenever an occasion demanded mass catering and the marshalling of a youthful population. Whether his substantial physical presence was meant to provide comic relief or inspire fear in the younger generation was never clear, but the usual result was the production of giggles rather than tears.

Rather than feeling he had been sent into exile, his position at the far end of the right-hand table extension gave Lugg a sense of tactical superiority. From there he could survey all the dinner guests and the meanderings of the waiters in and about them, secure in the knowledge that L. C. Corkran, in the same seat on the other extension, was guarding the left flank, and that Mr Campion was in his clear line of sight. He could, he felt sure, attract Campion's attention quickly and easily should the need arise, if only by flicking peas in his direction.

He was closely observing the wine waiters and mentally marking them out of ten, which he regarded as something of a professional responsibility, when he felt the soft tapping of a stockinged foot beating a tattoo on his right shin. His expression remained that of an Easter Island statue, and he waited until a gaggle of waiters swarmed in to remove plates and cutlery before he leaned forward under cover of the symphony of the chinking of china and the clash of metal.

When his melon-shaped head was within range of Precious Aird's left ear, he spoke out of one tiny corner of his mouth.

'If you want to play footsie, my dear, you'd best pick on someone your own size. You don't want my plates o'meat tap-dancing on your ankles.'

The American girl had known Lugg long enough to know that it was rarely worthwhile asking him to repeat or elucidate on any of his pearls of wisdom, but at least she had his attention.

'You've got to help me out here,' she hissed in reply. 'My neighbours are really heavy going.'

'Wot? The children not playing nice together? Come on, yer all old enough to drink so yer should know better.'

Precious exhaled through pouted lips and drummed the painted fingernails of one hand on the white linen tablecloth where her plate had been. Suddenly she decided on her tactics.

'Why, Mr Lugg,' she said loudly, 'it really isn't fair you perched on the wing-tip of this buffet bar with no one of your generation to chat to. How did you get the short straw and end up with all us young 'uns in the kindergarten?'

Lugg's massive head turned slowly on its axis, as if he was taking in the room for the first time.

'Just about everyone here's a nipper compared to me. If I was an MP, I'd be the father of the 'ouse, I would. That's why they put me here, to keep an eye on you young tearaways. It's my job to break up the food fights, make sure you eat your greens an' count the spoons after you've gone.'

Despite his air of professional indifference, Lugg had been keeping a close eye on his fellow diners on 'the kids' table' and indeed had been secretly pleased to find himself seated next to Precious Aird, who had proved only a few months before that she could not only 'look out for 'erself' (a most useful criterion in Lugg's book) but also was an enthusiast for British beer and the honourable custom of buying one's round (vital criteria).

Next to the American girl was the young Spanish woman, although she did not look particularly Spanish to Lugg. Admittedly only the wearing of a black silk mantilla and holding castanets would have instantly registered 'Spanish' in Lugg's mind, as she was as smartly dressed – 'Sunday best', he decided – as any respectable young lady of her age these days which, given what could be seen daily on the streets of London, was something to behold. She was, he guessed, roughly the same age as Mr Campion's son Rupert, but a more practised female eye might have observed that her two-piece dress suit in pink linen, with its princess line seams and a fitted jacket with wide lapels, shaped waist and matching belt might have, with the addition of a string of fake pearls and some white gloves, been worn by a woman twenty years older. A cynical female mind might have presumed that Señorita Vidal was making a conscious attempt to look as old, if not older, than her mother, and that she was well on the way to succeeding.

The young man seated next to Prisca Vidal did not seem interested in her fashion sense, deportment, or even her presence, except in the way it prevented him from sneaking frequent and all too obvious sideways glances across her in the direction of Precious Aird's lap. The reason for his interest was clear, as Precious' minidress rode up even higher than Carnaby Street had intended every time she made the smallest alteration to her position.

Lugg did not moralize; it was only-to-be-expected behaviour from a lad who was probably on the verge of being a 'first-year varsity man' after a dozen years in all-boys' schools. As long as he used his knife and fork properly, didn't get drunk and refrained from saying out loud what he was undoubtedly thinking, then Lugg saw no reason to be heavy-handed and interventionist. In truth, he felt quite sorry for the lad, whose name he had learned from the seating plan was Mr Robert Oncer Smith, although the boy's provenance and history was unknown to him. He was vaguely aware that he was one of Mr Campion's waifs, someone Campion had befriended on his travels, but he could not recall when or how. Mr Campion was prone to befriending any number of waifs and strays who would turn up on the doorstep months or even years later, quite often when they got parole.

Robert Oncer Smith must have thought the evening would be a memorable one the minute he set eyes on Precious Aird; eyes which seemed reluctant to give her more than a minute's peace. She was, after all, vivacious, attractive, exotically American, and almost exactly the same age as young Mr Smith, so his disappointment could only be imagined when he found himself separated from the object of his desire by the older (not *that* much older, he considered briefly) and rather prim and starchy figure of Prisca Vidal, who was uninterested in any form of small talk and whose rigid frame prevented him from communicating with Precious Aird, with whom he felt he could quickly establish a rapport. Unable to get the American girl within range of his witty and flirtatious repartee, Master Smith resorted to sulking quietly over his dinner.

He was sulking so effectively that it seemed almost too much of an effort to push stray peas around his plate, and not once did he catch Lugg's beady-eyed stare of disapproval. This annoyed Lugg to the extent that he was forced into, for him, the cruel and unusual practice of making small talk, if only to break the uncomfortable silence and stop Precious kicking him under the table.

'Come a long way for this do, have you, miss?'

Señorita Vidal responded like an automaton, and without lifting her eyes from the table.

'From Madrid. It was a very poor flight; a cheap one, I think, for my mother is cautious with money. It was full of English holiday-makers. Many were drunk and they all carried *burros*.'

'*Donkeys?*' Precious blurted.

'Toy ones, stuffed soft toys. Not real ones,' Lugg explained. 'Everyone going to Spain on holiday has to bring one back. No one knows why. That's a fair trek, miss. How do you come to know the birthday boy?'

Lugg flicked a glance towards the top table, as if he was heading a cup final goal.

'I do not know him at all. Tonight is the first time I have ever seen him.'

The woman seemed reluctant to offer any further information.

'I suppose he was a friend of your mother's then, from' – Lugg chose his words carefully, always a painful process, before settling on – 'way back when?'

'They met during the war.' It was a statement delivered with the maximum neutrality.

Genuinely pleased that the woman had made some sort of effort to come out of her shell, Precious was keen to keep a conversation going, but Robert Oncer Smith suddenly came to life and interjected: 'Was it one of Mr C's wartime adventures? I bet it was. He's just the sort of chap to have had a good war, I always thought.'

'There's no such thing as a good war, my lad, as I 'ope you never finds out,' said Lugg, giving him 'the look' he usually reserved for waiters who laid out dirty cutlery, landlords who pulled short pints and cab drivers who refused to go south of the river after dark. This time, there was no doubting that young Mr Smith knew he was under scrutiny, but his agony did not last long.

Lugg's ever-watchful eye had, when not boring into Master Smith's face, noticed a movement on the top table. Mr Campion, in something akin to a cross between pantomime and semaphore, was gesticulating with his hands to encourage action of some sort, reinforced by the tapping of a forefinger on the face of his wristwatch.

'Aye aye,' he said to his young audience, 'duty calls. Time for me to do me bit.'

Laboriously and with much wheezing and puffing out of cheeks, Lugg pushed back his chair and levered himself upright, causing a rare expression of surprise to disturb Prisca Vidal's sculptured visage. It was as if she was observing a South Pacific volcano emerging from the waves and becoming an island.

Once on his feet, Lugg braced himself and cleared his throat loudly. The rasping, gravel-filled sound was more effective than any High Court judge's gavel demanding order in the court. 'Me Lords,

Ladies and Hetcetras,' he began, with a portentousness befitting ill tidings, 'if we was down the pictures, this would be the intermission but 'ere, among such distinguished company, I 'as to refer to it as the *entremets*.'

There was a ripple of giggling and some whispered comments over Lugg's pronunciation, as if he were giving directions to the centre of a town in north-west France, all of which he ignored.

'Smoking between courses is now frowned upon by all them that believes in 'ealthy livin', but for them that 'as to, there will be an opportunity to satisfy their cravings in the reception room, where liquid refreshment will be available along with canapés, sweetmeats and dainties. A warning to the unwise, though. Be sure to leave room for pudding and cake!'

Under cover of the partygoers scraping back their chairs and searching jacket pockets and handbags for cigarette cases and lighters, Amanda saw her chance and leaned across her husband to clamp his left forearm with both hands, as if saving him from going over a cliff.

'Come and mingle with your guests, darling, and give these nice people a rest from your interminable historical meanderings.'

'Oh, *please*, Amanda, let him keep going. It's all getting really exciting,' pleaded Perdita, 'and showing us a side of Albert we knew nothing about.'

'He's not breached the Official Secrets Act just yet,' grinned Charlie Luke, 'but I'm keeping an eye on him and have the handcuffs ready in case he does.'

'I was thinking more of the sensibilities of Freiherr von Ringer,' said Amanda severely. 'It cannot be comfortable for him, this dredging up of old war stories.'

To Amanda's surprise, the German held up his hands, palms out towards her.

'Please do not distress yourself on my account, Lady Amanda, I am far from offended. In fact, I am greatly looking forward to the part of the story where I appear in person. So far I have been something of an "off-stage" character; often referred to but never appearing at the heart of the action. Please do not deny me my big entrance.'

'There you see,' said Mr Campion, 'my audience awaits and I cannot disappoint them. I must continue. A good story can't be stopped, even for *entremets*.'

SEVEN

Hush-Hush

England, Spain, France. August – September 1942

Of course, I had a lot more hoops to jump through before I was despatched on my most secret of missions, and the most arduous of them all was keeping things secret from Amanda. Mind you, she was good at keeping secrets from me, so I had absolutely no idea that she was pregnant with young Rupert. Much later she claimed that she had told me, or had dropped innumerable subtle hints which only a deaf-and-dumb drunkard would have missed, making it, as usual, all my fault.

Once the decision had been taken that I should go to France and make contact with Robert Ringer, I was sent on numerous crash courses. I mean, we couldn't unleash such a deadly weapon on the enemy as myself unless I was honed to perfection, could we? Consequently, dear old Elsie Corkran insisted that I tootle off to Scotland for training with some very beefy Commando types, who took an inordinate amount of pleasure in teaching me unarmed combat and something they called 'escape and evasion' techniques across vast swathes of damp and very prickly heather. They also had a variety of German pistols for me to play with, and a shooting range run by a grizzled corporal called Colgan, who took a particular interest in making sure I would be quickest on the draw when up against a charging Nazi. I'm afraid I disappointed him when it came to the accuracy of my marksmanship. He would tell me to get closer and closer to the target, which was a rather frightening life-size Hun made from cardboard, but was never satisfied that I'd scored a 'killing hit' with my borrowed Luger. Eventually he told me my best hope was to get up really close, almost nose-to-nose, and hit the blighter over the head with the gun.

Back in London, Elsie had fixed up another visit for me with our French friends to glean more local knowledge. Not the Second Bureau this time, but at the Free French headquarters across the park in Carlton Gardens, which was quite convenient for the RAC Club where General de Gaulle took his lunch.

I was kept waiting in a very comfortable drawing room with the latest issue of *La Lettre de la France Libre*, a twee little newspaper – more a parish magazine really – issued by the press service there. It was hardly riveting reading. Much more interesting were old copies of *Marseille-Matin* and the Marseille edition of *Le Petit Provençal*, which were hardly up-to-date briefing materials but did provide a flavour of what I might expect. Particularly worrying were reports of the Vichy government's *Interdits aux Juifs* or, more officially, *Le Statut des Israélites*, which excluded Jews from various professions and provided rather chilling simplified family-tree diagrams which identified which children were classed as Jews and which as 'non-Jews'. If both parents and all four grandparents were Jewish, then the situation was clear enough. If only one parent and two grandparents were Jewish, then a child was a non-Jew, but if a newborn baby was careless enough to have one parent and *three* grandparents who were Jewish, then he or she was clearly a Jew, or at least it was clear to the rather twisted minds to whom such things mattered.

Eventually a young staff officer with the temerity to be about half my age appeared and demanded to know how he could be of assistance, though he gave the impression that assistance was the last thing he had on offer. I spun him a yarn about needing to know the latest gossip from Marseilles, as I had to brief a Canadian diplomat who was about to be posted there. It was a thin story, but by that stage of the war I was getting pretty good at lying, and in a way he was pleased that someone had come seeking their expertise, as the Free French were surprisingly unpopular among the French population of London.

He produced a pile of paper from the depths of the press office and showed me what official documents now looked like, although they seemed to look exactly as they had before the war, except now the official heading *Republique Française* had a line drawn through it and the words *État Français* added in blue inked capitals. The obliteration of the very name of a proud republic must have stung every true Frenchman, and my young officer made it clear he had no time for Marshal Pétain and his Vichy regime of collaboration.

'You should always keep in mind,' he told me, 'that the police in Vichy regard Gaullists, communists, Jews, the British and then the Germans as enemies, and in that order.'

I felt he was being rather harsh on his compatriots, but I did not want to engage in a debate on French politics which I would most certainly lose. Oddly, we found common ground when, in among the papers and documents he was showing me, I spotted a small flyer for The French Club in St James's, where violinist Stéphane Grappelli was playing. That I could honestly say I was a great fan, and that I had seen Grappelli play in Paris at *La Grosse Pomme* before the war, boosted my standing with the Free French officer no end – possibly with the entire Free French organization – and he was nothing but charm and helpfulness after that.

He produced detailed street maps of Marseilles, which were useful for getting my bearings, or rather bearings which I could pass on to my 'Canadian diplomat', and he rattled off figures for the amount of bread, meat and sugar that were available on a Vichy ration book. I had to do a fair amount of mental gymnastics to compare grams and ounces, made more difficult by the fact that we rationed meat by price rather than weight, but on balance it seemed that we were doing better in London than they were in Marseilles, although of course they had wine . . .

I left Carlton Gardens with one final piece of advice from, by now, my new best Free French friend, for my non-existent Canadian diplomat friend.

'Be careful of dealing on the black market in Marseilles,' he confided. 'It is extensive and run by well-organized gangs of criminals from the Panier district. Those gangsters are making a lot of money from the war and they hate the Resistance and they hate the Free French. They are not to be trusted.'

'I have found,' I told him, 'that tends to be an occupational hazard with gangsters.'

My next port of call was on those jolly chaps in MI9, whom I half expected to be operating out of a garden shed in Cricklewood but were to be found occupying a floor of the Great Central Hotel opposite Marylebone Station.

These were the chaps, and they all looked like excitable chemistry teachers dying to show off an explosive gas to the Lower IVth, who specialized in gizmos and gadgets designed mainly to help shot-down aircrew find their way home. It was said they could knit you a pullover which, if you held it up to the light, would be a map of occupied Europe, and they could print an entire code book on the silk lining of one's bowler hat.

We all took rather a childish delight in teasing those eager-beavers at Nine, tempting them to come up with answers to quite ridiculous hypothetical problems. One of our lads had them going for quite some time, claiming that he couldn't possibly be parachuted into occupied Holland until the brain boxes at Nine had developed a piece of luggage in which he could carry not only his dinner jacket, dress shirts and cricket whites, but also *his butler*.

But we all took MI9 very seriously when they told us our escape routes. They knew nothing of the meat of my mission – I wasn't too sure I did at that stage – only that I might be in need of a safe way to get out of southern France. They gave me two; the first involving a route well travelled, as they put it, by escaping RAF types over the Pyrenees into Spain. For that I would need a good pair of hiking boots and details of how to contact my Spanish guide, which I had to memorize on the spot. The boots I had to find for myself.

The second escape option they offered was more problematic, as it went against what I had already heard: I could try and find passage on a ship out of Marseilles, working as a deck hand if necessary, by contacting the leading wheeler-and-dealer in the black market in the port, a man called Magnus Asher, who was, whether I believed it or not, an Englishman. That would, however, probably require a large amount of cash, as Asher was *that* sort of an Englishman and cash, like boots, I had to find for myself.

To help keep me alive they were very happy to provide me with a panoply of weaponry and survival equipment, all of which could be secreted about my person.

I told them straight off that I wasn't shopping for anything lethal, although the idea of a poison pen – a fountain pen which actually squirted poison rather than ink – did have a certain appeal. In the end, despite their best efforts at salesmanship, I settled on a pair of tiny compasses disguised as buttons, which could be sewn on to the suit I planned on wearing.

They were particularly disappointed when they offered me their latest design set of lock picks and I rejected them as I already had a set.

After that, it was a question of paperwork, by which I mean false paperwork, to create my new identity as a Canadian diplomat.

Fortunately, Elsie Corkran had a team of forgers on the pay roll, who were the best to be found outside Wormwood Scrubs, and I wouldn't have been at all surprised to find that most of them were well acquainted with the interior of that particular establishment.

Elsie had decided that I was to be Jean-Baptiste Hamelin, a name he had picked out of an obscure American history book dealing with the War of Independence, as they called it, and the Revolt of the Thirteen Colonies, as Elsie still referred to it. My namesake, the original M. Hamelin, had been a French Canadian who had, somewhat unsportingly, opted to fight for the revolting Americans rather than the good old British. The way Elsie put it to me made me query whether I was right in thinking that now it was 1942 and not 1776, and we were all fighting on the same side, at which Elsie told me to pull myself together and stop being an ass. 'There's no room for smart talk and horseplay when you're on enemy territory,' he had growled.

It was that admonishment more than anything which made me realize, as if someone had thrown a glass of cold water in my face, that although I might not, technically, be going behind enemy lines, I was indeed going to be in enemy territory. In the weeks since I had first chatted to good old Étienne Fleurey, when I could not help but be reminded of glorious, carefree visits to France in peacetime, I had become acutely aware that Vichy France was not a place I would wish to go on holiday, and that as an Englishman I might not be made welcome. And now Elsie had warned me about what Amanda called my 'most irritating bad habits' – or at least two of them – and the sudden, icy realization that I would be in an unfriendly foreign place and Amanda would not only have no idea where I was, but if she attempted to find out she would be lied to by people she thought she could trust.

At least I did not have to lie to her, for Amanda was far too sensible and knew that I could not divulge the nature of my work. Over our final dinner together she bit her beautiful bottom lip and pretended to be satisfied that I had been given an 'indeterminate posting overseas', as the jargon went. Brave girl that she was, she did not ask where or when I might return.

Once he had made sure Mrs Campion was safely located out in the country away from the main targets for German bombing, Mr Campion disappeared – to all intents and purposes – but a certain Canadian diplomat, a perfectly charming but rather bland sort of fellow you would pass in the street without noticing, called Jean-Baptiste Hamelin, began to make regular visits to Canada House. The visits were purely for the benefit of any enemy agents who may have been still active and lurking around Trafalgar Square. It was standard deception protocol, but I really don't think anyone noticed me, not even the real Canadians who worked there.

Then it was time to pack my bag, make sure all my false papers were in order and that I carried nothing about my person, not even a birthmark, which would identify me as Albert Campion, and I was ready for the off. I had even gone to the trouble of getting some new spectacles, really quite ugly wire-framed ones, and was cultivating a bit of a moustache on my upper lip which I hoped would be in full flower, and in fashion, by the time I got to France.

Elsie Corkran accompanied me in the drive down to Poole, quizzing me all the way on my plans and new identity, where I was booked on the Empire Flying Boat to Lisbon. They still flew a twice-weekly service even during the war, although the flight time could be anything up to eight hours as the planes took a wide detour, swinging out over the Atlantic to keep out of range of the Luftwaffe fighters based on the west coast of France.

Elsie said he was coming to Poole to see me off, though I suspect it was to make sure I actually got on the plane. If he did wave a handkerchief as we took off, I didn't see it. For the first part of the flight the flying boat's windows had their blinds firmly down to prevent the passengers observing any naval manoeuvres or shipping movements down in Southampton Water or the Channel.

After what was certainly the most uncomfortable flight I have ever experienced without actually being shot at, we landed in the River Tagus – which of course we were supposed to do as a flying boat – and a motor launch took me into Lisbon where I was met by one of our local agents from the Iberia Section, as MI6 now called its activities in Portugal and Spain.

Lisbon was quite a sight, so colourful and brightly lit up after London – no blackout here – but I didn't get a chance to enjoy the scenery. I was allowed a few hours' sleep and a bath in a cheap hotel and then hustled off to the railway station. Our local agent was terribly apologetic but insisted that Lisbon was such a nest of spies that I would surely come to somebody's attention if I loitered. He packed me on to a night sleeper train for Madrid, having made sure I had all the right permits and visas, and said I would be met by the head of the Iberia Section once I got to the Spanish capital.

As it turned out, that was an honour I had to forgo, although I have no regrets on that score. The head of Section was far too busy to meet-and-greet amateur field agents on unspecified missions who were simply passing through and treating the Iberia Section like a glorified travel agent, and so the sheriff sent one of his deputies to chaperone me, which was really a stroke of luck, as Kenneth Benton turned out to be a charming chap despite being about ten years younger than me, but he couldn't have been more helpful.

He was a career MI6 man – he'd retired only two years ago and taken up a new career penning thrillers, believe it or not – and, rather intimidatingly, compared to me, seemed to know what he was doing. One of his duties, of course, was to find out exactly what I was doing swanning through his patch; all I could tell him was that I was heading for Marseilles, which he knew full well as he had personally arranged my itinerary.

As to *why* I was going to Marseilles, I played to my strengths and was as vague as I possibly could be. Benton was not offended or annoyed; he would have expected nothing less than lies and obfuscation. It was that sort of world for us: everything was hush-hush, whether it really needed to be or not. Even among those of us on the same side, the rule was that it was best if the left hand did not know what the right hand was doing. Sometimes it was better if the left hand didn't know there was a right hand.

Getting in to Vichy was one thing, getting out quite another. Benton introduced me to Reuben Vidal as the answer to my problem, though my initial impression of that short, thin, weathered figure wearing a sheepskin waistcoat – which doubled his girth – and a greasy black beret, was that he could be an unemployed gardener looking for work.

He was, Benton assured me, a real 'mountain man', who knew all the old pilgrim trails over the Pyrenees and had been assisting escaping British airmen find sanctuary in Spain for more than two years. He traced the easiest routes with a nicotine-stained finger on a map for me, though it was often difficult to follow the contour lines through the cloud of smoke he produced. Clearly the mountain air agreed with Vidal's chain-smoking habit.

In all I spent three days in Madrid with Benton, who gave me some useful tips on arranging secret rendezvous and how to make sure I wasn't being followed, as well as briefing me on my travel arrangements. He also told a good story of how one of the Iberia

Section, a young lad on his first posting overseas, was convinced that the flamenco dancer in his local night club was using her castanets to send messages in Morse code to the Abwehr agents sitting in serried ranks at the bar. The novice agent had been wrong about the castanets but had unwittingly identified a club which the local branch of the Abwehr used as a place to hand over bribes to Spanish army generals, many of whom were receiving similar bribes from British intelligence.

Putting on his most serious and concerned face, Benton convinced me that our modest attempts at spy-craft were no laughing matter, as the Abwehr operated widely and with impunity in Spain.

'However,' he said sternly, 'you should be aware that some of their best agents are based in Marseilles. Those boys are sharp. If you're not careful, they'll have you spotted and picked up within half an hour of getting off the boat.'

I did not have the heart to tell him that I was counting on exactly that.

I suffered another interminable train journey across Spain to Barcelona, where I was grateful for Benton's advice to buy myself a broad-brimmed Panama hat, as the temperatures on the coast were even higher than those in Madrid.

Barcelona was hot, very hot and dusty and shabby, still recovering from its bombing by the aeroplanes of Franco's friends Hitler and Mussolini towards the end of the civil war. I was not there long enough to see much, but I did make sure I was seen wandering around the port area as conspicuously as possible, something of which Benton would certainly have disapproved.

He had managed to book me passage on the single-funnel steamer the SS *Maloja*, which was registered in Basel and owned by the Swiss Shipping Company. Now I hadn't realized that Switzerland had a merchant navy, but when war broke out they had wisely bought up what ships they could to ensure that their supplies from the outside world got through. The *Maloja* was a cargo ship with no special facilities for passengers or day-trippers, so I had to bunk in with the crew – mainly Portuguese but also a couple of Dutch who eyed me warily – and hope that the Swiss flag, the painting of the Swiss flag on the funnel and the word 'Switzerland' in large letters along the side, kept us free from air or submarine attacks from either side as we chugged across the Gulf of Lion at a nerve-straining speed of no more than nine knots an hour.

After a day and a night nervously scanning the waves or the sky for sight or sound of danger, I was mightily relieved when we shouldered our way into the Old Port of Marseilles, which was odd considering that I was now on enemy territory.

It did not feel like enemy territory; it felt like France – or, to be more accurate, it smelled like France. All dockside areas give off the pungent aroma of fishiness and spilled diesel oil, especially on a hot day, but the air of a French port will also contain the perfumes of black tobacco, melting butter and freshly baked bread, along with, it has to be said, the distinct tang of drains.

Jean-Baptiste Hamelin looked around the Vieux-Port, taking in its harbour walls and the solid forts which guarded them, its cranes swinging unidentified cargoes into the air and its ships – some bustling with activity, others which looked as if they had settled in to rust there – as if he had seen nothing like it in the world before. Which a Canadian diplomat on his first posting to Europe probably never had, and I thought I was giving a good impression of one, even though the imposter Albert Campion, who had been well briefed in London, knew that the port of Marseilles was now handling less than one-tenth of the tonnage it had in May 1940.

My papers, or rather those of Jean-Baptiste, were examined by a pair of surly port officials, and my single suitcase thoroughly searched, before I was allowed off the *Maloja*. I protested, good-humouredly, that this was no way to treat a visiting diplomat from a brother country such as Quebec, and shouted long and loud farewells to the crew, inviting them to Canada should they find themselves crossing the Atlantic. I doubt any of them understood a word I was saying, but there were enough pairs of ears within range to note that there was an unusual new arrival on the dockside and, like an idiot, one who didn't mind who knew it.

A uniformed *gendarme* on the Quai du Port, which was now being called the Quai Maréchal Pétain, directed me to the Hôtel de Ville, where my papers were checked more thoroughly this time, my suitcase opened and my underthings rummaged through once more without thought for diplomatic immunity. Once again, I went through a pantomime of being the amiable idiot, this time for a particularly seedy individual, with a moustache stained yellow with nicotine, and stubby fingers with inky nails, who wielded a set of rubber stamps as if they were deadly weapons which, for some unfortunates, I suspect they were.

My details were laboriously copied down on to various official forms under the watchful gaze of two leather-jacketed and well-armed militia-men, though from which security service or private army I could not determine; they did not look the sort who would engage in polite conversation. The bureaucrat with the rubber stamps and a leaky fountain pen asked me what my business was in Marseilles and, with a straight face, I told him I was a diplomat and therefore my business was my country's and not his, but it was no secret that I was en route for Vichy to take up my posting just as soon as I had used up the leave I was owed exploring Marseilles.

He stared at me in outraged wonderment that there were still such things as tourists these days, and I agreed with him that we were a dying breed and asked directions to the Hôtel Moderne. If I had requested that he carried my suitcase, I think he would not have been more offended but, having exchanged glances with his two militia thugs, he stamped my passport with far more violence than was called for and muttered directions which amounted to: 'Outside, turn left, keep going.'

I thanked him profusely, gave him a broad grin and even tipped my Panama in salute, happy in the knowledge that he would not forget me, but just in case he or his two heavies remembered me too quickly, I set off along the quay at a fair clip and did not look back.

I knew very well where my hotel was, though I made a point of asking the way from a pair of dockers sitting in the shade of a pile of crates, passing a bottle between them. From their accents they were certainly local, and from the way they eyed me up I was pretty sure they were memorizing a description of me with a view to selling it to a third party.

I walked on what was known as the Quai des Belges and, as it joined the Quai de la Fraternité, I climbed the steps out of the Old Port and headed inland into the city centre along what had been the most fashionable of streets, La Canebière. I walked over the very spot where the tramlines intersected and where, in 1934, the visiting King Alexander of Yugoslavia was assassinated, along with the French Foreign Minister who was sitting beside him in the official limousine. Not many people remember King Alexander nowadays, but he was hot news at the time as the assassination, by a lone gunman, was caught on film by the newsreel cameras and showed in cinemas all over Europe twice nightly, with matinees on Saturdays.

My hotel, which eight years previously might have given me a ringside seat, was only a few yards along La Canebière.

The Moderne was the sort of hotel where the plumbing did not live up to its name but its prices did, although the paperwork of registering and much copying of passport details came before the haggling. The guardian of the reception desk, a hunched toad of a man in a suit so worn it shined (apart from the lapels, which were coated in a fine sheen of grey cigarette ash), reluctantly accepted that a reservation had been made for me by the Canadian consulate in Vichy, and begrudgingly admitted that he had a vacancy, although from the number of keys gathering dust in the pigeon-holes behind him, he had several. Then came the haggling, as he demanded twenty francs a night for a room, and not even one with a view over the famous assassination site.

He must have seen me blanch, for he quickly added that he would accept Reichsmarks and the rate would be 5RM a night. Remembering my adopted identity, I asked if he was prepared to take Canadian dollars, but that seemed to confuse him and so I magnanimously agreed to his terms and forked out enough cash to cover me for a week. Thanks to the foresight of Elsie Corkran and the advice of Kenneth Benton in Madrid, I had plenty of cash secreted in the lining of my suitcase, and in a rather fetching money belt around my waist and, for emergencies, three 1937 gold sovereigns rather uncomfortably concealed in the heel of each shoe, which I liked to think helped my posture and added to my deportment.

In my musty, dust-filled room, I opened the windows to let in a breath of sea breeze – the only thing, it was said, which made Marseilles tolerable during the summer – then drew a bath, quite grateful for the tepid water provided by the hotel's groaning plumbing. Rinsing away the grime of that interminable journey by plane, train and then boat made me feel almost human again, refreshed and ready for the fray, or at least hungry.

Leaving nothing which I would mind being found by prying eyes or inquiring fingers, I set out to get the lie of the land, keeping the brim of my Panama pulled low until I found a shop on La Canebière which could sell me a pair of sunglasses. As a disguise, they did not put me in the Sherlock Holmes class, but the chances of running in to anyone in Marseilles who knew me were remote – or so I had convinced Elsie Corkran back in London, and almost myself in the process.

At a small *tabac* I spent fifty centimes on a copy of *Marseille-Matin* then splashed out on a pack of *Gauloises Bleues* and a box of matches, thinking that that was what a good French-Canadian would do. I took an impish delight in savouring the pungent black Syrian tobacco, knowing that back home Amanda would never have allowed me to light one up as the smell 'would hang on the curtains for weeks'.

At a sidewalk table outside the Café de Glacier, I drank *pastis*, smoked and read my newspaper from behind over-large sunglasses, hoping that I was being conspicuously inconspicuous as the world went by me on foot, bicycle, tram, and in strange adapted motor vehicles which now ran on gas rather than petrol. I ordered a second drink and made a point of showing off my out-of-town accent by asking the waiter if this was a good place for an early dinner. After checking that the management was not observing him, he lowered his voice and recommended a restaurant back down La Canebière, on the corner with the Place de la Bourse. Should I tell the maitre d' there that Pascal had sent me, I would be given a good table and Pascal, no doubt, would get a small commission.

I adhered to Pascal's instructions and, under the circumstances, my dinner was very acceptable: onion soup followed by a pale steak which might have been horse in a spicy sauce, served on a bed of cracked grains almost certainly of North African origin. The cold, thin white wine was eminently quaffable, and I was presented with a complimentary Armagnac to make up for the awfulness of the coffee by a waiter who muttered under his breath that all the good coffee had been 'diverted to Germany'.

So, I was sound in body if not mind, as I began a leisurely stroll back to my hotel as darkness fell, which seemed to be the signal for all traffic not afoot to disappear from the streets. I had gone no more than fifty yards from the restaurant before I was sure two of my fellow pedestrians, one on each side of La Canebière, were following me.

I could see the vertically hanging sign telling me that the Hôtel Moderne was well within sprinting distance, assuming of course that I could outsprint my followers. It would, though, be one way of proving they were after me and I was not just imagining things, and so I increased my pace to a fair clip.

What I had not counted on was that I had a third follower, who was very cleverly not behind me but in front, waiting in the shadows of a small side street; he was all too keen to make my acquaintance as I trotted by. Not that I appreciated his enthusiasm when he decided to attract my attention by means of a powerful punch to my stomach.

What followed was confusing to say the least. I had momentarily lost the ability to breathe and the laws of gravity seemed not to apply to me as I collided, horizontally, with the pavement. Something hard and painful in the chest area – a boot perhaps – propelled me into the gutter which, given how shamefully easy I was making life for my assailant, was quite appropriate really. A pair of knees landed on my chest, pinning me there, and then hands as delicate as meat hooks grappled at my jacket and shirt, despite the resistance I was putting up by pawing them away with all the ferocity of a tired, newborn kitten.

I concentrated on remembering how to breathe and attempted to heave my assailant from me, but he stuck to his task like a dead weight, his hands working his way through my pockets as we struggled in an eerie silence, apart from the pounding of rapidly approaching footsteps which I assumed to be his companions who had been following me. When a second pair of boots joined in the fun, I realized I was in for what an uncouth acquaintance of mine would have called 'a right good kicking'.

There was certainly a flurry of fists and feet in the general area of my head and the sound of my shirt being ripped open. In a flash of awful clarity, I realized that I did not have any chance of winning this fight. The shadowy figures who were attacking me were younger, heavier, fitter, and had used the element of surprise to good effect. Yet, just as I was sinking into the slough of despond, I was aware of the sound of an engine and the gleam of headlamps coming down the street.

Surely this would be my rescue. I was being thoroughly pummelled by two assailants in the middle of the equivalent of Regent Street in one of the largest cities in France. Even in London after the pubs had closed on a Friday night, you would think someone would have noticed. Perhaps the driver of the approaching car had, although my attackers seemed blissfully unaware and stuck to their task with gusto.

It was only when the car squealed to a halt so close to us that I could smell the exhaust fumes, that the pounding ceased, although a pair of knees still pinned me to the concrete. I had lost my glasses, my head was in the street and my legs were on the pavement, so my blurred, supine view of things was limited to the car's wheels, exhaust pipe and running board. And then a boot, a shiny boot which glistened even in the dark, descended from the running board so close to my face that I imagined I could smell the leather.

From somewhere miles above my head I heard a voice declaim in deep and threatening French, '*Lâchez-le, espèce de con*,' and then a quite distinct, loud plopping sound followed by a scream.

I registered two things before I must have fainted. I felt a splash of something warm and wet on my neck and chest where it was exposed through my torn shirt, and then, in hypnotic slow motion, I saw a single spent cartridge case bounce off the road an inch from my nose and roll away under the car.

The next thing I knew, I had been hauled to my feet and was being manhandled into the back of the car, my face pressed into the rough serge of what was certainly a uniform of some sort. I slid and was pushed across the leather seat; a body pressed in next to me and the car sped away.

An interior light was clicked on and I attempted to focus on my fellow passenger, my rescuer. I had been right about the uniform; it was that of an officer of the old Gendarmerie Mobile, sometimes known as the 'yellows' because of their gold insignia, complete with riding breeches and a peaked *kepi* hat. The wearer was calmly unscrewing a stubby black silencer from an automatic pistol, which really should have given me a clue.

I squeezed my eyes to help them focus on the face under the *kepi*.

'Robert?'

'Hello, Albert, welcome to Marseilles. Unfortunately, you've arrived too late.'

EIGHT

Unsafe Houses

Marseilles. September – October 1942

Policemen do not usually carry silencers for their weapons, unless they are up to no good or not really policemen.

'And you, my old friend, arrived in the nick of time,

although I was just getting the better of those thuggees and was about to teach them a lesson, once I'd got my breath back.'

'So I saw,' said my rescuer without much conviction, 'and I'm sure you would have done so had you not lost these.'

The gun and the silencer he had been holding had disappeared; he was offering me my spectacles, which were bent but mercifully intact.

'You are, sir, twice a life-saver,' I said, pleasantly surprised that the conversation was taking place in English, which somehow did not seem odd at all. 'What happened to my over-friendly welcome committee?'

'I thought it would save time if I shot one,' said Robert Ringer with a coolness which said much for his Cambridge education, 'so I aimed for the soft part of the shoulder. I'm afraid quite a bit of his blood splashed over you, but it seemed to do the trick. He and his friend took off for the docks at the gallop and did not look back.'

'What about the other one?'

'What other one?'

'There were three of them. I spotted two of them when I left the restaurant, and then one was waiting in ambush.'

'Oh, you mean the girl?'

'Do I? What girl?'

'The girl that was following the men who attacked you, not you. She hung back in a shop door when they jumped on you.'

'Are you sure? I know I'm a bit hazy . . .'

'A small figure in a seaman's jacket and wearing a beret, easily mistaken for a man. She was on the other side of the street. I think she was as surprised as you were when the other two attacked, and when she saw me, she disappeared fast.'

'And that was a girl? Are you sure?'

'I am, and I even know her name.'

Even confused and hurting as I was, I could not but admit that my estimation of German military intelligence had risen somewhat.

Our car journey lasted no more than ten minutes, but through such a twisted maze of dimly lit side streets that I completely lost any sense of direction. When we stopped, it was in front of a small, shabby hotel which wasn't mine. In the gloom of threadbare street-lighting and the shadows cast by the buildings crowded around it,

I could make out a sign bearing – in flaking paint – the words 'Hôtel Libéria'.

'I thought the Abwehr might have run to something a little more salubrious,' I said as Robert held the door to a small entrance lobby open for me.

'Oh, it does,' he said with a smile. 'We don't stay here, we just own it. To be pedantic, I own it – or rather my company does. It comes in very useful. Now let us find you a room and get you cleaned up.'

'But I have a room at the Moderne, a room I've paid for in advance, though I've only spent about five minutes in it,' I protested.

'And Jean-Baptiste Hamelin will remain registered there, but Albert Campion will operate out of here. This will be your safe house.'

'And is it safe?'

'Well, that depends . . .'

For all its air of general decrepitude, its well-worn carpets, wonky light fittings and a distinct smell of mould, the plumbing in the Libéria was superior to that of the Moderne, which I put down to German engineering, and I was grateful for it as I took my second bath of the day, soaping carefully around the bruises on my chest and arms, which were developing an attractive purple hue. A certain tenderness suggested I might have a cracked rib or two, but I decided not to investigate too closely on the principle that ignorance is often bliss.

I made a concentrated effort with cold water and a nailbrush to get the blood off my jacket, just grateful that it wasn't mine, but I realized that my shirt, now shredded and dark red, was beyond salvaging. I was to be grateful to the Abwehr for more than the plumbing, as a member of the hotel staff – almost certainly also a member of the Abwehr – had laid out a fresh set of clothes on the bed; and by 'fresh', I mean different.

I gathered that my identity as a smart Canadian diplomat was to be discarded in favour of that of an anonymous Marseilles working man who dressed in a blue shirt, dark brown cord trousers, a short and shiny leather jacket and, to complete the effect, a black beret and a blue and white spotted cotton neckerchief.

Robert von Ringer clearly used the Libéria as his personal wardrobe, for when I joined him in the hotel's small cocktail bar, he had changed out of his police uniform and was relaxing in an immaculate white linen suit, crisp white shirt and a Brooks Brothers' striped club tie tied in a perfect Windsor knot.

'I see you got first pick at the dressing-up box – and, yes please, I'll have a double,' I told him as he pointed a bottle of cognac and a glass in my direction.

'I thought it might be advisable for you to blend in more. Do you have another suit in your luggage?'

'Only a dinner suit,' I said, and immediately felt rather foolish. 'The sort of thing no diplomat travels without in case of formal occasions.'

Robert gave me a look of exasperation. 'Only the English would think a dinner jacket a good disguise for a spy. No matter: leave the suit you were wearing here and I'll have it cleaned and pressed. Tomorrow it will be better if you go about unnoticed as a dock worker or a deck hand on shore leave; your Canadian diplomat disguise drew too much attention.'

'It was sort of meant to. Those men in the street, they followed me from the hotel, I'm guessing.'

'From the moment you stepped off the boat this afternoon, actually.'

Robert really could be unbearably smug sometimes. 'I suppose your men were watching them watching me.'

'We've been watching you since you got off the flying boat in Lisbon.' He was not boasting, merely stating a fact.

'Then you had plenty of time to warn me or warn *them* off. It might have saved me a cracked rib or two, several bruises and a perfectly good shirt.'

'I wanted to see which one they were following: an innocent Canadian diplomat who mentioned the fact that he could pay his hotel bill in dollars, and was therefore a target of opportunity, or my old English chum who has come a long way to see me. Fortunately, they were robbers.'

'Fortunately?'

'I am sure they were after your money belt – please do not try and look surprised. It is obvious you were wearing one; your suit was too well cut to disguise it.'

'The local criminal fraternity, eh? Perhaps my reputation precedes me.'

'Let us hope not, but yes, those two are known figures in the Panier district. What did they take?'

Automatically, I patted my sides, which was ridiculous as these were no longer my clothes.

'My wallet, ration card, diplomatic accreditation and travel permits, but I did hang on to my money belt, though goodness knows how women put up with girdles.'

'And you still have those gold sovereigns in the heels of your shoes,' observed Robert.

'How do you know what I may or may not have in my footwear?'

'My dear Albert, you are not the first British agent to enjoy the hospitality of the Abwehr.'

It was then I decided to ask the question that really needed asking and could be put off no longer.

'Freiherr von Ringer, it is wonderful to be able to renew our acquaintance, but I really must know, am I your prisoner or your guest?'

'Both.'

One of Robert's staff took my photograph, a head-and-shoulders mug shot, up against a whitewashed wall; I was assured that my noble image would adorn a new set of false papers by the morning. The staff, whom I suspect were all Abwehr officers rather than hoteliers, were then dismissed, leaving Robert and me alone in the small bar/foyer area. We were, he assured me, quite secure, and there was no fear of interruption, so we should make ourselves comfortable with recharged glasses and 'put our cards on the table'.

I pointed out that as he had dealt the cards and my hand had probably come from the bottom of the deck, I would let him take the lead.

'First, I must thank you for coming here, at some risk to your person,' he said formally. 'You were the one Englishman I knew I could trust without question.'

'Trust with what, Dr Haberland?' My use of his pen name produced a satisfied smile. 'It seems a long way to come for a report on the progress of some French naval water babies.'

'I knew you would get the reference to the good Professor Haberland, and the French navy is certainly experimenting with new underwater equipment along the coast, but I wanted you here for another, more important reason: I need your help.'

'To do what?'

'To prevent a crime.'

'Is there a shortage of policemen in Vichy? I hear you have plenty in Germany . . .'

I knew, or I thought I knew, just how much I could tease Robert. When a man forgives you for scarring him in a sword fight, one assumes one has the measure of him. It was clear, however, that I had gone as far as I dare. He transferred his glass to his left hand and, with the forefinger of his right, traced the scar on the left side of his face.

'You gave me this,' he said. 'So you owe me something.'

'A re-match spiced with revenge after all these years? That's not your style at all, old chum.'

'No, not revenge, Albert, I meant what I said. I want you to help me prevent a crime and, in the process, hopefully prevent an innocent man being shot as a traitor.'

'That innocent man being . . .?'

'Why, me, of course.'

'I had a feeling you were going to say that, and now I simply have to hear you out. If you are sure there is no chance that either of us will be shot before morning, you'd better tell Uncle all about it.'

It would be pretentious of me, possibly heretical, to say that Robert von Ringer had experienced an epiphany, but it sounded that way as he told me the story of his transformation in a calm and rational, almost gentle, way. It was, like all epiphanies, an incident which first stabbed at the heart and then strengthened and resolved the spirit.

Until that night, I had no idea that Robert had a younger brother, Freddie, serving in the regular Wehrmacht as a junior officer in General von Manstein's 11th Army in Russia. Freddie was a good soldier, a promising officer, liked by his men, and a good German. He was not a good Nazi, however, and treated fanatical party members and organizations such as the SS with open disdain. He had been reprimanded more than once by senior officers with wiser, more cautious heads, who knew the power and vindictiveness of their political masters. Poor Freddie discovered those traits for himself during the German advance into the Crimea. It was at a place called Eupatoria, a resort noted for its spa and sanatorium, that Freddie von Ringer witnessed the execution – the massacre – of some 1,200 unarmed Jews, men, women and children, by dead-hearted, cold-eyed members of an SS 'Action Group'. Powerless to intervene and overwhelmed at the horror, Freddie peeled off his uniform tunic and began walking back to Germany. Of course, he did not get very far before he was picked up by the military police and returned to his unit to face charges of desertion. The charges were never brought as Freddie spent his last few hours writing a long letter to his brother detailing what he had witnessed (a letter he entrusted to a faithful company sergeant), and saying goodbye to the men in his company, before borrowing a pistol from a fellow officer and blowing his troubled brains out.

From the moment he read his brother's final letter, all Robert von Ringer's previously held doubts about the cause he was fighting for solidified into feelings of disgust and anger. He was aware that the murders his brother had witnessed were not the only horrors taking place on the Eastern front and, though his own sphere of operation on the tranquil Riviera was far removed from such violent atrocities, he began to bridle and protest when fellow Germans (and several Vichy officials) casually referred to Marseilles as 'the new Jerusalem of the Mediterranean' and suggested that Cannes should be re-named 'Kahn' due to the number of Jewish refugees who had fled south.

It was, he said, as if he had developed an extra sense. He became aware of the persecution of the Jewish people in a way, he was ashamed to admit, he had not been before, and it was a painful awareness as he realized he was powerless to do anything to alleviate it, however much he wished to appease the memory of his brother.

But at least his eyes were now open, which is how he noticed Nathan Lunel.

Lunel's name was raised at an Abwehr conference, not in France, but across the Mediterranean in Tripoli, in Italian-controlled Libya. The German intelligence service was active all across North Africa, operating freely in Vichy-run Tunis, Algiers, and in Rabat and Casablanca, and Nathan Lunel had come to the attention not just of the Tripoli branch office of the Abwehr but of all the Abwehr outposts in Tunisia, Algeria and Morocco. He was, it appeared, a frequent visitor to the sandy shores of Africa, though not as a tourist anxious to wander around Roman or Carthaginian ruins, but a man who rarely spent more than one day in any particular city, concluding his business as quickly as possible and then catching the first boat sailing for Marseilles. That his home port was Marseilles brought him within Ringer's sphere of influence. That his meetings in North

Africa always took place in French banks made him a figure of some curiosity. That he was always – always – accompanied by a Corsican gangster with an impressively long criminal record, made him a figure of considerable interest, as did his apparent ease when it came to getting travel permits and the crucial *laissez-passer* which allowed him to travel north into the Occupied Zone.

On his own initiative, and keeping his actions secret even from his immediate Abwehr colleagues, Robert began to track the many journeys across France and North Africa taken by Nathan Lunel over several months. He even arranged to travel on the same ship as Lunel and his 'guardian' on a return trip from Algiers; a voyage which was disrupted by warnings of lurking British submarines. Instead of Marseilles, the ship docked in Genoa, and the travellers chose to complete their journey by train, which involved an overnight stay in Mentone.

Thus had Robert found himself in the Hôtel Beauregard and in conversation with M. Étienne Fleurey while admiring framed photographs of a group of especially handsome Englishmen in happier, pre-war times. That had given him what the cartoonists call 'the light-bulb moment' and he realized that I was the answer to all his problems.

Well, perhaps not all, but possibly one, as it seems I was something of an expert.

'I'll have you know I have never been called an expert at anything!' I protested. 'There was a time when such an insult would have instantly brought forth a demand for satisfaction, but as you have undoubtedly kept up your duelling skills and I have not, I will let it pass as long as you tell me what the devil you are talking about.'

Coming across my smiling visage in the Beauregard had triggered more than one thought in Robert's mind, not only of our fencing days at Cambridge, but of the fame that had preceded me in German intelligence circles. I had, it appeared, been named in several confidential internal reports and memoranda as the main spanner in the works of a Nazi plot to drown the British economy in a flood of forged currency in the early days of the war.

I could not deny my involvement in that little escapade, although I had been somewhat distracted by suffering from amnesia and waking up a married man!

Modesty did not become me, said Robert, as the large-scale printing of fake currency (or 'off-white fivers', as Lugg would have said) was a plan, code-named Operation Andreas, into which the SD had put considerable time and effort.

At this point my host leaned forward in his chair and held out the cognac bottle to refill my glass, which was surprisingly quite empty. I had a feeling things were about to get serious and having a stiff drink to hand might be advisable.

'I am going to tell you a secret, a state secret,' said mine host as he lit a much-needed cigarette for me and one of his vile cigars for himself, 'an act for which I could be shot as a traitor.'

'I do hope you are not expecting a reciprocal arrangement, old chum, for I know absolutely no secrets worth knowing – not even my wife's weight, which is most closely guarded.'

'Please be serious, Albert,' said Robert firmly; so firmly, that I was.

I was aware, of course, of the rivalry between the SD, the SS's Sicherheitsdienst and the Abwehr, and I could well understand the glee in Abwehr circles when Operation Andreas failed, although my part in its downfall was fairly minimal. What I did not know until Robert took me, rather worryingly, into his confidence was that in July, a new counterfeiting initiative known as Operation Bernhard had been set in motion by the SD, utilizing the skills, under duress, of a large number of artists, engravers, plate-makers and printers currently enjoying Nazi hospitality in a concentration camp, many of them being Jewish with no option but to cooperate.

It is second nature for spies to spy on spies, and so the Abwehr began to take an interest in the SD's plans for manipulating Britain's currency, and one name, Nathan Lunel, cropped up more than once; and in the world of intelligence agencies, more than once made him a person of considerable interest.

Until the Vichy government imposed its anti-Semitic restrictions to curry favour with its Nazi neighbours, Lunel had held a senior position in a French bank with offices in Lyon and Marseilles. The fact that he could now travel freely from Vichy to Paris in the Occupied Zone, and then from Vichy to North Africa, suggested that he had friends in high places providing him with the necessary permissions and funds. Yet Nathan Lunel was not a known criminal, had no particular expertise in forgery or history of dealing in pounds sterling, so what use could he be to Operation Bernhard?

The answer lay in his visits to North Africa, and involved solid, old-fashioned undercover detective work by Ringer and a few trusted

Abwehr colleagues in Tunis and Algiers. Nathan Lunel was not forging money, he was *moving* money, as part of a highly unofficial operation mounted by certain members of the SD, based in Paris and working with a number of French industrialists (the sort who always prosper from war), some corrupt Vichy politicians and the criminal gangs that controlled the Marseilles underworld.

That was, I agreed, an unholy alliance, but corrupt policemen, if one could describe the SD as such, who worked with criminals rather than against them, were not unknown in any society, and corrupt politicians were *de rigueur* in every system, even one as imperfect as democracy. Yet among the many twisted ideologies which made up the insanity of Nazism, personal corruption or deviant behaviour was frowned upon and punished very severely, although there were convenient double standards inherent in the system. It was perfectly acceptable for the Nazis to steal an entire country, but embezzlement of even a few pfennings from NSDAP – Nazi Party – funds could result in summary execution; a party big-wig, one of the 'Golden Pheasants', as they were known, could amass a vast collection of priceless art, whereas an impoverished art student caught listening to jazz music could face a lengthy stay in a concentration camp.

If Robert was suggesting some form of criminal conspiracy, whereby the thieves were hiding their ill-gotten gains in North Africa (and personally I would have suggested Switzerland), then surely the wheels of diabolic Nazi justice and its agents should be put in motion. How could a middle-aged English dilettante, who was, after all, an enemy alien, if not a spy, possibly help?

'Precisely because you are English and an enemy,' Robert responded, 'and being a dilettante certainly helps, as no one who has met you will suspect you, just as no one would suspect Nathan Lunel.'

'I am not sure I follow the last part of your logic,' I told him.

With a shrug of his shoulders, he explained the gruesomely obvious. 'The SD is the intelligence arm of Himmler's SS. Who would believe they were trusting a Jew to move their money?'

I accepted Robert's rather distasteful point, but still could not possibly see how an enemy national with no practical powers and few attributes – other than his natural charm, of course – might help.

Robert stubbed out his cheroot in an overflowing ashtray and promptly lit up a replacement. 'I am a good German, like my brother was,' he said, 'and though I am no Nazi, I am no more a traitor to my country than you are to yours. What we are dealing with here, if I were to try and stop it, requires treason on my part. For you, it would involve only doing your duty. I would be put up against the nearest wall and shot – if the SS were feeling merciful. You might get a medal.'

I told Robert I was still somewhat in the dark, and if only he would use smaller words, I might understand what he was getting at.

'You must understand, my friend, that we are not dealing here with petty criminals intent on hiding their bad profits. What is the phrase you have in England for *Schlechte Gewinne*?'

'Ill-gotten gains.'

'Your German is good,' he acknowledged.

'Not as good as yours,' I conceded, which produced a brief smile.

'You must take this seriously, Albert, though I know that might be difficult for you. This is a conspiracy on a massive scale, which will bring huge profits to some very powerful people after the war – a war which Germany is certainly going to lose. It is a conspiracy which *depends* on the Allies winning the war and, when they do, this gang of thieves will profit immensely.'

After the long days of travelling, the excursions and alarums of the evening and, possibly, too much brandy, my brain abandoned its usual torpor and began to spark faintly into life.

'It's to do with those trips to North Africa, isn't it?'

'Exactly,' said Robert, with the satisfaction of a schoolmaster awarding house points to the straggler of the class. 'Lunel is opening fake accounts in banks all across North Africa and filling those accounts with money transferred from banks in both Vichy and the Occupied Zone with an eye to – as the Americans might say – making a killing. You do understand why, don't you?'

'Accountancy was never my strong point, old boy. At school I wasn't trusted with the tuck-shop takings, and my current employers keep me well away from the Christmas Club, so please enlighten me, unless it involves divulging state secrets, that is.'

'It almost certainly does, I'm afraid.' Robert did not seem at all afraid; he was irritatingly confident. 'Everyone, except perhaps our beloved Führer and his close circle of cronies, can see the way the war is going. It will not be long before the Allies attack in the west while the Russians keep us busy in the east; it is only a matter of where and when.'

I was not sure where this little homily was going, or happy with its direction, but as I was enjoying Robert's hospitality – and hopefully his protection – I allowed him the floor.

'And this is the point where we exchange secrets, or perhaps they are not so secret. Your raid on Dieppe last month was a bloody rehearsal for you, and we do not think an invasion will come in France – not yet, anyway. One theory is that the British will try and land a force in Portugal; it is an old ally of yours and your generals may still have fond memories of the Duke of Wellington and the Peninsular War.'

He must have noticed my eyebrows rise at that, but I kept them under control so as not to give anything away.

'We have a contingency plan for that: it is called Operation Isabella, which has a nice Spanish ring to it, don't you think? If the British land in Portugal, then the Wehrmacht will move into Spain to help our Spanish ally, General Franco.'

'Spain is neutral. Franco might sympathize with Hitler but he is not an ally,' I observed.

'He will be if the Wehrmacht says he is, but that is a remote possibility. Far more likely to happen is Operation Anton, the code name for the German occupation of Vichy France, and that will happen – not *could* happen but *will* happen – the moment the Allies, almost certainly led by the Americans, invade North Africa from the west. Morocco, Algeria and Tunisia are Vichy territories and soft targets. With the British army in Egypt, if they are taken then the Afrika Korps is trapped, but – more importantly for anyone with accounts in Vichy banks there – their funds will automatically be converted into American dollars . . .'

'Whereas, the banks in Vichy which come under the beneficence of a German occupation will have their assets converted into Reichsmarks . . .'

'And, given the likely outcome of the war, which would you prefer?'

'Just how many dollars might we be talking about?' I enquired, adding: 'Hypothetically, of course.'

'It could be millions. No one knows for sure except Nathan Lunel, who did the banking.'

'Then we must ask this M'sieur Lunel some serious questions.'

'That could be difficult,' said Robert gravely; very gravely. 'I told you that you had arrived too late, Albert, and I meant it. The

Vichy government decided to embrace National Socialist ideology last month and ordered a mass round-up of Jews with a view to deportation. Nathan Lunel is in a concentration camp.'

NINE

Entremets

The Dorchester Hotel, London. 20 May 1970

'Oo needs a palate cleanser when there's perfectly good wine still on the table?'

Mr Lugg's observations on the *entremets* intermission in proceedings went mostly ignored by those who heard them, and his feelings were not mirrored by his actions as he helped himself by the fistful from every passing plate of canapés – which he pronounced as if asking questions of primate behaviour. Only Precious Aird, armed with the innocence of youth and the enthusiasm of the American, felt confident enough to take him to task.

'My, what a grumpy-boots we are, and this is supposed to be a party! Well, I think it's all just swell, a real class act. In California, you don't get refinements like this, just a flunky pushing a sweet cart at high speed.'

'These ain't puddings,' sulked Lugg, 'they're hardly mouthfuls of anything. You've got a proper dessert to come and then there's cake.'

'You guys don't stint yourselves, do you?' As she spoke, Miss Aird deliberately averted her eyes from Mr Lugg's substantial girth. 'No wonder there are so many eating irons on the table.'

Lugg gave a quiet grunt, as if confirming his darkest suspicions. 'Yes, well, you Yanks never could handle cutlery, though the rules are pretty simple: start at the outside, work your way in towards where your plate goes and always keep the fork in the left hand. Anything else is just unnatural.'

'You've told me that three times tonight,' said the girl with an innocent smile. 'Maybe I'll get the hang of it before we get to the coffee and cigars.'

Lugg's bushy eyebrows arched like two caterpillars in a hurry. 'Cigars? You're not one of those females who smokes cigars, are you?'

'I will tonight, but only if you promise to look as outraged as you do now. I'm young and American: it's my duty to shock the older generation.'

Holding high a glass in her right hand, Precious plucked at the hem of her way-above-the-knee dress with her left, crossed one foot over the other and bobbed a dainty curtsey in front of the dinner-jacketed monolith.

'Cheek!' growled Lugg.

'I hope this old bulldog isn't worrying you, Precious,' said Rupert as he weaved through the throng towards them, narrowly avoiding a waiter with a tray of drinks and swerving to avoid Jolyon Livingstone who was bent over a plate of canapés, interrogating the angelically patient waitress holding them on their provenance.

'Oh, that's never going to happen, is it?' Precious chirped. 'Lugg has been tutoring me in something called "Hetiquette", which I intend to look up as soon as I can get to a dictionary. How's tricks down at the posh end of the table? We're kinda cut off way down there below the mustard.'

'The salt,' Lugg corrected. 'Below the salt.'

'Everyone's enjoying themselves, I think,' said Rupert hesitantly, 'but I'd be fibbing if I said there hadn't been a few sticky moments.'

'I could see that,' said Lugg. 'Only wish I'd stayed on at night school to do lip reading. Your ma not getting on with the French lady then?'

'It's not that they've come to blows or anything, but there's a definite coolness there. Madame Thibus is very tight-lipped about why she's here tonight, and Pa is doing his usual bonfire of the vagaries act, pretending it's nothing really to do with him, when of course it must be as it's his birthday party. And I've been charged with keeping the Spanish woman, Mrs Vidal, amused, though goodness knows, she's proving to be hard work.'

'So's her daughter – Prisca, is it? – down our end of the festivities,' said Precious Aird. 'She really comes across as someone who doesn't want to be here. She even made Robert the randy schoolboy look as if he's had a cold shower; not that he didn't need one. Who is that kid, anyway?'

'Don't ask me,' sulked Lugg.

'Somebody Pa unearthed as a schoolboy up in Suffolk a couple of years ago and has been keeping an eye on ever since. Pa says he comes across as a "moonstruck calf" whenever females are around, whatever that means.'

'I don't know what that means either, but I recognize the symptoms. He sure didn't cut any ice with Miss Vidal, though I reckon he wouldn't have if he'd had a blowtorch.'

'Like mother, like daughter, eh?' Lugg strained his neck out of his starched white collar in order to survey the surrounding crowd of talking heads. 'Where is the Ice Queen, anyway?'

'She's gone to the ladies' bathroom,' said Precious between sips from her glass. 'I don't know where the randy schoolboy is, but I ain't goin' hunting for him.'

'Young Oncer, if that's what he's called, is ensconced with Jonathan Eager-Wright over by the piano,' reported Rupert, 'in a deep discussion about mountaineering as far as I can gather. I overheard him say he'd read one of Eager-Wright's books on climbing techniques and, as that is the only subject under the sun on which old Jonathan is willing to engage in sociable conversation, he may be gone for some time.'

'I'll drink to that,' said Precious Aird to no one in particular; but then to Rupert: 'How's Perdita doin'? Enjoying herself down the dinosaur end of the table?'

'Oi, you! Less of the cheek,' warned Lugg.

'I was forgetting,' said Precious, 'I'm the one sitting with the dinosaurs.'

She reached out a hand towards a plate floating by, which contained the last two stuffed mushrooms in captivity, but a larger, much larger, hand shot out from a white cuff in a blur of movement and swept up the unsuspecting fungi.

'Age before beauty then,' said Lugg, before filling his gaping mouth.

The room throbbed with dinner-jacketed shoulders rubbing against each other, glasses tinkling with ice and occasionally colliding with jewellery, the ambient temperature growing due to cigarette smoke, almost as quickly as the rising volume of the chatter from glowing, well-fed and well-watered diners, grateful that the whistle had been blown for half-time.

The level of background noise was such that Mr Augustus Randall found himself almost shouting to make himself heard, although from the pained expression on his wife's face, Mary Randall was having no trouble whatsoever in hearing him.

'I've no idea what Albert was going on about,' moaned Guffy, 'giving that sermon of his. Why was he whispering?'

Not for the first time, Mary took a soothing approach.

'He wasn't whispering, darling, he's just naturally soft spoken. Not like you, who is only happy when you're yelling for the dogs to come to heel or bellowing across a field to make the cows come home. Monsieur Fleurey and I could hear him perfectly well. We really are going to have to get you fixed up with a hearing aid if you insist on eavesdropping.'

'I wasn't prying, just trying to follow the conversation. Thought that was what you were supposed to do at dinner parties. It's Albert's party and Albert was holding court, so I tried to pay attention in case questions were asked afterwards. Only caught one word in three, though. Something about the war . . .?'

Mary stretched out a hand and patted her husband's straining shirt front roughly in the heart area.

'Yes, my dear, Albert was talking about what he did in the war, but I don't think he expects you to take notes. It was quite fascinating. I had no idea he was involved in all that secret stuff.'

'Secrets?' bristled Guffy. 'He's not giving away secrets to a German, is he?'

'Not at all, dearest. Albert's talking about history. Things that happened more than twenty-five years ago, and from the way Albert tells it, that good German gentleman knew far more secrets than Albert did.'

'Good German? The only good German—'

'*Guffy, behave!*'

'Is one who brews beer. They make damn good beer, the Germans. And cars: their cars are absolutely first rate. What's the matter, darling, what did you think I was going to say?'

'Are they boring you, my dear? If they are, I have dozens of proven ways of keeping my husband quiet.'

Making no attempt to lower her voice, Amanda linked arms with Perdita and drew her free of the masculinity grouped around Mr Campion.

'I'm not bored at all, far from it; it's all jolly exciting. I had no idea . . .'

'No, not many people did. He's never been one for telling war stories. Perhaps he's feeling his age, and this party, with Robert here, gives him a chance to draw a line under things, bury hatchets, kiss and make up, or whatever men do.'

'They don't seem to have any hatchets to bury,' observed Perdita. 'It's hard to believe they were on different sides. They seem like old pals, even though Albert gave him that terrible scar.'

'It's always been difficult to stay angry with him for long,' conceded Amanda under her breath, 'no matter how hard one tries.'

'I wouldn't worry about him.' Perdita's voice betrayed nothing but adoration. 'He's having a whale of a time telling tall tales and he has his audience in the palm of his hands.'

Observing the phalanx of dinner jackets huddled around Mr Campion, Amanda pursed her lips.

'You're right about the menfolk hanging on his every word,' she confided to her daughter-in-law, 'but I have a feeling the tales are not quite as tall as you might think.'

'You haven't told us about the girl,' said Charles Luke.

'Sorry, what was that?'

Mr Campion had been briefly distracted by a passing Dr Livingstone who had picked an inopportune moment to mention the appeal fund for a new roof for the library of St Ignatius College, the previous roof having been lightened in both weight and value by audacious lead thieves. Having assured the master of his old college that a cheque would be in the post and that Dr Livingstone could certainly trust Coutts Bank if not A. Campion, Esquire, he turned back to his faithful followers who had been joined by Perdita, delicately shouldering her way back into the group.

'The girl,' Luke repeated, 'there was a girl in the street back in Marseilles, when that gang attacked you. Freiherr von Ringer noticed her . . .'

'Robert, please,' said Ringer.

'Don't get too familiar,' warned Campion. 'He's a policeman, you know.'

Luke persevered manfully. 'When you shot the man attacking Albert, you saw a girl who had been tailing him, although Albert hadn't spotted her. Actually, before you answer that, why did you shoot that chap? You had a gun, he didn't, and you were in the uniform of an officer of the law, were you not?'

'I told you he was a policeman,' said Campion.

'I wanted to make an impression,' said Robert von Ringer, and then laughed out loud at the expression on Luke's face. 'Forgive me, Commander, but the gangsters of Marseilles in those days respected neither uniforms nor the law. In any case, I was not a real policeman. And I had an ulterior motive.'

'You were coming to Albert's rescue, the situation was drastic, you had to shoot first and ask questions later . . .' Perdita spoke in a rush, betraying an enthusiasm which quickly embarrassed her.

'Naturally there was *that*,' said Ringer reasonably, 'but really I was thinking ahead. Yes, I wanted to get Albert to safety as quickly as possible, but I also wanted to be able to find out more about his assailants. A flesh wound would need treatment by a doctor and I would get to hear about it the next day through our network of informers.'

'The Abwehr always paid a better rate than we did,' said Campion.

Ringer nodded an acknowledgement to his host, then turned back to Luke. 'You asked about La Pucelle.'

Luke allowed his face to show his confusion. 'I'm sorry, who?'

'The girl who was watching from the shadows. We called her La Pucelle – the maid, as in *The Maid of Orleans*.'

'Oo, oo, I know,' exclaimed Perdita, hopping from one foot to the other and resisting the temptation to raise a schoolgirl-ish hand and cry, *Please, sir!* 'Because she was like Joan of Arc. You didn't burn her at the stake or anything, did you?'

'I think that was the English,' said Ringer, 'and we called her The Maid because that was her name in the Resistance, though we weren't supposed to know that. It came from her real name, which traditionally means "beautiful maiden".'

'That's quite charming,' said Perdita. 'What was her name—?'

'Corinne,' interjected Mr Campion. 'Her name was Corinne Thibus. It still is. She's over there being pestered by Hal Fitton. Perhaps we should go and rescue her.'

'That would be more than fair, Albert,' said Ringer. 'After all, she did rescue you.'

'I guess red hair runs in the family, huh?' said Precious Aird, who had found herself trapped between the most grotesquely mismatched pair of bookends she hoped she would ever come across.

'It's said to be part of the Fitton inheritance,' said the younger one.

'I don't have enough hair left to speak of, and it was never red, but then I'm not a Fitton,' said the other, older and much larger bookend.

'I'm Edward Longfox,' said the serious young man, offering one hand to shake while clutching a glass of orange juice in the other.

That clinched it for Precious Aird: the kid wasn't old enough to drink, which made him, she guessed, about seventeen years old. Being old enough in England, though not in her native California, Precious was acutely aware of such things, and on occasion had treasonously thought that life as a British colony might not have been that bad after all.

'So you're a Fitton?'

'I'm Hal's grandson. He's the Earl of Pontisbright,' said the boy, as though reading from a card, 'which makes Lady Amanda, his sister, my great-aunt, but I'm not allowed to call her that. She did once say, though, that she might respond to being called simply "Great".'

Master Longfox spoke with a completely straight, pale-skinned, freckled face, while Precious choked back a laugh.

'And I'm Christopher,' said the other bookend, who was twice the age and size of Edward Longfox. Precious, who had spotted both of them making a beeline for her from different directions, had stood her ground but offered a silent prayer that they would not actually collide when they reached her. 'And you are . . .?'

'An American,' said Precious smoothly. As she shook the older male's pudgy and rather damp hand, she asked: 'But not Christopher Fitton?'

'Oh, no, it's Campion. Well, it has been since Rudolph appropriated the name. I'm Albert's cousin and probably the black sheep of the family – well, more sort of grey than black, as I'm in public relations.'

'Oh, I see,' said Precious, though she did not.

'Young Edward here is the bright spark, from the brains side of the family, son of a very distinguished scientist.'

'Who died on an Antarctic expedition,' said the lad, but no deadpan comedian had ever delivered such a dark punch line with so little emotion.

'Edward has proved himself a bit of an inventor,' Christopher went on undeterred, as a good public relations man always should. 'Came up with some sort of cathode tube device which could read minds.'

'Really?' Precious heard her voice squeak into a higher register and quickly put the whine down to the wine she had consumed. 'Can you tell what I'm thinking right now?'

The red-haired youth became the red-faced youth.

'Oh, no, no, it was just a youthful experiment in controlled telepathy.' Edward spoke as if reading a witness statement in court. 'The results were deemed statistically insignificant and, in any case, the whole thing only worked on young minds.' He looked askance at the looming Christopher and for the first time showed a flicker of emotion. 'Older people were useless as subjects.'

Precious turned a beatific smile towards the older, clearly redundant point of their conversational triangle. 'And you, Christopher, you said that Albert had appropriated the name Campion, so is that not your name also?' Then Precious's eyes widened as she remembered. 'And you called him Rudolph, not Albert; what's the story there?'

'Well, you see,' Christopher lowered his voice to a whisper, 'the true family name is—'

'Snap to, let's be having you!' boomed Lugg from suddenly very nearby. 'This 'ere tea-break's over, so please form an orderly queue, then it's quick march to your tables and get your bibs back on!'

Only when all the guests, in a far from orderly fashion, had resumed their seats under the twin beams of Lugg's gaze, did the fat man lower himself with an audible sigh of relief into his own chair, which creaked in protest at the unreasonably heavy demands being put on it.

Precious Aird could hardly wait to confide in the big man whom she felt, for reasons not entirely clear to her, that she could trust implicitly. 'Hey, guess what? I think I've discovered a secret.'

'Well, you know what they say about secrets,' said Lugg, concentrating on a futile attempt to make his napkin stretch over his stomach.

'Three can keep a secret if two of them are dead? That was Benjamin Franklin, wasn't it?'

Lugg was nonplussed. 'And as he's dead now, his secret's really safe; but that's probably sound advice. Best way to deal with secrets is to not 'ave 'em in the first place.'

'I am told . . .' Precious paused for a dramatic effect she was sure would be lost on her audience, '. . . that Campion isn't Albert's real name; it isn't even Albert!'

Lugg concentrated on the empty table space in front of him, as if trying to conjure up his dessert by telepathic osmosis, or whatever

it was young Master Longfox had invented. With the tips of his
fingers he carefully rearranged his fork and spoon into what he had
assured Precious was called 'the starting grid' position, and only
when he was completely satisfied with their positioning did he reply.

'There's no secret there, my lass, or if there is it's a secret known
to all the high and mighty in the land, plus quite a few of the lower
orders, and even them that don't know they've got the vote yet, by
which I mean mostly the Picts and Scots north of Hadrian's Wall.'

'I didn't know!' Precious objected. 'So, what is Albert Campion?
Is it some sort of *nom de guerre*?'

'I've heard his Nibs refer to it as his *nom de plume*, but I can't
say my French is up to much.'

'Then what's his real John Hancock?'

'It's certainly not John Hancock, whoever he is, it's . . .'

A shiny black, dress-suited shoulder interposed itself between
the two of them and then a head, slick and pungent with Brylcreem,
lowered itself in parallel with Mr Lugg's giant orb, the effect
produced being that of a solar eclipse.

'Mr Lugg, sir,' said the waiter. 'Sorry to disturb, you being off-
duty, so to speak, but would you mind accompanying me to the
kitchens? There's a bit of a problem you could p'rhaps help us with.'

Snorting like a horse refusing a fence and shaking his head at
the unfairness of life, Mr Lugg rose majestically to his feet and
reluctantly took command.

TEN
Bouillabaisse

Marseilles, 1942

I had found myself up to my neck in a cauldron of simmering
stew, almost certainly a fish stew, this being Marseilles, and I
thought it imperative that I knew what was going on before
I jumped out of the pot and felt the flames nipping at my toes. Part
of my problem was that Robert, who superbly combined the
roles of old and distinguished friend with that of mortal enemy,

clearly thought I was as clever as he was. I therefore asked him to confirm the situation so that a bear of very little brain, to cite one of my heroes, could understand it.

There was a cabal – I could think of no better word – made up of serving officers of the SD, with easy access to 'appropriated assets' (mostly appropriated from Jewish sources), corrupt Vichy politicians making personal profits out of government supply contracts, and the well-established Marseilles underworld with all their traditional ways of raising funds. The cabal was moving its ill-gotten gains from both the Occupied Zone and Vichy into fake bank accounts in French banks in colonial North Africa, which not only 'washed' the cash to disguise its origin, but would also prove a sound financial investment if the invading Americans turned it into dollars rather than if the invading Nazis converted their deposits into Reichsmarks.

This was a criminal conspiracy, not a political operation nor a military stratagem, but in the current climate the forces of law and order seemed thin on the ground. The Marseilles underworld was a law unto itself; no one in Vichy government circles had the stomach for an investigation (as politicians rarely enthuse about turning over stones to see what corruption lies beneath), and any accusations against officers of the SD by officers of the Abwehr would be put down to inter-service rivalry and jealousy, possibly even treason. The criminals and the profiteers who made up this cabal were powerful and anonymous. Apprehending them would be as difficult as trying to handcuff an octopus, but I felt that Robert, with his web of contacts, must surely be able to identify the individuals involved, or at least have an idea of some 'usual suspects' – a group of people, as I understood it, the Vichy police were very fond of rounding up. But he protested that he was as much in the dark as I was.

'My Nazi overlords are skilled at covering their tracks when it comes to money. Our beloved Führer publicly rejects worldly goods and advocates the simple life, yet his deputy in the party, Martin Bormann, collects millions of Reichsmarks from the royalties on *Mein Kampf* and from putting Hitler's head on postage stamps, and the SS have a whole network of bank accounts under the name Max Heiliger, which contain loot and cash from Jewish homes. This cabal is even cleverer. Money is flowing from fake bank accounts in France to new, fake accounts in Tunis, Algiers, Oran and Rabat. The only person who knows the names of those accounts, and the real names behind them, is the man who opened them: Nathan Lunel.'

Given M. Lunel's current indisposition in a concentration camp, this did not bode well for us; nor indeed for him. But if Lunel had vital, and valuable, information locked away in his filing-cabinet banker's brain, why was he not using it as leverage to negotiate his release?

'You have to understand,' Robert told me, 'Lunel is a Jew. An SD or an SS officer could not be seen to negotiate with a Jew, and Vichy officials would see no reason to risk showing sympathy for one, especially one who has clearly collaborated with Germans in the Occupied Zone. The gangsters of Marseilles would certainly like to protect their investments, but even they cannot influence proceedings in a concentration camp, not now that the Final Solution is under way.'

I had not heard that sinister phrase before and, to my eternal shame, I did not pause to consider the full horror of its meaning, but instead gabbled on about the first thing that came into my head.

'Does the Abwehr not have the authority to interview a prisoner in a concentration camp – without arousing suspicion, that is?'

'It could have, but so could a Canadian diplomat researching for, say, the Red Cross . . .'

'I see,' I said, 'so I take it that Jean-Baptiste Hamelin, despite being assaulted and robbed, still has a role to play?'

'I think so,' said Robert, who clearly had thought about it, 'and he will need his stolen wallet, so we to have recover that, or rather Didier Ducret will.'

'And who, pray, is Didier Ducret?'

I might have guessed.

'You, of course, just as soon as you get your new identity card and work permit tomorrow. Didier Ducret is one of my most trusted employees, as a warehouseman and occasionally a driver; though as we are an important German import/export firm, that does not necessarily make him popular with his fellow Frenchmen. We shall make him come from Poitiers or Bordeaux, somewhere like that, which will explain why he does not have the local Marseilles accent and why he has to ask stupid questions to find his way around the city. Of course, the Ducret identity is only if you are challenged by the police or Vichy officials. Everyone has to have papers, and yours will be top quality, certainly good enough to fool the locals. In the evening, back at your hotel, you can be a Canadian diplomat. During the working day you will be Didier Ducret, scouring the back streets of the Old Port for a man with a flesh wound in his shoulder.'

'That shouldn't take him long,' I observed. 'How will he fill his time after lunch?'

Robert scowled at me. It was a scowl perfected long ago by disappointed schoolmasters and sergeant majors.

'I am sure you did not tell your colleagues in London that you were nipping over to France for a holiday with an old chum who just happens to be an officer in the Abwehr. You will have a contingency plan – some contacts here in Marseilles . . .' he held up a hand to forestall an interruption I had no intention of making, '. . . which I would not expect you to divulge. I have told you, I am not interested in making you reveal secrets, only obtaining your help.'

My immediate future prospects began to dawn on me and they were far from rosy. Here was I deep in hostile, if not technically enemy, territory, a lone British agent – oh, very well then, a *spy* – posing as a Canadian diplomat, who was being asked to pose as a part-time Frenchman using identity papers forged by German military intelligence. Such was my predicament, my starting point, my launching pad. I was to be no more than a bullet; but where was Robert aiming the gun?

'I get the distinct impression that I might be seen as doing your dirty work,' I told him.

'Then do not be seen doing it,' he replied with frighteningly Teutonic logic. 'If we meet on the street, we are enemies or, at best, strangers. In private, we must be allies if this conspiracy – this criminal conspiracy – is to be foiled. I hope you agree that it is worth foiling.'

'As a fencer, your weapon of choice was always the sabre rather than the foil, but perhaps that's just me being flippant.'

'It is; and it is a habit you must get out of. The people you will deal with in this matter do not have our famous German sense of humour.'

I was suitably chastised, or at least tried to look as if I was. I agreed that the cause, as outlined by Robert, was just, and that the cabal of thieves had to be exposed or their plans disrupted, but I was still not sure what I could do that the Abwehr could not.

'You will go into places I dare not visit, or at least not without a company of well-armed men to guard my back. You will find the contacts you have no doubt been given, those with Free French sympathies – I do not wish to know the details – and ask for their help in finding the man who took your wallet. That, of course, is your cover story.'

'My dear chap, I now have so many cover stories I feel positively smothered! Why do I need another?'

'Perhaps you do not,' Robert explained with the patience of a saint. 'Perhaps you have contingency plans in place; but if you followed the trail of crumbs I laid, London assumes you are here to gather information on the experiments in underwater diving being conducted by the French navy, correct?'

'Something like that,' I said, concentrating on not giving too much away and thinking how difficult this spying business was.

'In which case,' he continued, 'whatever plan you had for getting home to England – and again I do not need to know the details – was for you and you alone. Now you need to make contact with your networks here in Marseilles because you will need their help to get you *and* Nathan Lunel out of Vichy. It is vital to get the information he carries in his head to the Allies who will invade North Africa and take over the Vichy banks. I cannot do that, because I would not be trusted by the Gaullists and certainly suspected by the SD. You are not the only one surrounded by enemies, Albert.'

'Yet you managed to get Étienne Fleurey out of Vichy, through the Occupied Zone and across the Channel.'

'That was one man; though he is a quite charming fellow, I have to say he was a man of little importance. Nathan Lunel *is* important – to the powerful and dangerous people whose secrets he holds. They do not want him to fall into the wrong hands and would rather see him dead. It is a great irony that Nathan Lunel is, at the moment, in the safest place he could be: a concentration camp.'

I was getting the picture, slowly and fuzzily, but yet it was not quite the full picture and I decided to press Robert further. I never did know when to leave well enough alone.

'I still don't understand why Lunel has not traded what he knows about those bank accounts for his freedom, or why he hasn't just taken off on his own. If he has access to unlimited funds which officially don't exist, then money would not be a problem. He could have bought a new identity and a passage to Spain or Switzerland and travelled in style, I suspect.'

Robert vented his frustration by grinding the stub of his cigarillo into his ashtray with far more violence than was necessary.

'The problem is that Nathan Lunel will not leave France,' he said through gritted teeth. 'Not without his wife.'

I let that sink in and was about to ask Robert if there was any other minor detail it might be worth me knowing, but as usual he was thinking ahead of me.

'And the wife,' he said calmly, 'is missing.'

I hate to say it, but I slept like a baby under the roof provided by the Abwehr, though for nowhere near as long as I would have liked. I was gently shaken awake by a member of the Libéria's day shift, a muscular young man who looked as if he would rather be holding a machine pistol than a metal tray with a bowl of steaming coffee and a plate containing a round bread roll (stale), a smear of unidentifiable jam (possibly fruit-based) and a square of grease that could have been margarine, which, after all, was a French invention.

We had agreed that I should return to the Hôtel Moderne as soon as possible, before my absence was reported to the local police, and though my suit had been, remarkably, cleaned, brushed and pressed overnight, I still appeared as a complete scruff who had enjoyed a night out on the tiles. That was exactly the look I was going for, as my excuse for not using my room would be that I had fallen into bad company; the company in question being female, which would hopefully garner some sympathy from the toad-like French receptionist.

As it turned out, it was a harassed young man behind the desk at the Moderne who handed me my room key, though from his amphibian features, I suspected a family connection to the previous day's incumbent. He was not the slightest bit interested in my nighttime activities, no matter how much I spiced up the story of my imaginary tryst with a lady of the Marseilles night, not even when I made it *two* ladies of the night.

I resisted the urge to shave and brush my hair, and changed into the clothes Robert had supplied for 'Didier Ducret', which I had smuggled into my room at the Moderne by the cunning ruse of carrying them, wrapped in brown paper and tied up with string, under my arm. It was as Didier Ducret that I shuffled down to the harbour as the morning got under way, thinking myself into the character. Where Canadian Jean-Baptiste Hamelin would have *strolled* in all innocence, Didier Ducret was the sort who *shuffled*, and furtively at that.

I had a deadline to work to, having agreed to take lunch at the café on Joliette station, not on Robert's recommendation but at Robert's insistence, but apart from that I had been left to my own devices. As I made my way down to the Quai des Belges, I realized

why Robert had specified a station buffet bar: that would be far
more in character for Didier Ducret. The dashing Jean-Baptiste
Hamelin, a sophisticated and intelligent man-of-the-world (as I saw
him) would surely be more attracted to the establishments Ducret
was shuffling past as he made his way off La Canebière and on to
the Quai des Belges. On the corner stood the impressive brasserie
Le Mont Ventoux, and next door to it – under a garish striped awning
– the Café au Brûleur de Loups – the restaurant of the wolf-burner,
for some bizarre reason. Both, I knew, were hotbeds of intellectuals
and artists arguing about art and politics in a dozen or more different
languages, thanks to the influx of refugees. It was very fortunate
that there were two such establishments, as it was well known that
communists and surrealists did not mix well.

No, Didier Ducret would not feel at home there. His natural
hunting ground was further round the harbour in the dank narrow
streets of the Vieux Port quarter, which led through to the cathedral
and the big dock 'basins' of Joliette, Lazaret and Arenc.

If I had been the inquisitive Canadian tourist showing initiative,
I might have followed the tram lines along the quay and around
Fort St Jean which guarded the northern side of the entrance to the
old port. But a working man such as Didier Ducret would surely
be able to find his way through the backstreets. It would probably
not have taken him over an hour, getting lost at least three times,
but he would have emerged from that claustrophobic maze of stone,
brick and wooden shutters into the shadow of the cathedral, relatively
confident that he had not been followed.

Whether a real Didier Ducret would have paused to admire the
towers and domes of the cathedral, the Byzantine-Romanesque style
giving the building something of a Moorish feel, for as long as I
did was a moot point. It was an impressive building, as cathedrals
are supposed to be, and belied the fact that it had been completely
rebuilt only fifty or so years before. Ducret's perhaps uncharacteristic
interest in religious architecture did, however, have a reward on
Earth as well as Heaven, as it showed him that he had been guilty
of pride and overconfidence when he realized he had been followed
after all.

Having made sure I had a handful of coins for the offertory box
or collection plate – whichever confronted me first – I screwed up
my eyes to get them used to the lower light level and plunged into
the cool of the cathedral to seek sanctuary.

The young – frighteningly young – girl who had been stalking me so successfully had paused only long enough to produce a headscarf from somewhere to cover her hair (no good Catholic girl was ever without one) and was hot on my heels.

In her enthusiasm, she walked straight by the pew where I was kneeling, head bowed, inhaling a heady mix of dust and stale incense, her wooden-soled sandals clip-clopping down the nave. Fortunately, at that time of the morning, there was no service in progress, no priests or nuns, and only a few scattered devotees to be disturbed when I coughed loudly and indiscreetly.

The girl turned as if stung and let forth an expletive which she would certainly have to confess later; I estimated that particular expletive to be worth at least several hundred Hail Marys, with a few dozen more added because she had made no attempt at a theatrical hand-over-the-mouth reflex or looked remotely contrite.

'You think you are so clever,' she hissed as she approached my pew, 'but you have the luck of the fool.'

'I am told it is the best kind of luck to have, mademoiselle,' I said politely, moving along the pew penitentially to offer her space, 'but I admit I was told that by a fool. Will you not join me in quiet reflection and contemplation?' I deliberately avoided the word 'prayer' as, although in God's house, we were certainly not about his business.

Only when she had made the sign of the cross and knelt next to me did I realize how young the girl was; a mere 'slip of a girl', as my mother and several aunts would have called her, though I had never been quite sure exactly what that meant. I guessed her age at fifteen or sixteen. She wore a short-sleeved cotton dress, clean but frayed around the edges and with numerous sewn repairs, suggesting a hand-me-down from a mother or older sister. Her hair, bunched hurriedly under her headscarf, was black, curly and smelled faintly of olive oil. She displayed neither jewellery nor make-up, and was bare-legged, as most women were in a city where the climate eased the pain of black-market silk stockings costing four or five times their weight in gold dust.

I resisted the urge to ask why she was not in school, but some instinct told me that would be courting a danger that not even the sanctuary of the church could deflect. I decided to dispense with the pleasantries and put our relationship on a civilized basis of mutual respect.

'How long have you been following me? You seem very good at it.'

'Since you left your hotel disguised in those clothes,' she said, then shrugged her thin shoulders. 'It was not difficult.'

'Am I permitted to know why you are following me?'

'I have been ordered to look after you while you are in Marseilles.' She said it out of the corner of her mouth in that matter-of-fact tone which the young adopt when dealing with the obviously stupid older generation, keeping her eyes closed and her hand clasped in prayer. 'And from the evidence of last night, you are, M'sieur, in need of a guardian angel.'

'You were wise not to intervene.'

'I was not armed. Next time I will be.'

I have since thought that to have been an example of sheer youthful bravado, but at the time I was convinced of her sincerity, for such an angelic face in such a pious setting could not possibly be guilty of hubris or braggadocio.

'Why were you following me last night?' I whispered, curbing an idiotic impulse to suggest that we move into one of the confessional boxes.

She closed her eyes and rested her forehead on her entwined fingers. 'I was following the men who followed you. They work for a gangster called Pirani, and they had found you before I did – to rob you, it seems.'

'And they were successful,' I confessed. 'It might have been worse for me if the police had not arrived when they did.'

'Yes,' she said with something of a sneer, 'that was convenient, wasn't it?'

'Fortunate, I would say, from my point of view, that is. But why were you following the men who were following me? You said they found me before you did, which suggests that you were expecting me.'

'London told us to expect *somebody* – a person who might need our help.'

I put on my best tortured-owl face, an expression I have been told fits me like a glove – or perhaps that should be a slap with a glove.

'London?' I said, wide-eyed and clearly confused. 'But mademoiselle, I am from Quebec. I am Canadian.'

The girl turned her head lightly so that she could aim two very blue and very withering eyes on me from inside the frame of her headscarf.

'Please, M'sieur, this is a house of God. Your lies will not work here.'

She said I should call her La Pucelle – 'The Maid' – and I, of course, asked if that was as in The Maid of Orleans, who we knew from our schoolboy history books as Joan of Arc. Not only was she not flattered by a comparison, however tenuous, with a national heroine, she seemed to take it in her stride, and told me quite casually that her *nom de guerre* was simply because she came from Orleans, and had I not noticed her accent? She added that her real name was not Jeanne and she was now fighting for the English rather than against them.

I told her my name was Didier Ducret, although I was only just getting used to it myself, and that I was from Bordeaux (or should that have been Poitiers?), and she pursed her tiny lips and puffed out a breath of disbelief coupled with resignation.

It was one of the most bizarre discussions I have ever had. There we were, kneeling, hands (if not minds) occupied in prayer, eyes front, looking towards the altar, conversing in terse, sibilant phrases. We must have looked like a demented pair of ventriloquist dummies and, given the setting, I was rather surprised no one called for an exorcism.

La Pucelle was not giving much away; virtually nothing, actually. I quizzed her about who had sent her and how she had received instructions 'from London'. Through clenched teeth she hissed that she would not reveal her sources but that the information she had received had been accurate: she was to watch for a British agent who would pose as a Canadian diplomat and be easy to spot as he would appear both lost and stupid. This latter point, I felt, could easily have been withheld to protect my sensitivities, but my new young friend saw no reason to spare my feelings. I did not complain, for at least I now knew who she was working for.

She did not ask me how I had survived the assault of the previous evening, nor – fortunately – where I had spent the night, which showed either a sweet naïveté or a rather disconcerting lack of interest in my health and well-being. It was left to me to broach the subject, but she had given me an opening by mentioning the name Pirani as the employer of my unwelcome welcome committee, and she seemed happy to whisper fluently on that subject.

In the time it would have taken to recite a pair of the longer psalms, I learned that Paul Pirani was one of the senior predatory fish swimming in the murky waters of the Marseilles underworld, with a fin or a barbel in every criminal racket going. La Pucelle reeled off a litany of wrong-doings, including: drugs, extortion, smuggling, protection rackets, espionage, gun-running, corrupting policeman and judges, blackmail and 'slavery of women', by which I think she meant prostitution, though I certainly did not press one of such tender years for details.

The two thugs who had attacked me were known to be Pirani's henchmen, but robbery-with-violence on one of the main streets of the city was hardly normal behaviour for cut-throats such as they, who preferred to practise their trade in the dark passages and alleys abutting the docks. I accepted my cherubic advisor's assessment of the situation and was honest, if vague, when she asked me what my assailants had got away with: my wallet; some – but not all of – my money, and my papers.

'It was the papers they were after,' confided La Pucelle, her brow creased in concentration. 'That is why they did not use the knife.'

'Well, a dead visiting diplomat lying in the street might be embarrassing to the municipality,' I agreed earnestly, only to find myself quietly but very firmly rebuked.

'Do not be ridiculous! A *passeporte diplomatique* is a valuable thing, worth much money. They did not want to get blood on it!'

To say I was lost for words at the calm, matter-of-fact way in which this child had analysed the situation would not be putting too fine a point on it. Rudely, I stared at her, until she turned her head and met my gaze.

We looked at each other with pity, but we pitied each other for different reasons. She clearly thought she was in the presence of an idiot. I only hoped that, whoever she was, she was on my side.

Whether she was my guardian angel or my guard dog, The Maid was certainly dedicated to her task, and as following me covertly was now no longer an option, she opted to resume her duties by sticking to my side as if glued there. When I decided that we had stayed kneeling in the cathedral long enough – not for propriety's sake but rather the need to stretch my legs – she rose to her feet, crossed herself, shuffled to the end of the pew and genuflected with practised rhythm. Somewhat hypocritically, I followed her excellent example and, once outside in the weak but warming sunshine, she removed her headscarf like a conjuror and tucked it though the fabric belt of her cotton dress. Out of my jacket pocket, I pulled the rather greasy beret that the Abwehr's costume department had provided and placed it on my head at what I considered to be a jaunty angle. The Maid, her expression a cloud of disapproval, rose on her toes and reached up to straighten it and pull it down further over my ears. In silence, I deferred to her local fashion sense.

'Come,' she commanded, 'let us walk together and I will show you the error of your ways.'

'I thought we had just left the place where I might have received enlightenment,' I observed, but the girl was both dismissive and eminently practical.

'The church may look after your soul; I am concerned with your safety. We will walk together and when we talk I will call you "Papa" if anyone is close enough to hear us.'

There seemed little point in debating her orders – and disobeying was clearly out of the question – because as a stratagem it perfectly fitted my immediate needs. I could not, however, resist pointing out a minor flaw in my overconfident young mentor's plan.

'And should we be asked for our papers? Will it not be embarrassing that father and daughter have different names, not to mention that the father does not know his daughter's name at all?'

The thought troubled her only for as long as it took her bottom lip to jut out in a sulk, to quickly retract into an infuriatingly charming crooked smile.

'Then I will be your niece and call you Uncle Didier. You may call me Corinne.'

'That is a good name,' I said. 'It means "beautiful maiden", I believe, from the Greek *kora*.'

She seemed satisfied with that, if not impressed, looped an arm through mine and began to lead me away from the sanctuary of the cathedral, leaving me to ponder that if it was necessary for me to hire a temporary niece, why could I not have chosen a less bossy one?

Without any consultation on which parts of the old port I might wish to go sightseeing in, the girl steered me across the Place de la Major, passing uncomfortably close to the police station, and into the dank warren of streets through which she had followed me earlier. With her head occasionally bouncing off my shoulder in a simulation of filial affection, she chatted away in a sing-song tone which thinly disguised the dressing-down she was giving me.

'The street directly ahead takes you up the hill and into the Panier district. Had you gone that way instead of into the cathedral, you would have found yourself in the dark heart of Marseilles.'

It was not a phrase, I thought, which would come naturally to a fifteen- or sixteen-year-old who was not a native of the city, and I wondered where she had heard it.

'They call it that,' said my new niece, showing an uncanny ability to read my thoughts, 'because the Panier is controlled by the gangsters of Marseilles. Everything up there is owned and run by those rats, and the worst of them is Paul Pirani, whose men attacked you last night. You were close to wandering into their nest this morning, until I allowed you to see me and you ran into the cathedral.'

'That was most considerate of you,' I conceded, 'but what if I had scampered the other way, *into* the Panier?'

'Then I would have known that you were either a fool not to be trusted or we would have to tell London that they needed to send another agent. No one wanders innocently into the Panier; they take no prisoners there, and they hate those of us who resist Vichy most of all, as Vichy is good for business.'

'And you hate the Vichy government?' I asked.

'I despise the collaborators in Vichy,' the girl said with venom, 'but I *hate* the filthy Boches.'

The vitriol she put into those words – and hearing them spew from such a young, angelic mouth – gave me pause for thought. How was I going to break it to her that I had a lunch appointment with the filthy Boches?

ELEVEN

Flotsam, Possibly Jetsam

'Her name is Corinne Thibus,' said Robert. 'She is an orphan and has been wandering around Marseilles for over a year, being a minor irritant to the Vichy authorities and running messages for the communists. She is not considered a person of serious interest.'

I appreciated the background information but saw no reason to add to Robert's stock of it. Mademoiselle Thibus was not, I was sure, working for the communists but saw no reason to enlighten the Abwehr. It would be safer for my proxy niece if she remained a person of little interest.

It had taken all my extensive charm and powers of persuasion, not to mention several whopping great lies, to persuade my young companion to allow me an hour's furlough from my unexpected, though fascinating, guided tour of the shadowy and pungent backstreets of Marseilles. I spun her a yarn, being as vague as possible, that I had to meet a 'contact' (which was true) who might be frightened off (unlikely) if I turned up with a niece they knew I did not have.

I made her promise not to follow me and, to make sure she did not, I bribed her with a handful of notes and told her to get herself a good lunch and then meet me back at the cathedral in an hour. Hunger trumped duty and she confided that she knew a *boulangerie* where they would exchange *tickets* for bread for slices of pizza, though hard cash often did the trick if one wasn't carrying one's ration book.

I had watched until she had disappeared into the narrow streets, then doubled back towards the cathedral, checking every few minutes that she was following her stomach and not me. Skirting the giant building with its multiple Byzantine domes, I hurried on to the Bassin de la Joliette.

The harbour was working at perhaps a quarter of its peacetime capacity, with the majority of berths along its four piers empty of ships. The few dock workers and seamen drifting along the quayside eyed me suspiciously, probably suspecting I was after one of their jobs, but I pressed on towards the Joliette railway station, beyond sidings where empty goods wagons stood idly rusting, and entered the steam- and smoke-filled café there.

The café was cheap and popular, and clearly the majority of patrons were not there for the menu, rather to exchange or take delivery of suspicious packages wrapped in newspaper under the tables. It seemed it was a regular and blatant black-market palace, and I must have fitted in perfectly as none of the clientele gave me a second look. Robert too blended right in when he arrived dressed in oil-stained overalls, a patched and threadbare seaman's pea-coat and a dark blue fisherman's cap pulled down over his ears. He had a rectangular parcel wrapped in newspaper which he placed on the table between us.

He nodded a greeting and asked, in French, if the fish soup I had ordered was worth eating or 'the usual filth'? I shrugged non-committedly – it was not the sort of restaurant which received lengthy reviews – and he called towards the bar for a bowl of the same.

Scraping a rickety chair to the wobbly table, which I was trying to steady with my elbows and knees, Robert sat down and leaned in towards me.

'Speak French and speak it quietly.' He inched the parcel towards me. 'At some point give me some money and take them – it's a pack of cigarettes. Try and look suspicious.'

'I will do my best,' I said. 'I may need them, I've had a very stressful morning.'

I began what was no doubt a garbled account of how my shadow had turned into a fellow penitent and emerged as my niece-cum-guardian angel. Robert, of course, had known exactly of whom I was talking.

'She could be useful,' he said after he had told me her name and his suspicions of her political beliefs, 'if you think you can trust her.'

'I cannot believe that she means me any harm.'

'It is your life at stake, Albert. Do not be fooled by her age. In the northern zone we have taken casualties because many a careless soldier has seen a pretty young face and not the grenade she carries behind her back.'

'I am not a German soldier occupying her country,' I pointed out, 'but I promise to keep an eye on her handbag for unsightly bulges.'

'Do not joke about such things,' he scolded, 'but use the girl. She can take you to places in Marseilles which I cannot. Are you meeting her again?'

When I nodded, he said, 'Then ask her if she knows the English Seamen's Mission, because that is where you need to go as soon as possible.'

'Why?'

'Because my sources say that is where a certain gentleman with a nasty shoulder wound is in hiding.'

'That was quick work,' I said, giving credit where it was due.

'I told you, we pay very well. You must see if the man still has your diplomatic passport, because you are going to need it.'

'I am?'

'Most certainly. It will help you get into the concentration camp.'
'Excuse me, did you just say "*into*"?'

I made sure I was hidden in the shadows of the arches around the
cathedral's west door, before my hour's grace from my guardian
angel expired, so that I was able to observe her as she strolled
casually across the *place*, tying on her headscarf as she walked. She
was less than ten feet from where I was skulking when she stopped
and turned slowly on her heels, scouring the faces of the passing
pedestrians as if waiting for someone – an uncle, perhaps – to escort
her inside.

It had been my intention to disabuse her of the view that I was
the easiest of pigeons to follow, and also, perhaps, to sneak up
behind her and give her a bit of a fright. Standing within the aura
of that magnificent church, though, I decided not to be so childish
– and just possibly what Robert von Ringer had said about hand
grenades also affected my judgement. And so I compromised on a
discreet cough and a friendly 'Mademoiselle?' when I was within
two yards of her.

She still reacted as if stung as she turned to face me, and I could
not help but smile at the fact that the front of her dress was spotted
with pastry crumbs, which completed the picture of a guilty
schoolgirl.

Before she could speak, I said, 'I need your help, Corinne.'

Although Robert had told me roughly where the English Seamen's
Mission was situated, near the Joliette Basin not more than five
hundred yards from where we had met at the station, I doubt I could
have found it without Corinne Thibus, and certainly not gained entry
so quickly or so easily. Not that she was keen to take me there at
first. She was rightly suspicious of my mysterious private lunch; in
her position I would have been too. I was also aware of the warnings I had received in London about the need to be circumspect
about approaching or drawing attention to the Mission.

Her face set and her eyes unblinking, she grabbed my left wrist
and held on to it for dear life as she asked me to swear that my
reason for visiting the Mission would not endanger the Mission or
those who worked there. As such a thing was the furthest from my
mind, I assured her of my pure and noble intentions, which only
caused her to grab both my wrists and stare deeply and fiercely into
my eyes.

'Swear it! Swear that nothing you will do will place Pasteur Nevin in danger!'

'I have no idea who this Pasteur Nevin is,' I said, hoping that – as we were within the cathedral precincts – all my lies would be regarded as white ones, 'but my objective is to avoid danger wherever and whenever I can.'

'That is not always possible,' said the girl, with wisdom that belied her years.

Then she released her grip on one arm and led me by the other into her secret world.

Given that it had 'English' in its title, I could understand why the Seamen's Mission would not advertise its location; it was one of those places which you could only find once you had already been there. Corinne led me down the Boulevard Maritime, parallel to the Joliette Station, almost to the apex of where it met the Boulevard de Paris. To our left, a grid of railway lines and sidings, littered with wooden sleepers and strangely twisted pieces of abandoned metal, separated us from the Bassin d'Arenc, another of the port's near-empty docks which even the seagulls seemed to have abandoned. A single narrow street cut through to the dock which, at first sight, was a street of soot-stained warehouses or garages rather than houses, most with broken windows, shutters hanging at half-mast and tiles missing from the roof, where several of the mansard windows appeared in danger of collapsing and sliding into the guttering.

From the way she was chewing her bottom lip, Corinne clearly felt herself something of a Judas when she raised a slender arm and pointed to the third doorway along, where a square of yellow cloth was nailed to the frame of a sun- and salt-bleached door. Except that it wasn't a cloth, it was far cleverer. It was a naval flag, probably a yachtsman's version of the maritime flag for the letter Q, but flown alone was the signal indicating that a ship was free from disease and asking for a *Pratique* – a licence or permission to enter a safe harbour. It was a clever way to advertise, to anyone with a smattering of seamanship, that this house would welcome the lost and weary as long as they came free from contagion.

As we stood before the door with its flaking blue paint, I wondered if I would be welcomed as a lost soul or as a carrier of plague. Corinne raised a dainty fist and rapped a tattoo of blows, but whether it was code or not I could not tell.

We heard a bolt being withdrawn with a slow, metallic screech, and then a second bolt was pulled and the door seemed to sag with relief as it was pulled slowly inwards.

'My dear Corinne,' said a voice before the door was fully open; a voice with a worse French accent than even mine.

Its owner was a short, balding man, over fifty but not yet sixty, who had almost certainly at one time been described as 'chubby' and, inevitably, 'jolly', but whose clothes now hung on his slender frame as if they had been made by a short-sighted tailor who had transposed measurements in centimetres into inches. The jacket of his dark blue pinstripe suit hung off his shoulders like the wings of a bat, and the trousers were secured around his waist with what looked suspiciously like a length of skipping rope. His ensemble was completed by a black woollen sweater so thin and stretched that a white singlet or vest was visible through it, and a grubby dog collar which rose and fell with his Adam's apple as he spoke.

'What have you brought me today?'

'A lost soul, Pasteur,' said the girl, which I thought was taking a bit of a liberty.

The pastor put his head on one side and looked at me quizzically but without suspicion. 'Is that so?'

From the cobweb of an overcrowded memory, I salvaged a phrase which I hoped would prove my *bona fides*, and translated it into French on the wing.

'*Bless us thy servants and the fleet in which we serve that we may be a safeguard to such as pass upon the sea upon their lawful occasion.*'

The pastor smiled and opened the door wide.

'Naval man, are we?' he said in English. 'You'd better come in. Welcome aboard.'

The girl and I stepped over the threshold and into a gloomy corridor, which ended in a wooden staircase suggesting an even gloomier upper floor and to a small kitchen area with a single tap sink, a small spirit stove and a kettle. On the draining board were half a dozen oil or kerosene lamps waiting for dusk.

'Be it ever so humble,' said our host, closing and bolting the door. 'You are English, aren't you?'

'Canadian,' I said, on the basis that the less he knew, the safer it would be for him. 'My name is Jean-Baptiste Hamelin.'

'French Canadian, eh? You don't strike me as a Canuck, but then we get all sorts here. I'm Sandy Nevin, how can I help?'

'It would settle the butterflies in my stomach, Padre, if you were a little more circumspect when offering hospitality to strangers. Perhaps more suspicion is called for. Not that I am refusing your offer of help, for I genuinely do need that.'

Pastor Nevin smiled. 'I am flattered by your concern, m'sieur, but here we follow conscience, not common sense. Any piece of human flotsam is welcome to drift to our door, where they will not be turned away.'

'I could have been anyone.'

'Indeed you could, but as you came with Corinne and could quote the Naval Prayer, I was sure you could be trusted.'

'How did you know I was with the girl?'

'There is a window in the attic which looks down the street to the station. Our residents take it in turns to keep an eye out. We are not quite as trusting as you may think. Visits from the police are not infrequent I'm afraid, and when they happen, they tend to be rather disruptive, so we appreciate advance warning.'

'What are you saying?' complained Corinne.

In my enthusiasm to speak English, I had quite forgotten that the girl might not, and the realization that I had so easily and swiftly slipped into my native tongue produced a sickening wrench in my stomach and a memo-to-self to be a damn sight more careful in the future, if I was to be allowed one.

'Forgive us, little one,' said Nevin, reverting to French, 'we are being impolite. Tell me, why have you brought Monsieur Hamelin to our humble refuge?'

The girl's eyes widened at the name 'Hamelin', but thankfully she only said, 'He asked to be brought here. My orders are to help him if I could. We were not followed.'

'Orders from our friend in Toulouse?' asked the pastor, and the girl nodded silently. 'Then I am obliged to help if I can, and my first action is to ask the most important question: would you like a cup of tea, my dear chap?'

'What a good idea,' I said with too much enthusiasm, and Nevin beetled away into the corner to busy himself with kettle and tap. 'Do you have any problems getting tea? I hear that the tea ration in England is regarded as more of a threat than the Luftwaffe in certain quarters.'

Pastor Nevin's small frame shook as he chuckled, but it was a pleasant if hesitant chuckle; a chuckle he did not get much chance to use these days. He waved the kettle in the air, vaguely in the direction of outside.

'My dear sir, we are in a port, a rather large one. Most things can be obtained here – for a price – from the most exotic of locations. It would not surprise me if the tea I am about to brew was liberated from English prisoners taken by the Afrika Korps before it found its way on to the black market. Fortunately we do not pay for it; we gratefully receive gifts from those who avail themselves of our humble hospitality.'

'Then let me make a contribution to your upkeep,' I said, offering him the parcel Robert had given me at our meeting.

Pastor Nevin accepted the offering gratefully, carefully removing the two-day-old copy of *Marseille-Matin* wrapping paper, smoothing it out 'to read later'.

'American cigarettes!' he exclaimed with a huge grin. 'Thank you, they will come in very useful. Can I ask where you got them?'

'Diplomatic channels,' I said, tapping a finger against my nose and silently breathing a sigh of relief that Robert really had given me cigarettes, as I carelessly had not checked the parcel.

The pastor busied himself with the tea ceremony and then paused as his face contorted in dismay. 'But we have no milk!' he wailed, in an act of despair which would not have passed muster in even the most amateur of amateur dramatic societies. He frantically patted the pockets of his flapping jacket then plunged both hands into his trouser pockets. 'Corinne, my angel, run and buy some milk for us.'

'Allow me,' I said, taking my cue and producing a note from my wallet.

Corinne wrinkled her nose in disgust, but I thought it more an expression of the inbred French disapproval of putting milk in tea, rather than being asked to undertake a menial errand designed solely to get her out of the way so the grown-ups could talk.

She tugged the money from my hand, glared at me and left with a flounce. As soon as Sandy Nevin had closed and bolted the door behind her, he began to speak in English and, for the first time, I picked up a slight burr of a Highland Scots accent.

'We can speak English again, m'sieur. You are English, are you not? No Canadian face would light up at the mention of a pot of tea; they would demand coffee.'

'I must insist that you accept my Canadian persona, even if you do not believe it.' He nodded in agreement. 'But English would be the more efficient language for our dealings.'

'We are going to have dealings?' he asked with an impish grin.

'I certainly hope so, Pastor Nevin. Can I ask what you actually *do* here at the Mission?'

'We are a hostel for lost souls, both physically and spiritually, but in truth, mostly the physical. We can offer a roof and a bed and the prospect of a night's sleep without being torpedoed, dive-bombed or sunk to all the human flotsam which washes up in this great port.'

He held my gaze as he spoke, but it was a no more threatening look than would be dispensed by a rural vicar saying farewell to his flock after Sunday service. I decided to probe the country parson as much as I dared.

'Do you ever turn away a lost soul?'

'Someone in genuine distress? Never, though of course we do not shelter known criminals or enemy aliens who are, as the Americans would say, on the run.'

'By which you mean escaping prisoners-of-war or shot-down airmen?'

Somewhere deep in his oversized jacket he shrugged his shoulders.

'It would be against the law to shelter someone being sought by the authorities, and the police would be interested in anyone who might suggest such a thing. Especially a stranger who arrives unannounced and who may not be quite what he seems . . . Yes, they would be most interested.'

'I quite understand,' I said. 'You don't know me from Adam. I have given you cause to suspect my identity and absolutely no reason why you should trust me. All I can say is that I am bound to a higher authority to make sure that anything I do while in Marseilles does not endanger, embarrass or compromise the work of your Mission.'

Nevin graced me with a thin smile. 'I think I report to a much higher authority than you, my Canadian friend.' He let his eyes flick upwards, just in case I had not got the message. 'One who might judge that, by simply coming here, you have compromised our safety.'

'If He does, He will know that it was not my intention and allow me to prove it to you.'

'And how would you do that?'

'By asking one simple question of you, and if you cannot provide the answer I seek, then I will leave this refuge and forget I was ever here.'

The pastor narrowed his eyes, boring into my face. 'Do I have your word on that?'

'Absolutely.'

'As a Canadian?'

I accepted defeat; gracefully, I hoped.

'As an Englishman pretending to be a Canadian for the purest of reasons, and one who trusts you enough to admit that.'

'As a Scot who was brought up never to trust the purity of English motives, I am prepared to give you the benefit of the doubt. What is your question?'

'Would you happen to be sheltering a man with a bullet wound in his shoulder?'

The little man's emaciated face froze, his eyes, unblinking, still locked on mine, and for a full minute of thick silence I felt sure he would not answer me; possibly never speak again. But he did, though his voice was strained, as if invisible hands were strangling him.

'I cannot answer that.'

'Cannot or will not?'

'We offer a safe harbour here; not just a roof, but sanctuary. I cannot violate that. Sometimes I have to when the police force me. But you are not the police. In fact, I do not know who you are.'

'I have told you my name. To tell you more would not enlighten you and may endanger you and the Mission.'

'*And why would that be?*'

Who the Devil was that? And where had he sprung from?

After all the training I had received, my lords and masters in London would have been appalled at my performance in that moment. The fact that the voice had spoken in English – and had clearly been eavesdropping on Pastor Nevin and myself – had thrown a huge spanner into the creaking, slow-moving cogs of my brain. Otherwise, I was sure I would have followed the lessons drilled in to me by Corporal Colgan, my small-arms instructor at Commando school in Scotland, and dropped into a crouch, pulled out my pistol, turned and fired in one swift and fluid movement. My shot, naturally, would have scored a bullseye, were it not for the fact that I was not carrying a firearm and that the mystery voice did not come from behind, but *above* me.

The voice belonged to a man who had appeared with an impressive measure of stealth on the staircase. How he had got there was a trick that The Great Lafayette or Harry Houdini would have been proud of, as both Sandy Nevin and myself stood between the foot of the staircase and the firmly bolted front door of the Mission. Having successfully materialized as if from thin air, he had made himself comfortable by sitting on the top step, which gave him the equivalent of a front-row balcony seat from which to watch – and hear – the unwitting performance being put on by Pastor Nevin and myself and, judging by the arrogant smirk on fleshy lips framed by a dark, pencil moustache, he seemed to be enjoying the show.

'I don't believe we've been introduced,' I said, which was an idiotic thing to say but it broke the silence. 'My name is Jean-Baptiste Hamelin.'

'If you say so.'

He wrinkled his nose so that the hair on his upper lip wriggled like a caterpillar, as if an unpleasant scent had wafted up the staircase. He wore a three-piece suit which had been tailored for someone, though not him, and brown leather Oxfords, the sort issued to the British army (officers only). His feet were planted on the second step down from the first-floor landing and his elbows rested on his knees, allowing the fingers of both hands to meet in a triangle. His suit jacket hung open just enough to make sure I could see the shoulder holster tucked into his left armpit.

Pastor Nevin stepped up and exerted his authority as guardian of the Mission.

'I have asked you not to use the attic route before, Magnus. That's our escape route, not our front door. How long have you been there?'

'Long enough to hear the King's English spoken and the promise of a brew-up now the kettle's on. By the way, your little errand girl is sashaying down the street with a jug of milk even as we speak.'

Perfectly on cue, there was a rapid knocking on the street door.

'There she is,' said the man called Magnus with something of a leer. I imagined that he was the sort of chap who leered a lot, especially when young girls were involved.

I was perhaps being hasty – or perhaps I was merely saving time – by disliking Magnus Asher on first sight, for the armed man who had appeared without warning on the stairs only a few feet from me was certainly the British army deserter I had been briefed about in London.

The realization of that fact prompted my brain into first gear after it had been idling in neutral for too long. I deduced that our surprise visitor had not appeared on the staircase by some illusionist's trick. If he had spotted Corinne in the street, then he must have been looking out of one of the mansard windows which Nevin had said provided an early warning system. That, and the pastor's comment about the 'attic route' suggested that there was a way in, and out, of the Mission, at roof-top level from the adjoining buildings.

Sandy Nevin undid the bolts and opened the door to allow Corinne to enter. She carried a white porcelain jug with a starched white napkin covering it in one hand and the Franc note I had given her crumpled in the other. As she handed the jug to Nevin and thrust the note towards me, she burst into rapid French to tell us that a Madame Joubert, whoever she was, had refused to take payment for the milk as it was for the Mission, but whether there was any more to the story, we never knew, as her voice switched off the moment she saw the figure on the staircase. The look on her face was not one of starstruck admiration.

'What is he doing here?'

'The adults are having a private conversation, little one. Why don't you run along and play with the other street rats,' Asher answered her in French.

Before the girl could make a sound, though her mouth was open wide enough to accommodate a scream, Pastor Nevin gently took the milk jug from her with both hands and said quietly: 'It would be for the best, my dear.'

For me she reserved an icy glare, then turned and flounced out, her grip on the Franc note tightening so that it disappeared completely into her fist.

Asher had got to his feet and was slowly descending the stairs as quiet as a cat, and I noticed that he had buttoned his jacket coat, I would like to think so that the girl might not be frightened at the sight of the shoulder holster. But then, it was not the girls he was trying to impress.

I put his age at twenty-seven or twenty-eight, and although I had the advantage of a couple of inches of height, he came armed with greater width and several pounds of weight, all of it muscle rather than fat. He had a round, oddly childlike face, which had been weathered by the sun, and black hair which gleamed with some brand of vanilla-scented pomade. For a British army sergeant listed as 'missing' two years ago, he appeared to be doing rather well for himself, and would probably look equally at home sitting at a roulette table in Monte Carlo as he did in the seedy stairwell of a crumbling tenement in the docks of Marseilles.

He reached into the inside pocket of his jacket and grinned when he saw me wince, but he produced only a silver cigarette case which he clicked open and offered.

'You never answered my question,' he said as he shared a flame from a gold-plated lighter.

'Which question?'

'I asked why you told the padre here that his Mission could be in danger if you told him your real name, 'cos I'll bet a bottle of rum to a bag of toffees that it isn't Hamelin.'

'I can assure you that while I am in Marseilles it is, but I cannot prove it. That is the reason I'm here.'

'Now you've lost me, squire. You'd better come clean 'cos I don't like anything that might worry the good padre here.'

'There's no need for threats, Magnus,' said the good padre, more in hope than expectation as he recognized, as I did, a man who enjoyed making threats.

'I am a Canadian diplomat,' I said firmly, 'officially accredited to the Vichy government. Last night I was assaulted on the street and my passport stolen. One of the men who attacked me was shot and wounded by the police. I want my passport back and my information is that the wounded man may have sought shelter – if not sanctuary – here in the Mission. Rather than instigate a police search of the premises, I thought I would try and persuade Pastor Nevin to break the sanctity of the confessional, so to speak; but he would not.'

'You should have asked me,' said Asher with a smug smile.

'Magnus! We have rules about the people we shelter,' protested Nevin.

'Come off it, Padre. Rules is made to be broken, we both know that; and it seems a pity not to help such a nicely spoken gent, whoever he says he is.'

The pastor's response was through gritted teeth: 'We have rules, Magnus,' he repeated. 'Rules to keep us safe.'

Asher held up a hand as if to deflect the smaller man's criticism, but he fixed his eyes on me. 'No name, no pack drill; that's the rule here. Don't care who you are as long as you're flotsam or jetsam looking for shelter from the storm, though I was never sure what the difference between flotsam and jetsam was. I never said I'd give a name, in fact I don't know it, but there is a man with a bullet hole in his shoulder right here, up in the attic, right now. Come on, squire, let's finish our ciggies and I'll introduce you. Best if a sensitive soul like you stays downstairs, Padre. This might not go pleasant.'

I could have explained that flotsam was something washed off a sinking ship whereas jetsam was an object or objects deliberately thrown overboard, and though I was beginning to put Magnus Asher in the latter category, I bit my tongue as I followed him up the stairs.

The first floor of the Seamen's Mission extended over the ground floor of the building next door, and there was a second floor, the attic, on top of that. It was what a country solicitor would insist on calling a 'flying freehold' when drawing up the deeds for the land registry, though I doubted that any such legal niceties were of any concern to the current residents.

Not that anything was likely to worry the residents of the first floor, which was essentially one room with a toilet and sink at the end and six badly stuffed straw mattresses on the floor, three against each long wall. Four of the beds were occupied by sleeping figures, none of whom stirred as Asher and I creaked up the stairs. They gave off the sweaty perfume of men who have been sleeping rough, and where flesh was visible under the thin blanket each had been given, it was an unshaved chin or a pair of hands black with dirt. From one of the pallets, where the blanket had slipped from a sleeping figure, a lozenge of blue material – almost certainly an RAF uniform jacket – peeped out. Whoever they were, I saw no good reason to disturb them. They needed all the rest they could get.

I followed Asher up a second flight of stairs to the attic/mansard floor, which extended into a shadowy blackness. I guessed this attic connected with at least two more buildings, perhaps even to the end of the street. Light was provided courtesy of two mansard windows thick with grime and several missing roof tiles. There was no plumbing up here, only a chamber pot beside the one straw pallet on the planks laid across the beams to provide a floor. It was occupied by a man who appeared as near to death as is possible while still breathing.

He was shirtless and wore a singlet which was pitted with holes where moths had feasted, and splashed with brown, dried blood. His left shoulder was bandaged with clean white strips of linen and his arm pinned across his chest in a sling made from a far from hygienic towel. His face was the colour of faded parchment and his expression was one of a man who was halfway across the Styx before he realized he'd left his fare in his other trousers.

'Hello again,' I said, which got a reaction, but only from the man's blank eyes.

'I take it you two know each other,' Asher said, and the wounded man's eyes flashed in his direction. Now there was concern if not fear in them.

'Remember me? We met last night. Had a bit of a tussle in a gutter before being rudely interrupted by a policeman, which was lucky for me but not so much for you, but after our encounter I discovered I had lost something. A passport. I would dearly like to have that returned.' The eyes were on me, but were expressionless, like a shark's. 'Is any of this ringing any bells with you?'

The man squirmed on his straw mattress and nursed his sling with his working arm but remained stubbornly silent. Asher gave him ten seconds or so before moving closer to the sick bed until he loomed over the wounded man.

'He's not being very helpful, is he?' he said to me in English.

'Perhaps he'll talk to the police,' I said, having no intention at all of calling the local gendarmes.

Asher snorted back a laugh. 'This guy's a Panier gangster, a hood. Not a very good one, I admit, but the gangs in the Panier are not frightened by the cops; they own most of them.' He switched back to French. 'I think more direct action is called for.'

He raised his right foot and very slowly and deliberately brought the sole of his brown shoe down on to the bandaged shoulder of the man on the pallet. It was a shockingly cruel act, made more shocking by the fact that I witnessed it in silence.

The wounded man was anything but silent. He screamed, loudly.

Asher lifted his foot and the scream turned into a series of breathless sobs.

The wounded man thrashed around, his right arm flailing behind him and down the side of the straw mattress, then his right hand went under the mattress, groping blindly for something. My first thought was that the man had a weapon hidden under there, and perhaps Asher thought so too, as he raised his foot again, ready to stamp out any danger.

The man's hand reappeared and it was waving my diplomatic passport as if it were a white flag.

'There,' said Asher smugly. 'That wasn't so difficult, was it?'

TWELVE
For Want of a Sharp Knife

The Dorchester Hotel, London. 20 May 1970

'What a perfectly cruel and horrible man,' said Perdita. 'Yes, he was,' said Mr Campion.

Perdita turned sharply to face Robert von Ringer. 'Why didn't you shoot *him* instead of that poor man on the mattress?'

'Perhaps I should have,' said the German ruefully. 'It would have saved a lot of heartache and, technically, he was my enemy.'

'So was Albert,' observed Luke. 'Technically, that is.'

Ringer smiled. 'In the sort of war we were engaged in, terms such as "friend" and "enemy" often became blurred. True, we were working together, but had we been discovered doing so, we had agreed a cover story that we were really enemies, each trying to trap the other. In fact, we rehearsed a story that I had actually tried to shoot Albert on two occasions.'

'It was a jolly good story,' Campion chipped in. 'Very dramatic, and I was incredibly brave on both occasions, escaping a hail of bullets by the skin of my teeth. When I eventually got back to London, I told the story constantly and got lots of free drinks out of it. Now eat your pudding and drink your wine. All this reminiscing means we're lagging behind the rest of the trenchermen.'

Perdita looked at the circle of almond and lemon meringue roulade centred on the plate in front of her and briefly considered its potential impact on her figure, which she liked to keep 'stage ready' (for she could, when roles were thin on the ground, still pass for a teenage *ingénue*).

Mr Campion, who could still – blast him – fit into his 1945 de-mob suit, gently nudged her wine glass closer to her hand.

'Do try the wine, dear. It's a '67 Château d'Yquem and quite outstanding.'

Perdita took a sip, savoured the wine and then picked up her fork and spoon. In for a penny, she thought – as long as it didn't result in a pound on the hips.

'Well, thank goodness the little girl you befriended didn't see any of it,' she said between spoonfuls. 'Is that really her down the table, talking to Amanda? She was The Maid, as you called her?'

'Yes, it is and yes it was,' said Campion, 'and I'm afraid she saw other things which were much worse.'

'And did things which were worse,' said Ringer softly.

The concentration on dessert resulted in a temporary hiatus in the volume of the clatter of knives and plates and background chatter, but Guffy Randall was still having trouble listening in on the story unfolding on the top table.

'Perdita is trying to get that German to shoot somebody!' he hissed towards his wife.

Mary Randall, registering the rising eyebrows of Joseph Fleurey, and the fact that his spoonful of roulade had paused a good inch below his chin, moved swiftly to defuse the situation and lower her husband's blood pressure.

'I'm sure you misheard, Guffy. It might be time to have your ears syringed again. Anyway, I'm not sure you should be eavesdropping – or trying to.'

'They were definitely talking about shooting somebody,' Guffy persisted in a rasping whisper.

'Well, if they were, it was probably one of Albert's stories – you know what he's like. Gangsters, gunmen, pirates, burglars, fast cars, being chased up hill and down dale; Albert had a fund of adventures in his sprightlier days. I think he's secretly disappointed no one ever wrote a book about him.'

Joseph Fleurey leaned in and lowered his voice conspiratorially: 'I think Monsieur Campion and Herr Ringer are telling war stories, about their time in Marseilles.'

Mr Randall made a slight snorting sound as he sipped his wine.

'That'd be a rum do. Albert's always kept quiet about his war. Why is he bending Perdita's ear with it now?'

His wife shrugged a delicate shoulder.

'I know she was always curious about what Albert did in the war. Perhaps she pestered him so much he finally gave in.'

'But why now, at a birthday party?' Guffy persisted.

'Perhaps he has assembled the right audience,' said Joseph Fleurey quietly.

'You know they're talking about you,' said Amanda to Madame Thibus.

'What woman does not want to be the centre of attention?' said the Frenchwoman. 'Especially when the attention comes from two such distinguished gentlemen.'

'You said you met my husband during the war. Was that when you met Herr Ringer also?'

'No, I became interested in his career after the war.'

Amanda made a conscious effort to keep a high-pitched note of alarm out of her voice.

'Not in your professional capacity as a lawyer . . . *une avocate*?'

Madame Thibus diverted her eyes downwards towards her plate when she answered. 'Not exactly.'

Charlie Luke scraped his plate squeaky clean, drained his glass and found he could contain himself no longer.

'So what happened next? Don't keep us in suspense.'

Mr Campion smiled benignly. 'Such was the rather bizarre life we led in those days that the moment I regained my diplomatic passport saying that I was Jean-Baptiste Hamelin, a Canadian, I became Didier Ducret, the Frenchman who worked as a warehouseman in the Old Port for a very understanding boss.' He winked cheekily at Ringer. 'Though, come to think of it, I never got paid . . .'

'I don't follow, Albert. Could you possibly be less vague?'

'Is the idea of me having an actual job so unbelievable, Charlie? I assure you, I was honestly employed – without pay – in Robert's import-export business for a week, and it was an eye-opener, I can tell you.'

'What was? Seeing how the other half lives?'

'Please, Charlie, curb your socialist tendencies. I had to keep a low profile. When I used my room at the Hôtel Moderne I was Jean-Baptiste Hamelin, but really that was only for bed-and-breakfast. During the day, I was Didier Ducret, an itinerant warehouseman grateful for a job but not averse to the odd bit of pilfering of the stock.'

'I always suspected as much,' observed a straight-faced Ringer.

'Some very interesting goods, not to mention chattels, moved through that import-export business, Robert. Quite a lot of the exports seemed destined for the Afrika Korps in Libya, and I do admit on one occasion I was tempted to steal a pair of Afrika Korps pyjamas, as they seemed better quality than my own threadbare ones.'

'It was important for Albert to stay out of sight during the day,' Ringer told Luke. 'He had very quickly come to the attention of some very bad people, and I could not protect him properly, or not without raising the suspicions of my own side.'

Ever the policeman, Luke probed further: 'The gangsters of this – what did you call it? – Panier district. The man who took Albert's passport was one of them?'

'Exactly, and one gang in particular, run by a man called Paul Pirani, who had the local police in his pocket. He did not take kindly to one of his wounded men being tortured by Albert.'

'That's outrageous!' stormed Perdita. 'Albert didn't touch that hoodlum, it was Asher!'

'I'll bet that wasn't the story Pirani was told,' said Luke. 'I think Albert was portrayed as the villain of the piece.'

'How did you know?' Ringer turned to Luke, genuinely curious.

'I've been pulling wide boys and petty crooks for almost twenty years. Wharf rats from Marseilles to Limehouse, they're all the same when a job goes wrong: they blame somebody who isn't there.'

The German nodded in professional agreement. 'Albert was safe when working at the warehouse and at his hotel, where I had a man undercover in the kitchens, but out on the streets he was at risk until I could arrange a meeting with Nathan Lunel. Then we could make a plan.'

'And this meeting was to take place in a concentration camp.' Luke did not make it a question.

'Well done, Charlie, you've been paying attention,' said Campion cheerfully, 'and this is where the story gets really exciting!'

'I do hope it has a happy ending,' purred Perdita.

'Oh, I never promised you *that*, my dear. It's a war story, after all, and wars are not happy things. Anyone who pretends . . .'

Mr Campion faltered, his attention caught by a movement at the far end of the room where the large and unmistakeable figure of Lugg was attempting to squeeze behind the row of diners, his girth causing no more problems than a tidal wave in a narrow gulley.

'Oh dear, I see the dinner-jacketed shadow of doom approaching and, from the look of it, he hasn't touched his pudding, so he'll be in a bad mood. He's making a beeline for us, so we must have done something wrong.'

Wheezing slightly from his exertions and the numerous apologies he had been forced into making for ruining the digestion of innocent diners, Lugg eventually made it to the top table. After nodding his obeisance to Lady Amanda as he shuffled by, he drew himself up – and out – to his full bulk and loomed over Campion's left ear.

'There's a problem,' said the fat man, in what for him counted as a subtle whisper.

'The roulade not to your liking? Or is it something really serious? We haven't run out of wine, have we?'

'The maître d' called me out for a quiet word,' said Lugg patiently and rather proudly, 'and my professional expertise.'

'Short of staff in the washing-up department, are they? That's not like The Dorchester. Now, The Savoy . . .'

'Something's gone missing from the other room where we're supposed to repair to for the dancing and the rest of the frivolities.'

Charles Luke pricked up his ears. 'Stolen? Do we have a thief at the party?'

'P'rhaps,' grunted Lugg, 'but mebbe it's a bit more serious than petty thievery.'

'Come on, old fruit, spit it out. That hangdog expression of yours is bringing down the mood – and it is my birthday.'

'Birthday without a cake at the moment.' Lugg's tone was lugubrious, his face resembling that of a suicidal bloodhound.

Campion did a theatrical double-take. 'Somebody's stolen my cake?'

'Not the cake, the knife that was put out for the ceremonial cutting. Flash thing it was, brought out specially for the occasion. Bone 'andle and a fourteen-inch blade honed to perfection. Could be a nasty bit of kit and do some serious damage.' He paused dramatically before adding: 'In the wrong hands.'

THIRTEEN
The Devil's Banker

Camp des Milles, Aix-en-Provence. October 1942

I don't know how Robert did it and didn't want to know. Should anything go wrong, the less I knew, the better. He must have pulled a few strings with Abwehr headquarters in the grand Hôtel Lutetia in Paris, where James Joyce had written parts of *Ulysses* and where, before the war, I had enjoyed a level of hospitality I was sure would not be offered to me now. I did not press Robert for details, just as he never pressed me on the methods I used to keep in contact with London. It was not a question of trust between two gentlemen, which I hoped we were, but Robert was just as much in danger from the Gestapo and its Vichy acolytes as I was if things went wrong, so the less we knew of each other's secrets, the less we could betray under torture.

However he managed it, by bribery, bullying or coercion, Robert had arranged what he had promised, or threatened, to do; he was taking me to a concentration camp, but no prisoner had been delivered into custody in as much luxury as I was. We travelled in a cream-coloured, chauffeur-driven Panhard et Levassor Dynamic limousine, the chauffeur being one of Robert's men from the Hôtel Libéria, and I was sure I had also seen him lurking around the staff entrance of the Hôtel Moderne. He was difficult to miss, not because he was big, small, or deformed in any way, but because of where he sat. The Panhard was a battleship of a car which could seat nine people in comfort, but the unusual thing about it was that it had the steering wheel in the middle of the dashboard rather than to the left or right. However quirky the design, the Panhard – which the French affectionately referred to as a 'Pan Pan' – provided a very comfortable ride for the thirty-kilometre drive north towards Aix-en-Provence.

There was also room in the car for a huge wicker hamper which, disappointingly, contained only packs of cigarettes and bottles of cognac, and was not a picnic basket as I had hoped, but a bribe for the duty commandant we had to deal with.

We may have been driving through Cézanne country, but we had a grimmer destination than rolling fields of lavender. We were expected at a former tile factory near the village of Les Milles, which had become infamous as the Camp des Milles, an unsavoury holding pen for several thousand Jews rounded up that summer by the Vichy authorities, keen to impress their Nazi overlords.

Robert's field grey uniform, despite few insignia other than the obligatory eagle holding a swastika badge over the right breast, and the impressive Panhard got us through the main gates with only silent resentful looks from the militia on guard there. The main prison was a large four-storey brick building, with two tall chimneys rising from the rear, which resembled one of those giant wool mills in the West Riding of Yorkshire before it acquired its covering of soot and coal dust.

To get there, our driver steered the Panhard down a corridor of two-metre-high barbed-wire fences, behind which were penned hundreds of silent, shambling men in civilian clothes, many clutching cheap suitcases and most poorly dressed for the approaching winter. I asked Robert what was going to happen to them and he answered, through tight lips, that they were 'in transit' and would be moved north into the Occupied Zone. Indeed, many already had been. When I pressed him as to what happened to them then, he replied grimly, 'Nothing good.'

The camp official who greeted us had put on his best uniform but, although it was hung with a rack of medals and yards of gold braid, he could not match his German visitor for military modishness. He did not resent this; rather he seemed deeply respectful and keen to ingratiate himself, especially after he took charge of the hamper in the Panhard. From then on he could not have been more helpful and was far more keen to impress his German visitor with the efficiency of the camp than to question the presence of a Canadian diplomat, or why said diplomat should want to talk to 'the Israelite' Nathan Lunel.

Robert and I had agreed that I should talk to Lunel alone. An immaculate, well-pressed German military uniform might impress a sycophantic Vichy prison warden, but was not likely to be welcomed by a Jew imprisoned for nothing more serious than simply being a Jew.

Our interview took place in a windowless cell which had been furnished with two chairs and a folding card table. The bare brick walls were stained with damp, and a single wall lamp in a metal cage provided the only light. If the cell contained a listening device, I had no idea where the microphone was hidden. Robert was of the opinion that the camp did not run to such sophisticated equipment, but while I was waiting for Lunel to be extracted from the main prison population, I scoured every inch of that claustrophobic brick box as best I could, looking for tell-tale wires.

I made sure I was seated, legs crossed, on one of the creaking chairs, and that I was looking relaxed, unaggressive and sympathetic when the door clanged open and Nathan Lunel was pushed, unceremoniously, into my presence.

He was a small man; balding and dishevelled, his clothes filthy and torn, with the ripped pockets of his jacket flapping loose. He looked a good ten years older than he was. But then, given the circumstances, who could blame him? He gave off that rank odour of dirt and sweat which is known in certain circles as 'prison smell', and his entire body shook with nerves. He stood to attention in front of the table, removed his black beret and twisted it nervously in both hands over his stomach, while quivering like a squirrel trying to eat a walnut before he is discovered by other hungry squirrels.

'You are Nathan Lunel?' I asked in a neutral tone, trying to be official but not intimidating.

He nodded nervously. 'Yes, sir.'

'My name is Hamelin. I am a Canadian diplomat accredited to the Red Cross,' I lied – quite smoothly, I thought. 'Please sit down. We have much to discuss.'

He glanced over both his shoulders, as though expecting a guard to truncheon him into a sitting position, before scraping back the chair and shuffling his knees under the table. In his lap he continued to strangle the life out of his beret.

'Do you speak English?'

He glanced at me with pity, as if thinking, *better than you speak French*, but he held his tongue and said only, 'Yes, sir, I do.'

'Then let us speak it quickly and quietly, Monsieur Lunel. How are they treating you?'

'As a Jew,' he said grimly.

'I am sorry. There may be a way to . . . alleviate your situation.'

He frowned at that. 'I mean, there may be a way to have you removed from here.'

'I understood your words, sir but being removed from this place is a fate which has already been planned for me and my fellow prisoners.'

'That particular fate can be avoided.'

'I seriously doubt that.'

I glanced around the cell and at the door, to make sure the sliding metal peephole had not moved. I was still unsure about hidden microphones, but it was a risk I had to take as I had no idea how much time I would be allowed with the prisoner.

'Monsieur Lunel, I know what you have been doing this past year. The bank accounts, the transfers, the trips to Algeria, Morocco, Tunisia. You have been working for some very unsavoury clients.'

I thought I saw his lips twitch, but it was only the briefest shadow of a smile.

'That is the lot of bankers, M'sieur Hamelin. Is it not the case in Canada?'

'You do not seem surprised that I know of your activities.'

'Why should I be? The web I was caught in was a big one. Too many people are involved, powerful people, and the sums involved are large, very large. It was inevitable that the conspiracy would be found out.'

'You knew it was a conspiracy, but you still facilitated it?'

'What choice did I have?' I realized it had been a stupid question and Lunel had every right to be indignant at it. Instead, he answered it with sad resignation. 'I am a Jew and Jews have no rights or choices any more. We hold our jobs, our property, our lives, only on the whim of others. I am here talking to you because a guard with a stick and a pistol ordered it.'

'I appreciate that, m'sieur,' I said, noticing that he was no longer calling me 'sir', which I took to be a sign of progress, 'but I have no whip or truncheon to threaten with. I can only ask you to trust me. I must ask you to trust me.'

He was silent, reading my face intently. I removed my glasses and placed them on the table between us; a gesture to indicate that I was not hiding behind them.

'How?'

'By telling me about the conspiracy and the cabal of men behind it.'

'Cabal – that is a good word for them,' he acknowledged, 'but I cannot tell you much about them.'

'Cannot or will not?'

'Cannot because I do not know who they are.'

'I find that hard to believe. You were their banker and, I think, given your present circumstances, any attempt to protect client confidentiality is both inappropriate and pointless.'

'Would it do me any good if I knew their names and told you? I think I would be dead before dawn. My clients, as you call them, know how to protect their investments. They are powerful. Some are high-ranking SS officers, some are politicians, some are gangsters.'

'But you do not know their names?'

'Not their real names, only the counterfeit names they used to open bank accounts. My task was to transfer those fake accounts to new fake accounts in Vichy banks in Africa.'

'But you know *those* names?'

'Of course. And' – he lowered his voice – 'the account numbers.'

I sat back in my chair to let what he had said sink in along with the fact that he was volunteering the information in the first place.

'Such information must be very valuable,' I said. 'Valuable enough to buy your way out of here, I would have thought. I believe such things are possible.'

Now it was Lunel's turn to sit back in his chair, though he was far from relaxed. If anything, his body stiffened, as if expecting a blow.

'I cannot do that. Not as long as they hold my wife.'

I took a deep breath and tried to retain my external composure, but internally I was kicking myself for my stupidity. I had thought of Nathan Lunel as merely a cog in a devilish machine, and if I could disrupt or somehow loosen that cog, then an enemy would be disadvantaged. I had forgotten – or worse, never considered – that he might also be a human being with feelings for things far more noble than the war or money.

'Was your wife taken in the same Vichy round-up you were?'

Lunel nodded. 'She was arrested and put in the Centre Bompard. It is a hotel near the *terminus du port* now used as a prison for women, but she was removed from there.'

'How? And by whom?'

'How is anything done in Vichy? By corruption, and by a man who makes a career of crime and corruption; the prince of Marseilles' gangsters, Pirani.'

'I have had some dealings with him myself,' I said, 'albeit indirectly. If he is such a power in the land, why has he not also arranged for your release?'

'Why should he? Since the round-ups, no Jew can move as freely as I used to and he knows I will do nothing about the accounts because he has my wife. Whatever Vichy or the Nazis have planned for the Jews here probably means I will soon be a problem he does not have to worry about.'

'But if . . .' I said, trying not to give away how big an 'if' it was, 'it was possible to arrange for your escape, not just from here but from France, accompanied by your wife, of course, would you be prepared to share your knowledge of the cabal's accounts?'

He leaned forward, and his knuckles whitened as he gripped the edge of the table. 'I can do better than that. I have kept a ledger.'

'And you would be willing to trade it for two safe passages?'

'I will hand it to you personally as soon as we cross the border into Switzerland or Spain . . . or even Canada, M'sieur Hamelin.'

I did not rise to his Canadian jibe, though I did not begrudge him it. 'You would not be tempted to use the information in your ledger and access the cash yourself?'

Lunel relaxed his grip on the table, flexed his fingers and exhaled. 'Those accounts are tainted, Mr Canadian Diplomat, and I am not so stupid that I do not know where the funds in them came from. I would not touch them if my life depended on it, though my life is not worth very much.'

He placed a fist on the table, not demanding anything, simply showing he had come to a decision.

'In fact, my life is worth nothing at all; it can be forgotten. I will make a gift of my ledger if you can only get my wife out of France.'

'You are offering me a substantial prize, M'sieur Lunel, without knowing who I represent or whether you can trust me.'

'What choice do I have? If I must put my trust in someone, it might as well be you. At least you have not threatened me or demanded a share of the profits from those accounts – and the profits will be great, enough to tempt any man.'

'But not you?'

'They reek of corruption, and I have no wish to smell that stench again.'

'Which is why those North African accounts must be exposed,' I said.

'And as soon as possible.' Lunel spoke softly. 'There cannot be much time left.'

He scrutinized my face closely, but it was my most impermeable 'poker face' – not that I had ever played poker, but it sounds so much more dramatic than adopting a 'four no trumps' expression.

I knew what Lunel was fishing for: the date of the American invasion of North Africa when those counterfeit accounts would blossom in value as francs became dollars.

'I think the sooner we act, the better,' I said.

In the light of what happened subsequently, it seems incredible that at that moment I was suspicious of Lunel and began to doubt everything to do with him. Despite his incarceration and obvious discomfort in Les Milles, there was always the possibility – or so my training in the secret black arts had taught me – that a good story or 'legend' could also be a perfect trap. What if Lunel was where he was *only* to fish for the date and location of the American invasion of North Africa? And if he was, was he doing it in collaboration with Robert and the Abwehr, who had smoothed my path into this very prison? Robert involving me on the basis of an old friendship and the false assumption that the War Office was stupid enough to trust me with any sort of vital information.

That was the way we were supposed to think: trust no one and assume only ulterior motives. I looked at the pale, drained figure of Nathan Lunel, sitting across the table from me, and thought of my old friend Robert Ringer and what they both had risked – and were going to risk – and decided that to doubt them was the way of madness. If I was to stay sane and retain my faith in humanity which, after all, was what we were fighting for, I would believe in them both and be proud to be on their side.

'M'sieur Lunel, your wife . . .'

'Astrid. She is much younger than I. You must say you will protect her.'

'If I can, of course I will. Is she from Marseilles?'

'No, from Pau in the Pyrenees, but we were both in Marseilles when the round-ups started. And before you ask, she knows nothing of the African accounts, or of the ledger.'

'You are sure that Paul Pirani is holding her?'

'Astrid is his insurance policy. He knows I will do nothing without her, but make her safe and I will give you everything. You *must* get my wife out of Vichy, and soon: there is not much time.'

Again, I assumed Lunel was fishing for the timetable of the North African invasion, but I was wrong. 'I have no idea how much time we have, m'sieur. I am not privy to the plans of generals and statesmen.'

Lunel shook his head. 'You do not understand. You must get Astrid away from Pirani and out of Vichy before the birth.'

'Excuse me?' I said rather aimlessly.

'My wife is pregnant.'

'How far along?'

'Seven months, perhaps a week or two more.'

He read the expression on my face.

'But she is young and strong. She will do whatever is necessary to survive. Survival is the only weapon we Jews have these days. All you have to say to her is, "Nathan says . . ." and she will trust you and do whatever you tell her to do. Get her out of Vichy, M'sieur Hamelin, or whoever you are, and you will have the Lunel Ledger. It does not matter about Lunel himself: just save Astrid and our baby.'

'If I can, M'sieur Lunel, I will save all three of you. Be prepared to move at a moment's notice.'

He spread his hands wide, shooting the frayed cuffs of his shirt like a sad magician proving he had nothing up his sleeves.

'I do not have much to pack and my freedom of movement is somewhat limited.'

'Forgive me, I should have said be prepared to be moved. The commandant here will receive a transit order for you. It will be to another prison, I'm afraid, but one which offers, shall we say, some advantages to us.'

'You can do that?'

'I have influential friends,' I said. 'Let us leave it at that. With luck the orders will be issued in the next three days.'

The small man rubbed a hand over his balding pate. 'Then you have three days to rescue Astrid.'

Was the little man – the prisoner – bargaining with me? 'You are convinced that Paul Pirani has her?'

'Yes, I am sure. She was betrayed to the police by Pirani's partner, a most evil man. An Englishman without honour and without a country. His name is Magnus Asher and he is very dangerous.'

I had not gone blithely into my interview with Nathan Lunel without a plan, or at least the glimmer of one. It was now time to reveal it to Robert as the gates of Les Milles shrank in the rear-view mirror of the Panhard.

'What are the chances of getting Lunel transferred to the camp at Rivesaltes near Perpignan?'

'You are thinking of the Spanish border,' said Robert.

Indeed I was. I had been briefed on the camp by Benton of MI6's Iberian section. Originally used to house refugees fleeing from Franco's Spain in 1939, the Rivesaltes camp, only forty kilometres from the border, had been pressed into service by the Vichy regime as a holding pen for prisoners of any ilk, and no doubt 'undesirables' such as the Jews. Benton had assured me that the Perpignan area offered the best options for the 'extraction', as he put it, of anyone wishing to get out of Vichy France, either on foot into the Spanish foothills of the Pyrenees, or by ship to Barcelona or Valencia.

'Rivesaltes is not an option for Lunel,' Robert said, 'or at least not a healthy one. The Jews there have already been transported north to the camp at Drancy outside Paris. Where their final destination will be I do not know and do not like to think. There is an alternative, though, if you are keen to go walking in the mountains.'

By referring to 'walking in the mountains', Robert meant the numerous routes used by escaping British POWs or shot-down aircrew, but he was far too much the gentleman to ask for details.

'There is another camp,' he continued, 'and it is a place you do not wish to go, but it could serve our purpose. It is the camp at Gurs, which is perhaps eighty kilometres from the border with Spain. It too was built to accommodate refugees from the Spanish Civil War, but Vichy has encouraged a much wider clientele to enjoy its facilities, which mainly comprise mud and barbed wire.'

The camp at Gurs offered several advantages to us if not to the present residents. It was close to Pau, a fine city nestling in the approaches to the Pyrenees and, according to her husband, the home town of Astrid Lunel. To get there one would travel via Toulouse, which would have been on my itinerary anyway, as it was the hub of covert Free French activity in Vichy and I would need their help. Best of all, Gurs was far enough from Marseilles to be beyond the reach of Pirani and the gangsters of the Panier, and also, if we were lucky, the other shareholders in the cabal's activities.

'Can you get Lunel transferred to Gurs?'

'Easily,' said Robert. 'My department can provide authentic-looking movement orders. No one questions when a German decides the fate of a Jew any more.'

'So we can get Lunel into the camp at Gurs, but can we get him out?'

Robert allowed his eyebrows to dance an impromptu jig.

'I have an idea about that – though you will not like it – but your immediate concern must be Madame Lunel. That problem you must handle yourself, Albert. It would be difficult for me to interfere directly, without arousing the suspicions of my Abwehr colleagues, or indeed Vichy counter-intelligence, who have arrested far more German 'spies' than they have British ones, or even communist agitators. I will help in any way I can, but I must remain in the wings. The British Secret Service must take centre stage when it comes to Madame Lunel.'

'Have no fear, old chum,' I said, oozing confidence. 'I intend to employ all our vast resources in Marseilles to rescue Lunel's wife.'

I really did not have the heart to tell him that the sum total of the resources I could call upon were a retired naval chaplain and a teenage girl, neither of whom had reason to trust me as far as they could throw me.

'There is one thing, though. Could I possibly borrow a pistol?'

On our journey back to Marseilles we spoke English because our driver did not, even though his central driving position made it impossible to ignore him. The pink, closely shaved neck above his shirt collar seemed to have a hypnotic effect on the both of us.

'What did you think of my little Jewish banker? More importantly, what did he think of you?'

'He is very clever and had me spotted as soon as he saw this distinguished profile,' I admitted, turning my head to look out of the window at the countryside floating by, so that Robert had the benefit of my best side.

'He recognized you? I appreciate, my friend, that you move in exalted circles, but I am surprised that you are so well known among provincial French bankers.'

'Oh, he didn't recognize me for *who* I am – he's never seen me before in his life, and I've never seen him – but he spotted *what* I was straight away, and it was rather flattering. He saw me as hope; hope for him, his wife and their unborn child. The first hope he had seen in a long while. It was remarkable, really, as I could have been anyone: a spy for the cabal to see if he had talked; an undercover Vichy cop; one of your chaps from the SD or the SS or the Gestapo. I could have been any one of a dozen people not worth trusting, and yet he trusted me.'

Robert's eyes were fixed on our driver's neck as he spoke. 'You said he was clever. Perhaps he saw through the cloak of deliberate vagueness and flippancy which you have perfected over the years and realized that under that polished veneer there was a good man, a just man, trying not to be recognized.'

'I said he was clever, not a genius.' Like Robert, I also concentrated on our driver's pink neck and our conversation took on the atmosphere of the confessional. 'I think he realized I was his last hope. No one else would come after me, other than those wishing him dead. It did not really matter who I was: I was his last resort.'

'And do you accept that responsibility?' Robert asked, his eyes still front.

'I prefer to think of it as the two of us together, working from different angles, being Lunel's last resort.'

As he considered this, Robert produced his cigarette case and offered me an evil-looking black cigarillo, which I politely declined. He cranked down his window as he lit up, even though the interior of the Panhard was so big it could have offered a separate No Smoking section.

'You are assuming that the personal safety of Nathan Lunel is our primary objective, are you not?'

'And his pregnant wife,' I added, then recanted, 'but I know very well what you mean. If the cabal's money-changing scheme in North Africa is to be thwarted, then the lives of two little people, or even three, matter as little as a mote of dust in a giant's eye. Having given my word, I would like to think we can beat the cabal and save the Lunel family.'

Robert blew a perfect smoke ring, which hung in the air before being pulled out of the open window.

'You are the eternal optimist, my friend, or perhaps just naïve.'

'In the past,' I admitted, 'many people have cut to the chase and called me downright stupid. For the first time in forty-odd years, I think I am willing to concede they may have a point.'

FOURTEEN
Free French Connections

Robert had estimated that it would take him three days to arrange the transfer orders and transport to move Nathan Lunel from Les Milles to Gurs, but my deadline was tighter than that: we had to assume that Pirani and the cabal had eyes and ears in the camp and, once Lunel appeared to be slipping out of their sphere of influence, they were likely to react violently. Most at risk would be Astrid Lunel.

I had to save her, but first I had to find her, and to do that I had to break several rules, expose my admittedly paper-thin cover, and put perfectly good and innocent people in harm's way.

I needed help and I hoped it would come from a source of which Robert was unaware, for, although I trusted him, I could not expect others to. It was time to pull a name out of the hat, or perhaps the beret, and call upon the services of Olivier Courteaux, the Free French's man on the ground in Toulouse. The camp at Gurs would be in his operational area, and Toulouse was a good 250 miles from Marseilles, which I hoped was well outside Pirani territory.

I had no doubt that Courteaux knew I was in Marseilles, and that Corinne Thibus was the watch dog he had set on me. The girl had confirmed as much the moment she had identified my accent as 'bad enough to be Canadian' – the very line which Colonel 'Passy' had used in my briefing with the Deuxième Bureau in London. I had read our file on Olivier Courteaux before leaving London, and knew he was rated highly as a resourceful and intelligent agent who had, in peacetime, been a respected journalist; respected in the sense that he had written regularly and perceptively on the dangers of fascism in Europe, being particularly scathing about the rise of the Action Française party and the Rexist movement in neighbouring Belgium. It was said that the Vichy government, Nazi Germany and the Communist Party all wanted him dead, which was surely the best character reference a chap could ask for.

It had been dinned into me that the way to contact Courteaux was via Sandy Nevin at the Seamen's Mission, but only if I was in dire straits and on the strict understanding that my actions would not compromise 'the good padre', as Asher had called him; and just thinking that made the hairs on the back of my neck stand up. I was pretty sure young Mademoiselle Thibus would prove the ideal conduit to Courteaux and, though I might have to go through the Seamen's Mission to find her, the collateral damage to Sandy Nevin would be minimal.

On that count, as a strategy, it was an utter failure.

Robert and I agreed that the Panhard was far too distinctive a vehicle to risk being seen in around the Old Port area, so I was dropped off on the edge of an industrial area north of the railway tracks leading into the St Charles station. I was confident I could follow my nose towards the docks, despite the distraction of a huge tobacco factory and at least two distilleries where business seemed to be booming.

I was suited and booted as a smart, suave Canadian diplomat should be, and that was fine as I walked through the St Lazare district, but the nearer I got to the Joliette docks I began to feel that I would be less conspicuous as the more down-to-earth working man Didier Ducret. My Ducret ensemble was back at the Hôtel Moderne, however, and I decided I did not have the time for a detour and a quick change.

So it was the well-dressed Jean-Baptiste Hamelin who approached the door of the Seamen's Mission, glad to see the welcoming yellow Q flag still displayed, but also desperately trying to remember if Corinne Thibus, when she led me there, had used a secret or coded knock. If she had, I had not paid enough attention, and so I settled on something I felt sure a former naval chaplain would appreciate: dit-dit-dit, dah-dah-dah, dit-dit-dit, the international SOS call sign in Morse Code, which had been first adopted by the German government several years before the *Titanic* needed to use it.

My distress call, unlike the *Titanic*'s, was answered promptly; in my case by the sound of a bolt being drawn and then the door creaking open to reveal the cherubic face of Pastor Nevin.

'My, my, if it isn't our Canadian friend,' he said with a thin smile.

'If that is indeed who you are today. I thought we had seen the last of you.'

'I am the proverbial bad penny – or should that be bad *centime*? – in that I always keep turning up and, as always, I am seeking your help.'

'The last time you came here,' he said sternly, 'you brought violence into this house.'

'That was not of my making, and I am genuinely sorry if I caused distress in any way to yourself or the Mission.'

The door opened another six inches to allow the Pastor to vent his anger directly into my face.

'You tortured a wounded man who was seeking sanctuary here.'

'You mean the man who attacked and robbed me in the street? I did not torture him; I did not even raise my voice to him. It was your friend Magnus Asher who took the route of cruelty.'

It was difficult to judge whether that had shocked him or confirmed a suspicion, but either way Nevin's grasp on the door relaxed and it swung gently inwards.

'You had better come in off the street.'

'You believe me?' I asked as I crossed the threshold.

'I am aware that Magnus can be ruthless,' he said quietly, avoiding my eyes. 'He has had to be to survive this long, but he has always protected this Mission. You, I do not know, but I do not think you are a ruthless man, or a violent one.'

'I will take that as a compliment,' I said as I squeezed by him into the small hallway which doubled as a communal kitchen – evidenced by the lingering aroma of boiled vegetables. Automatically, my gaze swept up the open staircase on which Magnus Asher had appeared like a pantomime villain.

'Don't worry,' said the pastor, 'we are alone. The Mission has no guests at the moment – at least not until after dark tonight.'

'Please, Padre,' I raised a hand to silence him, 'the less I know about the goings-on here, the better. I have no wish to bring any further distress to the Mission. Do me one small favour and I'll be out of your hair for good.'

'When being asked for, favours are invariably small; when granting them, they tend to be less straightforward. What is it?'

'I need to find Corinne Thibus.'

'May I ask why?'

'I would rather you didn't.'

Nevin raised his eyebrows.

'Then I assume it is not Corinne you really want, but Olivier Courteaux.'

If we had been playing chess, my next move would have taken some time.

'Can I take the lawyer's escape and say I can neither confirm nor deny that?'

'Then perhaps it is a case of me knowing as little as possible, but there is something you should know – about Corinne.'

'That she is very young for the work she does?'

'That is certainly true,' said Nevin, 'but in wartime, the young always take the brunt of the hardships, and to survive they become hard themselves.'

'It sounds almost as if you are suggesting that the girl could be dangerous.'

'I am not suggesting it, I am telling you it as a fact. And, despite her youth, she is madly and deeply in love with Olivier Courteaux. If you do anything to endanger him, you will have Corinne to answer to, and you have no idea how dangerous that young lady can be.'

The lady in question certainly looked young, but far from dangerous, as she served behind the counter of a thinly stocked *épicerie* on the Rue des Honneurs, though I pitied any of the glum-faced shoppers who did not have the correct *tickets* in their ration books.

Sandy Nevin had reluctantly parted with the information that Corinne lived in the back of Madame Joubert's grocery shop, earning her keep by helping out the ageing proprietress in any way she could. At first glance it did not seem that her workload would be too onerous, as most of the shelves were only half full of goods. There was, as always, a queue just in case new stock had arrived, but it comprised a dozen silent women waiting patiently more in hope than expectation, in stark contrast to the unruly crowds which gathered, often queueing around the block, outside every *boulangerie* each morning.

Corinne was wearing a shapeless brown smock coat and her hair was scraped back into a straggling ponytail tied with a piece of red ribbon. I was sure she had spotted me as soon as I had entered the shop, but she made me wait my turn, ignoring me like a true professional shopkeeper, until I had edged up to the counter and she demanded to know what I wanted.

I told her something off-ration and, without a change of expression, she pointed to a crate of unlabelled wine bottles, saying simply, 'It's Algerian,' as if that explained everything.

'Do you have any wine from Passy?' I asked quietly. 'I understand it is very popular in Toulouse.'

Her face when it turned towards me was as expressionless as a blank headstone in a cemetery. 'Then perhaps that is where you should go.'

Having first convinced herself that I had enough cash for the rail fare, we left for Toulouse first thing the next morning. She had shown no surprise at my approach and had immediately recognized the importance of my dropping the name 'Passy'. Among Free French activists it was a magical word, and almost as effective as if I had General de Gaulle himself at my shoulder vouching for me.

Corinne, of course, showed no reaction in front of Madame Joubert or the women in the shop, but under her breath told me to return two hours later when the shop would be closed, and then proceeded to sell me a bottle of red wine whose origin was as dubious as its price was exorbitant. Almost as an afterthought, she advised me not to spill any on 'that expensive suit'.

I made my way to the Hôtel Moderne, where I changed clothes and identities, and it was as the far more suitably attired Didier Ducret that I returned to the grocery as night was falling. Corinne was waiting for me in the shadows of the poorly lit street and wasted no time on pleasantries.

'I have telephoned Captain Courteaux and he is willing to meet you. I think he was expecting you, but he cannot leave Toulouse so we must go there. There is a train early in the morning. Bring money for the tickets and meet me at Gare St Charles at seven o'clock. If we are questioned, we are uncle and niece and you are taking me to Toulouse with a view to entering a convent.'

'You or me?' I asked, drawing a look of utter disgust.

'We have used the story before and the police have accepted it without question. Perhaps I look as if I am the sort of girl who should be in a convent.'

I thought it both polite and safest to say nothing.

In many ways travelling by train in Vichy was preferable to a rail journey in wartime Britain. There were no blackout restrictions and the absence of a curfew meant trains could run later, plus they were not overcrowded with bored and sullen troops moving aimlessly from one army camp to another. True, there were more police – many more – on the station platforms checking identity cards than you would find while waiting to board the 4.50 from Paddington. Most of them seemed to take only a passing interest in their duties and gave the identity papers of the shuffling passengers no more than a desultory glance. Although they were well armed, as officials of authority they were far less intimidating than the average Great Western ticket inspector.

Our journey, thanks to numerous unexplained stops, took almost five hours, and the bulk of it was observed in the silence one might expect between prisoner and guard, or uncle and convent-bound niece. Only once, after some diplomatic questioning, did Corinne let slip something of her relationship with Olivier Courteaux.

A precocious reader, the young Corinne had discovered Courteaux's take-no-prisoners style of journalism while still at school, and idealism soon turned to infatuation, which would flower into happy-ever-after as soon as the war was over. Corinne was content to wait, though whether that was for an Armistice or Olivier's acceptance of his fate was unclear. She added that 'not being French', I could not possibly understand how a woman could love a man almost fifteen years older than herself, which amused me, but I did not disabuse her.

I did not get the opportunity to explore Toulouse's old town, known as 'the pink city' because of its buildings built with terracotta bricks, as Corinne took my hand and dragged me out of the station, across the road and into a small café, which was as dark and dingy on the inside as its soot-encrusted windows suggested it might be. If it had a name, I was not aware of it; it was simply one of those basic, unpretentious and totally anonymous establishments which could be found near factory gates or railway termini in any city of any size. Being France, customers would be more likely to have a glass of red wine rather than a mug of tea in front of them, and the advertising material pasted to the walls was certainly more exotic, but essentially the same sort of 'caff' could probably be found in London, Birmingham or Glasgow. Its clientele would be predominantly male and working-class, and strangers would be recognized immediately.

Thankfully Corinne did not seem to be a stranger there and, by dint of the fact that she was still holding my hand, acted as my passport and, judging by the suspicious stares of the rough-looking customers, also my bodyguard.

Through a hanging cloud of blue smoke and the distinctive scent of caporal tobacco, Corinne pulled me through a maze of small tables, each occupied by a lone male customer with a bowl of coffee or soup in front of them, and a packet of Gauloises or Celtiques within easy reach.

Without warning, Corinne released my hand and skipped, positively skipped, the last metre or so to a table near the end of the chrome-topped bar, bending over almost double to throw her arms around a seated figure, with whom she exchanged kisses on both cheeks. When he stood to disentangle himself, I could see that the man being so enthusiastically greeted was perhaps thirty years old; tall, thin, and sporting a healthy tan and a dashing pencil moustache. He had something of the Errol Flynn or the Clark Gable about him, and I think he knew it.

I waited politely for he and Corinne to exchange greetings – or devotions of love – in rapid, whispered French, and discreetly surveyed the café to observe the reaction of the clientele to this overt display of emotion. There was none. Every customer continued to eat, drink or smoke as if nothing untoward had happened. Perhaps nothing untoward had, and it was only my straight-laced English sensibilities which had been disturbed. I tried to look impervious as Corinne snaked an arm around his shoulders and maneuvered herself with considerable wriggling until she was seated on his knees.

'Do not be alarmed, M'sieur Canadian,' said the film star, 'you are among friends. Every man here fights for General de Gaulle and most of them are armed.'

I acknowledged him with a short bow and noticed the pack of cigarettes nesting next to his coffee cup.

'And you are clearly their officer,' I said, 'because you smoke Gitanes. It is something the British – and the Germans – noticed in the last war. French officers smoked Gitanes while enlisted men smoked Gauloises. You must be Captain Courteaux.'

I held out a hand and he shook it without rising from his seat, where he was anchored by Corinne.

'You come to me from Passy,' he said, 'which is a high recommendation.'

'*He* recommended *you* most highly, should I find myself in trouble and in need of a resourceful friend.'

'And you are in trouble, m'sieur . . .? I do not think you gave your name.'

'I did not, which was rude of me. The name Didier Ducret will have to do, I'm afraid, and if I am not yet in trouble, I certainly will be without your help.'

He whispered something in Corinne's ear and the girl stood up, smoothed her skirt and flounced off behind the bar counter and into the kitchen. Courteaux pushed a chair away from the table with his foot.

'Sit, and tell me how I can help, which I will if you can convince me that nothing you are involved in is contrary to the honour of a Free France.'

'On that you have my word, though – as you do not know me – you can put little value on my word.'

Courteaux leaned back in his chair and, with the forefinger of his right hand, stroked the line of his moustache. It was a gesture I suspected he had practised in a bathroom mirror.

'I may not know you, M'sieur Ducret, but Passy does – and he knows your name is not Ducret. Nor is it Hamelin, for you are neither French nor Canadian. Passy's view is that you are too well known in London to pretend to be someone and something you are not.'

I did my best to appear crestfallen, although I was secretly relieved that Courteaux had had the foresight to check my credentials, probably by radio, with his superiors in England.

'I always considered that I was rather good at appearing to be something I was not,' I sighed, 'but I suppose I should be grateful that Colonel . . . that Passy . . . vouched for me. I take it he did vouch for me?'

'For you personally, yes, but not for your mission here in Vichy, about which he has no knowledge. Why are you in France?'

'That I cannot tell you, at least not in detail,' I said, noting that Courteaux stroking or tracing the line of his moustache was probably a nervous tic rather than simple vanity. 'All I can say is that what I am doing will not harm France; or at least not the France you are fighting for. There are some in Vichy and others in Marseilles who will be harmed if my actions succeed, and they will do anything to stop me.'

'We have no friends in Vichy and only enemies in Marseilles. How can we be of help here in Toulouse?'

'I intend to get two people out of France and into Spain. I cannot

stress how important it is for France that they do get out. One I
will bring from Marseilles, the other will be collected from the Pau
area. I have an escape route over the Pyrenees already agreed, but
I will need transport, a safe house, and someone I can trust to
establish a line of communication with my Spanish contact.'

Courteaux reached for his pack of Gitanes, extracted a cigarette
and lit it from a match struck on his thumb nail. It was another
move he had practised in front of a mirror.

'That is all? You do not require my help in Marseilles?'

'I was assuming that Marseilles was not in your operational area.'

'It is not, but I have already assigned one of my best men to
assist you there.'

'You have?'

'But of course, you know Corinne. Where is she? I think we
should eat before your train back to Marseilles.'

The girl took her leave of Olivier Courteaux only after an extended
bout of hugging and cheek-kissing, and we strolled back to the
station, side by side, as the afternoon waned and a chill wind curled
down off the distant mountains. From the café, Corinne had collected
a sausage-shaped seaman's bag, which she carried slung across her
chest like a bandolier, the crispy ends of two long baguettes
protruding from the open end, which she had said were provisions
for our return train journey.

Only when we were walking along the platform awaiting the
arrival of our train did she raise the subject of my mission.

'Olivier has ordered me to help you,' she said seriously. 'There
is someone you have to get out of Marseilles.'

I looked up and down the platform to make sure we were alone.
There were policemen at the station entrance checking papers, but
none within earshot.

'A woman,' I said, pausing to point at a faded timetable peeling
off a noticeboard in case we were being observed, 'who is currently
a prisoner of the gangster Paul Pirani.'

'In the Panier?'

'I presume so, but that's where I need your help, to find out
where she is being held.'

'This woman is important?'

'Vital.'

'And she is an Israelite?'

I concentrated on the timetable as if it were the most fascinating example of hieroglyphic inscriptions.

'Yes, she is Jewish. Does it matter?'

I was not sure what answer I should expect, but it was certainly not the one I got.

'And she is expecting a child.'

'How did you know that?' I hissed, resisting the urge to abandon the charade of examining the timetable, pick the girl up by the shoulders and shake her violently.

'Pirani sends one of his men to Madame Joubert's shop every day for milk and eggs. He does not like being treated as a servant to what he calls a "dirty Jewess" who should not be allowed to bring "more of her kind" into the world.'

'Can we find out where he takes the milk?'

'I already have. He was easy enough to follow one morning. He goes to one of Pirani's houses in the Panier. You will need me to find it for you. Alone in the Panier you would be lost in one minute and assassinated in two.'

Now I did tear myself away from the timetable poster and I stared at the girl, lost for words and only vaguely conscious of the fact that our train was pulling into the platform in a cloud of smoke and steam.

I touched Corinne lightly on the shoulder and said, 'Come on, let's find a good seat.' As we walked down the platform, side by side, past the big, black panting engine and heading towards the carriages, a white fog of vented steam engulfed us briefly, and I could not resist adding: 'You know, this could be the start of a beautiful friendship.'

An hour into our journey, Corinne pulled one of the baguettes from her duffel bag, broke off a chunk and handed it to me. There was a faint sheen of something liquid smeared over parts of the crust and the bread smelled of something other than yeast, a smell I recalled from my enforced Commando training course in Scotland. Many was the time I had dipped fresh French bread into dishes of olive oil, but I had never before eaten it coated with gun oil.

FIFTEEN
After Eight

The Dorchester Hotel, London. 20 May 1970

'Y ou will not be familiar with the legendary Sten gun and how we thought it would win the war for us,' said Mr Campion, with the resigned air of a university lecturer addressing an early morning tutorial.

'What a ridiculous thing to say, Albert. How could Perdita possibly be expected to know about guns and such?'

Mr Campion turned to mollify his wife. 'You are absolutely right, my dear. Perdita is blissfully young and mercifully ignorant of such things, but I was talking to Robert.'

'Who I am sure is too well mannered to tell you when you are boring him. I really have no idea what has brought on all this talk about the war, anyway.'

'Your husband may be a lot of things, Lady Amanda, though rarely boring,' said the German politely, 'but I have to disappoint him when I say I was very familiar with the British Sten gun. Unlike Albert, I found myself on the wrong end of one more than once during the war.'

'Ah, but do you know the story of the genesis of the Sten?' asked Campion, warming to his theme.

'I think you're going to tell us,' observed Charles Luke.

'I am, for it is a story of British pluck and ingenuity, and I shall tell it while we have our coffee and fashionably thin chocolate mints.'

Campion leaned back in his chair and signalled the hovering waiters to begin their assault on the empty coffee cups lined up along the table, each saucer already armed with a brace of mints in square paper envelopes.

'They say necessity is the mother of invention, but an unexpected gift from an unlikely benefactor also helps,' Campion began. 'When the war started we – that's us, the plucky British – were terribly unprepared. We were short of most things, and particularly, if you were in the army, there was a lack of sub-machine guns. We had some American ones, Thompsons, and they were much sought after, as everyone fancied themselves as a Chicago gangster from the Roaring Twenties; even dear old Churchill, who was photographed cuddling one and trying to look like George Raft.'

Unseen by Campion, Perdita mouthed a silent *Who?* towards her mother-in-law, who raised her eyebrows and quietly shook her head.

'Just when our need was greatest, a mystery benefactor stepped in to help. Actually, it wasn't much of a mystery: it was Mussolini; well, in a roundabout way it was. You see, our early victories – our only victories – had been in North Africa against the Italians, and our chaps in the desert had captured not only thousands of Italians, but millions of rounds of Italian ammunition. The problem was that the ammo was nine millimetre, a calibre which didn't fit any standard-issue British firearm – so there was a need to invent one and thus the Sten was born. It had to be simple to use and able to be mass-produced quickly and cheaply. Almost immediately, a mythology developed around the gun. You could drop it in a river and drag it through mud and it would still fire. On the other hand, there were those who said the Sten was prone to jamming if the magazine was fully loaded and recommended thirteen bullets rather than thirty-two. Famously, a Sten gun jammed during the assassination of Heydrich in Prague in 1942, but millions were made and many thousands dropped to Resistance fighters in occupied Europe.'

Perdita's jaw dropped, but she glanced across the table to where Corinne Thibus was deep in conversation with Rupert and Astrid Vidal before she spoke and, when she did, she kept her voice low, suppressing both surprise and indignation.

'Are you telling us that the teenage girl on that train with you was carrying a machine gun in her bag?'

'Well, she was supposed to be my bodyguard and we were going into a rough district, so it was probably for the best. But it wasn't just any old Sten gun, it was a prototype of the Sten Mark 2S.'

'The Silent Sten,' said Charles Luke involuntarily, blushing as four faces turned to stare at him. 'We confiscated a batch of them from a firm of Maltese gangsters in Soho in 1947. They'd been lifted from the small-arms factory at Enfield, but thankfully never used in anger. Nasty things.'

'I'm still not sure what we're talking about,' complained Perdita.

'What Charles means,' said Campion, 'is a Sten gun with a built-in silencer, which made it a particularly dangerous weapon in the right – or should that be wrong? – hands.'

Perdita was suitably horrified. 'You mean a teenage girl was walking around with a machine gun which could kill people *quietly*?'

'There was a war on,' said Robert Ringer before Mr Campion could.

'But do we have to talk about it?' Amanda's voice sent a chill eddying down the crisp white tablecloth. 'This is supposed to be a birthday party, not a regimental reunion. You really must pay more attention to your other guests, Albert, especially the younger ones. Look, young Edward is trying to attract your attention, almost certainly to tell you how bored he is with proceedings.'

'Oh, I very much doubt that,' smiled her husband. 'Young Master Longfox has been anything but bored, making googly-eyes at Precious Aird all evening.'

However reluctantly, Edward Longfox had abandoned his place at the table near the American girl and was making his way down the room to the top table.

'He looks to me a very serious young man,' observed Robert Ringer.

'Oh, he is,' agreed Mr Campion, 'and he looks to be a young man on a mission.'

It was clear that Master Longfox was steering a course directly for the Campions, carefully avoiding the other diners, and the waiting staff performing acrobatics trying to pour coffee into cups rather than over guests. When he reached the top table, he placed himself squarely behind the senior Campions and coughed politely, just in case they had not noticed his looming presence.

'Happy birthday, Great Uncle,' he said with great solemnity.

'Thank you, Edward. Have you eaten well?'

'Very well, thank you.'

'Not having coffee?'

'I do not take stimulants of any sort,' said the young man with the seriousness of a junior funeral director. 'Which is why I am currently free to act as Mr Lugg's messenger boy.'

Campion focused on the far end of the left wing of the table.

'Ah, yes, Lugg – a man who has never stinted on stimulants, at least not the liquid ones. Where is the old rogue? He seems to have disappeared, which is quite a trick for a man of his bulk. In his dinner suit and dress shirt he might blend in to a pod of orcas, but otherwise he's usually hard to miss.'

'He's with the kitchen staff . . . something to do with checking the cutlery. He was rather preoccupied, but he wanted me to tell you that the *dis-koh-thee-kway*, and he pronounced it like that, is being set up in the reception room.'

'I will translate for Robert's benefit,' said Mr Campion.

'Robert speaks perfect English,' said Amanda pointedly.

'Yes, but Lugg doesn't. He was referring to the *discothèque* which I have hired to entertain the younger members of the party or those, like myself, who are not necessarily sound in wind and limb, but are young at heart. The music will be raucous and loud enough so that even Guffy Randall can hear it.'

Campion beamed beatifically into the silent, slightly stunned faces of his immediate audience.

'Did you know,' he began, as though the thought had just occurred to him, 'that we get the word *discothèque* from the French? Well, obviously; but the original ones, during the war, were places where people met to dance to music which had been banned by the Vichy government.'

'And we're back to the war!' said Amanda, shaking her head in mock despair.

SIXTEEN
Commando Raid

Marseilles. Late October – early November 1942

Our train eventually stumbled and wheezed back into Marseilles several hours after dark. We were tired and hungry, and I had no wish to visit the Panier before I had a chance to do some reconnaissance in daylight. To my surprise, Corinne agreed with me. Perhaps the euphoria and spring-in-her-step, so obvious in Toulouse when in the presence of her beloved Olivier, had dissipated on the long, slow train journey in my company, but she opted to return to her bed in the back of Madame

Joubert's shop in the Rue des Honneurs. That way she could get a few hours' sleep and be on hand in the shop in the morning if Pirani's man came to buy milk.

I saw her to the shop, wished her goodnight and, once I was sure she was secure inside, I did my best to disappear into the Stygian darkness of the narrow streets and then surprised myself by finding my way to the Hôtel Libéria without getting lost more than twice. It took far longer than it should have as I was nervously looking over my shoulder most of the time, paranoid that I might be seen making a beeline for an Abwehr safe house by a compatriot of Olivier Courteaux. It would indeed be difficult to explain how I was helping our Free French allies by collaborating with our German enemies.

I did not recognize the tall man behind the reception desk at the Libéria at first, as I was more familiar with the back of his neck. It was the driver who had taken us to the Camp des Milles in that rather spectacular Panhard and from somewhere I recalled that Robert had called him Erik, but his surname and Abwehr rank I never knew.

Thankfully, Erik remembered me and, having ascertained that I spoke German well enough, he told me that Freiherr von Ringer was away from Marseilles but had left instructions that I was to be assisted in every way possible, and before I could reveal my shopping list of favours, Erik reached down behind the desk and produced a cardboard box, smaller than a shoebox, which he handed to me without comment. It did not contain shoes, but a Walther PPK automatic pistol – the safety catch thankfully on – and a spare magazine.

With Teutonic formality, a short bow and a click of his heels, Erik asked if I would be requiring anything else.

I adopted what I thought was my most charming demeanour. 'Yes, please. Could you get me a car for tomorrow night along with enough petrol for four hundred kilometres? Oh, and it had better not be the Panhard. I need something less conspicuous and something you won't get angry about if it doesn't come back in one piece.'

The Panier district was once described as 'an ant hill with none of the home comforts', and so it had been for nearly two hundred years after the middle-class of Marseilles had moved out to more fragrant areas, leaving the Panier to become, as its name implied, a basket full of immigrants, seamen, dockers, dope-dealers, thieves and prostitutes.

The streets were narrow, dark, pungent and steep, with deep steps and iron hand rails running down the middle. It was not a place from which one could make a quick, or even a slow, getaway by car. Which was why I needed Corinne, or so I told myself. She would help guide Astrid Lunel out of the Panier and to the Hôtel Moderne, where my Abwehr taxi would be parked. A pregnant woman walking with a young girl, even late at night, would be noticed less than one being dragged along by a furtive middle-aged man desperately trying not to get lost in the Old Port. It was my plan to be the advance guard when it came to the actual rescue and then the rearguard for the escape. I was loathe to involve young Corinne in my pseudo-military campaign, but I could not see how I could manage it alone – even finding Pirani's hideaway in the maze of the Panier after dark might be beyond me – and, in any case, I seriously doubted that Corinne would agree to be left out of the action now that it, and I, had the blessing of her idol, Olivier Courteaux.

We had conducted a reconnaissance mission in daylight, getting as close to our target as we dared, or at least what Corinne assured me was our target: specifically, a tall, thin house with a warped and faded green door at the top of three stone steps in a narrow canyon of an alley where adjoining houses with overhanging balconies and window boxes helped limit the natural light. The alley gave off the distinct aroma of rotting vegetables and bad sanitation, and the presence of a large dead rat in the gutter near the door suggested that even the seagulls found the place unsavoury.

I never doubted that Corinne had correctly identified Pirani's hidey-hole, not because she felt obliged to help me, but because she was keen to impress Olivier Courteaux. Still, I was relieved to have my faith in the girl confirmed when, as we were observing that shabby green door, it opened and a man emerged. He was dressed in standard French workman's clothes – complete with beret – and puffing on a Gauloises. He looked neither left nor right, but walked quickly down the hill, confident of his territorial rights and moving with a swagger, despite his left arm and shoulder being encased in a sling made from what appeared to be the remains of an old shirt. The last time I had seen him he had been screaming as Magnus Asher's foot had descended on that shoulder.

Corinne confirmed that he was not the man who had complained about having to do the shopping at Madame Joubert's, which meant that Astrid Lunel had two guards. To make sure, the girl and I watched the house from the shadows at the far end of the alley, but apart from 'shoulder man', who returned carrying a string bag clinking with bottles, there were no other comings or goings.

Once it was dark, I made the girl show me the quickest way out of the Panier, down the hill and across the Place Daviel and into the crumbling tenements of the Old Port, threading our way through to emerge on to the Quai Maréchal Pétain near the Hôtel de Ville. From there, I led the way to the Hôtel Moderne and insisted we had something to eat to keep our strength up, which Corinne seemed determined to do. Noting her appetite, I realized we might need provisions for our escape from Marseilles and, in good military style, I volunteered the girl as quartermaster, palmed the required funds from my wallet and slid them across the table.

As I did so, our waiter – an ancient specimen with fallen arches and body odour strong enough to fell an inquisitive ox – approached to inform M'sieur that there was a telephone call, which M'sieur could take in the *cabine* near the reception desk if he so wished. Trying not to look surprised, M'sieur agreed to take the call as long as the provision of food to the mademoiselle continued uninterrupted.

I was not expecting a telephone call, and of course there wasn't one. The receiver of the telephone in the *cabine* was out of its cradle, acting as a paperweight holding down a single sheet of paper on which was written *extérieur*. Even I could follow such simple instructions and, having checked I was not being observed, I strode outside.

Thirty feet from the hotel doorway, a tall figure in a trench-coat and fedora signalled me to approach. He had positioned himself under a street lamp to add to the dramatic effect, and then heightened the tension as I approached by plunging his right hand deep into the pocket of his coat.

I was ten feet away from him when I realized it was my Abwehr chauffeur Erik, and that what he was pulling from his pocket was a set of car keys.

We conversed furtively in whispered German, and I learned two things: that there was a Citroën 7CV ready for my use, with extra petrol in cans in the boot, parked around the corner, and that Robert had sent me the message: 'Our mutual friend is moving west tonight'.

I thanked Erik, took the keys from him and returned to the hotel dining room.

'We have to do it tonight,' I told Corinne as she demolished a pastry of uncertain origin. 'I fear we don't have much time.'

*   *   *

I could not tell Corinne why we were now on a deadline, but if Robert had secured the transfer of Nathan Lunel out of the Camp des Milles, it was only a matter of time before Pirani's network got wind of it, which meant that Astrid Lunel would be in danger, and so our clock was ticking.

When my Abwehr friend Erik had given me the keys to the Citroën, he had added a small bonus by telling me that the car was 'known' to the local police and was unlikely to be stopped or searched within the city. Outside Marseilles was, of course, another matter, nor did it make the car immune from the interest of other parties, but I decided it was worth the risk to leave the car in the Old Port, nearer to the Panier, hopefully making our escape that much easier.

Around nine o'clock that evening, it began to rain heavily; the stinging, swirling sort of rain generated by a squall out to sea. It would clean the gutters of the Panier and hopefully keep pedestrian traffic to a minimum. I decided it was time to launch our little Commando raid.

Corinne led the way up the hill through the rabbit warren of alleys into the Panier. She wore a headscarf and a long woollen coat, no stockings and rope sandals to cope with the rainwater running down the streets. The coat disguised her slender frame and the Sten gun strapped across her chest.

My Commando instructor in Scotland, the red-faced Corporal Colgan, would have had a plan for storming the house in the alley, which would no doubt have involved tossing grenades in through the first-floor windows and covering crossfire from two machine guns. Our plan was much simpler: Corinne would knock on the door and then run away. I would then wave my pistol in the face of whoever opened the door and we would enter in a civilized manner and commence negotiations.

Corinne knocked on the door, and when a voice growled, 'Who is it?', she answered, as we had rehearsed, in her best girlish voice, that she was delivering clean clothes 'for the lady'. The door was unlocked and opened by a tall, dark figure. He was male and bearded, but I could make out little else before Corinne poked the Sten gun from out of the folds of her coat and shot him in the foot.

Although momentarily stunned by Corinne's improvisation on our original meticulous plan, I sprang into action, knocking down the silenced barrel of the Sten and pushing Corinne aside to get at her victim. It was not altruism on my part. The single shot had been a quiet *plop*, but a man with a bullet in his foot was almost certainly going to scream the house down and wake the neighbours.

He had stumbled and fallen backwards on to the floor, his hands scrabbling at his left boot, already slippery with blood. I dropped to one knee by his shoulder, removed a small revolver from his waistband and pocketed it, then clamped my left hand across his mouth and waved my pistol in front of his staring, frightened eyes. I spoke rapidly and hoped that he was paying attention through the shock and the pain.

'Keep quiet and we will send for a doctor. Make a noise and you will not enjoy breakfast. Do you understand?' He nodded enthusiastically. 'Where is the woman?'

His eyes flicked upwards, which given his position could have meant anything, but I assumed he was indicating an upstairs room and the sound I could hear was Corinne already running up the wooden staircase. I girded my loins and charged after her.

They had been keeping Astrid Lunel in a small bedroom at the back of the house. The shutters on the single window were closed and fastened by a looping chain and padlock. The single weak light bulb showed there was a bed, a chair and a washstand with a large china bowl and jug. On the bed lay a figure covered with a bulky eiderdown; in the chair sat a man with his arm in a sling and an expression on his face which said: 'Oh no, not again!' In the doorway stood Corinne, legs apart, brandishing the silenced Sten gun, her left hand around the canvas sleeve on the silencer, which prevented the user from being burned as the barrel overheated, something the gun was prone to do when set to fire on full automatic. Corinne had wisely set the gun to single-shot mode. Corporal Colgan would have been proud of her.

'Madame Lunel,' I announced, asserting what was left of my authority, 'you will come with us now. Please do not let this young lady frighten you. You will be safe with us.'

The eiderdown on the bed began to billow and a dishevelled female face emerged as if gasping for air.

I turned to the man with one arm in a sling, who was staring down the barrel of Corinne's Sten.

'As for you, my friend,' I told him, 'my advice is that you should be *very* frightened of this young lady. If you give her any excuse she will happily put a bullet in your other wing. If you follow us out of this house, I cannot guarantee her aim will be so kind. If you doubt me, ask your compatriot downstairs by the front door.' His eyes widened at that. 'And he might also appreciate you fetching a doctor before he bleeds to death,' I added as an afterthought. 'Are you armed?'

He shook his head at Corinne, if only to show he was not entirely frozen with fear, but the girl had already moved on to her next objective, the figure on the bed still cowering under the eiderdown.

'Get up, woman! Now! You are coming with us!' she snapped.

I thought her approach to be harsh and unkind, but it seemed to work, as Astrid Lunel shook herself into action. In the bed she had been fully clothed apart from her shoes. She swung her legs over the edge of the bed and reached an arm under it in an attempt to find them, but her condition restricted her movement.

I slipped my pistol into my pocket and knelt down to help her. As I placed her feet into her shoes as gently as I could, I looked her in the eyes and whispered in as calming a voice as I could muster.

'Madame Lunel, Nathan says you must trust me. I have come to get you away from this place and reunite you with your husband.'

'Nathan?' she said in little more than a croak.

'Yes, Nathan. His release from prison has been arranged by some friends of mine and you will see him soon, but not in Marseilles. We must get away from the city tonight. I have a car waiting.'

All we had to do now was get to the car.

We didn't make the end of the alley before we heard the first shouts and the first lights began to come on, producing a chequerboard of illuminated squares on the wet streets; but in this game of hopscotch, those would be the most dangerous areas. It seemed we really had kicked an ants' nest.

Our intention had been for Corinne to assist Astrid Lunel down the hill with me acting as rearguard, but our roles were quickly reversed. Whether through hunger, exhaustion or sheer fear for her condition, Astrid seemed incapable of putting any strength or urgency into her stride, and we made progress only when I wrapped my arm around her generous waist and began to half drag, half carry her.

'Hurry! Stay in the shadows! Keep in to the left! They are gaining!'

Corinne, who now seemed to be directing operations, barked her orders from behind us. Exactly who, or how many were chasing us,

I did not know, so intent was I on making sure Astrid did not stumble or fall as we ran into yet another wet and smelly canyon between the looming buildings. To give the woman her due, she kept going, her breathing heavy and erratic, her legs pumping. Not once did she complain or cry out.

Not even when the first shots rang out and echoed through the rain.

I would like to say we ran through a hail of bullets, or that I turned in one swift movement (in homage to Corporal Colgan again), dropped to one knee and returned fire with deadly accuracy, but I have never been good at battlefield heroics.

Fortunately, Corinne was.

When an incoming bullet thwacked into the brickwork of the nearest building a few feet above my head, I pushed Astrid into a doorway, covering her as best I could with my body while fumbling for the pistols in my pockets. I turned my head to look back up the alley to locate our pursuers, only to find that Corinne was ahead of me.

She was down on one knee in the middle of the alley, the Sten gun at her shoulder, aiming up the incline we had just stumbled down. When she fired, it was on full automatic, and the sound was a continuous popping noise, rather like a distant motorbike revving up. I saw her shoulder judder and shake with the recoil, and even heard the tinkling of spent cartridge cases as they were ejected, bouncing off the cobbles through a cloud of cordite smoke, until the gun gave a loud click on its empty magazine and fell completely silent. From where she had been aiming there came the sound of breaking glass and a distinct, and rather satisfying, howl of pain. Then Corinne herself yelped like a kicked dog, flung the Sten away from her body and put her left hand to her mouth where it had been burned by the hot barrel.

'Go!' she said, her voice muffled as she sucked at her hand. 'That will not hold them for long.'

We were all soaked from the rain as well as hot from our exertions and, within a few minutes of piling into the Citroën, the atmosphere inside the car had become a steamy fug, as if we had allowed a pair of Labradors fresh from a dip in a duck pond on board.

I drove with one eye permanently fixed on the rear-view mirror, looking for following headlights, and one eye negotiating the main streets of the city, heading north and west.

Corinne sat in the back seat, breathing loudly and rapidly and nursing her burned hand. Astrid Lunel was slumped down in the passenger seat, perhaps instinctively so that she could not be seen from the street. She had pulled her coat tight around her and clasped her hands, with fingers locked across the bump of her stomach.

'Am I allowed to ask who you are?' she said at last.

'Of course, *madame*. My name, at least for the moment, is Didier, and I represent the government of Great Britain. The young lady in the back, who acts as my guide and moral compass as well as my bodyguard, is Corinne.'

'And I,' said the girl rather grandly, 'represent the government in exile of the Free French.'

In the dark I gave Madame Lunel the benefit of my most disarming smile. 'So you see, Astrid, you are in the best possible hands. Within the hour we will be clear of the city and by dawn we will be well on the way to Toulouse.'

'Is my husband in Toulouse?'

I could not bring myself to tell her that – if all had gone well – Nathan Lunel had exchanged one concentration camp for another.

'Not exactly,' I said with studied vagueness.

'Then I have no intention of going there,' she said firmly. 'You will drive on to Pau.'

'That's an extra two hundred kilometres!' wailed my guardian angel in the back.

'If you want what my husband has, you will take me on to Pau.'

'Why Pau?' I asked, feeling that I already knew the answer.

'Because I intend to have my baby at home,' she said, then closed her eyes and fell immediately asleep.

After four hours of driving, peering through the darkness and the rain, I felt I needed to follow Astrid's example and pulled off the road. I estimated that we were twenty or thirty kilometres short of Montpellier and, from memory, possibly in the commune of, ironically, Lunel, which had once been a noted centre of Jewish learning.

Corinne, who seemed not to require sleep, demanded a weapon if she was expected to stay on guard, so I passed her the revolver I had liberated from Astrid's guard with a sigh of resignation and the request to wake me at the first sign of trouble. Then I settled down in my seat as best I could, closed my eyes and dreamt of splashing through long puddles while running down dark corridors, being chased by shadows firing quiet machine guns.

I was woken just before dawn by Astrid Lunel jabbing an elbow into my ribs and Corinne pushing a stale croissant into my ear.

'You should eat,' said the girl. 'We already have. Pity we have no coffee.'

'Yes, it is,' I said, removing my spectacles and rubbing the sleep from my eyes. 'Good morning to the both of you, by the way.'

The rain had cleared, blown out to sea by the early stirrings of the annual mistral and, after topping up the fuel tank from one of the petrol cans in the boot, we set off again. We encountered little civilian traffic other than agricultural lorries or tractors pulling trailers, and the police and military trucks which passed took no interest in us. In the Aude valley I stopped at a farm so that we could buy goat's milk and cheese, which went some way to softening the stale bread which now comprised the bulk of Corinne's iron rations. We did what all tourists did and marvelled at the sight of the hilltop citadel that was Carcassonne, and then, on the run in to Toulouse, tracked down a telephone in the sole café in a village so small it could not boast a church so that Corinne could make a rendezvous with her field commander and the love of her life.

Not that the main platform of Toulouse station was the place I would have chosen for a lovers' tryst, but it seemed a safe enough place for a conference of war. There were fewer police hanging around than there had been in Marseilles, which was perhaps due to the fact that we were coming up to lunchtime, that most noble and sacred period of the French day which, during peacetime, seemed regulated by law to a minimum of three hours.

I linked one of Astrid Lunel's arms through mine and held on tight, not sure how she would react to contact with yet more strangers, even if they claimed to have her best interests at heart. I knew that she would only trust us if we reunited her with her husband, and could not blame her for that.

Olivier Courteaux stood waiting for us in the middle of the platform, a small suitcase at his feet, his raincoat buttoned and belted, a black beret carefully sloped. I almost looked around to see where the cameras were, for surely this was Clark Gable auditioning for the part of a French secret agent, and I wondered if he saw me as a Leslie Howard, approaching to give him his cue, but for once Leslie Howard was ignored.

The Frenchman took Corinne in his arms, lifting her off her feet and kissing her on both cheeks; then, having replaced her, he politely shook hands with Astrid Lunel.

'Madame, we are here to help you on your journey.' He reached down, picked up the suitcase and offered it to her. 'I have brought you some clothes. They are not fashionable, and they are not new, but they are clean.'

Astrid took the case in silence and held it in front of her stomach, both hands on the handle, as if it was a bomb.

'Corinne will show you the ladies' toilets and help you change,' said Courteaux, at which point Corinne held out her hand to me and demanded change for the washroom attendant. Clutching a fistful of coins, she took Astrid by the arm and led her down the platform, walking directly towards two uniformed policemen who seemed suspiciously idle but clearly curious about the approaching pair of females.

'Don't worry about the *flics*,' said Olivier. 'They are my men.'

'That was very thoughtful of you, as were the clothes for the lady.'

'Corinne suggested it when she telephoned. I hope she was useful to you in Marseilles.'

'Very. Invaluable, you might say. She is a very brave girl. Perhaps it would be best if she did not go back to Marseilles for a while as she has made enemies among the Pirani gang.'

Courteaux shrugged his shoulders and smiled a film-star smile. 'Those of us who fight with General de Gaulle have enemies everywhere. Corinne knows how to take care of herself.'

'She does,' I agreed, 'but the Pirani gang will be very angry to have lost Madame Lunel and they will lash out.'

'Why is this woman so important to them? And to London?'

'That I cannot tell you, but please take my word that she *is* important, and I have promised to reunite her with her husband and get her out of France.'

'You will use one of the pilgrim trails, over the mountains?'

'That is my plan.'

'You must move quickly, before winter – or the baby – arrives.'

'I know, and must ask one more favour of you. Can you get a message across the border to a contact in Spain for me?'

'To Reuben Vidal?'

I did my best to suppress my surprise. 'You know of him?'

'Naturally; he is not only a good anti-fascist, but he is also the best guide you could have to take you across the Pyrenees. We have used him many times to help escaping airmen who have been shot down, but I do not think he will take kindly to helping a pregnant woman.'

'He seems a good man as well as a good guide,' I said.

'Vidal has never betrayed us, which is why he still lives and moves freely in France.' I could not doubt the tone in Courteaux's voice. 'What is your message?'

'Tell him that his Canadian friend will be coming from the direction of Pau within the next five days. Those words exactly, please.'

Olivier nodded in acceptance of his task.

'You are meeting the husband in Pau?'

'Not exactly,' I said, as I had to Astrid. 'Monsieur Lunel is currently languishing in the concentration camp at Gurs.'

Now it was Olivier's turn to try and control a dropping jaw and eyebrows suffering from St Vitus's Dance.

'And just how are you going to get him out of *there*?'

'I am afraid, my friend, that is secret – top secret.'

So secret I did not know myself.

SEVENTEEN
Saying Cheese

The Dorchester Hotel, London. 20 May 1970

'Had you any idea that the rather suave French lady seated next to your mother used to rush around pulling guns and shooting gangsters with your father when she was a teenager?'

'Well, there was a war on,' said Rupert, in a failed attempt to stem the flow of words gushing from his overexcited wife.

'And they were doing it to rescue a woman who turned out to be pregnant! Fancy, putting a pregnant woman through that!'

'We mothers-to-be had to put up with a lot in those days.'

The younger Campions turned in response to Lady Amanda's voice.

'Don't you dare look so shocked, Rupert,' scolded his mother. 'You were not found under a gooseberry bush. I was pregnant with you for the regulation nine months at almost the same time as Madame Lunel was pregnant, or Señora Vidal as she became; the lady you have been sitting next to all evening. It's amazing we wartime mothers survived at all, what with absentee husbands, the air raids and rationing, not to mention the ingratitude of one's offspring.'

'Did Pop know?' Rupert asked hesitantly. 'When he was absent in France?'

'Oh, he knew.'

'Yet he still went on the mission to Marseilles?' Perdita was shocked.

'Of course he did; he was doing his duty, and he certainly did a lot more good out there than he would have done sitting at home in England moping around making sure I didn't pick up heavy objects or take in ironing. As you so rightly observed, Rupert, there was a war on.'

'So that's what this is? It's a reunion for all Pop's wartime buddies?'

'No, it's not a reunion,' smiled Amanda, 'it's a birthday party, and if you two would get a move on and lead the charge in to the next room, we can have birthday cake, once we've got the awful, grinding formalities out of the way.'

'You mean there will be speeches?'

'Worse than that.' Amanda put her fingertips on to her son's face and gently pulled his mouth into a smile. 'There are going to be family photographs. Say cheese.'

Slowly the diners decanted themselves into the adjoining reception room, which appeared to be being transformed into something between a dance hall and a photographic studio. Thin blackout curtains had been drawn across the large windows to block out the lights of the traffic on Park Lane, chairs and tables had been removed or pushed against the walls. At either end of the space created there was an altar. One was a drab affair, a black table groaning under the weight of square boxes of electronic equipment, the centrepiece of which was a rectangular co-joining of two record-player turntables. The table was flanked by large, floor-standing speakers, and behind it stood a metal tree, from the branches of which were suspended a variety of light fittings with coloured bulbs flashing slowly. Leaning over the turntables, earphones clamped to his head and his fingers caressing a large vinyl disc, was a skinny youth in a white T-shirt lost in concentration.

The second altar at the opposite end of the room was a far more welcome sight for the bulk of the guests present. This table was covered with a crisp white cloth and, centre stage, on its own wooden plinth in splendid isolation, sat a square yard of birthday cake, its shining white surface adorned not with candles but with large Roman numerals in thick red icing in the shape LXX.

Fussing around the table, vainly attempting to marshal the main members of the Campion family, was a middle-aged man wearing a pearl grey suit, a bouffant hairstyle and a very expensive Hasselblad camera from a sling around his neck.

In an increasingly strident voice, his commands punctuated by loud clicks from the camera shutter, the photographer eventually captured a series of images of Mr Campion with Lady Amanda, then joined by Rupert and Perdita, then by Amanda's brother Hal and sister Mary, with Guffy Randall belatedly united with his wife after failing to hear the numerous calls for his presence at the cake table rather than the bar.

The rest of the guests shuffled into a scrum on what was to become the dance floor, waiting in polite expectation for the next stage of proceedings.

'Are they not going to cut that splendid cake?' said Dr Jolyon Livingstone to no one in particular.

'I think that will be done off-stage, so to speak,' said Robert Oncer Smith who, being an ambitious undergraduate, had already identified the sole master of a Cambridge college in the room. 'That Lugg chappie – a bit of a vulgarian – claimed that they couldn't find another knife strong enough to cut through icing as thick as that, so they've sent out for a cutlass. Of course, he could have been shooting me a line.'

'I know Lugg of old,' said Dr Livingstone, 'and he is famous for the lines he shoots, aimed at unwary young people. I have, however, never considered him a vulgarian; at least, not out loud and within his hearing, which is said to have bat-like qualities.'

To Dr Livingstone's amusement, Master Smith gave the predict-
able guilty reaction of looking rapidly over both shoulders, but the
vulgarian in question was nowhere to be seen. His absence had,
however, been noticed in another section of the crowd.

'How come Mr Lugg isn't in the photographic line-up? Don't
family retainers count as family?' pondered Precious Aird, who had
attached herself to Charles Luke.

'Lugg has a natural aversion to line-ups, and to having his
picture taken,' said the policeman, 'with good reason, given
his history.'

'So where is he?'

'Find out where they keep the port and you'll probably find Lugg.
He will have taken shelter there to avoid the speeches and, under
normal conditions, I'd be hiding there with him.'

Monsieur Joseph Fleurey, being involved in what might be termed
the hospitality industry, was possibly the only person in the room
aged over thirty familiar with the concept, and equipment, of *'le
disco'*, and was taking a professional interest in the sound system
hired in by The Dorchester and, being not that much over thirty, a
personal interest in the stack of records waiting to be played. The
titles represented an eclectic cross-section of British and American
pop music, and Fleurey was envious of the fact that many of the
discs were not yet available in France, although apprehensive about
how the selection of music on offer would go down with the present
audience.

'Chiaroscuro,' murmured the man standing next to him.

'Excuse me?'

'It's the name of this devilish contraption,' said L. C. Corkran.
'It's stencilled down the side of that speaker, which looks big enough
to damage the walls of Jericho. Fancy name for a purveyor of ear-
bashing sounds purporting to be music, Chiaroscuro. Something to
do with light and shade in paintings, isn't it? Leonardo Da Vinci,
Caravaggio, those chaps.'

Unsure whether this was some sort of test, Joseph said, 'I believe
so. I think it's rather a good name for a disco, but I did not expect
to find one here tonight. A military band, perhaps, or one of your
English sing-songs around the pub piano, but not the Rolling Stones
and Manfred Mann.'

'Albert's been talking about the war, I suppose,' conceded

Mr Corkran. 'Bound to, given the guests here tonight. Myself, Madame Thibus, Señora Vidal, yourself as a proxy for your father . . . all connected to Albert by the war.'

'And the German gentleman, Ringer?'

'Yes, him too.'

'Is he still here? I would like to meet him.'

'Robert's popped outside to smoke one of his terrible cheroots. Can't light one up indoors; they taint the curtains. Look out, we're being called to order for the speechifying. Best look keen; only polite, and it puts off the ghastly music for a bit.'

'Speeches should be short, brief, to the point, preferably over before they begin and, above all, short. They come in useful at the opening of Parliament but rarely once Parliament is in session. They are traditional at weddings and obligatory at funerals, but at birthdays they are usually prefaced by tiresome, off-key renditions of "Happy Birthday" – that inexplicably popular dirge which does nothing but remind the subject of his own mortality.

'I therefore decree, without let or hindrance, that there will be no singing of that gruesome anthem tonight. Nor, as the more observant of you will have noticed, are there to be any candles on this splendid cake. This is not because I no longer possess the lung capacity to extinguish them, but because such would be the number required that, once lit, they would constitute a fire hazard. The bakers of this splendid cake have, however, provided a useful *aide-mémoire* should I have forgotten my age. For anyone present not blessed with a decent education, I should explain that the numerals LXX are Latin for "21 Again", and I will brook no other translation, as it is my birthday.

'You will have noticed – or if you haven't, you soon will – that I have laid on a discotheque so that we may bop and boogie the night away. This will not be to everyone's taste, I know. Indeed, if it becomes too raucous I may well retire to my chambers where a *chaise longue* – just like the one my mother used to call her "fainting couch" – has been prepared.

'I beg the indulgence of those of my generation who will no doubt find the music on offer too loud and too fast and the songs incomprehensible, but this part of the evening's entertainment is for the youngsters here, though the young at heart are more than welcome to join in. And before anyone starts to complain about the music, I beg them to remember that when we were young, our parents said exactly the same things about us attempting the Black Bottom or the Jitterbug, and we dismissed them as old fogies.

'So my instructions, nay my orders, are that everyone should enjoy themselves, and for those who really do find the music intolerable – and yes, I am looking at you, Guffy – the bar will remain open. Until dawn, I'm told.

'It only remains for me to thank you all for being here tonight. Some have travelled many miles, and for reasons which are ancillary to any birthday celebrations, and I would like to thank them personally.

'Firstly, my old friend Freiherr Robert von Ringer, with whom I shared many adventures from undergraduate to . . . where is Robert, by the way?'

There was a comprehensive shuffling of feet and turning of heads, Mr Campion's audience acting as a single entity; or almost, until the crowd parted, and a large, mostly rotund shape advanced like a juggernaut.

'The German gentleman,' announced Lugg in his most favoured sepulchral tone, 'has been incapacitated in an incident just outside the front door of this 'ere h'establishment. Incapacitated with a knife. An ambulance 'as been summoned but the hotel management think it wise to call in the police as well.'

'I'm already here,' said Commander Charles Luke, stepping forward.

EIGHTEEN
A Place You Do Not Want to Go

Pyrénées-Atlantiques. Early November 1942

The British have always loved Pau, and the Scots are probably to blame for that. In 1840, a Scottish doctor called Alexander Taylor published a book on how the climate and mineral waters of the city had cured him of typhus. Naturally, a boom in sickly, but well-to-do, British visitors followed, and many of them must have been Scots, as by the 1860s they had established an eighteen-hole golf course; a sure sign of Caledonian imperialism. It was a relaxed place where one leisurely ritual followed another. What better, after a round of golf played in all your Victorian formal finery, than a stately promenade along the magnificent Boulevard des Pyrénées, the concrete and stone balcony which girdled the old city and provided spectacular views of the distant mountains? For the more inquisitive tourist, the stone handrail which ran the length of the boulevard had a series of V-shaped depressions at irregular intervals. By bending down and looking along the depression, the viewer was given a clear sight-line of a particular peak which an accompanying engraved plaque helpfully identified. Especially popular among young male visitors was the game of making a lady friend admire the peak named the *mamelon de singe* and then demand that she translate the name plaque.

Astrid Lunel spoke little on the drive from Toulouse, apart from giving directions to the family apartment once we had reached Pau. Her husband had told me that had been their home, although both were caught in Marseilles during the round-up of Jews. I asked her if she thought the Pau apartment would be safe, as I had no idea what the Vichy line was on the property of its Jewish victims. If the example of Germany was anything to go by, an awful lot of 'confiscation' or 'appropriation' had gone on which in any civilized context would have been labelled as pure theft.

She told me that ownership of the apartment had been put, legally, in the name of a Madame Prisca Henneuse, a widow of the First War and the concierge of the building, in late 1940 – Madame Henneuse being a family friend of the Lunels and totally trustworthy. There was no doubt at all in Astrid's mind that the apartment would be clean, warm and welcoming when we arrived, and it would be the first place her husband would head for once he was free of the clutches of the Pirani gang and Vichy.

I did not have the heart to tell her that her husband was still firmly in the clutches of Vichy, if not his criminal employers, but I was delighted that we had a base in Pau. The camp at Gurs was only thirty or so kilometres away, and Pau was the perfect jumping-off point for an escape route through the mountains into Spain, providing we could beat the winter, not to mention the small matter of obtaining Nathan Lunel's freedom.

Exactly how all this would be accomplished was still in flux, and I was both delighted and relieved to learn that the Lunel's apartment was equipped with a telephone.

The concierge, Madame Henneuse, proved to be exactly the faithful family retainer Astrid Lunel had promised, and their greeting was a genuinely warm one. The apartment had been kept spotless during the Lunels' absence and Madame Henneuse had resisted the temptation to move in, although she had every legal right to do so, preferring to remain in her two-room lair by the front door of the building. She may now technically be a woman of property, but her needs were few and, after all, she was the concierge and had her basic duties to perform: intimidating visitors and deterring tradesmen.

I was introduced to her simply as 'M'sieur Didier' and described as 'a family friend'; I would be staying only for a few days until we were joined by her husband and then we would all be leaving, and for good. Madame Henneuse looked both relieved and apprehensive at the news and interrogated Astrid about the health of both the forthcoming baby and the mother-to-be, accompanied by much fussing and the brewing of some rather unpalatable herbal tea.

When Astrid declared that she needed to bathe and find some clothes which made her look less like a gypsy fortune-teller, I managed to get Madame Henneuse alone and, using all my natural charm, got her talking about the Lunels. She did not need much encouragement, as she was relieved to have the opportunity to talk about them in the present tense after months of uncertainty.

Nathan Lunel – a true gentleman if ever there was one – and Astrid had left Pau in June that year. Nathan often worked away for long periods, and it was only natural that he would want his pregnant wife close to him, although at that time she was hardly showing.

The three of them had discussed the possibility of Vichy action against the Jews and taken what steps they could. The round-up, when it came, caught the Lunels in Marseilles, but left their Pau apartment – now no longer in their names – intact. A local Vichy official (at this point Madame Henneuse made as if to spit at the very thought) had called round to check if there were any Jews in the building and had been sent away with several fleas in his ear. No one else had visited the apartment or enquired after the Lunels that summer.

I explained that there might be some strange comings-and-goings over the coming days and discretion would be required. I need have no fear of that, Madame Henneuse assured me, as 'her' Astrid had told her that I was the bravest man she had ever met and had promised to get her and her husband out of France.

With such a glowing character reference, and several portions of Madame Henneuse's excellent *boudin noir* stew inside me, I slept like a log that night in the smaller bedroom of the apartment. I greeted the morning with a bowl of real coffee and some freshly baked rolls served with home-made apricot jam. Madame Henneuse, in my eyes, was proving herself to be invaluable, and with a view of the majestic Pyrenees from the casement windows I found it difficult to believe there was a war on.

But there was, and I had to get on with it.

The telephone in the apartment was working and I placed a call to the Hôtel Libéria in Marseilles and asked to speak to the manager.

'This is Ignatius Saint of Trinity Street, Cambridge,' I said to identify myself and indicate that I was alone and could speak safely in the code Robert and I had established.

I had spoken in English, and if Robert was in any way compromised, he would answer in French or German, demanding to know who I was and what the Dickens I was talking about.

'So, you are safe?' he answered in good, safe English. 'All of you?'

'All present and correct and quartered safe out of danger.'

'In Pau. A beautiful city, don't you think?'

'How did you know?'

'A guess; but remember, I have been taking an interest in Nathan Lunel for some time. I know about their apartment in Pau and I knew you were heading in that direction, so I took the precaution of having a man watch the place.'

'You have a local office?'

I was sure I could hear Robert smile down the wire.

'We like to know who is coming and going over all those escape routes to Spain, but Pau is perfect for our purposes and I would have suggested it myself as a base of operations. I can be there by this evening.'

'That sounds ominously like you have a plan.'

'I have, and you won't like it.'

Robert gave me an address and more things to worry about before cutting the connection, which required me to place another call, this time to a café in Toulouse, to a number which Olivier Courteaux had made me memorize as we stood on the station platform.

This time I identified myself simply as 'Didier' and asked to speak to 'Javel', which was Olivier's code name based on the Paris metro station system favoured by the Free French. I was told to telephone again in one hour and eventually had Courteaux on the line.

'I have important news,' I said.

'As I have for you,' he countered.

'But first I must know if our young friend is safe.'

'Yes, she is safe here with me. She sleeps all day and eats whenever she wakes.'

'Good. Keep her close. Actually, send her away, far away. On no account let her go back to Marseilles. She would be in great danger there.'

'Why?'

'She has made a big enemy there, in the Panier.'

'We all have enemies there,' Olivier said lightly, but there was concern in his voice. 'Have they taken the loss of their guest badly?'

'Very badly, and it is worse than that. During the . . . removal . . . of that guest, there was shooting, and one of the casualties was Paul Pirani himself.'

'Fatally?'

'No, but he will walk with a limp from now on.'

'A pity. You should have been a better shot.'

'I was not the one shooting and I did not know it was Pirani who was chasing us, but on the general principle, I have to agree with you. The Panier gang have already started a campaign of revenge. They suspect the girl and are hunting her; the first place they went was the shop of Madame Joubert.'

'Be assured, I will keep Corinne close,' said Courteaux, 'but now you must listen to me carefully. The word from our Spanish friend is that you should look to the Ilhéou valley and the black lake beyond Pont d'Espagne. He will be watching for you at noon on the Pilgrim's Way the day after tomorrow, and for the next three days. He said you would understand.'

'I do. Thank you for that.'

'Good luck, my friend. Keep safe.'

'You too – and keep the girl safe also.' I took a deep breath. 'There is something else I must tell you, but you cannot ask me how I know.'

The Frenchman did not hesitate. 'Agreed.'

'Pirani's people have also visited the Seamen's Mission, which Corinne knows well.'

'We all do. Pastor Nevin is a good friend to France.'

'Not any longer, I'm afraid,' I said with a heavy heart.

I told Astrid Lunel not to leave the apartment, use the telephone, or answer the door to anyone who had got past her loyal guard dog of a concierge, and to keep away from the windows while I was away. She looked at me with amazement and not a little scorn; it was rapidly becoming her favourite facial expression where I was concerned. With some disdain she explained that as a Jew she knew only too well how to go unnoticed, but she had no intention of leaving the apartment as she had to prepare it for the return of her husband – the very return I had promised her.

I left her just before dusk, after Madame Henneuse had given me directions to the address Robert had given me. It was a hotel near Pau Château, once the home of Henry IV, known to the French as 'good king Henry' and to generations of English schoolboys as the man who declared that Paris was 'worth a mass', which is the sort of thing schoolboys remember even if they have no idea what it meant at the time it was said.

Le Postillon was an old coaching inn, now a hotel, and had no connection other than in my infantile brain with the famous translation from a Hungarian guide book that 'my postillion has been struck by lightning', which surely ranked with *la plume de ma tante* as one of those phrases which should by law be in the vocabulary of every cosmopolitan traveller.

I did not know if Le Postillon was the Pau headquarters of the Abwehr or simply a place where Robert liked to stay, so I did not go blundering in there. Rather, I observed the place from a nearby café until a familiar Panhard drew up to the door and decanted Robert and two large suitcases. As the limousine pulled away, I noticed that it was the faithful Erik who was driving, and not for the first time reflected on the irony that in that moment my two most reliable allies in the vicinity were members of the enemy's intelligence service.

I watched the doors of the hotel for another ten minutes, eking out a small glass of red wine which the café proprietor clearly thought should have been replenished by now, then strolled across the street and into Le Postillon and asked if a Dr Haberland was in his room.

With an efficiency which suggested German rather than French management, I was told that *Professor* Haberland was in residence and expecting a visit from a Jean-Baptiste Hamelin. Thinking quickly on my feet, I remembered that was me and was shown to a room on the first floor.

'I'm glad you are safe, my friend,' Robert greeted me after stubbing out one of his odiferous cigars in the blue china saucer which served as an ashtray. 'It would be wise not to return to Marseilles.'

'I have no immediate plans to do so,' I said, 'though I assure you it was not I who attempted to assassinate Paul Pirani. I've never met the man and I usually insist on being formally introduced before I try and shoot someone.'

'Unfortunately, Pirani lives, and his men have turned the city inside out looking for Madame Lunel, the girl who shoots badly, and you. The Seamen's Mission was one of the first places they went to and your countryman Sandy Nevin took the brunt of their anger.'

'Pastor Nevin had nothing to do with it.'

'He knew the girl and he knew you, that was enough. That is why they tortured him before they killed him.'

That was one detail Robert had left out of our telephone call.

'He could not have told them anything,' I said, feeling weak and rather useless.

'Oh, do be realistic, Albert. Pastor Nevin was a conduit for escaping prisoners and airmen and he had many contacts with those who resist Vichy. He knew, or would have guessed, that you and the girl would contact the Free French in Toulouse.'

With more defiance than I truly felt I said, 'That doesn't mean Nevin told them anything.'

'I know what they did to him and would say that in all probability he did; before he died.'

'Asher,' I said.

'Excuse me?'

'Magnus Asher. He saw me at the Mission and the girl was there too. He was also involved in Lunel's financial transfers and in getting Astrid out of the Jewish round-up. I suspect Mr Asher's name will feature in Lunel's ledger of accounts. He has a vested interest in this business.'

'Which could make him more dangerous,' said Robert thoughtfully. 'Especially if he knows of the Lunels' apartment here. We must assume that by now his contacts in Les Milles will have told him that Lunel has been moved to Gurs. The Gurs camp is only thirty kilometres away and Pau is a gateway to Spain. He will make the connection.'

'Then we had better move fast. You got Nathan into Gurs easily enough, but how do we get him out?'

'Through the front gate,' said Robert, heaving first one then the other suitcase on to the bed, flicking the catches and lifting the lid, 'wearing these.'

Each case contained a pair of shiny black leather jackboots, a black peaked cap and a black uniform with diabolic silver piping and insignia.

'Albert, you're about to join the SS.'

The next morning saw us being driven out of Pau, with Erik once again our chauffeur, only this time he had exchanged the Panhard for a black Mercedes military staff car to give our expedition a more official feel. Erik was in a nondescript Wehrmacht uniform but there was no pennant flying over the bonnet. Official, but not ostentatious. Any possibility of us travelling unnoticed would quickly go up in smoke if the Mercedes was stopped and the passengers in the back seat examined. German staff cars were not unknown in Vichy, especially this close to the Occupied Zone running along the Atlantic coastline, but SS officers in full uniform were still liable to cause a stir. Neither of us carried pistols, at least not openly, as technically we were in friendly territory.

Robert had assured me that the uniforms were essential. They would give us unquestioned access to Gurs, where many of the Vichy guards had been trained by the SS in concentration camp efficiency, and throughout Europe it was known that it was never prudent to disobey the bullyboys of the SS.

When Robert had arranged the transfer of Nathan Lunel out of Les Milles, he had done it with a subtle combination of bribery, threats and fake documentation, which identified Lunel as a person of some interest to the SS, who would be collected by them from his new home in Gurs for 'onward transportation' – a phrase most Vichy officials and police had learned not to question.

He assured me that the paperwork was in order, or at least

well-enough forged to impress the officials at Gurs, and two SS
men in an official-looking car with a driver would be above suspicion. It was Robert's way of explaining why I had to be there
partaking in that horrid charade. It was not a question of sharing
the risk – that I accepted completely – it was the fact that while
one SS man might be suspect, two officers in an official car with
a driver were clearly an arrest squad.

I accepted the need for the masquerade, but it still made for an
uncomfortable journey, sitting in the back of the Mercedes with
that infamous black peaked cap on my knees, its gruesome death's-
head insignia grinning up at me.

It could have been my imagination, but I was sure I smelled the
camp at Gurs, a sour stench of dampness, smoke and open drains,
before we saw it. Perhaps it was only the overwhelming sense of
dread which closed round me like a clammy evening mist. I put it
down to having to wear that hated uniform, and the fact that it
allowed us the impunity to enter that 'place you do not want to go',
as it was known, to rescue just one of the thousands of inmates,
none of whom deserved to be there. I was further affected by Robert's
last-minute briefing speech which, although necessary, was ignoble
at heart, and nowhere near as inspiring as Harry's exhortations
before the walls of Harfleur.

'Albert, you must remember that for the next few hours, you are
a person of rank within the SS. I hesitate to use the word "officer"
for that would imply that they behave with some shred of honour.
They do not, which is why they are feared and not respected. You
must think yourself into the role, old friend. You must act as if your
orders are always obeyed instantly and never, never questioned. You
do not take orders from any Vichy official or soldier, whatever their
rank. The prisoners you ignore, for there is only one we are interested in, and he is a Jew; therefore, you do not acknowledge him,
certainly not as someone you have met before but also not as a
human being. He is a Jew, and if he looks you in the eye or fails
to remove his cap, your instinct will be to strike him. If somebody
does strike him down, you do not help him up, understand? Do you
think you could do that?'

'With difficulty,' I said, 'but I know I must try.'

The road which bisected the camp was long and straight, like an
aerodrome runway, flanked by flat fields which had been scoured of
vegetation and were now simply squares of mud. To our left the road

was lined with telephone poles which, with a low sun behind them, could prove a hypnotic danger to the unwary driver as they flashed by, adding another layer of unreality as the camp itself came into view.

The line of poles continued into the distance, but suddenly the space between them was filled with a wire fence. There were no watchtowers or machine-gun posts or minefields that I could see, and the wire fence, not much higher than a tall man, was made up of large squares like farmyard chicken wire. At first glance it would seem the easiest of obstacles to climb, the spacings in the wire forming a perfect ladder, but then I noticed the strands of barbed wire woven through the fence in large X-shaped patterns. This boundary fence protected a landscape of grey windowless wooden huts, six straight rows on each side of the road, stretching off almost as far as the eye could see and, between each row, a street of mud. Had it not been for the humans shuffling aimlessly through the ankle-deep mud – men, women and children, all wearing several layers of clothing; and, on the corners of alternate barrack blocks, ramshackle outdoor kitchens with tables and portable wood-fired stoves – the whole camp could have been a chicken farm built by the giant at the top of Jack's beanstalk.

I had not imagined the smell of open drains.

Our car was stopped at a drop-down barrier operated by two dissolute, unshaven figures in police uniforms covered by long military overcoats, possibly surplus stock from the first war several sizes too big for them, their hems thick and heavy with dried mud.

Neither looked to have the inclination or energy to unhook their rifles from their shoulders, and seemed bored with their lot in life, even as they shuffled towards the window Erik had rolled down and through which he was offering a sheaf of documents. Only when the lead guard leaned in to take them and bothered to raise his eyes did he recognize the two uniforms occupying the back seat.

From there on, things moved with commendable promptitude, as one of my old house masters would have said. A telephone call provoked the appearance of a senior camp official; clearly senior, as he was vastly overweight and his uniform was relatively mud-free.

We were asked – not told – to leave our car on the road and to report to the administration office, a white wooden building similar to the chicken huts of the barracks but with windows, a chimney and a wooden boardwalk from road to door over the mud.

On that short walk over that bouncing boardwalk, I felt as if a thousand eyes were fixed on me, or rather on the uniform I was wearing, but I followed Robert's lead, careful not to let any emotion – and certainly not sympathy – show.

Inside the office we were greeted by what I assumed was the duty officer, a swarthy individual in a uniform I did not recognize, although a wine connoisseur could probably have identified the stains down the front of the tunic. I felt no compunction at all in following Robert's example and disdainfully refusing to return the handshake offered by our odious host. I was, after all, only acting in character.

After glancing at the paperwork Robert had thrust at him, our Vichy gaoler issued orders to his minions to fetch the prisoner, then settled himself primly behind his desk.

'So, *mon colonel*, what is so special about this Jew? We have many Jews here now. This camp was designed for illegal immigrants – Spanish Republicans, communists and renegades from the International Brigade – but now we have an equal number of Jews and more arriving every day. May I ask why this particular Jew?'

'Because he is a person of interest to the Reich,' growled Robert. 'That is all you need to know, and I am not a colonel; my rank is Sturmbannführer.'

Our host asked no more questions after that, taking a concentrated interest in the few scraps of paper on his desk to while away the uncomfortable silence. Robert, imperiously, turned to me and said in German: 'Obersturmführer, put your cap on straight.'

I snapped to attention once I remembered that was the rank – lower than his, of course – Robert had assigned to me, and straightened my hat, pulling the visor low over my eyes. It was something we had discussed in the car. Hopefully the shock of seeing the SS uniforms would prevent Lunel from recognizing me, at least initially, but it was wise to hide as much of my face as possible and, as he was a Jew and I was a Nazi, I had perfectly good reasons not to look him in the eyes. I could only imagine how I would feel to suddenly discover that the dashingly handsome Pimpernel Smith figure who had offered hope and freedom had turned into the hated enemy.

'I thought he was going to have a heart attack,' Robert said in English once we were in the car.

'So did I,' said Nathan Lunel.

He and I were in the back seat, Robert riding next to our driver Erik. I think Nathan had recognized me within a few moments of being pushed into the administration office, made to remove his wool cap and confirm his name and prisoner number to the Vichy official. Fortunately, the sight of two men in those black Satanic uniforms froze his nerve-endings and his vocal chords, so that his voice was little more than a croak as he acknowledged his name and was signed over into Sturmbannführer Ringer's custody; a ceremony which for me conjured up the image of a transaction at a slave sale on the docks of Savannah.

'How did you manage to get me transferred here?' he asked, even while we were still within the camp confines, motoring on the long straight road lined with telephone poles and wire.

'I told you I had friends in low places,' I said, and saw Robert shake his head, even as he was lighting one of his cheroots which I was sure had been dipped in tar during their manufacture. 'The rest was a game of bluff, and I've always been rather good at that.'

From the front of the car came a snort of mild derision and a cloud of acrid smoke. Perhaps Robert had a point, as I realized that the inside rim of my SS cap, which I had taken off and rested on my knees, was stained and damp with sweat.

Of the three of us, Nathan Lunel seemed to have recovered his wits the quickest.

'Where do we go from here?'

'To Pau, to collect your wife.'

His face blossomed, and he seemed to grow back into the clothes which had fitted him before prison.

'Astrid? You got her out?'

'I said I would, and with the help of some brave Frenchmen – and women – she is now safe in your apartment in Pau, gossiping with Madame Henneuse, who has kept the place immaculate. It was a clever move to sign the apartment over to her. Who else knew about it?'

Lunel shrank back into the upholstery of the seat. 'Magnus Asher did,' he said bitterly. 'He knew everything. The man is an evil spider with a large web.'

'Then Pau will not be safe. We will move on quickly.'

'Into Spain?'

'It is a hard road and will not be easy for Astrid in her condition.'

Lunel allowed himself a smile.

'Do not worry about my wife. She is a strong woman and her condition is just one more reason for us moving quickly.'

'I have a better reason,' said Robert, jabbing a finger at the car's windscreen. Then he rolled down his window and stuck out his head, looking to the sky.

Only then did I hear the sound of a low-flying airplane engine, and I quickly followed Robert's example, lowering my window and leaning out into the car's slipstream.

Almost directly above us was a Fieseler Storch, a 'stork', although they always reminded me more of a mayfly: the small, single-engine spotter plane beloved of the German military. I could clearly see the black cross with white border on the fuselage and the swastika on the tailfin.

Beside me, Nathan Lunel had shrunk in his seat and was trying to squeeze himself into the footwell behind the driver's seat. 'Are we under attack?'

'No, don't worry,' I tried to reassure him, 'the plane is unarmed.'

Indeed, it had already flown over us, following the road to Gurs.

Robert threw his cigar out of the window and turned in his seat, his face like granite. 'We have less time than we thought,' he said.

'What does he mean?' Lunel asked, his voice cracking.

'That plane was acting as a forward observer for the army,' said Robert. 'The German army has activated Case Anton. The Wehrmacht is invading Vichy France.'

'Which means in turn,' I said, 'that the Allies are in the process of invading North Africa. There could be something of a run on the banks there unless we can stop it.'

NINETEEN
The Scar Outlives the Wound

The Dorchester Hotel, London. 20 May 1970

A woman screamed. It was a shrill falsetto of a scream; a scream of surprise rather than pain, and undoubtedly female in origin. In the general confusion of jostling bodies and turning heads it was some moments before the vocalist was identified as Sophia Longfox, and a good minute before her father, the

Earl of Pontisbright, managed to shoulder his way through the crowd to comfort her. By the time Hal reached his daughter, the concerned guests who had gathered around her had relaxed somewhat, having assured themselves that she was not herself physically injured.

Sophia confirmed this by pointing frantically towards the door of the hotel – the raising of her statuesque arm resulting in a tinkling of jewellery – and directing the onlookers, as her son Edward later recalled (quietly) 'like an insane traffic policeman'.

'What is it? What's out there?' demanded Hal Fitton, placing firm hands on Sophia's shoulders.

His daughter gulped air before answering, the revellers crowding round her, hanging on her every word and dramatic pause.

'A body . . . There's a body lying on the ground . . . I popped out for some fresh air and almost fell over it . . . There's a knife sticking out of him . . . I think I've got blood on my shoes . . .'

'Stabbed? Somebody's been stabbed? Look to one of the foreigners!'

'Johnny, really!' scolded Lady Carados. 'How can you say such a thing?'

'Stands to reason,' bridled her husband. 'There's German, French, Spanish, even Americans here tonight: who knows who they are? Everyone else is family, or friends of family, and none of us would think of spoiling a party with a surprise homicide.'

'Actually, that sounds just the sort of stunt Albert would pull,' observed Jolyon Livingstone, who had attached himself to Lord and Lady Carados as the party had drifted out of the dining room, 'if half the stories of his undergraduate pranks at Cambridge are to be believed.'

'Seventy's too old for pranks and tomfoolery,' said Johnny Carados gruffly, 'and everyone says he became much more serious after the war. Can't see him putting on a show with a fake corpse. Damn bad taste at a birthday party, if you ask me.'

A minor earthquake in the form of Magersfontein Lugg pushed his way through them, a biblical parting of the water performed by a dinner suit stuffed with rocks.

'There ain't no corpse, fake or otherwise, leastwise not yet. A nasty flesh wound in the back and a crack on the 'ead as 'e fell over and hit the steps. He'll live.'

Lugg was already beyond them, the crowd deciding that avoiding his oncoming momentum was the better part of valour.

'Who?' cried Dr Livingstone at the expanse of Lugg's broad back. 'Who's been stabbed?'

'The German gentleman, Baron von Ringer, only the flamin' guest of honour after 'is nibs, that is,' grumbled the big man without turning his head.

'See!' Johnny Carados pounced. 'I told you it was foreigners!'

'There's nothing you can do, Albert, so stay out of it,' said Amanda. 'Charles has everything under control.'

'But I need to be sure Robert is all right,' said Mr Campion, removing his spectacles and polishing them furiously with his handkerchief.

'The ambulance men are taking good care of him,' said Luke. 'Once they've got him settled in hospital, I'll have the Yard send a man to sit with him.'

'In case somebody tries again?'

'Perdita, don't be so melodramatic.'

'It's her job, darling,' said Mr Campion quietly, 'but Charles is right to consider all eventualities, that's his. Personally, I don't think there will be any further incidents of being stabbed in the back, except perhaps on grounds of party politics.'

'How do you know he was stabbed in the back?' Luke pounced.

'A shot in the dark, my dear Clouseau, as they say in the pictures. I have no gory details, but here comes Lugg. He's sure to have.'

Mr Lugg eased his Titanic bulk through the bobbing surf of concerned and panicky guests with serene calm, and docked himself firmly next to the Campions, leaning forward so that his report could be heard in private.

'Well this is a shindig they won't forget in a hurry. Mind you, half of them think it's part of the after-dinner cabaret.'

Mr Campion fixed the big man with his best owlish stare. 'Thank you for that quite superfluous observation, Lugg. Have you got anything remotely useful to tell us?'

'Only what you've probably surmised yerself by now,' said Lugg, doing his best to look offended. 'That it was an inside job.'

He turned imperiously on Charles Luke and waved a sausage of a finger over his shoulder, indicating the murmuring crowd behind him. 'Got your Warrant Card with you, Charlie? I reckon you should make a start questioning this lot.'

'Don't you – of all people – tell me how to do my job,' said Luke severely. 'You're sure it wasn't a spur-of-the-moment thing? Well-to-do hotel guest wearing a dinner jacket steps outside for a cigar, some passing young hooligan on a motorbike thinks he can wave a flick-knife around and relieve him of his wallet, then things turn nasty. It happens, you know, and not just in Soho.'

Lugg wrinkled his nose and pursed his lips, savouring his moment. 'You didn't get a close look at the knife, did you? I did. It was the same knife that went missing this very evening, during dinner. Why do you think we haven't cut the cake yet?'

Luke narrowed his eyes and bit his lip. 'I'll make sure no one leaves. Albert, I may need you if any of your guests turn ugly.'

'My dear Charles, most of them are naturally ugly, but it's only skin deep. I'm sure they will behave.'

As Luke pressed his way towards the door, reassuring and calming the guests as he went, Amanda reached for her husband's hand.

'Albert, what happened to Robert – it's not got anything to do with those war stories you've been telling all night, is it?'

Campion automatically took her hand in his and patted it reassuringly. 'I'm sorry, darling, but I'm afraid it probably has.'

TWENTY
Menu Pèlerin

Pau and the Pyrenees. November 1942

Astrid Lunel screamed, then burst into tears and began to swing both clenched fists when she saw her husband for the first time in more than three months. It was a reaction I had not anticipated and for a moment thought I must still be wearing my SS uniform.

But for once I was not to blame, nor even the target. Indeed, I might not have been in the room with them. My presence was blissfully ignored as the pregnant wife berated the hapless husband, not just with her fists but with a stream of invective which would have made a docker blush, even a Marseilles docker.

Since we had been buzzed by the spotter plane, Nathan Lunel had spent most of the journey from Gurs hunched, half on the seat, half in the footwell of the Mercedes. Uncharitably he reminded me of a large, hapless gun dog, the sort that is a bad traveller and simply cannot get comfortable enough in a car to fall asleep. I also felt guilty that my nose detected a doggy aroma coming off his soiled clothing.

Only when we reached Pau did he sit up straight in his seat and risk looking out of the window. Even then, he flinched when a pedestrian looked directly at the car and positively squirmed when we saw a gendarme.

At Le Postillon we left him in the car under the protection of Erik while Robert and I hurried inside and up to his room to change back into more civilized clothing.

'Did you notice the staff glaring at these uniforms when you picked up your key?' I asked him as I struggled to de-boot myself.

'I am a German in France, I am used to being stared at,' he said, pulling on his suit trousers.

'You don't think the news . . .?'

'I doubt it. We would have seen more people on the street and more police, but I will not know for sure until I contact my superiors.' He barked out a laugh at a private thought. 'Or I could wait until the evening news on the BBC and find out what my own army is doing.'

Then as he began to tie his shoelaces, he became more serious.

'I may be recalled to Marseilles as soon as I report to the local office, so it is perhaps best if we say goodbye here. I realize that from now on, your journey will take you on one of the well-trodden escape routes which you should not reveal to an enemy, so it is best if I do not know the details. Is there anything I can provide to help you on your way?'

'Petrol,' I said as I continued to change back into Didier Ducret. 'I will need more petrol, enough for two hundred kilometres.'

Robert smiled as he tied a blue silk tie.

'Which means you will be driving no more than *one* hundred kilometres, unless you intend to take your car up mountains where there are no roads. Still, it is always good practice to spread disinformation about one's plans.'

'You will, though, forgive a freshman spy for trying, won't you?'

'Freshman?'

'Well, undergraduate then, trying to impress his professors.'

'You give me too much credit and yourself too little,' Robert said, easing himself into his jacket. 'Tell me where you left the car and I will have Erik make sure it has fuel. I'll leave you to escort Lunel to his apartment and his wife and to do what has to be done with his ledger of bank accounts. I trust you to do that, Albert, because you know what is at stake.'

Robert fastened the middle button of his suit jacket and examined the results of his rapid costume change in the full-length mirror on the room's oak wardrobe.

'I will try and justify your confidence,' I said, hopping on one foot as I struggled with my own clothing.

'Then I will wish you good luck and say goodbye in the hope that we will meet in more convivial times.' Robert clicked his heels together, gave me a curt bow and held out his right hand.

'You have my thanks,' I said, 'and my warmest wishes. Please do take care of yourself. This stupid war can be quite dangerous at times, and you must promise to survive so that we can continue our friendship in peacetime. But please forgive me if I do not shake your hand, as it is absolutely forbidden – by all the laws of etiquette, form and good manners – for an Englishman to shake hands when he is not wearing trousers.'

Nathan Lunel took the battering and the abuse being dished out in equal proportions by his wife with great stoicism and only the occasional grunt of pain. A younger man might well have let his wife continue to exorcize her pent-up emotions until she had exhausted herself, but Lunel was of an older generation and calmed the storm as quickly as he could by pinning his wife's arms to her side and talking slowly and patiently to her. Eventually he took her head in his hands and brought her forehead to his lips in a chaste but loving gesture, for he was of the generation which frowned on displays of emotion in front of strangers; in this case, me.

'Madame Lunel,' I said, 'I told you I would reunite you with your husband, but we must plan for the next stage of our journey and we must do so with all haste.'

I was not sure either of them had heard a word I had said. Astrid was now stroking her husband's head as he bent over to rub his cheek over the curve of his wife's pregnant belly.

'Jean-Baptiste is right, my love,' he murmured dreamily, 'we have to leave Pau.'

'Who is Jean-Baptiste?' asked Astrid, equally dreamily.

'Your wife knows me as Didier Ducret,' I said quickly. 'I answer to both names.'

'And no doubt several others,' said Lunel.

I refrained from telling Lunel how right he was; and from offering him any examples.

'When we get to Spain, I will reveal my true identity,' I offered, 'but only if you insist, and only then if you ply me with dry sherry. Until then, call me what you will, but you must accept me as your tour guide and leader.'

'He has looked after me well so far,' said Astrid, 'and he has kept his word about bringing you home to me.'

I nodded my appreciation of the generous character reference and half expected her husband to second it, which only proves it never pays to be too pleased with yourself.

'He is being well rewarded for his trouble. In fact, he has charged a very high price.'

I knew Lunel had been through a lot and was speaking more out of nervous relief rather than anger, but even so I decided to lay down the law.

'My reward is to foil a criminal conspiracy whereby evil men will profit, for me it is a duty and an obligation. Your reward is three tickets to freedom. *Three*, M'sieur Lunel: remember your unborn child. That is your duty, your obligation now. If you think we have made an unfair bargain, then perhaps we should renegotiate terms.'

He looked at his wife and slipped an arm around her shoulders.

'I am sorry if I sound ungrateful. You will get my ledger just as soon as my wife is safely in Spain.'

'When we are *all* safe, my dear,' Astrid corrected him, but it was to me that she flashed a warning look.

'The ledger is here in Pau?'

'It is nearby,' he said carefully. 'But you will not find it without my help.'

I could not help but bridle at that. 'I was not planning to steal it, merely trying to ascertain that it was at hand, because we cannot stay here long. I suggest you ask your wife if she would kindly draw you a bath and find you a change of clothes. Outdoor clothes, a good coat and stout shoes or boots. We will have some rough walking to do. Take a bag, but essentials only. Some food would be good and a bottle of brandy perhaps. It will not, I am afraid, be an easy journey for one in your condition, madam.'

'Let me worry about my condition, m'sieur.' Astrid patted her midriff bulge. 'My little passenger will not slow us down.'

I had my reservations about that but kept them to myself.

'Are we allowed to know where you are taking us?' Lunel asked.

'I don't see why not; you should learn the route we intend to follow.' I left off the caveat 'in case anything happens to me'. 'Do you have a map of the Lourdes area, out towards Cauterets? As large a scale as possible.'

They both looked as puzzled as if I had asked them to describe a spiral staircase without using their hands, but Nathan snapped out of the trance first.

'Madame Henneuse will have. She and her husband were great cyclists before the last war. I doubt if the terrain has changed much since then.'

'Not where we're going,' I agreed.

Astrid busied herself preparing Nathan's ablutions before disappearing downstairs to raid Madame Henneuse's map-drawer. She returned clutching a faded, much-folded road map with a torn cover, which extolled the health benefits of a day cycling out on the open road, but also the labour-saving benefits of the latest Singer sewing machine, should the lady of the house decide to stay at home.

When Nathan finally emerged from the bathroom, he was wearing a wool dressing gown over rather gruesome lime-green silk pyjamas, his cheeks red and stinging from an aromatic aftershave and his remaining hair wet and slicked back, revealing a large proportion of exposed dome.

Astrid had cleared the dining table and I laid out the map, regretting only that I did not have a swagger stick or pointer, as that would make it seem more of a proper briefing.

'We go by car to Lourdes and then—'

'*The Song of Bernadette*,' said Nathan.

'I beg your pardon?'

'*The Song of Bernadette*. It's a novel about Catholics and Lourdes, written by a Czech Jew called Franz Werfel. He used to live near Marseilles.'

'Used to?'

He shrugged his shoulders. 'Who knows now? He was a writer whose books were burned by the Nazis.'

'That alone is reason enough to fight them,' I said, 'and perhaps he got out before the round-ups. What we have to do is make sure we get out while we can. That does not involve making side visits to places of interest such as Lourdes, whether out of literary curiosity or religious devotion. We go from there to Cauterets.'

My finger traced the road south, the lines on the map getting thinner and the contours more intimidating. 'Beyond Cauterets there's a tourist spot with a view – a "panorama" – known as the Pont d'Espagne. There we leave the car and trust to our sturdy footwear, because from there we will be hiking, mostly uphill, carrying anything we might need, so if you have rucksacks all the better. Should we need it, and I think we might, there is a shepherd's refuge – a hut – where we can stay overnight. It is not, I am told, equipped with many comforts, in fact none at all, but the conditions cannot be worse than those you have had to suffer in recent weeks. From there, a sprightly step up a mountain path and we can look over into Spain. By which time our Spanish guide should be looking down on us. His name will be Vidal, by the way.'

'You are taking us on the old pilgrims' way, aren't you?' said Lunel.

'One of them. There were many routes over the Pyrenees for those on pilgrimage to Santiago de Compostela. We are treading in the footsteps of the devout.'

'We are hardly pilgrims going about our devotions, we are fleeing for our lives as the Jews fled out of Egypt to escape Pharaoh.'

'I hope that doesn't make me Moses,' I said. 'That is altogether far too much responsibility.'

Madame Henneuse, with supreme ingenuity, had conjured up a spicy stew with chunks of belly pork, and joined us for what she had guessed would be the Lunels' last meal in Pau. There was wine, naturally, and a good bottle too, from Nathan's own stock which she had guarded closely in the months he had been gone. As he opened it and proposed a toast, wishing ourselves a *bon voyage*, he told Madame Henneuse to drink or sell the remaining bottles and not to hold any foolish notions about saving things for their return.

The old woman sniffed loudly and dabbed her eyes with a ball of lace handkerchief when Astrid added that she should treat the furniture as her own and if need be sell it or burn it as fuel, should the winters be harsh.

Miraculously, she produced a small bag of coffee beans which, she said, she had 'hidden away like a squirrel', and Astrid, squealing in delight at the prospect of a pot of real coffee, grabbed them and hurried off to the kitchen to brew it. Her husband offered to help and followed her.

When we were alone at the table, Madame Henneuse spoke to me directly and with a steely passion.

'The way we have treated our Jews is shameful. The Lunels have always been kind and generous people. When my husband was killed by the Boches, M'sieur Nathan found me the position as concierge and always made sure I had money for the doctor, even for the church, though it was not his religion. I look on him as a brother; when he took Astrid for his wife, he asked my opinion before he did so.

'At first I hesitated, because she is so much younger than he is, but I could see that she felt for him as much as he did for her. They have not had long together and now there is a child on the way. Astrid is strong, Nathan is not as strong as he thinks he is. You will take care of them, m'sieur? Whoever you are, you must.'

'I will do my very best, madame,' I said, and then there was the sound of the door buzzer being pressed repeatedly and Madame Henneuse froze in her seat.

'Allow me,' I said, rising from the table and closing my hand around the butt of the pistol in my jacket pocket.

'Who is this?' Astrid's voice was nervous and high-pitched.

'This is Professor Haberland,' I said quickly, taking my hand out of my pocket. 'He is an ally.'

'He is a German,' said Lunel.

Having taken no more than two steps into the dining room, Robert was faced with a scene which could have been mistaken for an interrupted séance. There was Madame Henneuse, the fraudulent medium, seated at the table, quivering nervously, as if her trickery had just been exposed. Behind her, clutching each other in the kitchen doorway, the Lunels were playing the part of the hidden assistants, suddenly revealed, who made the creaking and knocking noises at the appropriate times and cooked up ectoplasm as and when required. All that was missing was the sickly smell of scented candles.

'Do you have it?' Robert asked me.

His tone indicated that he was anxious, not to say nervous, which in turn made me nervous, and my right hand remained deep in my jacket pocket clutching my cold metal comforter.

'I'm told it is nearby and easily accessed.'

'Then get it and go. Go now if you can.'

'He is frightening me,' Astrid told her husband.

Robert drew himself up and nodded in turn to both women, while I offered a silent prayer that he would refrain from clicking his heels in salute.

'Madame Lunel and Madame . . .' he began.

'Henneuse; loyal family retainer and concierge,' I supplied in English.

'Forgive me if my arrival has frightened you,' said Robert in French. 'I wish you no harm, in fact quite the opposite. I wish you a safe journey out of France, but I urge you to go quickly. Now, if possible; but by first light at the latest.'

'It is the invasion?' Nathan found his voice.

'Invasion?' Madame Henneuse's face began to melt.

'Of North Africa,' I said quickly, before her hopes got too high.

'Somehow the Americans have assembled an invasion fleet of seven hundred ships which have sailed across the Atlantic and are landing troops in Morocco and Algeria.'

'An unpleasant surprise for you, I imagine,' I said.

'A surprise, but not an unexpected one.' Robert was in no mood for flippancy. 'As a security measure, the German army is already crossing from the Occupied Zone to take control of Vichy France. I expect that our advance armoured units will be entering Marseilles at around four o'clock in the morning. By lunchtime, there will be loudspeaker vans on the streets of Pau announcing the end of Vichy; a curfew will no doubt be imposed and movement restricted.'

Lunel was automatically suspicious of such news coming from a German he had only seen previously in SS uniform.

'What if the Americans fail in their landings?'

'That is unlikely. In the short term, the landings will face only half-hearted opposition from French troops, many of whom will not want to die for Vichy and will go over to the Free French.'

'*Vive la France!*' said a joyless Madame Henneuse, folding her arms and planting her elbows on the table in a stubbornly patriotic gesture, indicating 'and there's an end to the matter'.

'The Americans will secure their beach-heads one way or another

and begin landing men and material. The Afrika Korps is already
hard-pressed in Egypt and Libya and will now have a new enemy
in the west. Supplying them will become impossible as the Allies
pour ships into the Mediterranean and establish superiority in
the air. Our Italian friends will not prove much of a hindrance to
them, and the war in North Africa will soon be over.'

'A fact which will not be lost on our friends in the cabal,' I added.

Astrid tugged at her husband's arm.

'What is this cabal he speaks of?'

'The men I was forced to work for,' said Lunel. 'The depositors,
as I called them; the names in my ledger.'

She stared, unblinking, towards Robert and me, as if we had
entered under the door rather than through it.

'The ledger is what they want, isn't it? It is the only reason these
men are helping us. What else would make a German and an
Englishman work together? Do they want those bank accounts for
themselves?'

I felt Robert stiffen next to me, but before he could leap to our
defence, Madame Henneuse, of all people, did so.

'My God, girl, does it matter why they are helping you? Who
else is going to? France's Israelites have few friends now, and if
the Boches are coming, they will have many more enemies.'

The old woman levered herself up from her seat, placed both her
hands on her stomach, pushed out her hips and faced Astrid.

'You are no longer allowed to think about anything except saving
what you carry inside you. If these men can get you and your child
to safety, go with them. Do not question their reasons. Do not
question anything. Just go!'

Lunel took his wife's hand and kissed it. 'Madame Henneuse
talks complete sense, my dear. Start packing.'

'Good,' said Robert. 'Now I will leave you to your preparations.
It is best that I do not know the details of your journey. Will you
see me out . . .' he paused and then remembered, 'Didier.'

'With pleasure, Professor.'

As we walked down the stairs to the front door and Madame
Henneuse's temporarily deserted concierge outpost, I asked Robert
how he had gained entry.

'I had a local man watching the place. Being a good German,
he was efficient and acquired a spare key from the electricians
who rewired the building last year. The Abwehr does not kick

doors down unless it really has to; unlike the Gestapo, who do it for fun.'

'It is odd to hear the words "Gestapo" and "fun" uttered in the same breath,' I said. 'I suppose we'll have them on our trail now like a pack of Beagles.'

Robert put on his schoolmaster face. 'Do not make light of the Gestapo, Albert. I strongly suspect that some of the accounts in Lunel's ledger belong to high-ranking officers and, like all the cabal, they will think that their investment is about to pay off in dollars. You must hurry and get the ledger to the Allies. You are sure Lunel has it?'

'So he says.'

'Make sure you relieve him of it before you turn him loose in Spain.'

'And if he refuses to hand it over?'

'Shoot him and take it,' Robert said without hesitation.

'I doubt that will be necessary, Nathan cares too much about his unborn child. And in any case, I could not shoot an unarmed man.'

'Do not be so sure, Albert. When the time comes, you will do what you have to do.'

'And on that cheery note, old chum, we had better say goodbye again.'

As we solemnly shook hands, Robert pulled me closer in. 'Good luck, my friend. Remember, you will be alone until you reach Spain. Anyone following you is almost certainly an enemy. You carry the fortunes of many dangerous men with you; think of it like that. And they may be closer than you know.'

'You mean among the invading Wehrmacht?'

'Perhaps, but I was thinking more of the scum Lunel associated with in Marseilles.'

'Pirani?'

'I'm sure he would slit your throat if he could, but he is incapacitated with a bullet in his leg. It is his attack-dog, the Britisher, who worries me more.'

'Magnus Asher?'

'Yes. A deserter, a traitor, a crook and almost certainly the man who tortured Pastor Nevin before killing him. My men in Marseilles tell me that he has not been seen for two days. For all we know, he could be here, right now.'

Robert's rather gloomy valediction had me glancing over my

shoulder as I herded the Lunels through the dark streets to where I had left the Citroën. Robert had been as good as his word and the car had been refuelled, with a spare can in the boot.

I insisted that we all tried to get a few hours' sleep before we departed, if only because I was exhausted and knew I had to drive the next day. I doubted very much that the Lunels would attempt to do a moonlight flit without me, but just to be sure, I slept on the chaise longue only a yard or so from their bedroom door. They would have had to shin down a drainpipe or virtually step over me to make their escape, and I doubted Astrid, in her condition, could do either.

We sneaked out of the apartment building an hour before daylight, like burglars, with bags slung over our shoulders. Being the only one with no personal possessions other than the pistol in my pocket, and no spare clothing, other than a pullover borrowed from Lunel's wardrobe, my suitcase having been left in my hotel room in Marseilles as a cunning diversion, I carried the expedition's iron rations: some spiced sausage, a small cheese, a packet of hard biscuits, two very heavy screw-top glass jars filled with *confit de canard*, a pot of *rillette* and a bottle of brandy, the whole lot cushioned by balled-up pages of newspaper to prevent breakages and clanking.

Madame Henneuse had done us proud yet again, and I felt a twinge of guilt by even wondering if we could trust her. From the map she had provided and what she must have overheard, or been told by Astrid, she knew as much about our escape route as any of us. As we could not take her with us, not that she would have gone, I risked all the Gallic indignation in the world by asking her to promise not to speak of the Lunels' reappearance in Pau.

By some miracle of navigation, I steered us out of the city without mishap. If we were seen, it was only by a baker hurrying to light his ovens and, by the time we reached Lourdes, the morning's bread was already being queued for by lines of women clutching their ration books and no doubt offering silent prayers to Saint Bernadette that the line would move faster and that the baker had made enough to go around.

'Will there be snow in the mountains?' Astrid asked from the back seat.

'On the high peaks I think there is always snow, but I am no mountaineer,' I answered. 'I do have a friend who is, and he always said that climbing in the Pyrenees was no more difficult than a strenuous walk in the hills of Scotland, and the weather was usually better here.'

To be honest I had no idea what my old chum Jonathan Eager-Wright thought about climbing the Pyrenees, but it was necessary to instil some confidence into the Lunels, both of whom – one by age and a sedentary occupation and the other by pregnancy – were ill-suited to the trek that lay before them.

As dawn broke, and the granite peaks of mountains older than the Alps loomed even closer, the burden I was placing on the Lunels began to weigh heavily on me. I had impressed upon them to wear several layers of clothing and their most sensible, toughest shoes, but I realized that both had been physically weakened by their months in captivity. In comparison, despite a public school diet in my youth and wartime rationing, I was a positive Olympian. Still, I reasoned, they had the best possible incentive to face the rigors ahead: survival.

They must have found the prospect daunting, for they were ominously quiet during the journey, and it was not until we were beyond Lourdes and on the twisting and ever-rising road through Argelès-Gazost and a dozen straggly hamlets towards Cauterets, that Nathan finally broke his thoughtful silence.

'These are pretty farms.'

'It is all beautiful country here,' I said.

'It seems so clean. The air has a quality I had forgotten, or perhaps never appreciated before. Will I ever see France again?'

'I do not see why not,' I said with, I hoped, conviction. 'The war cannot last forever and there can be only one outcome – the Germans will be defeated, and France will be free.'

'You are sure of that?'

'As sure as I have ever been about anything in my life.'

'Sure enough for *three* lives?'

'Four,' I said. 'Don't forget the baby.'

I drove on through the pretty village of Cauterets which, if my calculations were correct, would be the last pocket of habitation in France we would see. From there on, the road became narrower, hardly a road at all, and that would soon become a track and we would have to abandon the car. If we were lucky, we might see a shepherd stalking the hillsides, perhaps even a wild chamois, which were known locally as *isards*. If we were very lucky, we would encounter no other humans, not even fellow pilgrims.

Those pilgrims who had come this way over the centuries would surely have appreciated the beauty of the tall pines, meadows, bubbling streams and glistening waterfalls as we approached the Pont d'Espagne – and then there was the bridge itself, an impressive stone arch spanning a rushing sluice of white water. It was the perfect place to stop for breakfast, gather our strength and gird our loins for the climb ahead.

I pulled the car over to the side of the road just before the bridge and we walked to the middle of the span, where I balanced my bag on the stone parapet and began to unpack our picnic.

'Our *Menu Pèlerin*,' I announced. 'Perhaps not an authentic pilgrims' menu but the best we can do in the circumstances. Madame Henneuse has provided everything except cutlery, but I have a penknife we can share. I suggest we save the brandy until we get higher – and colder.'

'How much higher do we go?' asked Astrid.

'In height about another two thousand metres. In distance, perhaps six or seven kilometres.'

I checked my wristwatch to find it was not yet ten o'clock, yet it had already seemed like a long day.

'I suggest we make a start as soon as we cross the bridge. I am hoping the trail will be marked. In fact, there are so many trails from here, my only concern is picking the right one. I propose we keep going until noon, so let us eat our breakfast, put our best foot forward and whistle a happy tune as we go. I must say, this *rillette* is delicious . . . Oh my goodness, how stupid of me! I never thought, fool that I am, about our food. It's not kosher is it?'

'Do not worry,' said Nathan scooping up some of the potted meat with a biscuit, 'we are not strict. We find we draw less attention to ourselves that way, and Madame Henneuse knows our tastes.'

'She seems to be a positive angel.'

'She is one of the few French citizens I would trust never to betray us,' said Lunel, then corrected himself. 'No, the *only* one.'

Conscious of the fact that by all the 'tradecraft' I had been taught by my lords and masters in intelligence, in Madame Henneuse I had left a classic 'loose end', I only hoped that my tutors were wrong, and Nathan Lunel was right.

We crossed the bridge. As soon as I could, I pulled off the road – now an unmade, rock-strewn track – and parked close to an exposed piece of granite as big as a double-decker bus. I did not bother to lock or disable the Citroën as no one could follow us in it, and hopefully some passing pilgrim would find a use for it. It would be a crime against such beautiful scenery if it was allowed to rust to death and remain an eyesore on the landscape.

The first part of our trek was easy enough, essentially through meadows along the floor of a small valley, with only the occasional exposed granite boulder to hint at what was to come. The biggest obstacles we faced were the streams we had to cross, and Nathan's insistence that his pregnant wife must not attempt to jump, even though she protested that she was perfectly capable of doing so, and to be lifted and passed over from one set of male arms to the other. I suspected that if I had been wearing a cloak, Nathan would have expected me to lay it down if the going got muddy.

Our progress slowed dramatically as soon as we reached the first scree slope, and the muscles in my legs told me in no uncertain terms that we were now walking up an incline of forty-five degrees; my heels registered every slip and twist of walking over a stony surface.

I took the lead by default, keeping one eye constantly open for the small stone cairns which marked the trail, many of them adorned with scallop shells, the traditional symbol of the true pilgrim. The other eye was always over my right shoulder on Astrid, who was being gently pushed up the slope by her husband, although – of the three of us – his was the reddest face and his breath rasped loudest, something which would not ease the higher we climbed.

At noon we stopped to rest, eat and break open the brandy at the foot of a scree slope, the steepest incline we had yet faced.

While the Lunels ate, I scrambled up the slope to scout the easiest route, a sort of zigzag tack across the stony surface, and at the top took my bearings. Directly ahead, across a small meadow, the landscape became even more rugged, with the openings of five valleys converging, each one offering a narrow funnel up into the mountains proper.

I returned to the Lunels, scrambling sideways down the scree, my shoes filling with small stones and dust.

'If I have my bearings correct,' I said with more confidence than I felt, 'there are five valleys ahead, and the one we want is the middle one. We follow the trail through it until we see a lake and a refuge – a shepherd's hut, most likely – but I am told it can offer shelter if not comfort should the weather turn. In that respect, we have been very lucky so far.'

'You seem very familiar with the terrain,' said Lunel.

'I was well briefed. This route has been used by shot-down airmen for over a year.'

'Do the Germans know of the route?'

'I hope not, but others may.'

'You are thinking of that other Englishman, Asher. He would help British prisoners-of-war escape to Spain, if the price was right.'

'He seems to have had a crooked finger in many a pie,' I said, realizing that the phrase probably meant less in French than in English. 'Let us not worry about him, let us concentrate on the task ahead. When we find the refuge, we can rest before our final climb, but we must find it while we have daylight. Try and follow in my footsteps but be careful, the ground is loose and slippery. Best you hold my hand, Astrid.'

Despite her condition, and the fact that she was wearing battered black leather dance shoes from which the metal taps had been removed, hardly Eiger-appropriate footwear, Astrid proved to be made of strong stuff, and her progress up that slope would have impressed even Corporal Colgan at his Commando school in Scotland. I felt sure Astrid would have earned a grunt of approval from the way she tackled that scree slope. But I would have received several demerits, if not one of his infamous bawlings-out, because while I had been so concerned for Astrid, I had temporarily forgotten Nathan, bringing up the rear.

We were painfully close to the top when he slipped, his right leg buckling under him and his arms flailing as he tried but failed to keep his balance and he tumbled back down the slope, screaming. All I could do was grip Astrid's hand even more tightly and look on helplessly as Nathan slid, rolled and bounced all the way to the bottom in an avalanche of small, sharp stones.

'Stay here. For God's sake, stay here. I'll get him.'

I pulled Astrid over the top of the slope and forced her to sit down on level ground, thrust my bag into her arms and set off at reckless speed down the slope.

I could see Nathan was in a bad way well before I reached him. His face was covered in dirt and blood from a dozen or more cuts and scratches, and he had lost the flat workman's cap he had been wearing. He was lying in a foetal position, his arms reaching down towards his left foot, which was bent at a sickeningly unnatural angle.

'Is it broken?' I asked, leaning over him and hopefully shielding him from Astrid's viewpoint above us.

'I do not think so, merely a sprain,' he gasped.

'A bad sprain. Can you stand?'

I pulled him upright, realizing for the first time how little he weighed and how his clothes hung on quite a slender frame, his months in a camp having taken their toll.

'Put your arm around me and we will take it slowly. We can stop whenever you need to. You'd better let me carry your bag.'

'No!' He clutched at the hemp satchel which had somehow stayed hooked over his shoulder. 'Until my wife is safe in Spain, the ledger stays with me.'

His eyes flashed, his jaw jutted, and his moustache bristled as he stared me down. I did not want to play the bully, but he needed to be brought to heel.

'Monsieur Lunel, you are lame and out in the wilds with nowhere to hide. To go back the way we came will only be to meet people who wish you harm, added to the fact that Vichy France probably no longer exists and is now run by the German army. I have identity papers and I have friends who will help me get out of France; you have neither. I have a pistol, you do not. If I wanted to take your ledger, what could you do about it?'

The fight went out of him with a sigh which could have been a balloon deflating.

'Nothing,' he said at last, his body slumping into mine. 'Absolutely nothing. We are in your hands entirely.'

He opened his bag and rummaged inside, retrieving a black leather-bound notebook, no bigger than a cheap paperback book, its cover tied closed by a bootlace strip of red material.

'Here, take it,' he said. 'It contains all the numbers and names of the accounts I opened on behalf of members of the cabal in banks in Casablanca, Rabat, Oran, Algiers, Tunis and Tripoli. Stop those accounts and you will foil their scheme. If you wish for the real names behind those account transfers . . .'

He tapped the side of his head with a finger. 'They remain in here.'

'Your ledger will help us stop the conspiracy from succeeding,' I said, 'and your memory would make sure the perpetrators face justice. Both are valuable assets and, being greedy, I would like to secure both. So put the ledger back in your bag, Nathan, and your arm around me, and let's get up this damned slope. It's awfully bad manners to leave a lady sitting twiddling her thumbs.'

For the third time I crabbed my way up that scree incline. The going was slow, with Lunel often a dead weight against my shoulder. He could not put any pressure on his left foot, and the higher we got the more terrified he became of slipping again. I was virtually carrying him over the last twenty yards of the climb, but he made an effort when he saw Astrid at the top, her arms out as if to catch him.

In the upper meadow, I laid him down and let Astrid minister to him as best she could, though I advised her not to try and remove Nathan's left shoe as we might never get it back on again. While she was fussing, I flexed my aching muscles and wandered off until I found a small stream cascading over an exposed lump of granite. I took a long drink of ice-cold water and then soaked my handkerchief so that I could clean Lunel's face.

'He cannot walk,' Astrid said as I wiped away the grime and dried blood.

'He has to,' I said. 'There are some trees up ahead and with luck we'll find a walking stick for him. For the moment, tie his ankle tightly with something. His belt if need be.'

I checked my wristwatch and then looked up at the sky. Clouds were rolling in over the peaks, the temperature was definitely dropping and the light was going. I began to worry about how ill-equipped our expedition was. We had no blankets or sleeping bags and little food. The terrain we were about to cross could provide us with water – we could hear a constant bubbling of streams and waterfalls – but little in the way of food. The only thing we had on our side, and perhaps I was clutching at straws here, was that the skies were empty of German spotter planes.

We crossed the meadow slowly but relatively easily, with Lunel and I stumbling along as if participating in a drunken three-legged race. We then followed the middle valley of the five which opened before us, and the going became narrower and stonier, with jagged rocks rising to each side of the narrow path.

My lungs told me that we were gaining in altitude, and they complained even more when I was forced to carry Lunel piggy-back when he began to fade and finally faint with pain and exhaustion.

The trail eventually brought us to a small plateau, a geological comma in the mountain range. There was a lake there, a lake of still, lifeless grey water, and small stone hut with a chimney but no windows and a door made of rough planking.

The sun was dipping behind the mountains as I pushed open that flimsy door, with Lunel still clinging to my back, his arms around my neck. I sank to my knees and Lunel yelped as he rolled off my back.

'Be it ever so humble,' I wheezed, 'this is no place like home.'

TWENTY-ONE
Message for Emil

The Dorchester Hotel, London. 20 May 1970

'Nobody's seen nuffink, then? That's what you're saying?'

'Spare us the double negatives and let Charlie speak,' said Mr Campion.

'I'm afraid Lugg's got it in one,' said Luke. 'Not the way I would have reported it in a magistrates' court, but basically that's the gist. I have talked to most of your guests but only briefly, hardly proper interviews.'

'Not packing yer notebook tonight? I suppose it would spoil the cut of yer penguin suit.'

'Albert, do tell Lugg to shut up,' said Amanda, glaring at the fat man rather than her husband.

'I have, but it didn't do much good.'

'Then tell him to fetch us a drink or get some music going. We can't have people standing around with long faces like washerwomen on a wet drying day. This is supposed to be a party, not a funeral. It's not a funeral, is it, Charlie?'

Luke shook his head and motioned the senior Campions to come closer to him. Lugg, excluded and dismissed, sniffed loudly and shuffled off in the direction of the nearest waiter.

'When we moved from the dining room to here, the seating plan went out of the window and everybody was milling around. Herr von Ringer headed straight out of the hotel for a smoke; I saw him go myself. Maybe he wanted some fresh air.'

Mr Campion smiled weakly. 'With those terrible cheroots he puffed, he could have done with a demilitarized zone. I think he was being polite; going outside to protect us from the fumes.'

'Whatever his motive,' Luke continued with the professional air all expected of him, 'he left the building of his own volition and, as far as anyone knows, was minding his own business, having a smoke. Who followed him out is the interesting question, for as Magersfontein Holmes over there has pointed out, the knife used to stab him came from inside the hotel, most likely purloined by one of the party guests.'

'Can we totally rule out the kitchen staff? Lugg said the knife had gone missing from the kitchen.' Mr Campion removed his spectacles and began to polish the lenses with his handkerchief.

'My gut feeling is we can,' said Luke. 'They're all wearing chefs' whites and surely would have been noticed walking through the mass of your guests to get to the front door. But of course, I can't be sure until I get some men here and we take detailed statements.'

'Is it going to be a long night, Charles?' asked Amanda. 'I'm thinking of our guests. They were expecting some dancing and frivolity, not a murder enquiry.'

'Don't be too sure about that. I've overheard a couple of your guests suggesting that this is Albert's idea of an elaborate party game.'

Mr Campion bridled at the accusation. 'How dare they! Would I ruin the cutting of my own birthday cake for the sake of a cheap stunt? How ungrateful. Didn't any of them see anything useful?'

Luke took a deep breath and recalled the mental list he had made. 'Well, Mrs Longfox certainly did, but only after the fact. She says she popped out for some fresh air, and more or less tripped over the victim. The hotel would normally have a doorman or two on duty, but it was all hands to the pump for the staff, moving furniture and setting up your disco, so no one actually saw her going out, let alone Ringer. Her father the earl, by the way, is kicking up rough with the hotel management, saying how disgraceful it was to have a body dropped at the feet of his daughter like that.'

Campion replaced his spectacles and turned to his wife. 'Have a word with your brother, would you? Calm him down.'

'You know what Hal's like,' said Amanda, 'but I'll pour oil on troubled egos. Go on, Charles, what else?'

'Not much, I'm afraid. Guffy Randall and Eager-Wright were

having an argument about the current state of English rugby, having been trounced in the Five Nations, and how could we possibly let both the Welsh and the French win? Your sister Mary was helping Lady Carados find a rogue earring and Johnny Carados, Dr Livingstone and your nephew Christopher were talking politics and were therefore oblivious to anything else. You might have thought the two youngsters, Edward Longfox and the student Oncer Smith, would have kept their eagle eyes open, but they had them zero-ed in on the American girl, Precious. So nobody noticed anyone making a surreptitious exit, following the German gent with a carving knife, nor anyone coming back with blood on their hands.'

'What about Elsie?' said Mr Campion. 'He normally notices things.'

Luke hesitated and tried to look shamefaced, an expression unfamiliar to his invariably solid countenance. 'I may have distracted Mr Corkran. I was pumping him about Ringer. They were on the same side after the war when they worked in intelligence and were in Berlin when the Wall went up. Albert's war stories got me interested in him – sounded a fascinating chap. Suffice it to say, we didn't see anyone stalking Ringer; not that we were expecting anything like this to happen.'

'I notice,' said Mr Campion, 'that you haven't mentioned my other foreign guests, apart from the magnetic Miss Aird.'

'I haven't talked to them yet. Thought I'd better have a word with you first, see what the form is.'

'I wouldn't be too worried about the diplomatic niceties, Charles. You are a policeman and there seems to have been a crime. You are the representative of law and order and you are on the spot, therefore you must investigate. As to my guests, they are all here as private citizens, though I believe Madame Thibus's presence was negotiated by the French embassy.'

Luke's eyes narrowed, and he studied his friend in a way he knew from experience was effective in disconcerting the guilty.

'Are you saying that you did not invite Corinne Thibus personally?'

'It was suggested that I invite her.' Campion was deliberately vague. 'I have not seen her since 1942.'

'When she proved herself fairly adept at violence,' said Luke, 'if your reminiscences over dinner are to be believed.'

'Charles!' Amanda reprimanded him. 'There was a war on then.'

'Against the Germans, I believe.'

Mr Campion shook his head. 'Don't jump to conclusions, Charles. By that logic, the majority of men in this room probably had an argument with a German thirty years ago. They even tried to drop a bomb on old Lugg during the Blitz but their aim wasn't up to much.'

'Speak of the Devil,' sighed Luke, noticing the juggernaut approach of the bombproof Mr Lugg.

'Sorry to h'intrude on a conference I wasn't invited to,' he declaimed with the solemnity, but none of the dignity, of one of Landseer's Trafalgar Square lions, 'but I bring a message for 'is 'onour the birthday boy.'

Mr Campion allowed Lugg five seconds of imperious smugness.

'Then let us have it; or do we rely on telepathy?'

Lugg, the unlikely carrier pigeon, puffed out his chest and delivered his message.

'The German gentleman was taken across the river to St Thomas's and, on the orders of Mr Luke here, a young constable of the noble Metropolitan Police was assigned to his bedside on hand-holding and bedpan duty . . .'

'Don't be coarse,' warned Amanda, and was studiously ignored.

'Anyways, this particular PC is called Dillon, Gerald Dillon, whose dad, Mike 'Sweetheart' Dillon is an old mucker of mine and custody sergeant at Love Lane nick.'

'Get on with it,' growled Luke.

'So, as I have a sort of family connection, when young Gerald telephoned the front desk here at the Dorchester, he thought it would be a better bet to communicate important information to someone he could trust.'

'And any day now we will find out what Constable Dillon wanted to tell us,' said Mr Campion. 'I pray that Robert's life is not hanging on your extended prolongation – and that's not a *double entendre*.'

'First off, no Germans have died while I've been relaying this message, nor are they likely to. Initial medical opinion is that Herr Ringer suffered only a flesh wound. By some fluke or sheer amateurishness, the blade missed all vital arteries and didn't penetrate all that deep. The doctors are more worried about the bang on the 'ead your mate got when the doorstep came up to meet him. They're keeping him in for tests – concussion and such like – but he come around long enough to dictate a message to PC Dillion, though it sounds to me he was raving a bit.'

'Dictated?'

'Made him write it down; that's dictation, innit? Made sure of the wording he did, 'cos it was in German. Told young Gerald it was "a message for Emil" but then said that was you, so oo'se this Emil?'

'It's a character from *Emil and the Detectives*, which Robert and I used as a sort of code during the war. Emil was the boy detective in the book. Even though it had pictures, I don't suppose you've heard of it.'

'Now you're being rude, Albert,' said his wife.

'Nonsense, I once got Lugg a book for Christmas and he said thank you, but he'd already read one.'

'Ho, very droll. Do you want to hear the message or not?'

Lugg's fat fingers squirmed into the breast pocket of his jacket and produced a square of paper. Like a stage magician playing for time, he slowly unfolded the square into a sheet of Dorchester notepaper.

'I wrote this down just as it was said to PC Dillon and he said it to me. It's in German, so it's no wonder it makes no sense: *Für meinen Vater*. That's it, that's the message for Emil.'

Lugg turned the paper over and displayed the three words to the trio who had clearly been expecting something more dramatic.

Lady Amanda and Luke remained nonplussed. Only Mr Campion seemed to consider the message had significance.

'Right then, old fruit,' he said, taking the note from Lugg's paw. 'Have a word with that young tearaway running the disco – I'm not sure whether he's a Mod or a Rocker, so be careful not to upset him. Tell him he can start up the music so people can get dancing, or at the very least gyrating.'

Amanda looked in genuine puzzlement at her husband.

'Albert, you're surely not thinking of providing entertainment after what's happened?'

'No, darling,' said Mr Campion, 'I'm providing a distraction.'

TWENTY-TWO
The Way of St James

Pyrénées Occidentales. November 1942

Pilgrims are a generous bunch, at least in my limited experience.

The stone refuge in which we took shelter was a basic structure with few, if any, home comforts, but at least it was dry. It must have been visited by hundreds if not thousands of pilgrims taking the road to redemption via Santiago de Compostela over the years, and many of them had left a little something behind, perhaps for a return journey or for the use of the next caravan of holy walkers. There were numerous crucifixes, some pale and withered, made from cleverly twisted palm leaves or bull rushes, others from two thin strips of wood and a single nail, and several stout walking sticks or staffs brought up from the treeline and then abandoned or forgotten before the next phase of the journey. There was even a besom-type broom made from pine-tree branches, tied together with a strand of rusty wire, to help pilgrims keep their hovel clean for the next set of visitors. That would come in very useful as the last lot of pilgrims appeared to have been a flock of sheep, judging by the fronds of dirty white wool, and other sheddings, left behind before their sheltering shepherd, or his dog, rounded them up and moved them on.

Most pilgrims had arrived far better equipped than we had and had brought candles with them. Whether for practical or religious purposes I did not know, but many a candle had been lit in that refuge, and devout pilgrims had left behind a generous collection of stubs scattered about the hut. There was also a thin, burst and stained mattress made from a sack which some pilgrim had dutifully carried, determined to have a comfortable night's sleep on the mountains, only to have it soaked by rain or being dropped in a stream. The hessian material had split and the straw intestines had spilled out, probably helped by the nibbling of sheep.

There was enough light left in the afternoon for me to take stock of our thin resources and face the fact that we would be staying in the refuge overnight. From our bag of provisions, I took the glass jar which had held the duck confit eaten at our 'picnic' and told Astrid to go to the lake, rinse it out and bring it back full of water while I screwed up the newspaper which Madame Henneuse had used as padding and stuffed it in the hut's stone fireplace.

My reasoning was that once darkness fell, we could risk a fire, as the smoke from the chimney would not be seen. It could, of course, be smelled on the otherwise clean mountain air, but I reasoned that might help keep animal predators away, if there were any. Human predators, of course, were another matter, and might be attracted but, purely for keeping up morale, I felt the risk worth taking.

Using the besom, I swept into the fireplace anything which looked remotely flammable: pine needles, strands of wool, dried sheep droppings, twigs, the remains of the burst mattress and several pine cones, and then broke up three of the abandoned walking staffs. It was a pathetic reserve of fuel and the fire did not last long; but as we sat on the hard floor, it gave us the illusion of heat and some comfort as we shared out our dwindling provisions.

'I don't suppose anyone noticed if there was a red sky,' I said, chewing on a crust. 'It's a saying, at least it is in England, that a red sky at night is a shepherd's delight – a forecast of good weather for tomorrow.'

'Is that how you predict the weather in England?'

I could not see Lunel's face clearly now the fire had died, and the only light in the hut came from one of the candle stubs – a generous inch-long one I had found, yet I felt there was a new calmness in his voice.

'In England, it's as good a way as any,' I said.

'What do they call you in England?'

'Albert.' I saw no reason not to admit to it, now the end of our journey was in sight – or hopefully would be, come the dawn.

'I would like to visit England, Albert.'

'I don't see why you should not,' I said. 'The man you will meet in Madrid is called Benton. He will be most interested in the contents of your ledger and the Allies will be most grateful. If you want to go to England until it is safe to return to France, I am sure it can be arranged.'

'We may not wish to return to France,' said Astrid from the shadows.

'The Germans will not be here for ever.'

Astrid let out a snort of derision. 'Our problems of late have all come from fellow French citizens. The policemen who arrested us were French. The guards in the prisons and camps were French. My captors in Marseilles were French. I am no longer a Frenchwoman, I am just a Jewess. It may be best if my baby is not born here.'

I said nothing, judging it not the moment to point out to her that a very brave French girl had been instrumental in her escape from the Panier.

'Come and sit next to me, my dear,' said Lunel, 'and let us try and get comfortable as best we can. Tomorrow you will be in Spain. Is that not so, Albert?'

'If my calculations are correct, we should meet Vidal, our Spanish guide, at the top of the ridge directly ahead of us. It is not an easy climb, but we are on the Way of St James and the track has been successfully followed by thousands of pilgrims in the past. If they could do it, so can we, for are we not pilgrims in a just cause?'

Neither of them said anything, but I could hear rather than see the two of them huddling closer for warmth and comfort, and then my candle stub guttered and went out and the only sound in the hut was that of their breathing, deep and regular, as exhaustion overtook them.

I pulled my coat tight around me and sat propped up against the wall opposite where I judged the door to be. With my right hand around the butt of the pistol in my jacket pocket, I wondered how long it would take sleep to claim me.

I had just enough time to realize that Nathan had said, 'Tomorrow you will be in Spain' and not, 'we will be in Spain', before it did.

When I awoke, I was stiff, cramped and disorientated. Only a thin sliver of light around the frame of the door told me that dawn's alarm clock was as reliable as ever. It was still dark and gloomy in the windowless hut, so I slowly negotiated my way to the door, careful not to step on one of the sleeping Lunels.

There was a thin frost on the ground which made the exposed lumps of granite sparkle like diamonds, but the lake was free of ice, albeit icy cold when I knelt to wash my hands and the stubble growth on my face. That had the effect of a double-espresso coffee in terms of blowing away sleep's cobwebs; I was determined to get my body, and my circulation, moving.

A brisk walk to the end of the stony, saucer-shaped plateau brought me to the foot of a proper mountain. A cairn of piled stones and vague indentations in the ground indicated that the pilgrims' trail continued steeply upwards from here on. It was no north face of the Eiger, but it was a mountain, not a hill, and my heart sank at the prospect of trying to get the Lunels up it. I knew Reuben Vidal would be up there somewhere waiting for us, but he would not wait for ever, and he had no way of knowing that I had a pregnant woman and a man with only one working foot in tow.

Still, things could be worse, I told myself, though I was not sure how.

Back in the refuge, Astrid was struggling to help her husband stand, an exercise which seemed risky for both of them, so I intervened as gently as I could, putting an arm around Nathan's waist and taking his weight.

'How's the foot this morning?' I said in my best bedside manner.

'Much better,' winced Nathan.

'Liar!' said his wife. 'The ankle is broken and turning blue. He cannot walk.'

'Let's get him outside into the light,' I said. 'I'll see if I can make . . .' I fumbled for the word in French, '. . . splints and find a walking stick.'

We sat him down gently on a large square rock, his short legs dangling over the edge so I could clearly see that Astrid's diagnosis was painfully accurate.

'Perhaps soaking in cold water might help,' I suggested. 'We could sit you over by the lake . . .'

'No, that will not cure me.' He used my arm in an attempt to lever himself up but, as soon as his swollen foot touched the ground, his face twisted in an animal grimace, the breath hissed between his teeth and he sank back on to the rock. 'Nothing will.'

I thought for a moment he had fainted and, because I had no real idea what to do at that moment, I brusquely ordered Astrid to fetch the brandy from the hut. As soon as she was out of earshot, Lunel's eyes flicked open and locked on mine.

'You must leave me.'

'Don't be ridiculous, I can help you.'

'You cannot carry me up there,' his eyes flicked towards the surrounding peaks, 'not if you are carrying Astrid also.'

'Nonsense, she's proved herself as strong as me if not stronger. Between us we can do it. It will not be easy, but in a few hours we can have you in Spain and safety and I can get help.'

He shook his head. 'If you think that, then take Astrid. Make sure she is safe, then come back for me.'

I thought of the climb ahead and did some rapid mental arithmetic. 'Even if nothing went wrong and the weather held, I doubt I could get back here before nightfall.'

'I am not afraid of the dark,' he said calmly.

'Are you not afraid I might not come back?'

His gaze came back on to my face, though his eyes were watering with pain.

'You will return for my ledger once Astrid is safe. That was our agreement. You can have my ledger once my wife is safely out of France. I do not matter. Did you not give me your word?'

'Yes, I did Nathan, I did; but won't you at least try?'

'No, I will only be a hindrance. Take Astrid and make sure she is safe, then come back for me.'

'I promise I will,' I said.

'Your word again?'

'Certainly, if you trust it.'

'I do. You have got us this far, Albert; I trust you to get my wife and child over the border. Nothing else is important; nothing.'

For a moment I could not speak, I merely studied the man lying splayed out in front of me. He had been threatened and bullied into criminality, persecuted and imprisoned. Deprived of his possessions and citizenship and his wife held hostage, he was little more than a husk of the comfortable, middle-aged businessman he should have been, had the war not intervened. Now he lay injured, unable to walk unaided, miles from anywhere in inhospitable surroundings, and he was entrusting a stranger with the one thing he held most dear.

He spoke again before I could think of anything to say. 'I think you would come back for me even if I did not have the ledger, M'sieur Albert.'

'You think too much of me, Nathan, because you are truly a good man.'

'I think you could be one, too.'

I helped him hobble back inside the refuge and made him as

comfortable as possible, propped against the wall by the fireplace. With the door open, he would have light during the day, but I found a pair of surviving candle stubs and placed them within reach and made sure he had matches for them. I emptied my bag of what little food we had left and made a pillow of it for the back of his head.

There was little enough to share out. I left him the brandy, the scrapings in the last jar of *confit*, the butt-end of a salami and half the sourdough biscuits. When Astrid was fetching more water from the lake, I pulled the pistol half out of my pocket and showed it to him.

He shook his head vigorously. 'No, thank you. I may be tempted to use it. Now please leave me alone with my wife for a few minutes.'

I did as I was bidden. After no more than five minutes, Astrid emerged, buttoning her coat over a mismatched but practical ensemble of sweater and ski pants.

'I wish I had better shoes,' she said, as if she did not have a care in the world.

'So do I,' I said, determined to keep things light, 'but at least your ski pants are fashionable, aren't they?'

'They should be, the amount they cost. They're by Lucien Lelong the designer.'

'Do you ski?'

'No, but I am interested in *couture*.' She hitched her bag over her shoulder. 'Shall we make a start?'

And so we did: two unsuitably dressed pilgrims putting their best badly-shod feet forward on the Way of St James, looking for what all pilgrims seek: hope.

For the first two hours, Astrid was absolutely superb. Uncomplaining, she set a cracking pace, even when the trail took us higher and every intake of breath burned the lungs.

The boulder-strewn terrain made for harder and slower progress, and at times the trail had us squeezing between giant stones which had only a narrow gap between them. When Astrid stumbled and fell three times within fifty metres, I insisted that she rested and drink from a small rivulet of water trickling over the rocks, then pressed her to eat one of the ration of biscuits I was carrying in my jacket pocket.

'Not far now,' I said, trying not to look at the next section of the trail, which seemed to be almost vertical.

'You should eat something also,' she said. 'I insist. We are not moving until you do.'

'You will make a very good mother, madame,' I said, nibbling on a biscuit.

We pressed on. The sun, now high in the sky, provided little warmth, and yet I was sweating profusely. I offered to carry Astrid's bag but she refused to relinquish it, although she did take my arm and allow me to pull, sometimes drag her up the steepest parts of the path.

I began to stumble and fall myself; on one occasion putting a four-inch tear in my trousers. My lungs were on fire, my calves ached and my hands were pitted with cuts where I had steadied myself against sharp rocks. Our progress had become painfully slow and was getting slower. On the early part of the climb it had been possible to look back and see the lake, the saucer-shaped plateau and the refuge diminishing beneath us, but the trail had twisted in among larger rocks following the line of an old stream bed, and our view was obscured. In many ways it was a blessing as I had enough to worry about on the climb ahead, without thinking of a return journey to collect Nathan. I resisted looking at my watch, preferring to use the sun as my clock and convincing myself that if there was daylight, there was a chance.

At my insistence our rest stops became more frequent, as I became more and more concerned about Astrid. Her complexion was deathly pale and her arms were locked around the bulge of her midriff, as though she was trying to carry the weight of her pregnancy in her clasped hands. On certain sections of the trail, I extended my arm for her to pull on, using it as a sort of guide rope. On the very steep slopes she allowed the indignity of me pushing her from behind.

At some point after noon I sat her down to rest on a square metre of stone-free ground. It was the only flat surface I could see, as the next stretch of the trail was not only steep but strewn with large boulders, some the size of London buses. Without the comforting sight of a marker cairn, no pilgrim, however devout, would have attempted to cross that stone minefield.

I warned Astrid as she allowed herself to be pulled to her feet to be careful. The last thing I wanted to happen was an ankle injury, although in that rocky moonscape, the odds of sustaining one were high.

With our arms linked like an old married couple, we picked our way carefully through the maze of rocks, and it became more of a maze as we progressed, the boulders so large that we could not see round or over them, and edging between them was like squeezing into a series of narrow canyons.

That steep and difficult section of the trail, which I would always think of as 'The Maze', was the point when I began to despair. The climb was exhausting, with Astrid seeming heavier with each step, and the disorientation of being able to see nothing but the next rock looming in front or the one just passed behind adding to my general light-headedness.

I was sure I was hallucinating when I convinced myself I could smell smoke. Not wood smoke or the reek of a smoking volcano – there were neither trees for wood nor active volcanoes in the vicinity, as far as I knew – but cigarette smoke and particularly the bitter scent of black, Continental tobacco.

I stopped and put my back against a cold piece of granite, pulling Astrid into my side and gesturing, with a finger to my lips, for her to be silent. So as not to frighten her further, I slipped the pistol out of my pocket and held it down the side of my leg.

I strained my ears, but the silence of the mountains was absolute now we had ceased crunching and stumbling up the pilgrims' path. Then I thought I heard something – a trickle of small stones dislodged by a boot, perhaps, from somewhere close ahead of us, but all I could see was yet another large chunk of granite blocking our way.

I tensed and leaned out from the rock in order that my body covered more of Astrid's and faced whatever was coming.

The boulder in front of us didn't move, but it seemed to sprout an arm – an arm in the shape of the barrel of a rifle.

'*Hola!*' said the muzzle of the carbine. '*Llegas tarde!*'

'Astrid, meet Ruben Vidal,' I said, slipping the pistol back into my pocket as a leathery face appeared around the granite. 'He's our guide and he's rather cross because we're late.'

Reuben Vidal was a small man with a big heart. If he was surprised to find me with a pregnant woman in tow, he did not show it. He gave a 'better-get-on-with-it' grunt, thrust his rifle at me and began to guide, almost carry, Astrid over the rocks and up the slope.

We had been closer to the summit than I had imagined. Not the summit of the mountain – that still towered over us – but at least that stony ridge. From there the trail went into a gentle descent and curved around the edge of a stand of trees about five hundred feet below.

Going downhill was a pure treat for my legs, and Astrid felt confident enough to release Reuben's arm and stride out under her own steam, although she stayed close to him as he maintained a constant patter of soft Spanish which I could barely follow, other than that he was saying something about not having far to go.

He spoke only the truth as he had set up a camp just inside the copse of trees, a camp which I did not spot until I fell into it.

'This is cosy,' I said.

He shrugged. 'I have been waiting for three days.'

Reuben had made himself at home, his temporary shelter consisting of an army pup tent camouflaged by pine branches, with a groundsheet, a sleeping bag and a Primus stove. Astrid and I sank down by the stove as if it was lit and we were expecting to warm our hands over its kerosene flames, although in truth I was enjoying a personal fantasy, imagining the nice hot cup of tea I had been missing since I left London.

Our swarthy mountain man, however, had far more practical ideas, and began to unpack the rucksack he had pulled from the tent.

'I have soup to warm,' he said in mangled French, brandishing a metal flask, 'and chicken, sausage and cheese if you are hungry, and' – he pulled a bottle from the pack like a magician – 'wine, too. Otherwise rest here before we go on.'

'You have truly provided a feast for hungry pilgrims,' I said, 'so let us eat. Tell me, are we in Spain?'

'Not quite,' answered Reuben, lighting the stove and laying out the food on the brown paper it had been wrapped in. 'Another two kilometres perhaps, down the valley. The going is easy and there is a house, where a shepherd who brings my supplies lives. We can sleep there and, in the morning, go down to the village of Baños de Panticosa. I have a car there and the road takes us to Zaragoza and from there, Madrid.'

Astrid's eyes were fixed on the roast chicken Reuben had produced and I realized the woman must be starving, so I pulled off a leg and gave it to her, ripping a chunk of breast meat for myself.

'We will eat and thank you for your hospitality,' I told him, 'but you must take Astrid on alone. I have to go back.'

'Back? Into Vichy?'

'Only as far as the refuge down towards Pont d'Espagne. We left her husband there with a broken ankle and he needs my help. I promised him I would return for him.'

'There is no need,' said Astrid, wiping chicken juice from her lips with the back of a grubby hand.

'I gave him my word.'

'You made Nathan a promise to get me to safety in return for his ledger. I judge you have accomplished that.'

She pulled her bag closer and from it produced a black, leather-bound notebook, identical to the one Lunel had shown me in the refuge. As she held it out, offering it to me, I noticed that it was not quite identical; the red leather fastening had been replaced with ordinary string.

'This is Nathan's ledger?' I asked, taking it from her.

'One of them. He kept two. He said it was his double-entry system for extra security. He told me to give it to you once I felt safe. He does not expect you to go back for him.'

I am ashamed to say that I was concentrating on examining the notebook to make sure its contents were genuine to react immediately to what Astrid was telling me. But eventually it sank in.

'But we cannot leave him in that hut; he may be discovered. Even worse, he may not be discovered before winter sets in.'

'It was his choice. It was his wish.'

Vidal, who had been following this exchange as if watching a tennis match, took a long swig from his wine bottle then handed it to me.

'I will come with you,' he said slowly. 'We can make a stretcher out of the tent and carry this man if he cannot walk. If he is important.'

'He has a broken ankle,' I said, 'and he is important. But he is not as important as this.' I waved the notebook in his general direction. 'Though may the Good Lord forgive me for saying that.'

'That is what Nathan thinks,' said Astrid. 'He trusts you to do what has to be done.'

Nathan Lunel had trusted me; that was the problem. But he had specifically trusted me to get his wife to safety. That, I felt, I had done.

I thrust the notebook at Vidal. 'You must get this to Señor Benton in Madrid and as quickly as possible. Speed is of the absolute essence.'

'Why?'

'It has to do with the American landings in North Africa. This book is a ledger containing the names and numbers of bank accounts there. Tell Benton that when the Americans take over the banks, they must freeze these accounts. Astrid will be able to tell him more.'

Vidal's face lit up with childish enthusiasm and I realized that, stuck up here in the mountains, he would not be aware of the latest war news.

'The Americans are coming? Does that mean the Germans will now invade?'

'I do not know if they will invade Spain, but they are already taking over Vichy.'

'I hope they do,' he said. 'I would like to fight Germans.'

I had not appreciated until then how much younger than I he was.

'Do not wish for violence. It tends to come unbidden. As a great philosopher once said: do not declare a war until you have already won it.'

Reuben's brow creased, and I wondered if he had understood, but Astrid certainly had.

'That is stupid. Which "great philosopher" said that?'

'Me.'

As an attempt to lighten the mood in our little camp it was not a success, so I returned to the business at hand.

'Astrid, rest while you can, then go with Reuben and stay with him all the way to Madrid, where another Englishman called Benton will look after you. I will try and get Nathan there somehow. Do not wait for us, do not look back, do not waste a moment. Do you both understand?'

They nodded in unison, like a pair of scolded children promising good behaviour in perpetuity to a particularly strict teacher.

'Reuben, please give me what food you can spare and throw in that bottle of wine if you are feeling generous.'

I stood up and, out of habit, brushed down the front of my trousers.

Reuben also got to his feet and looked at the sky. 'If you get back down and find your friend, you will not get him back up here before nightfall.'

'I might,' I said, showing a flash of bulldog spirit, or perhaps petulance. 'I may look weak and feeble' – I simply could not recall the French for *wiry* – 'but I have the heart of a lion and the feet of a mountain goat, though I admit they are carrying a lot of blisters at the moment.'

Reuben shook his head slowly. Either he had misunderstood me or simply thought I was mad. It was difficult to tell.

'I will leave the tent here for you, but you may need this.'

He offered me his rifle; an elderly bolt-action short carbine which may have been a family heirloom.

'No, thank you, I need to travel light. In any case, there are few barn doors for me to miss around here.'

His face did not crack at that either. One of us was clearly not convinced by the fluency of my French.

Having told the two of them not to look back, it was the first thing I did when I reached the edge of the copse of trees. Astrid was on her feet and Reuben was slinging bags and his rifle over his shoulders. Perhaps Astrid had rested enough, or Reuben was being strict and anxious to get moving; either way, they were on the move, and I was happy to see them walk off through the trees towards safety. For me, that was one part of my mission completed.

The second part now commenced with me navigating the boulder-strewn maze section of the slope, but down rather than up this time. In many ways the descent was more painful on my feet, as the last thing I wanted to do was twist an ankle, and my shoes, which would have looked smart on any boulevard, offered little support or protection against the granite teeth chewing at them.

I stumbled often, and the palms of my hands were pockmarked with pinpricks of blood where I had grabbed at the larger rocks to slow my downward momentum. I was already regretting my claim to having the feet of a mountain goat. If I had, they were the two-toed hooves of a very old, very drunk goat.

When he at last found a few square centimetres of flat ground blessed with a few strands of grass, this drunken old goat collapsed to his knees and began retching and breathing in equal measure. I had no idea what the lifespan of a mountain goat was, but this one was definitely getting too old for larking about on the hillsides.

It was while I was indulging in this moment of self-pity that I noticed, through a gap in the boulders, a glimmer of something way below which did not seem as solid as the bulk of my very solid surroundings. I staggered to my feet and scrambled on top of a lump of granite the size of a car, from which vantage point I could see down the trail and, in the distance, the lake and the small meadow with the refuge where we had left Nathan Lunel.

I could not see the hut itself but I felt that I could almost lean out and touch the surface of the lake as it reflected the weak afternoon sun. To do so, however, would have involved pitching head-first from my rock and tobogganing down the scree on my chest, which seemed a rather drastic course of action, and with that thought came the realization that I was becoming light-headed either due to dehydration or the altitude or both. More than once I thought I heard the sound of an engine echoing off the mountains but, no matter how hard I looked, I saw no sign of a spotter plane and put the sound down to a fevered imagination.

There was nothing I could do about the altitude, but I did find a tiny stream and slaked my thirst before carefully continuing my descent, keeping my feet side-on to the slope despite the agony in my ankles.

Eventually I came to the top of the last scree face leading down to the meadow with the lake and got my first clear sight of the hut, albeit no bigger than something out of a child's toy farmyard set.

It was just as we had left it early that morning, except it was not and I knew there was something seriously wrong. I halted my crab-like gait, took off my glasses and wiped them, and then my eyes, with my grubby handkerchief. There was a thin wisp of smoke coming from the stone chimney, despite the warning I had given about lighting a fire during daylight. I was not sure whether the smoke was substantial enough to be seen from the air by my imagined spotter plane, but if I could see it from that distance, so could others.

And others had come to the refuge, but not by plane.

Parked outside the hut, leaning against the wall near the open door, was a motorbike, almost certainly the source of the engine noise I had heard.

I did not believe that pilgrims on the Way of St James had taken to riding up the trail on motorbikes, no matter how anxious they were for redemption, so I cast caution to the wind and charged downhill.

No one was more surprised than I when I made it to the bottom of the slope without breaking an ankle, or my neck. Finding my balance on the relative flat of the meadow was like finding my sea-legs on a boat that had just left the safety of Dover Harbour and turned into a Force 8 gale in the Channel, but I forced myself into a shambling, staggering run.

I was still at least five hundred metres from the refuge when I heard the shots.

The figure which emerged from the refuge was a black hobgoblin, the sort of demonic figure seen in the corner of a Renaissance painting of purgatory or hell. It took me several breathless moments to realize that the demonic figure was a man wearing black leather from head to foot, who was in the process of pulling on gauntlets, then dropping a pair of goggles from the leather helmet over his eyes. There was no possibility at all that, at that distance and wearing such garb, I could identify the figure who was mounting the motorbike and kicking it into life.

But I knew who it must be.

I pulled the Walther from my pocket and had the presence of mind to flip off the safety catch before sinking to my knees and attempting to take aim. The black-clad figure had not seen me, or if he had, did not feel threatened in the slightest, as he manoeuvred the bike away from the wall of the refuge, revved the engine loudly and steered it in a half-circle and headed down the pilgrim's trail towards Pont d'Espagne.

My finger was on the trigger of my pistol, but I did not fire. It was no moral problem, it was simply a question of ballistics. The target was too far away for my pistol to be effective and I cursed my rejection of the loan of Vidal's rifle.

I could still hear the rasp of the motorbike's engine bouncing down the valley as I reached the refuge's door, already half knowing what I was to find inside.

In the crude fireplace were the blackened paper ashes of what had been Lunel's ledger, or at least one of them. Next to the fireplace, sitting propped against the wall almost exactly where I had left him, was Nathan Lunel, his body still warm.

There was one bullet wound in his chest and one directly between his eyes. Either would have achieved the desired result.

How long I stayed there I do not know.

I sank to the hut floor, against the wall opposite Lunel. I apologized to him for being too weak, too slow, too old. For regretting I had not sent Reuben Vidal in my place. He would have gone, probably relishing the challenge, and he would have been stronger and more sure-footed than me. Reuben would have heard the motorcycle coming and, with his rifle, protected the defenceless Lunel. I admitted I had failed him and broken the promise he had not held me to and his silence admonished me.

On the plus side of the account, I had got Astrid to safety, and I thanked him for the trust he had in me in providing her with the second ledger, which was on its way into safe hands. The information it contained would reach the Americans before the banks in North Africa were liberated and the accounts frozen and then appropriated. The members of the cabal would be exposed, and retribution would follow.

A noise disturbed my reverie – or perhaps it had been a soliloquy: the crunch of footsteps approaching the entrance to the refuge.

Daylight was fading and suddenly reduced even further as a uniformed figure appeared in the doorway. The uniform was unmistakably German, as was the pistol in the hand which preceded the body, as was the voice.

'Albert?' said the uniform. 'Is that you?'

'It's good to see you, Robert,' I replied in English, 'or I think it is. Is it?'

'You have nothing to fear from me, Albert, although technically you are now an enemy combatant in civilian clothes in the territory of the Third Reich and that means I could shoot you as a spy.'

'Please don't, Robert, at least not yet.'

Robert holstered his pistol and stepped into the hut. He produced a small metal flask from the breast pocket of his uniform tunic – a Wehrmacht uniform, not the black SS one we had worn forty-eight hours ago. The flask contained cognac and I was grateful to take a long swig.

'I could have offered you some Spanish wine,' I told him, 'but I think I lost my bag coming down the mountain.'

Robert crouched down on his haunches in front of me so that the dead, accusing face of Nathan Lunel was hidden from me.

'What happened, Albert? Did Lunel not give you the ledger?'

'Nothing like that. Lunel played it with a straight bat the whole time. The ledger and Astrid Lunel are by now in Spain and making their way to Madrid. How goes the invasion?'

'Yours or ours?' said Robert with a weary smile.

'Either.'

'The American landings have encountered some resistance from Vichy French forces, but nothing that will inconvenience them unduly. Case Anton is in full swing and our troops are meeting no opposition. I have been ordered back to Marseilles to expand the Abwehr office there.'

'So what are you doing here?'

He reached for the flask which I reluctantly returned to him. 'Firstly, tell me what happened to Lunel.'

'Nathan broke his ankle on the climb up here and could not go any further. He insisted I made sure Astrid was safe before coming back for him. I delivered Astrid into the hands of our Spanish contact and started back down. Before I could get near enough to do anything about it, a man on a motorcycle turned up and shot him.'

'And the papers in the fire?' Robert was as observant as ever.

'A second ledger. Don't worry, Astrid is carrying a copy. Lunel must have wanted a duplicate as something to bargain with in case he fell into the wrong hands.'

'He did. Magnus Asher, the one man he couldn't bargain with. A man who wanted the ledger destroyed to protect his investment.'

'I know,' I said. 'It must have been him. I remember being told that he was a dispatch rider before he took his leave of the British army, so the motorbike would have been a natural choice of transport and the only vehicle that could get up this trail. Thing is, how did Asher know we were on this particular pilgrim's way? Come to that, how did you?'

'Asher paid a call on Madame Henneuse at the Lunels' apartment this morning. She knew enough to tell him the direction you had taken. Remember, Asher had a lucrative sideline in helping people escape into Spain across these trails.'

'Madame Henneuse would not have betrayed the Lunels!' I protested.

'Not without a severe beating, a very severe beating. I had a local man watching the building and, when he felt something was wrong, he called me. Asher had gone but Madame Henneuse was able to tell me what had happened.' His voice dropped into a solemn drone. 'It was the last thing she did. I called a doctor for her but it was too late, then Erik got the car and we set off after him, but he had too much of a start.'

Anger overcame fatigue and frustration and I struggled to my feet with Robert's help. 'Asher is a loathsome creature. We can't let him get away.'

'He hasn't,' said Robert calmly. 'Got away, that is. He is at Pont d'Espagne being guarded by my faithful Erik.'

'You captured him?'

'No, he surrendered to us. We stopped to examine the car you abandoned there and heard the motorcycle coming down the trail. As soon as he saw our uniforms, he presented himself to us and said that as good German soldiers we might be interested in an escape route over the mountains used by Jews. He had even killed a Jew attempting to escape the round-ups and could give us full details, even show us the body, to prove what a friend of the Reich he was.'

'Did you shoot him?'

'No.'

'What a shame,' I said.

TWENTY-THREE
A Perfect Hatred

The Dorchester Hotel, London. 20 May 1970

The music, when it began to float from the large speakers of the discotheque equipment, was surprisingly gentle and reassuring to the more mature party guests. Having seen the equipment being set up, they had feared the worst excesses of guitar-twanging and screamed lyrics, such as they had experienced when subjected to Radio 1 as played on the transistor radios that every builder and plumber carried these days or, horror of horrors, when they had accidentally tuned their televisions into that appalling youth orgy that was *Top of the Pops*.

The younger guests, accepting they were in the minority, graciously put up with Nat King Cole and Duke Ellington, knowing that the disc jockey, who was of their own age group, almost certainly had more modern and more lively records up his sleeve for later, when the older crowd had drifted away or been carried off to their beds.

The strains of smooth jazz and the accompanying gentle (so far) strobe lighting served Mr Campion's purposes perfectly. Prying eyes and ears like radar dishes were distracted, allowing Campion to huddle in conference with his inner circle of Amanda, Luke and Lugg, the latter there by virtue of the simple fact that he refused to move away.

'Now let's clear up the question of our foreign guests before your boys in blue arrive to give everybody the third degree,' Campion addressed Luke. 'I am working on the premise that the family and friends contingent, not to mention the odd gate-crasher' – he glared at Lugg – 'are the unusual suspects in the assault on Freiherr von Ringer. As far as I am aware, none of the domestic guests, with the exception of Elsie Corkran, knew him from Adam.'

'And you had never mentioned your wartime connection,' said Luke.

'Not even to me,' Amanda whispered.

'I saw no reason to dwell on my unhappy wartime experiences,' Campion replied.

'Until tonight.'

'That's right, Charlie, and there's a reason for that, which I'll come to. First, though, put your policeman's helmet on and hear me out.'

Luke, who had not worn a policeman's helmet for many a year, nodded his acquiescence.

'Well then, we can dismiss Joseph Fleurey, who had no idea who Robert was and in any case was too young for the war.'

'So the assault on Ringer has to do with the war?'

'Yes, Charles, I'm pretty sure it has.'

'I knew it!' exclaimed Lugg, who then fell silent and red-faced as three pairs of eyes turned on him.

'What about Fleurey's father?'

'Well done, Charles, you remembered the note from Robert. Except it did not refer to my old chum Étienne Fleurey, who owed his arrival in England and the safety of his family to Robert. I can't really see a motive there.'

'Surely you can't suspect Corinne?' said Amanda. 'She seems delightful: frightfully bright and far too sophisticated to stab a man in the back.'

'But quite capable of shooting a few, if Albert's war stories are to be believed,' Luke observed dryly.

'That was then,' said Mr Campion, 'this is now. Corinne had no direct contact with Robert, at least not while I was in Marseilles, though perhaps she did later, but I can assure you her motive for being here tonight is not remotely to do harm to Robert – quite the reverse, in fact.'

Lugg pursed his fleshy lips and pushed his face aggressively into that of Charles Luke. 'Did you follow that? Because I sure-as-shooting didn't.'

Luke did his best to ignore him and turned on Campion. 'Then why is Corinne Thibus here? Didn't you say her presence was requested by the French Embassy?'

'I did,' said Mr Campion, 'and this is where I have to blush and giggle in the manner of a schoolgirl – something I was always rather good at. The truth is Corinne Thibus is here tonight to give me a medal. It was supposed to be a surprise for everyone.'

Amanda, open-mouthed, grasped her husband's arm. 'Oh my goodness! Not the *Légion d'honneur*?'

Mr Campion patted his wife's hand gently. 'Not quite, my love. It's the Order of Liberation, which I'm told comes a close second. They don't give many to foreigners, just the important ones like Churchill, Eisenhower, the late King George, and me. It's for services to France during the Occupation, and it seems part of the reason I got gonged was down to Robert putting in a good word for me.'

Luke made as if to speak, paused, thought, and then spoke. 'You're getting a French medal for resisting the Germans on the testimony of a German army officer?'

Mr Campion allowed himself a weak smile. 'Yes, funny old world, isn't it? I knew the story would come out one way or another tonight, so I thought I would pre-empt the speeches and tell Perdita the story, as she was the only one who has ever expressed an interest in what I did in the war.'

Lugg's temper and complexion bubbled up like magma. 'Strewth, that's rich! You've kept schtum about all this for twenty-five years, not saying a word no matter 'ow 'ard people tried to wheedle it out of you. Anyone wiv eyes could see you'd changed when you came back from the war, but you never let on what happened to yer.'

'Until tonight,' Luke pointed out.

'Well, I thought I had better get my side of the story out before Madame Thibus started tongues wagging when she made her presentation. That, of course, has now been postponed as she specifically wanted Robert von Ringer to be present.'

'Did she now?' Luke could not prevent his policeman's eyebrows from rising.

'Don't give me that look, Charlie,' said Mr Campion. 'Madame Thibus is in the clear.'

'Are you sure, dear?'

Now three pairs of eyes turned on Amanda. 'You call her Madame Thibus,' she said, 'but that's her maiden name, isn't it? She never married?'

'Not as far as I'm aware, darling, but that's not a criminal offence as far as I know, even in France.'

'Mebbe it should be,' grunted Lugg, who was ignored.

'What happened to that Free French man who helped you in Toulouse? The one she was madly in love with as a girl?'

'Ah-ha!' grinned Campion. 'So, you were listening to my memoirs over dinner!'

'It was difficult not to. The sound of your voice can be quite . . .'

'Sonorous? Distinguished? Hypnotic?'

'I was going to say persistent. Olivier, that was his name.'

'Yes, Olivier Courteaux, and Corinne was indeed infatuated with him.' Mr Campion became serious. 'He was a real hero and did get his fair share of medals. Sadly, they were awarded posthumously. He was killed by the SS; members of the Das Reich division who went on the rampage in the Dordogne in 1944. Put up against a wall and shot out of hand in a place called Souillac. There was a memorial service for him and other heroes of the Resistance after the war. General de Gaulle was there, as was Elsie Corkran, I believe.'

'It must have hit Corinne hard,' said Amanda. 'She was still very young.'

'It spurred her on to become a lawyer,' said Campion, 'special-izing in war crimes. She eventually tracked down a couple of the SS men who had been in the firing squad and brought them to justice. She was tenacious in that regard.'

Luke pressed the point Lady Amanda had left hanging in the air. 'Consequently, Madame Thibus has little love for Germans . . .'

'You're giving me that "Anything you say may be taken down" look again, Charlie. As I understand it, Corinne's enquiries about Nazi war criminals received the full cooperation of the West German security services and a certain Robert von Ringer, who had already proved himself to be no Nazi. He's the one who should be getting the medal. In fact, our government should have given him one or two.'

'Well, if you're sure Corinne did not have the motive to stab Robert . . .'

Amanda began the unasked question, but it was Charles Luke who finished it as a statement. 'That leaves the Spanish lady, Señora Vidal. I'd better have a word with her. Where is she?'

'Over there, near the bar,' said Campion, 'talking to Perdita. She's a bright girl, Perdita. I think she might have guessed already.'

'Guessed what?' Luke asked sharply.

'That you really should be talking to the daughter.'

Quietly and unobtrusively, Campion, Amanda and Luke made their way across the hotel foyer, now an ad-hoc dance floor, through the crowd of chattering, drinking and even occasionally dancing guests. As it was impossible for Lugg to be inconspicuous under any circumstances, he was dispatched by a circuitous route to the Park Lane doorway where, in case a suspect should try and flee the scene, he was to use his considerable bulk to block the exit.

By the makeshift bar, Perdita was nursing a glass of white wine and Señora Vidal was, judging by the ashtray she held, chain-smoking. They were both silent and looking slightly furtive as Luke and the Campions approached.

'Astrid, we need to talk to you,' said Mr Campion, 'but before we do you should know that Mr Luke here is a senior British policeman investigating the attack on Freiherr von Ringer. You will be pleased to hear that my friend is not seriously hurt and is recovering in hospital, from where he sent me a message which I believe is what he heard just before the attack.'

Señora Vidal stubbed out her cigarette and carefully placed the ashtray on the bar, then turned and squared up to Mr Campion, her eyes on his, unblinking.

'Yes?'

'Whoever attacked Robert Ringer said, "For my father", just before striking with a knife taken earlier from the hotel.' The small woman remained impassive even as Campion pressed on. 'Who else here tonight would say such a thing, except someone who blamed the Germans for the death of a father, moreover a father they never knew? Where is Prisca, Astrid?'

There was still no reaction from the Spanish woman, and Campion felt Luke push out his chest and flex his shoulders as a prelude to entering the fray, but it was Perdita who broke the deadlock.

'She's in their room upstairs. Her mother smuggled her up there in the general confusion. I think she must have blood on her, as Mrs Vidal has a very damp red handkerchief in her handbag.'

'How very observant of you, my dear,' Campion said with pride. 'Keep an eye on this one, Charlie, she could be after your job.'

'It was all my fault,' said Astrid Vidal. 'Prisca must not be blamed.'

'I'm afraid she may have to be,' said Luke. 'This is a very serious matter.'

Campion turned his head in to Luke and spoke quietly. 'Robert is not the sort to press charges against a girl who is possibly unhinged and his injuries are not life-threatening.'

'A crime is a crime,' said Luke out of the corner of his mouth.

'Blame me!' cried Astrid. 'I confused her. I should have told her everything or nothing at all, then this would not have happened.'

'She asked about her father, didn't she?' Amanda said gently.

Astrid nodded her head violently and fumbled for another cigarette, instantly happier to be able to talk to a woman of her own vintage.

'When she was twelve or thirteen I told her about Nathan, my first husband, and how he had been killed during the war. She knew well enough that Reuben Vidal was not her father – we married when Prisca was five – and that she was really French, not Spanish; but as she learned about the war and heard stories about the persecution of the Jews, she wanted to know more.'

She scanned the faces watching her, appealing for understanding. 'I did not tell her about the bank accounts in Africa that Nathan had been forced to set up, nor about his involvement with the gangsters of the Panier. I said that after the first round-ups of Jews in 1942, we had decided to escape from Pau, over the Pyrenees and into Spain, where she was born and where I met and later married Reuben.'

She looked at Campion and, for the first time, her gaze fell away. 'I am sorry, Mister Albert, but I did not tell her fully of your part in our escape, valiant though it was.'

'I understand,' said Mr Campion. 'I failed to get Nathan to you in Madrid and I was unable to tell you the circumstances personally. I am sure you were very angry with me.'

'Yes, I was angry – and vengeful. I never told Prisca that she would not have been born if you had not helped me over the mountains but, worse, I told her that we had fled from Pau pursued by a German officer of the SS called Haberland and that Nathan had been killed during our escape. She convinced herself that Haberland had killed Nathan, and I did not correct her perfect hatred of him.'

'She may have hated the name Haberland,' said Campion, 'but she had never seen Robert before, had she? So how did she connect the two?'

'I told you, it was my fault. When I saw the German tonight, I recognized him even after all these years, and I said "Haberland" out loud before I could stop myself. I did not think Prisca would do anything or even remember the name.'

'But you, Astrid, you knew that Robert, or "Haberland" as I introduced him to you in your apartment in Pau, helped your escape. He did not kill Nathan: you know who did.'

'Yes, they told me I was a widow when I reached Madrid,' the woman said with sharp venom, 'and that you had sent a report saying that his body had been taken to Cauterets and he had been buried there as a Christian.'

'I am sorry I could not see you in person . . .' Campion faltered. 'But I was delayed. I have regretted that ever since, though it is far from the only thing I regret from those years.'

'Then help Prisca now.'

'I will try, Astrid, I will try, but it is up to Charles here.'

'Let me call in a WPC and we'll take a statement,' said Luke professionally. 'I'm assuming Prisca is not a flight risk.'

'I very much doubt it,' said Campion, 'and she would have to be driving a tank to get past Lugg guarding the front door.'

'Then leave things to me and you get back to your guests.'

'Do you know, Charles, I'm not in a party mood any more.'

But parties, once started, have a habit of carrying on to the bitter end, and Mr Campion's birthday jag was no exception, even though there was no presentation of medals or long speeches of honorification, and much of the vulgar action which could have prompted juicy gossip took place off-stage. A subdued Prisca Vidal, accompanied by her sobbing mother, had been escorted from the hotel by a uniformed constable and a female PC via the kitchens and a rear exit. The majority of the partygoers, now dancing to or complaining about the increased volume of the disco's output, failed to notice their going.

The Campions did the rounds of the non-gyrating guests, exchanging pleasantries and receiving thanks and congratulations in profusion. Mr Campion stressed at every encounter that for a seventy-year-old, beauty sleep was needed, and though his bedtime would soon beckon, music and refreshments would continue unabated.

Only when it was time for the hosts to slip away to their suite did they find themselves in a secluded corner with Rupert and Perdita.

'You go to bed, Pops,' said Rupert. 'I'll make sure they all get home safely and Lugg will make sure nobody steals the silver.'

'Thank you, my boy. I'm sorry we had to skip over the medal presentation. I like a good presentation, especially when I'm getting the medal. Oh, and also the cutting of the cake. We never did that; and I really do like cake.'

Amanda patted her husband's arm, which was curled around her waist. 'We can have cake tomorrow,' she cooed, 'and have it all to ourselves, and I'm sure they'll put your medal in the post.'

'I'm just sorry I never got to hear the end of your war story,' said Perdita.

'Is your wife actually fluttering her eyelashes at me, Rupert? I think you should have been stricter when she was a puppy.' Campion beamed as his son blushed. 'But don't worry, one should never refuse a friendly audience, as you two thespians know very well.

'Truth is there's not much more to tell. After I found Nathan dead in that hut and realized that I had failed him, I was pretty useless. I let Robert take command and he got me down to Pont d'Espagne where the cars were. I was too exhausted to face going back up the pilgrim's trail again and Reuben and Astrid would have been long gone even if I had tried.

'Robert found me a bath, a bed and some clean clothes, and then passed me on to the Abwehr office in Perpignan. The Abwehr were a bit like Boots the chemist: they had branches everywhere. From Perpignan they arranged passage for me on a merchant ship steaming to Barcelona. I think Robert had told them I was a double agent being planted to infiltrate the Iberian Section of MI6, which is exactly where I reported when I arrived. By then, Lunel's ledgers had been acted upon and the bank accounts frozen, and Astrid and Reuben Vidal had left Madrid – Astrid to have her baby in peace out in the country and Reuben back on pilgrim duty in the mountains, though he clearly kept a fond eye on Astrid.'

'At almost exactly the same time I was struggling alone, without any guardian angel, to produce you,' Amanda told Rupert, reaching out to ruffle his hair.

'And what about Magnus Asher?' Perdita asked.

'I told Charles you had a natural copper's inquisitiveness,' said Campion. 'But a character like Asher is not worth worrying about. He was not mourned.'

'But what happened to him?'

'I told you, Robert and Erik had taken him into custody and he was dealt with. Now I really must go to bed.'

Perdita looped her arms around her father-in-law and kissed him on the cheek. 'It must have been awful for you, that horrible journey up and down the mountain only to find Nathan dead. No wonder it affected you. Everyone says you had changed when you came back from the war.'

Mr Campion returned the kiss and he and Amanda took their leave.

In the lift going up to their suite, Mr Campion caught sight of himself in the mirror fixed above the elevator buttons.

'No, it wasn't that,' he said.

But he said it to himself.

By retiring when they did, the Campions missed the sight (though Lugg did not) of Commander Charles Luke of New Scotland Yard tripping the light fantastic with Madame Corinne Thibus on a crowded and rather humid dance floor to music which neither recognized, though both admitted the beat was infectious.

When it became clear that the energetic disc jockey did not require time to reload but was able to slip from one thumping anthem into another without pause, Luke signalled that they should find something to drink out of line of fire of the speakers.

Once in an area which offered both alcohol and relative quiet, Luke asked the Frenchwoman if she could clear up something that was bothering him.

'In France,' smiled Corinne Thibus, 'that would be a prelude to an offer of dinner and seduction, but here in England and you being a policeman, I suspect not.'

The policeman, relieved that Lugg was well out of earshot, albeit edging his way nearer around the edge of the room, as if supervising a high-school dance, decided that small talk – even if he were any good at it – would be wasted on Madame Thibus.

'I understand you are a lawyer,' he said.

'You understand correctly.'

'And you specialize in prosecuting war criminals.'

'I do.'

Luke took a deep breath and plunged in.

'Did you ever investigate Robert von Ringer?'

'Is this professional curiosity, Commander?'

'You could call it that, though in English we'd say it's me being nosey.'

'That sounds honest, so I will satisfy your curiosity and the answer is yes, I did investigate Ringer, just as I did hundreds of Germans who occupied France during the war, but no crimes were ever laid at his door.'

'And the investigation was thorough?'

Corinne Thibus sniffed haughtily. 'Very. I am very thorough, especially when it came to suspects who were based in Marseilles. Remember, I was there during the war, as was Albert, and there were plenty of collaborators and criminals in Marseilles.'

'People like Magnus Asher?'

'Exactly. He should have been investigated by you people at Scotland Yard or MI5 or whatever you call it, as he was a murderer, a traitor and a war profiteer of the first order.'

'What happened to him?'

Her eyes lit up with surprise. 'Did not M'sieur Campion tell you?'

TWENTY-FOUR

Peccavi

Near the Pont d'Espagne, Hautes-Pyrénées. November 1942

'Are you sure you have him secure?' I asked Robert as I stumbled and fell against him for the hundredth time.

'We did not have to capture him – he seemed delighted to see us and keen to offer us his services. I think that officially makes him a traitor to your country.'

They say revenge is a dish best served cold, but the prospect of vengeance was a delightfully warming apéritif. The prospect of confronting Magnus Asher after the helpless despair of watching him ride away from the scene of Nathan Lunel's murder was the thing which had warmed my blood and pumped life back into screaming leg and thigh muscles.

Even so, I could not have attempted that descent down to the Pont d'Espagne as darkness began to fall without Robert's solid shoulder to lean on. I lost count of the number of times I might have fallen flat on my face or walked into a tree. Even more frightening was the prospect of tripping over a rock or my own leaden feet and rolling down a slope into one of the torrential streams which tumbled towards the bridge where they met in a picturesque cascade. In this area of France those streams were named as *Gaves*, from an old Gascon word, though quite why that sprang into my befuddled mind at that time was beyond me.

I decided I was hallucinating and reality was slipping from my grasp, when I saw lights ahead of us, flickering and flashing through the dark pillars of trees, and I must have croaked a warning to Robert, who was breathing heavily as he struggled to keep his feet and me upright at the same time.

'Erik,' he said, as if that explained everything, but my misty brain needed more detail. 'Erik has turned the lights of the cars on.'

As we got nearer, I could make out an amphitheatre of yellow light provided by the headlights of two vehicles, the Citroën I had abandoned on the edge of the bridge and the Mercedes my German rescuers had arrived in.

Robert called out in German to announce our arrival and Erik responded smartly, probably clicking his heels as he did so, shouting that everything, as was only to be expected, was in order.

I released my hold on Robert, determined to confront what lay ahead on my own two feet, as we stepped into the pool of light.

Magnus Asher was in the centre of that artificial amphitheatre, sitting cross-legged against his motorcycle, balanced on its footstand. He wore his leather riding gear – boots, three-quarter-length coat and helmet with goggles attached – but I no longer saw him as a dark hobgoblin. If anything, I saw him as a defeated gladiator on the arena floor, his victorious opponent, Erik, standing over him pointing a pistol at his head, as if waiting for the decisive thumb signal from his emperor.

Asher himself did not seem unduly worried by his predicament, at least not until I moved closer and recognition dawned.

'Where's the bitch Jewess?' he snarled up at me.

'Safely away from you, you evil bastard.' I spat the words and felt Robert tense beside me. I also realized that my right hand had automatically gone to the pistol in my jacket pocket.

Whatever reaction I had expected from a man at such a disadvantage, it was not the one I got.

Asher's face relaxed and he smiled. It was the most terrible grin I had ever seen, and a very bad strategic move on Asher's part.

'Well, she can't hurt me now, can she? Shame you went to so much trouble to get her out of the Panier. You and that bloody girl caused a lot of aggravation. If Pirani gets his hands on her, he'll gut her for putting a bullet in his leg. And none of it was really worth it, was it, Mr Canadian Diplomat or whoever you are?'

'I wouldn't be too sure of that,' I said. 'You don't appear to be in the most advantageous of positions just at the moment.'

Again the smile. 'Have you not met my new lords and masters? The Germans are in charge of Vichy now and there are many in the Gestapo and the SS who know how helpful I can be to them.'

'Naturally you have offered your many talents to their service.'

'Of course,' he said with a sickly smoothness, 'to these officers here.'

'The first ones you ran into after killing Nathan Lunel. That shows an enthusiasm which would be commendable were we not talking high treason.'

Asher snorted in derision at the suggestion, but his overconfident expression began to melt away as Robert began to speak, in English, as if reading from a court charge sheet.

'Treason . . . desertion from the British army . . . collaboration with the enemy . . . black-market profiteering . . . gangsterism . . . corruption of government officials, even if they were Vichy . . . currency manipulation . . . conspiracy . . . kidnapping . . . and, of course, murder.'

I joined in the indictment. 'At least three counts: Nathan Lunel, Pastor Sandy Nevin and Madame Henneuse. Does that last name mean nothing to you? She was the Lunels' housekeeper in Pau. She died. You beat her to death. She was an innocent civilian and defenceless, just as were Lunel and Sandy Nevin. You picked your victims carefully; none of them could fight back. It's a pity you didn't pick your new friends as carefully.'

Now he showed fear, as his eyes flicked to Erik, towering over him, and then Robert, who was unsnapping the flap of the holster on his belt. When Asher looked back to me, he found a third pistol pointed at him.

Erik could not have followed much as we had spoken in English, but he was a good soldier and took his lead from his officer, and did not pause or flinch when Robert switched to German and gave him his orders.

'Get this piece of shit on his feet, we're taking him into the trees. Push the bike off the road and turn the cars around; leave the engines running.'

'*Jawohl, Herr Hauptmann!*' snapped Erik, as if he had been straining on the leash, and he unceremoniously hauled Asher to his feet.

'Walk.' Robert swiped his pistol in front of Asher's twitching face and indicated the direction we had come from.

For the second time I followed the pilgrim's trail, but this time only as far as the treeline, at which point Asher spun round, his hands up in mock surrender.

'Wait! I have money.'

'Not any more,' I said, and I think that struck home harder than the fate he must have realized he faced.

'Keep going,' Robert ordered, and Asher entered the trees.

From behind us, we heard a car start up, and the light silhouetting us swirled away as Erik moved one of the cars, but there was still enough to illuminate the trudging figure of Magnus Asher.

'That's enough,' said Robert. 'Turn around.'

He levelled his pistol at Asher. The distance between them was little more than ten feet.

I stepped forward to be next to Robert and slipped the safety catch off my Walther.

Robert looked at me out of the corner of his eye and spoke softly. 'I will do this, Albert.'

'No,' I said. 'Together.'

Our weapons barked as one.

I was shaking as we walked back to the stone bridge where, below in the dark, we could hear the rushing of water even over the sound of the idling engines of the car.

'At any other time and in any other place, what we just did would be called murder.'

'Perhaps,' said Robert, 'but war changes things.'

About the Book

The idea for the basic plot involving banks, money, Vichy France and North Africa in 1942 came from that thriller-writer supreme, Len Deighton, over lunch in a Japanese restaurant just off Regent Street in June 2014. When I decided, in 2017, to adapt it for a Campion story, to partly explain Mr Campion's 'hush-hush' wartime work, Len graciously 'gave' me the plot, though I have no doubt he would have made a better job of it than I have.

I am immensely grateful to Marcel Berlins for sharing his family history and experiences of life in Marseille (NB: not Marseilles!) in 1942.

This is fiction, but the character of Sandy Nevin was inspired by the heroism of the Reverend Donald Caskie (1902–83), known as 'The Tartan Pimpernel', at the real Seamen's Mission in Marseille, who survived capture by Vichy, Italian and German security services – and a Gestapo death sentence – to return after the war to his beloved Scotland.

Students of the period may also be reminded of the wartime career of the traitor Harold Cole, who evaded capture for the last time when he was shot dead by French detectives in Paris in January 1946.

The MI6 officer Campion meets in Spain, Kenneth Benton (1909–99), really did serve in the Iberia section of British intelligence's Madrid office in 1942, and his immediate boss was indeed Kim Philby. After a thirty-year career in MI6, Benton retired and began a new career as a thriller writer. He served as chairman of the Crime Writers' Association 1974–75, succeeding Dick Francis.

The expression Mr Campion uses in chapter four describing MI5 as 'a sort of jumped-up gendarmerie' is stolen from the novel *A Captive in the Land* by James Aldridge, published in 1962 by Hamish Hamilton, the dust jacket of which was designed by a certain P. Youngman Carter, Margery Allingham's husband.

In chapter twelve, Campion mentions that he was tempted to

steal a pair of 'Afrika Korps pyjamas'. As a young British soldier just after the war had ended, my friend Philip Purser, the television critic and thriller writer, was issued a pair of Afrika Korps pyjamas from a captured supply depot. He often boasted that they lasted him for over a decade, long after his National Service was over.

I have taken to heart Agatha Christie's famous comment that all Margery Allingham's books had their own separate and distinctive background and shape, and so have attempted a different narrative structure for this one. I always appreciated this would be a risk and I am indebted to my former publisher, Edwin Buckhalter of Severn House, a dedicated Campion fan, for having faith in the experiment.

Sources

Donald Caskie: *The Tartan Pimpernel*, Oldbourne Books, 1957.

Jacques-Yves Cousteau: *The Silent World*, Hamish Hamilton, 1953.

Michael Curtis: *Verdict on Vichy*, Weidenfeld & Nicolson, 2002.

Isabelle Janvrin & Catherine Rawlinson: *The French in London*, Wilmington Square Books, 2013.

Simon Kitson: *The Hunt for Nazi Spies – Fighting Espionage in Vichy France*, University of Chicago Press, 2008.

Mark Mazower: *Hitler's Empire*, Allen Lane, 2008.

Robert Mencherini: *Ici-Même – Marseille 1940–1944*, Editions Jeanne Laffitte, 2013.

Ian Ousby: *Occupation*, John Murray, 1997.

Colin Smith: *England's Last War Against France*, Weidenfeld 2009.

Edward Stourton: *Cruel Crossing*, Doubleday, 2013.

Mr Campions War
11/29/2018